LORD OF THE ISLES

"Ms. Scott's diverse, marvelous, unforgettable characters in this intricate plot provide hours of pure pleasure."
—Rendezvous

"Scott pits her strong characters against one another and fate. She delves into their motivations, bringing insight into them and the thrilling era in which they live, and proving herself a true mistress of the Scottish romance."
—Romantic Times BOOKclub Magazine

"Amanda Scott writes great tales [set] during this turbulent time in Scotland history."
—RomanceReviewsMag.com

"A fine fourteenth-century romance . . . fans will appreciate this tale of marriage starring the wrong bride."
—TheBestReviews.com

"This historical romance gives us a wonderful look at the country and its people. An enjoyable read."
—RoundTableReviews.com

"A good book . . . a readable story with a well-done plot."
—FreshFiction.com

more . . .

"Perfect for readers who enjoy romances with a rich sense of history."
—Booklist

"A fabulous medieval Scottish romance."
—Midwest Book Review

"A marvelously rendered portrait of medieval Scotland, terrific characters, and a dynamic story."
—Romantic Times BOOKclub Magazine

"Great mix of romance, adventure, humor, courage, and passion—a very captivating read. One can almost hear the bagpipes playing . . . a MUST read."
—TheBestReviews.com

"A wonderful history of the Scottish isles that carries through with its promises to the very end."
—RoadToRomance.ca

"Powerful . . . so exciting! Wonderful! Loved it."
—RomanticReviewsMag.com

"Irresistible! . . . Passion, danger, and even a murder mystery are intertwined to create constant intrigue."
—BookLoons.com

"As usual, the author has created a very believable set of characters, a vivid setting, and a wonderful love story."
—RomanceReadersConnection.com

Knight's
Treasure

AMANDA SCOTT

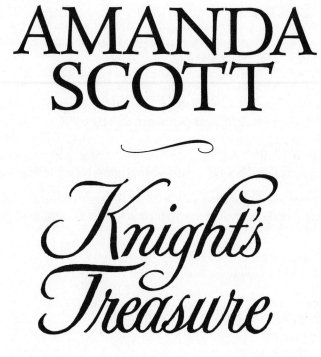

Knight's Treasure

WARNER
FOREVER

NEW YORK   BOSTON

Warner Forever is a trademark of Time Warner Inc. or an affiliated company. Used under license by Hachette Book Group, which is not affiliated with Time Warner Inc.

Cover design by Diane Luger
Book design by Giorgetta Bell McRee

Warner Forever
Hachette Book Group USA
1271 Avenue of the Americas
New York, NY 10020

Printed in the United States of America

ISBN-13: 978-0-7394-7927-8

To Nancy & Charles Williams
for countless reasons and with great affection

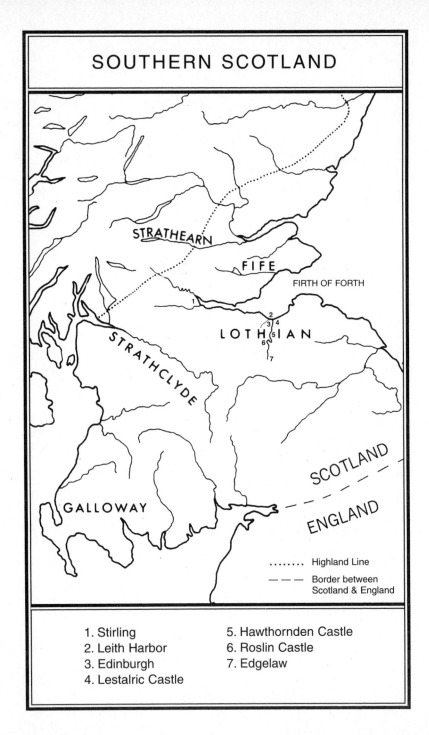

SOUTHERN SCOTLAND

STRATHEARN

FIFE

FIRTH OF FORTH

LOTHIAN

STRATHCLYDE

SCOTLAND

ENGLAND

GALLOWAY

.... Highland Line

— — Border between
Scotland & England

1. Stirling
2. Leith Harbor
3. Edinburgh
4. Lestalric Castle
5. Hawthornden Castle
6. Roslin Castle
7. Edgelaw

Author's Note

For those among you who make studies of British titles and like to understand them, please note that Sir Robert of Lestalric, although a baron and entitled to be addressed by lesser folk as "my lord" or "Lord Lestalric," would commonly (in the fourteenth century) have been addressed by his peers as either Sir Robert or Lestalric and referred to as such or as Sir Robert of Lestalric, or as Sir Robert Logan of Lestalric.

The key is that in the fourteenth century Sir Robert's status as a knight was what set him apart from his fellow noblemen (i.e., landowners, primarily barons). Eventually, as protocols evolved over centuries, a baron Lestalric would commonly be known as Lord Lestalric or "my lord" and informally addressed by his peers as Lestalric.

Prologue

~

Two Miles Northeast of Edinburgh, March 1371

I hope ye've gained wisdom in your four years away, lad," Sir Ian Logan, second Baron Lestalric, said sternly to his younger son.

Sir Ian stood before the huge fireplace in Lestalric Castle's great hall, his silk-shod feet planted well apart, his thick arms folded across his chest. A rich crimson velvet doublet, silken hose, and gold jewelry proclaimed his wealth, just as the frown on his face revealed his doubt that his hope had been fulfilled.

Standing on the nearby dais, his heir, William, was a fair copy of his sire with the same proud posture and substantial, richly attired body. He, too, scowled at the third party in the chamber as he said, "We hope ye've found at least enough wisdom to tell us the damnable secret ye've kept to yourself since ye left here, Robbie."

"Whether ye've the wisdom or no, ye'll tell us, and straightaway," the baron snapped. "I command ye."

The baron's younger son, Sir Robert, halfway into his eighteenth year, was six feet tall and extremely fit, for he had just returned home after earning his spurs on the field of battle. His temper stirred at being confronted so, but equal dismay aided him in suppressing it. He had arrived at Lestalric two hours before, hoping to succeed at last in marrying the love of his life and knowing he needed his father's aid to do so. But he could not obey Sir Ian's command.

All three men were dark-haired, hazel-eyed, and bore a strong family likeness, although Rob's height was greater, his shoulders broader, and his hips slimmer than those of the other two. Only a few feet of the rush-strewn floor divided the three, but four years and dozens of similar confrontations before stood between them as well.

Rob, in travel-stained breeks and muddy boots, never having learned to communicate well with the other two, felt as if they were miles apart. Absently, he rubbed the plain gold ring on his left little finger as he tried to think what to say.

"Well?" Sir Ian demanded. "I ha' asked ye a plain question. Any *loyal* man o' this family would answer it straightaway."

Again his temper stirred, but Rob said with forced calm, "You know I am loyal, my lord, so you must likewise know by my silence that I cannot answer you."

"I told you so, Father," Will said. "He was nobbut thirteen when he went away, and the taunts he hurled at me then meant nowt. Why would our grandfather ha' revealed aught to him that he did not tell you or me? Grandfather said himself that he'd told Rob nowt of any import."

"Be silent, Will," Sir Ian ordered without looking away from Rob. "Did ye no hear me say earlier, lad, that the Steward will soon be crowned King o' Scots?"

"I heard you," Rob said. "I don't know what that has to do with me, although I expect we'll all be attending his coronation at Scone Abbey."

"And ye ha' nowt to say that could add to the splendor o' that occasion?"

"No, sir. What could I possibly know about the King's crowning?"

"Will ye tell me your grandfather passed no useful information to ye?"

"He passed a great deal of useful information to me," Rob acknowledged. "However, he talked mostly of the old days here at Lestalric and of hiding in caves and playing tricks on English invaders, raiding their supplies and such. Sakes, he must have told you all those same tales, and Will, too."

Rob looked at his older brother, who was still glowering, and said, "I do apologize for my taunts that day, Will. But you'd made me angry, and well do you know it. In any event, Grandfather told you those same tales, did he not?"

"Aye, but ye ken fine we're no talking o' pranks to annoy the damned English. They ha' kept out o' Scotland now for nigh forty years, since those days he spoke of, except for a brief foray twenty years back when our lot nearly captured their third King Edward. What o' family secrets, though? What d'ye ken o' them?"

Rob shook his head. "I'd expect family secrets, if we had any, to have gone to our father as heir to the title, and thence to you. Surely, no one would confide such to me.

Recall, too, that our grandfather died two months after he sent me to Dunclathy."

"So he said nowt to you o' his father and uncle wha' were friends wi' the Bruce," the baron said. "Nor o' things the two o' them might ha' done for the man?"

Rob frowned. "I know that my great-grandfather, Sir Robert Logan, whose name I bear, and his brother Sir Walter, whose name our grandfather bore, were with the Bruce at Bannockburn. I know, too, that they both went with the good Sir James Douglas and Sir William Sinclair after the Bruce died, to carry his heart to the Holy Land as he had asked them to do."

"Aye, sure, for that be why our crest bears a heart proper on it like that o' the Douglas," Sir Ian said. "But what else d'ye ken o' them?"

"I know that on the way, our two kinsmen were killed in Spain with Sir James and Sinclair, and that Sir William Keith and other survivors brought their bodies and the Bruce's heart home again. What I do not know is how any of that can have aught to do with what you have asked of me."

Sir Ian's eyes narrowed, and he stared intently into Rob's eyes, but Rob had been withstanding even sterner looks for four years. He met it easily.

"So ye ken nowt," Sir Ian said with a heavy sigh. "'Tis a pity, because I'd hoped to advance ye. I'm told ye've been looking to wed the lady Ellen Douglas. Sakes, I'm told ye dared to talk wi' her about it a year ago, when ye spent a day wi' the Douglas at Tantallon but didna visit your own father nobbut a few miles away."

Rob said tightly, "You know I had no choice in that. I rode in Sir Edward Robison's fighting tail when he went to confer with the Douglas about English Border raiders who were becoming increasingly daring."

"Aye, well, 'tis still a great pity that ye ha' nowt o' import to tell us now."

William looked smug.

Rob remained silent, fighting to retain control of his unpredictable temper. He wondered if they could hear his heart thumping with the effort.

"Well?" his father snapped. "D'ye want the lass or no?"

"You must know I do," Rob said. "What's more—"

William interjected lightly, "Ellen's a snug handful, to be sure."

"Hold your tongue," Rob snapped. "Recall that you speak of a lady and that you are no longer head and shoulders taller or four stone heavier than I am."

"I can still best a stripling like you."

Rob did not spare him another glance, thinking that whatever else Will had learned during his years of training with the Earl of Douglas, he had not learned chivalry. As far as he could tell, his brother had not changed a jot since they were fifteen and thirteen, when Will had lorded it over him at every turn, even calling him a bairn when he'd cried after their mother's death. How Rob had hated him then!

On the other hand, Rob thought the Order had taught him all he needed to know in life except one important thing: how to keep his temper in check. Sir Edward Robison, the commander he had served at Dunclathy, would have had something scathing to say about his impulsive reaction four years ago to Will's teasing, but Sir Edward did not know about that and if Rob had his way, he never would. Nor would Hugo or Michael. His two best friends were ever ready with advice and censure if a man deserved either.

As he struggled to restore calm to his mind, Sir Ian said, "I'm thinking ye can put that lass straight out o' your head now . . . "

William's expression grew smugger, warning Rob of what was to come.

". . . because without more to offer her ladyship than your fine new spurs, I'm thinking she'll do gey better to marry our Will."

"She doesn't want him," Rob blurted before he could stop himself.

William laughed. "She's got nowt to say about it. I'm heir to Lestalric, not you, and she's Lady Ellen Douglas, daughter of the most powerful man in Scotland."

Rob opened his mouth and clamped it shut again.

"Will's right," the baron said. "Moreover, if ye've nowt else to offer, ye're nobbut a damnable disappointment to me and no worth exerting m'self for."

Longing to reply in kind, Rob kept his teeth tightly together.

Still grinning, Will said, "You cannot have met the lass above three times in your life. If you think she'd want a scarce-tried knight when she can have all that Lestalric offers instead, you're the same witless fool you were at thirteen, Robbie. Even if she did want you, her father would demand more for her and she would obey him. But it won't come to that. Ellen has already accepted me."

Rob looked at his father, but Sir Ian just shrugged.

"Tell me, my lord," Rob said stiffly. "Had I been able to answer your question about this mysterious secret you think my grandfather told me, what would you have done? If Will has already offered and been accepted by Lady Ellen, then . . . "

"Faugh," his father said. "Had ye done aught to deserve the lass, I'd ha' spoken to Douglas about ye taking her instead. A man does what is politic, lad. Will kens that. If ye dinna ken as much after all your fine training, ye dinna ken nowt."

"So if I had known such a secret and shared it, you would have passed it on to Douglas to gain his daughter for me instead of Will. Is that it? Or would you have let Will tell him, to add to his own stature and assure *his* match with Lady Ellen?"

Arms akimbo now, and chest puffed, Sir Ian jutted his chin and said, "Aye, and what if I had? In troth, I'd ha' used it to further the Logans' interest as best it could, and wi' the right information, I'd ha' seen ye *both* wed to Douglas lasses. 'Tis nobbut plain fact that any secret your grandsire held, the Douglas *should* ken. 'Tis his right as the most powerful descendant o' the good Sir James."

"Then I'm sorry I cannot oblige him," Rob said with a stiff nod, turning away.

"And where d'ye think ye be going?" Sir Ian demanded.

Turning back, Rob snapped, "I'm bidding you adieu, my lord. I'll not be back."

"Aye, well, dinna come back then," Sir Ian retorted. "And dinna expect nowt from me in the future, either!"

Furious, but still struggling to contain it, Rob said, "I *don't* expect anything. As I'm such a disappointment, you should be glad to see the last of me!"

"Aye, well, I am, then!" shouted Sir Ian.

As he rode away from Lestalric, Rob did not look back, but thoughts of the angry exchange and a strong sense of betrayal continued to plague him, and never more so than when it occurred to him that although the first secret his grandfather had confided to him had naught to do with Lestalric, the second one did.

The key to it lay within the castle itself, and now that he had vowed never to return, he might never learn what that secret was.

Doubtless, though, it was just some family treasure or other. If so, even if he did find it, his father or Will would claim it. Nevertheless, for all his effort to restrain his wretched temper, it had been his undoing again. So, whatever course he took next, it should be one to teach him humility.

On that thought, he knew just where he would go, for although his father and brother had rarely made him feel at home, one family in Scotland always did.

Chapter 1

Stirling Castle, April 1380

The Earl of Fife, hereditary governor of Stirling Castle and third son of the King of Scots, sat behind the large desk in his audience chamber, sternly regarding the well-dressed young man who stood before him. Fife was a good judge of men, and this one seemed more confident in his presence than most. Fife's formidable personality and ever-increasing power intimidated most men—with good reason.

"Who sent you here to me?"

"I came of my own accord, my lord," his visitor said. "I own, though, that I came to you because I think we can help each other. I am told that, rightfully, you should be heir to the throne of Scotland but must bow to a lesser man."

"It is true that I am more capable than my brother Carrick will ever be of ruling this country as it should be ruled," Fife admitted. "However, Robert the Bruce set the order of succession years ago and ordained that it must go to the eldest son."

"But the Scottish Parliament can alter that order, can it not?"

"Aye, if one could persuade them to do so."

"I'm told also that you are a religious man, a follower of the Kirk of Rome."

"That is true enough," Fife said.

"If the Pope were to support you instead of the Earl of Carrick as the next King of Scots, would that not increase your chances of persuading the Parliament?"

"Aye, sure, but what would his holiness ask of me in return?"

"We seek information about the death of a cousin, the son of my late father's brother. He disappeared whilst trying to find and return an item of some value to the Kirk of Rome. His own men believe he died at the hands of certain Scottish nobles."

"What is this cousin's name?"

"Waldron of Edgelaw, my lord."

Fife leaned forward. "And these Scottish nobles. Do you know their names?"

"The Sinclairs, my lord, likewise cousins of Waldron on their mother's side."

"I did hear rumors about his death," Fife said, "but my sources told me that from all they could learn, he died in a fair fight. Tell me more of this item he sought and why you think the Sinclairs had aught to do with his death."

"First let me assure you that if you can aid me, his holiness will be grateful. You may be sure of great financial reward as well as holy favor."

"Then something of *great* value is involved," Fife said. "What is it?"

His visitor nodded. "They told me you were astute,

my lord. 'Tis true that what Waldron sought was of enormous value, but it does belong to Holy Kirk."

"Aye, sure, and I'd faithfully see it returned," Fife promised. "But what is it?"

"Treasure, my lord, stolen from the Kirk nearly a century ago by the Knights Templar. Those who sent me believe the Sinclairs guard it now. Likewise, a woman now in their care but who is soon to marry and depart for the Highlands spent a fortnight with my cousin right before his death. Her name is Lady Adela Macleod."

Fife was thinking. He said musingly, "Sir William Sinclair was one of the men who attempted to carry the Bruce's heart to the Holy Land."

"Aye, sir, and a Templar."

"Perhaps, but you are the second man in as many weeks to speak to me of hidden treasure. I must think on this. Return tomorrow, and we'll discuss it further."

Roslin Castle, Thursday, May 10, 1380

"Smile, Adela. We brides should look happy on our wedding day!"

Lady Adela Macleod turned to her younger sister, Sorcha, who was certainly beaming brightly enough for both of them. But although Adela tried to obey her command, she knew her own smile was feeble at best.

She had hoped that her second wedding, unlike the first, might proceed without undue fuss or drama. However, although she knew that Roslin Castle's highly trained guardsmen would prevent the kind of trouble that had cut short her first ceremony, she had already seen more fuss and ado than she liked. And she knew that before the day was over, she would see more. Nervously, she fingered the gold chain necklace her mother had given her the year before she'd died.

Sorcha reached to push back a long, thick strand of Adela's straight honey-blond hair that had managed to slip over her shoulder to the front of her tightly laced golden velvet gown. Letting go of the chain, Adela stood quietly, even submissively. Sorcha's pearl-trimmed caul and the simple blue, shoulder-length veil that matched her silk gown concealed her own curlier, amber-golden hair.

Adela reminded herself that fuss had been inevitable. Not only were there now two brides and bridegrooms instead of one couple, but when one's hostess was a powerful countess in her own right, one had to expect such an occasion to merit extraordinary pomp and circumstance. And when one's younger sister had married the countess's favorite nephew by declaration a fortnight before, one could scarcely cavil when the fond aunt and one's own fond parent insisted on a double wedding to sanctify both marriages properly.

Even her father, Macleod of Glenelg, had had little say in today's wedding plans. His word was law back home in the Highlands, but Adela had not expected him to object to anything, because he planned soon to wed a widow in comfortable circumstances, which included a fine house in Edinburgh, seven miles away. The royal court was presently in residence there, and she knew that Macleod would do nothing that might stir gossip or jeopardize his own nuptial plans.

She had therefore understood from the outset that this wedding would be a grander occasion than her first attempt, which had taken place in the Highlands mere weeks after the death of the first Lord of the Isles. But the result was beyond anything she had anticipated. Her hostess, Isabella, Countess of Strathearn and Caithness, and the rest of the powerful Sinclair family had spared no expense.

Adela had not mourned any lack of splendor the first time. But after all the effort and expense, and in view of her own considerable gratitude, she thought it a pity that she could not feel more enthusiasm for this wedding.

As she waited near the chapel entrance with Macleod and the other members of the wedding party while the small but noble audience crammed into the chamber began to quiet down, she wondered why she did not care more. After all, other than the much larger group of friends and kinsmen unable to squeeze into the tiny chapel but assembling now in the castle's great hall for the wedding feast to come, nothing but the setting had changed—and Sorcha's role, of course, and Sir Hugo Robison's presence today at Sorcha's side.

Adela's bridegroom remained the same. And a generous, kind man Ardelve was, too. He was fond of her, she knew, and would make few demands with which she would not willingly comply.

So far, he had asked only that she manage his large household in Kintail near Chalamine, her family home. It was a responsibility that she expected to enjoy far more than the near decade of running her father's much less manageable household.

Although Sorcha insisted that Ardelve was too old and pompous to make a good husband, Adela liked him. To be sure, he was nearly as old as her father, had been twice married and widowed, and had a grown son older than she was. But his children had raised no objection to the marriage, and his cousin, Lady Clendenen, the wealthy widow whom Macleod intended to marry, stood in the front row now with an approving smile, waiting for the ceremony to begin.

As a result, Adela believed her marriage to Ardelve would be as happy as anyone could wish. So what, she asked herself, was wrong with her? Why did she not feel *something*?

She normally felt things deeply, and she normally expressed those feelings easily. One had to do so, after all, if one was to manage a castle full of servants, let alone to manage such an unruly sibling as Sorcha had been or a father as blustery as Macleod could be. Even the youngest of her sisters, the elusive Sidony, had required just the right degree of Adela's self-expression. But now—

So lost in thought was she that when Sorcha touched her arm again, she started violently and nearly cried out.

Sorcha's smile faded to a worried frown. "Pinch your cheeks," she said. "I vow, you look as pale as chalk. Is aught amiss? Does your shoulder still hurt?"

"Nay, it has healed," Adela said, ignoring the ache that lingered from an injury a fortnight before. "I'm quite well."

"You don't look it," Sorcha replied with her usual candor.

"Easy, lass," Sir Hugo said, laying a restraining hand on her shoulder.

Not, Adela mused, that anyone—even the tall, handsome, imperious Hugo—could restrain her sister unless Sorcha chose to allow it.

Hugo smiled as he said, "Doubtless you are recalling the last such occasion, Lady Adela. But no raiders will interrupt today's festivities, I promise you."

Since he controlled Roslin Castle's security, Adela knew he meant what he said. Politely if automatically returning his smile, she said, "Indeed, I have no such fear." She could hardly tell him she felt nothing at all, that it was as if she were in a dream, disembodied, watching four unknown figures about to walk to the altar.

The look that crossed Hugo's face then nearly matched the deepening frown on Sorcha's. Adela saw his hand squeeze her sister's shoulder a little harder, as if he sensed without looking that she was about to speak.

For a wonder, Sorcha kept silent.

Hugo said quietly, "You should not wonder if you do not feel a bride's usual excitement, lass. It can be only natural for you to feel wary now. I've seen similar reactions in brave men after one battle, about to face another. I warrant it must be much the same for you now."

"Pray, sir, do not concern yourself," she said. "What happened to me cannot possibly match aught that occurs in battle. I suffered no hurt, after all. I do not believe he would ever have harmed me."

Hugo's grimace revealed his disagreement, but he did not contradict her. He said, "I think the piper is about to play."

Macleod had stood quietly beside her, taking no part in the conversation. Now he said, "Aye, lass, and we're to go first, ye ken, after your maidens. So hold your head high. Ye look well, even if ye're no wearing blue for good luck."

Adela took a deep, steadying breath before she said

with forced calm, "I pray you, sir, do not tell me blue is a luckier color than yellow-gold, for I don't want to hear it. Last time I complied with your superstitions. I even agreed not to marry on a Friday that fell on the thirteenth of the month. Only recall what those precautions won me."

"Aye, sure, but it might ha' been worse had ye no worn blue. Never ye mind that now," he added hastily. "That gown becomes ye. It brings out the green flecks in your eyes and makes your hair look like golden honey flowing down your back."

Adela tried to ignore the thought of sticky honey oozing down her back, reminding herself that he rarely paid compliments and was thus out of practice.

He held out his arm to her, and the fact that her maidens were walking up the narrow aisle between flanking rows of standing guests, nearing the altar, recalled her to her wits. Obediently, she placed her right hand on his forearm and waited.

Sorcha and her younger sister Sidony had served as Adela's bride-maidens for the first wedding, but she and Sorcha had four attendants this time, three of whom they scarcely knew.

Sidony, blue-eyed and fair, looked beautifully serene as she led the way in, wearing a gown of pale rose. The next two were Sir Hugo's younger sisters in lavender and pale green. The last was their cousin, another niece of Countess Isabella's, in a straw-colored gown. All three had arrived only the day before.

Sorcha and Sir Hugo were already legally married, having taken advantage of the ancient Scottish tradition of simply declaring themselves husband and wife. Therefore, they would walk to the altar together. Sorcha had said she couldn't imagine why they need marry again. But Countess Isabella had declared that she intended to see them properly wed by her own priest, and that had been that.

When the four maidens had taken places on each side of the shallow steps leading to the altar, where Ardelve and Isabella's chaplain waited, Adela and Macleod walked up the aisle toward them. Sorcha and Sir Hugo followed, all accompanied by the piper's tune.

Although only a few years younger than Macleod, Ardelve was a handsomer, more dignified-looking man with a trim beard and grizzled dark hair. For the occasion, he wore a high-crowned, white-plumed hat, a black velvet, sable-trimmed robe belted over parti-colored hose, and fashionable pointed-toe shoes.

Standing straight and proud beside Isabella's chaplain, he watched his bride walk toward him, and when his gaze met hers, he smiled.

Adela replied with the same smile she had summoned up for Hugo but did not look away from Ardelve, grateful to have the excuse to avoid meeting the eye of any onlooker. She lacked the energy to smile and nod, and just wanted to have the ceremony and subsequent feasting behind her.

She reached the halfway point aware only of her hand on Macleod's arm and of Ardelve's smiling face before her. Then, an abrupt movement to her right and the clink-clink of something falling to the chapel's flagstone floor caught her attention.

Turning her head, she looked straight into the jade-green eyes of one of the handsomest men she had ever beheld.

He had finely chiseled features, gleaming chestnut hair that curled slightly at the ends, broad shoulders, a tapered waist, and muscular, well-turned legs. And he displayed the three latter features to advantage in an expertly cut forest-green velvet doublet and smooth yellow silk hose. His cap bore a curling bright yellow feather.

He had begun to bend down, so he had certainly dropped something. But whatever it was lay where it had fallen, because as Adela's gaze collided with his, he froze. Then, slowly he straightened, his gaze still locked with hers.

His remarkable green eyes began to twinkle. Then, impudently, he winked.

Startled, she wrenched her gaze away and sought Ardelve again, relaxing when she saw him, still smiling calmly. She did not look away again.

The piping stopped when she reached the two shallow steps that led up to kneeling stools awaiting the bridal couples before the altar.

"Who gives this maiden to wed this man?" the priest inquired.

"I do—Macleod o' Glenelg, her father," Macleod said clearly.

The priest beckoned to Adela, and releasing her father's arm, she went up the steps to stand by Ardelve. Sorcha and Hugo followed, taking their places at her left. All four faced the altar.

Isabella's chaplain stepped in front of them. After a long moment of silence, he said, "I be bound to ask first if there be any amongst ye today who kens any just cause or impediment to a marriage betwixt Baron Ardelve and

Lady Adela Macleod. If ye do ken such, speak now or forever hold your peace."

Adela shut her eyes, for it had been at this point in her first attempt to marry Ardelve that the interruption had occurred.

Today, aside from brief shuffling of feet, silence reigned.

Because Sorcha and Sir Hugo were sanctifying an existing union, the priest did not ask the same question about them, and Adela was glad to note that they both seemed blissfully happy.

She had seen them only once since their declaration, because immediately after Hugo had declared them married, they had removed to Hawthornden Castle, a mile down Roslin Glen to the north. Three days later, Adela had accompanied her sister Sidony, their elder sister Isobel, and the countess to pay them a bridal visit. But she had not seen them again until that very morning.

Isobel, now Sir Michael Sinclair's wife and thus daughter-by-marriage to the countess, stood in the audience with her husband and his mother. There had been no time for their other three sisters to travel to Roslin for the wedding.

When the priest spoke Adela's name, she wrenched her attention back to the ceremony, responding as he bade, and doing so calmly and clearly. The ceremony was mercifully brief, and although the nuptial mass to follow would last the usual time, she could recite her responses by rote and would not have to think.

When the priest declared them husbands and wives in the sight of God, Ardelve took Adela's hand in his and did not let go until they took communion.

When the mass came to an end, Adela hoped no one would ask what she had been thinking about or if she had enjoyed her wedding. The entire ceremony and service had registered little more in her mind than mere passage of time.

Isabella did not allow the bridal couples to linger but whisked them off to the great hall to receive their guests and begin the wedding feast. Laughter and music greeted them long before they entered, because the festivities had already begun.

Musicians in the minstrels' gallery played lively tunes until the bridal party appeared in the doorway. Then Isabella's chamberlain stepped forward.

"My lords, my ladies, and all within this chamber," he bellowed. "Pray rise to make welcome Lord and Lady Ardelve, and Sir Hugo and Lady Robison!"

As cheers broke out and the music resumed, Adela noted that two long boards for guests extended from the dais where the high table stood nearly the full length of the lower hall. Space had been cleared on the near side of the hall for the entertainers Isabella had hired to perform during the feast.

As they walked through the clearing to the dais with the others, Ardelve bent his head to Adela's ear and murmured, "I would speak privately with you, my lady wife, afore we feast. If you will oblige me, Isabella has offered the use of her solar."

"As you wish, my lord," she said, hoping she had not done something to vex him already. Remembering her reaction to the green-eyed man, she dismissed that. Ardelve had shown no sign of being a possessive husband or a jealous one.

Crossing the crowded dais, they approached the door in the center of the wall behind it, skirting the high table, which would soon groan under the weight of gold and silver platters and trays of food, and jugs of whisky and wine, not to mention the guests' goblets and trenchers that were already in place.

A Sinclair gillie thrust the door to the solar open for them.

Nodding to the lad to shut it behind them, Ardelve led Adela away from it, then said without preamble, "One hesitates to speak to a lady about her looks other than to compliment her, my dear. But all this splendor seems to have tired you. If you want to leave, I'll gladly make our adieux and retire now to our bedchamber."

"'Tis kind of you to offer, sir, but it would be unkind of us, not to mention most ungrateful, to do such a thing after Countess Isabella has put so much effort forth to honor us."

"Faugh," he said. "Isabella does what she does for Isabella or for Roslin. In truth, I am weary myself. But if you are sure you are feeling well . . . "

"I am, sir," she said. "I am a little tired but no more than that."

He looked searchingly at her, then said, "If it is any relief to your mind, you have naught to fear from me on this night or any other. If you want time to adjust to our marriage before taking up all your wifely duties, I will understand. I am in no great hurry, Adela, and would understand your preference for a more peaceful place to get to know your husband. Do you take my meaning, lass?"

"Aye, sir, I do," she said, aware that she was blushing. "My sister Isobel explained what my duties will be. You

are most kind, but I want children, and I have no objection to taking up my wifely duties whenever it shall
please you. Moreover, if you do not *want* to stay for the
feast, you have only to say so."

He patted her hand. "I am content," he said. "My
household stands in great need of your woman's touch,
and I have need of that, too. Your thoughtfulness only
makes me look forward more eagerly to our years together. You are right, though, to remind me that everyone
here worked hard to provide our wedding feast."

"I, too, am impatient for our return to the peace of the
Highlands, sir."

He smiled again. She thought his smile a particularly
charming one and responded this time with her first natural smile of the day. No matter that Sorcha thought she
was making a mistake. Sorcha, after all, had married
Hugo, a man who always wanted his own way and made
no secret about it.

Since Sorcha's nature was much the same, Adela was
certain that sparks often flew between them. With
Ardelve, she was certain she would enjoy a more peaceful, more comfortable life.

He touched her shoulder, and then, as she turned toward the door, he moved his hand easily to the small of
her back. She was astonished at how reassuring it felt
there as they moved to rejoin the boisterous company.
They took their places at the high table next to Sorcha and
Hugo, the four of them standing behind chairs at the central places of honor facing the lower hall. Looking at the
other guests nearby, Adela congratulated herself on her
decision to marry Ardelve.

Members of the Sinclair family comprised much of

the company on the dais, and thanks to Countess Isabella's insistence, the seating order was unusual. Instead of the traditional arrangement with all the men at the left end of the table as viewed from the lower hall, and all the women at the right, the countess had declared that the bridal couples should take central place, with all others deferring to them.

Therefore, Isabella stood on Ardelve's right, with her eldest son, Henry Sinclair, owner of Roslin, on her right.

Henry was also Prince of Orkney, a Norse title inherited through his mother's family. In Scotland, though, even the heir to the throne—not to mention lesser men of the royal family—were earls and thus took a dim view of anyone else in the country claiming the title of prince. So, in Scotland, Henry was Earl of Orkney.

Beyond Henry stood Macleod with his intended wife, Lady Clendenen, between them and an empty space at Macleod's right. Her ladyship, reluctantly entering her fiftieth year, was a plump, personable woman with fair, smooth skin, nut-brown hair, and pleasant features pleasantly arranged, who claimed kinship with everyone of importance in Scotland. Her lively brown eyes often twinkled, but to her ladyship's oft-spoken chagrin, she lacked height. Even Adela, at just a couple of inches above five feet, was inches taller than Lady Clendenen. Standing now beside Henry, who was well over six feet, the plump little woman looked diminutive.

Sorcha stood on Adela's left with Sir Hugo beyond, then Isobel, Sir Michael Sinclair, and Hugo's father, Sir Edward Robison, flanked by one of his daughters on Hugo's side and an empty space at the end. Everyone at the high table faced the other guests, who had all gathered around the two long trestles extending from the dais.

After the countess's chaplain had spoken the grace-before-meat, the company noisily took seats, the carvers entered to the accompaniment of Prince Henry's pipers, and gillies began bustling about with jugs of wine, ale, and whisky.

Adela sat quietly, speaking only when someone spoke to her. After a time, she caught sight of the handsome young man she had noted in the chapel.

He was speaking to one of Sir Hugo's sisters, the elder, she thought. But the two girls' gowns and veils were of similar color and style, and they were nearly the same height, so she could not be sure.

Glancing past Sorcha at Hugo, she was not surprised to see his frowning, intense gaze fixed on the same couple. She was certain he must be a most protective brother and had no doubt that he would have stern words for his unfortunate sister. Adela sighed. To think that her own sisters had once expected her to marry him!

Turning to Ardelve, she smiled as she shifted aside to allow a gillie to pour wine into her goblet. When the lad stepped back, she began to reach for it but pulled her hand back when she remembered there would be toasting.

Beside her, Ardelve said, "Take a sip or two, lass. No one will mind. The carver is flashing his knives, but they'll be piping food from one end of this hall to the other for a while yet, so I'd also advise you to eat some bread with your wine."

Another gillie, overhearing, instantly offered rolls from a basket.

Adela took one gratefully, tearing off a bite-size piece and eating it before she tasted her wine. It was fine claret, she was sure, but her sense of taste seemed to have deserted her along with the rest of her senses.

Ardelve also sipped wine, and when the ceremonial presentation of the first course ended, Adela was able to eat in peace, buffered on one side by Sorcha and on the other by Ardelve. Gillies kept food and wine flowing, musicians played, and the company remained noisily cheerful. The claret was heady for one who rarely drank more than half a goblet of any wine, and Adela began to relax.

At her left, Sorcha chatted merrily with Hugo, and doubtless most improperly, too. Adela had noted that the two seemed to talk about any subject that entered their heads, and she could not approve. In her opinion, people—ladies, at least—should display more decorum. But she had long since stopped trying to persuade Sorcha of that. She just hoped her irrepressible sister would do nothing to make the countess regret her unusual seating arrangement.

"Where is Sidony?" she asked when Sorcha next turned to her. "I've not seen her since we came into the hall."

"I'll wager she went upstairs to look in on our new nephew," Sorcha said with a grin, referring to Isobel and Michael's firstborn child, now a fortnight old. "She spends more time with him than with anyone else, and you can see how relaxed Isobel is. Had her bairn been lying upstairs alone all this time, she would be fidgeting by now." Stopping a passing gillie, she asked for more wine.

"Dearling, you should have let Hugo give him the order," Adela said.

"He is talking to his sister Kate," Sorcha said.

Adela saw that the girl she had seen flirting with the handsome stranger was now sitting between Hugo and Sir Edward. The latter was chatting with the lady on his left, so she decided Hugo must have summoned Kate, because he was talking to her and looking very stern.

Kate looked annoyed, too, as well she might, Adela mused, remembering that she herself had once emptied a basin of holy water over Hugo's head when she had had enough of his lecturing. Trust the man, a notorious flirt himself, to call his sister to order for harmless flirting.

Adela recalled, too, that people besides her sisters had expected her to marry Hugo and she had even considered doing so. Now she wondered at herself. She liked him very much. He was handsome, charming, and a famous swordsman.

But he had an annoying tendency to order people about, and she preferred not to have orders flung at her. Sorcha dealt with him better than she ever could.

Ardelve would suit her better. She would live close to her own home, see old friends and family whenever she liked, and he was wealthy enough to provide every comfort. Moreover, he never snapped orders at her.

She turned to smile at him again.

He was staring at his goblet as if he considered refilling it, but he sensed her gaze, for he turned his head and said, "I think this wine has turned. But I'll not complain, for you are so beautiful that I believe I must be the most fortunate of—"

To her shock, his face froze, except for his lips, which opened as if he gasped for words to finish his sentence, and his right hand, which clutched his chest. Then, just as she realized he *was* gasping for air, he slumped awkwardly against Isabella.

The countess exclaimed and tried to hold him, but he collapsed to the floor.

Adela stared in shock.

"Sakes, I didn't think he was even in his cups," Sorcha exclaimed.

"He isn't," Hugo said, leaping up and moving swiftly to Ardelve's side.

"Adela, turn away, my dear," the countess said in a firm voice. "And, prithee, try to compose yourself, for you do not want to cause a stir. Indeed, I am sure this can be naught that should distress you."

"His eyes are open, but I do not think he sees me," Adela said without looking away.

Hugo still knelt beside Ardelve, but after only a cursory examination, he looked up and said gently, "I'm sorry, lass. I'm afraid he's gone."

She gasped, and tears sprang to her eyes.

Isabella signed to the minstrels in the gallery, and they began to play a lively tune. Startled, Adela looked up to see a trio of jugglers run into the clearing in the lower hall. Acrobats followed, doing flips.

As she began to turn back to Ardelve, she saw that although nearly everyone had turned to watch the entertainers, at least one person had not.

The man with green eyes was looking at her.

Chapter 2

⁓

The white linen cloth on the table draped to the floor, so the activity behind it remained out of view of the company in the lower hall. But Adela had no doubt the stranger had noticed Ardelve's collapse. And if he had, others had, too.

Before turning back, she noted uneasily that the stranger was getting to his feet. She hoped he did not intend to approach the dais, but she dared not watch him, lest even such slight interest draw notice.

A gillie and one of Hugo's henchmen knelt by Ardelve. The henchman's lean, muscular form and dark, neatly trimmed beard looked vaguely familiar, but Adela paid him small heed. She kept her gaze fixed on the body of the man who had so briefly been her husband.

Lying at the center of barely controlled chaos, Ardelve looked only peaceful.

Gillies poured wine, served food, and made themselves useful. Taking their cue from their betters, they attended their duties as if nothing else were happening.

In the lower hall, jugglers juggled while acrobats did flips and cartwheels. People laughed and cheered them as the minstrels continued their merry tunes.

At Adela's right, Isabella chatted with Prince Henry as if Ardelve had simply excused himself for a few minutes. But Ardelve still lay where he had fallen.

Hugo's henchman glanced up at Adela just then, again stirring that tickle of familiarity. Then he touched Hugo's arm and said something to him.

Looking over his shoulder, Hugo met her gaze briefly before turning to his wife. "Sorcha," he said, his voice carrying easily despite the general din. "I think perhaps you and Adela—"

"Nay, Hugo," Isabella interjected, turning from Prince Henry but looking as if she spoke to Adela rather than to Hugo. "They cannot both go. Nor Isobel. You should remove Ardelve to the solar for now in any event, since you three can easily do so without causing alarm."

"But her ladyship should not stay here, madam," Hugo said, his kinship and long-proven loyalty to the Sinclairs giving him license where others would dare take none. "To ask that she remain is unfair to her. Nor should you expect her to stay with . . . with him in the solar until we can arrange matters more suitably."

"I agree," Isabella said with a slight gesture to her right that brought Lady Clendenen at once to stand by her chair, smiling as if naught were amiss. Without a blink, she stepped carefully out of the way of Hugo and his helpers.

Standing beside the countess as she was, her ladyship was only a head and a few inches taller. She was, however, a good many inches wider than the willowy Isabella.

Her expression, although remaining cheerful, revealed her concern.

"What can I do to help, madam?" she asked with a glance at Adela.

"Take Lady Ardelve up to her chamber, Ealga," Isabella said. "If you take the northwest stair corridor yonder, anyone who notes your departure will assume the two of you mean to visit the garderobe tower. A casual departure will give those who may have noted Ardelve's collapse to think only that he suffers from an excess of wine, especially when Hugo helps Einar and Ivor carry him into my solar."

The name Einar was familiar, too, but Adela lost interest in Hugo's henchman when Lady Clendenen said, "But, surely, when Adela fails to return . . . "

"By then, most will have forgotten the incident. Those who recall it will assume that the bride and groom simply arranged a ruse to let them slip away for the usual purpose. Few of our guests have been in the solar, after all. Even fewer will recall that it opens only onto this dais."

"Why, that is true, for that chamber is a quite new addition, is it not?"

Adela heard their words but paid scant heed, feeling compelled to watch the men prepare to move Ardelve. Lady Clendenen's touch on her shoulder a moment later startled her so she nearly leaped off her chair.

"Forgive my smiling after so tragic an event, Adela dear," her ladyship said. "But we must try to look unconcerned unless we want everyone in the lower hall to know what is happening. If that happens, both the concerned and the curious will instantly surround us. But if we can manage to look as if naught is amiss, they will carry

Ardelve out quietly, as if he were in his cups. Then, the feasting can continue."

Adela nodded, grateful for the chance to get away. As she stood, Sorcha said quietly, "Do you want me to go with you?"

Adela glanced at her. "The countess said—"

"If you want me, I'll go, no matter what anyone says," Sorcha said firmly.

"Nay," Adela said. "She's right. 'Twould create a stir, and I don't want that."

"Very well. Then I'll come to you as soon as I can get away."

"Smile at her, Adela," Lady Clendenen said quietly.

With difficulty, Adela directed a wan smile at her sister, then turned to join her ladyship, noting with relief that Hugo and his man had lifted Ardelve out of her path and were taking him into the solar.

"Look at me, dearling, or at the floor in front of you," Lady Clendenen advised as they passed the others.

"Thank you for your kindness, madam," Adela murmured.

"Sakes, my dear, you need use no such formal tone with me. We'll be close kin when I wed your father, so I already think of you as my daughter."

"Thank you," Adela said again, finding it hard to keep looking ahead or at the floor, because she had a most inappropriate urge to see if the handsome stranger still watched her or if he had left the chamber.

Sharp movement from her companion as they neared the west end of the dais drew her to see Lady Clendenen signal repressively to someone. Following her gaze,

Adela saw the tall, broad-shouldered figure in the forest-green velvet doublet and yellow hose turning away.

He glanced over his shoulder, then paused when he caught her eye.

"You need speak to no one," Lady Clendenen said, putting a small but firm hand under Adela's elbow as they stepped off the dais and urging her thus to walk more briskly toward the nearby archway.

"Do you know that man, madam?" Adela asked, believing her companion would need no further identification. "I own, I do not, although I saw him earlier in the chapel. I also saw him speaking briefly with Sir Hugo's sister Kate."

"Aye, sure," Lady Clendenen said with her cheerful smile. "For is he not *le chevalier* Etienne de Gredin, one of my own kinsmen? Sithee, he is a distant cousin on my mother's side and likewise kin to le Duc d'Anjou. He tends to be a trifle encroaching, but he is a most charming and amusing creature withal."

"He is French then."

Lady Clendenen shrugged. "Most of us have French blood in us, do we not? However, Etienne's people came over with the Conqueror, as did the Sinclairs' and my own. His father, before he died, was envoy to France, and I warrant Etienne has as many kinsmen in France as he does here. He travels there frequently. But then many young men of good birth who have access to boats do, do they not? He wants to meet you, which is doubtless why he had the impertinence to approach. But then, he does not know it was impertinence, because he does not yet know of Ardelve's death. Nevertheless, I cannot allow him to annoy you at such a difficult time."

"Thank you," Adela said. "I do not want to talk to any-one."

"I'll present him another time," Lady Clendenen said. Then, with a direct look, she said, "I hope you do not mean to mourn overlong, my dear. Ardelve would not want that, not for a lass of your youth and beauty.

"Indeed," she went on before the astonished Adela could speak, "you must not shut yourself away or waste your attractions. A woman of your years requires a hus-band to be respectable. But I shall say no more about that now. I shall chatter away, to be sure, but you need heed none of it."

It was as well that she added the last, because Adela could think of nothing to say. That her ladyship could even raise such a subject seemed outrageous, but Adela was sure that any reply she might make would only be more so.

"Such an odd way for Ardelve to go," her ladyship went on as they entered the stair hall and approached the stairway in the thick walls forming its northwest corner. "Still, I doubt he would object much to it if one could seek his opinion."

Motioning for Adela to precede her up the stairs, she added without pause, "It is certainly a better passing than my late husband's. He was wounded in battle, poor man, and it took him months to die. To my mind, Ardelve's was a gentler way. Not that you will thank me for saying that. Indeed, your mind must seem befogged now, but we will talk again when you can think clearly. In the mean-time, I'll just keep talking to put off anyone else who might approach us."

Adela let her prattle on, although they met no one

other than a hastily curtsying maidservant before reaching the bedchamber that, until that morning, had been Adela's alone since her arrival at Roslin.

When she opened the door, the crackling fire on the hooded hearth drew her attention at once. Since she assumed that a chambermaid or gillie had lighted the fire to warm the room, the sight of a man turning sharply from the bed made her gasp and clap a hand to her breast.

Making a swift, deep bow, he said, "I pray ye'll forgive me, Lady Ardelve. I didna expect—"

"Mercy," Lady Clendenen exclaimed, putting a hand to Adela's shoulder and urging her into the room. "'Tis a wonder we did not startle one another witless, Angus. It quite slipped my mind that you'd likely be here, putting all in readiness for your master and his lady."

"Aye, sure, Lady Clendenen. But, surely, the feasting ha' only just—"

"Angus, a dreadful thing has happened," her ladyship interjected. She explained hastily.

"The laird be dead?" The man frowned heavily. "But he had nowt amiss wi' him earlier, nowt that I who ha' served him these thirty years past could see."

"Nevertheless," Lady Clendenen said on note of warning, "Ardelve is dead, Angus, and we must look after her young ladyship now."

"Aye, sure, me lady," Angus said. "But me duties now lie wi' me laird."

"They do, and you may go to him at once. But no one in the lower hall must suspect the tragedy. I warrant most of them believe he just took too much drink."

"Beg pardon, me lady, but the laird ha' kinsmen here,

ye ken. Some o' them will take it gey amiss an ye dinna tell them at once."

"Those who must be told will be told," Lady Clendenen agreed. "But few if any members of his immediate family were able to come on such short notice."

"Aye, 'twas done in a blink." He frowned. "We'll take him home, o' course."

"Arrange it as you will," she said. "I know you'll see it done as it should be."

Adela shivered at the thought that everyone would expect her to escort her husband's corpse on its long journey home to Loch Alsh. "How . . . how *will* we manage that?" she asked.

Angus was already out the door, but Lady Clendenen said briskly, "You, my dearling, will manage best by letting Angus look after Ardelve. I know I am not truly your mother, of course, but you would be wise to heed my advice."

"I am grateful for it, madam. You must know far more about such situations than I." Meeting Lady Clendenen's astonished gaze, Adela grimaced. "I beg your pardon," she said. "I should not—"

"Bless you," her ladyship said with a chuckle. "You need not fret when you say just what you think to me. I am of that same ilk, myself."

"But I should not—"

"No more apologies, for I mean to speak plainly myself," Lady Clendenen said. "Your pallor alarms me, child. I know all about your dreadful abduction a few weeks ago. 'Tis because of it that I fear you might look on this tragic incident as an excuse to immure yourself in Ardelve's castle. That will not do at all."

"But duty requires that I accompany him home, madam, and see him buried."

"I do not recommend it," her ladyship said. "But may I suggest that you will feel better if you wash your face and hands? I am sure there is no hot water in here yet, but there must be cold water in that ewer on the washstand. Let me wet a cloth for you whilst you sit on that stool by the hearth. Despite the fire, it is chilly in here."

Deciding that matters had been taken out of her hands if, indeed, she had ever held them, Adela obeyed, realizing only as the fire's warmth began to penetrate that her hands and feet were icy cold.

Holding them out to the warmth, she said nothing until her ladyship returned to her with a damp cloth, and then only to express her thanks.

"Here is a towel, too," Lady Clendenen said, laying a small one across Adela's lap before moving to the window. "Sakes, what happened to our sunlight?" she demanded, sweeping the curtains aside, "I swear I saw no sign of this murk approaching when we crossed the courtyard earlier."

Adela lowered the damp cloth to see curling wisps of mist outside the window. "How thick is it?"

"Thick enough that Isabella will find herself with more overnight company than she expected."

"That won't trouble her," Adela said. "Hugo will be annoyed, because if it gets too thick, he'll have to take the guards off the ramparts and send them and any number of others into the glen to keep watch over the approaches to the castle."

Lady Clendenen shrugged. "I've seen fog in these parts so dense that one could scarcely see one's hand before one's face even in daylight. 'Tis bad near any river, and especially so here with the Esk flowing right round three quarters of Roslin's promontory. The lads will not find it so murky in the woods."

Adela pressed the damp cloth against her forehead. Despite the chill, it felt good against her face. And with the cloth over her eyes, she felt a sense of badly needed solitude, if only while her companion remained silent, gazing out at the fog.

Hearing movement of her ladyship's return to the fire, she lowered the cloth.

"Do you feel as if you could talk a bit now?" Lady Clendenen said as she returned the towel to the wash-stand. "I do not think we should put it off. Sithee, my dear, 'tis your future at stake. I'd not have you make a muddle of it."

The last thing Adela wanted was to have to listen to more advice. But neither did she want her ladyship to prod her more about her feelings when the plain truth was that she still felt nothing. That she had been shocked at Ardelve's death was certainly true, but the sensation had passed with surprising speed.

That was not a fact she wanted to admit to his cousin, regardless of how kindly the woman felt toward her. She was distressed at the lack herself and could only imagine what Lady Clendenen would think of such an unfeeling bride. So, with nothing else to say, she kept silent.

Drawing up a second stool, her ladyship settled herself on its cushioned seat and stared into the flames before she said, "I know things are happening quickly. You've scarcely had a moment to think, but people are going to want to know what you mean to do, my dear, so you would be wise to have a plan. Did Ardelve explain the settlements he made or suggest what he might expect you to do in such a case? Not that he expected any such thing to happen today," she added with a grimace. "But he was a sensible man. I know he left you enough to insure your comfort."

"I paid no heed to the settlements," Adela confessed. "He arranged them with my father. 'Tis the usual way, I'm sure."

"Well, they did discuss some of them with me," her ladyship said. "For example, with regard to an allowance—"

A double rap on the door barely gave them warning before it opened and Lady Sidony Macleod erupted into the room, her pink skirts still rustling as she said impulsively, "I just heard, Adela, and they said you had come—"

Stopping short in visible dismay, she bobbed a curtsy to Lady Clendenen, adding, "I beg your pardon, my lady! I ought not to interrupt, but I just learned what happened and feared Adela would be all alone. I should have known someone would be with you, dearest," she added, moving to hug Adela. "How can I help?"

"Sit with us, of course," Adela said, knowing Sidony would be hurt if she sent her away. "How did you hear?"

"I was looking after Isobel's baby, but his nurse returned and said I ought to go down," Sidony said, pulling another stool up beside Adela's. "So I did, but when I heard what had happened, I came right here to you. Isobel said she and Sorcha will come as soon as they can. Others have begun to ask questions, she said. I do not know how anyone thought they could conceal Ardelve's death for long."

Adela suppressed a sigh. Much as she loved her sisters and respected Lady Clendenen, she longed for solitude.

Sidony looked guiltily at Lady Clendenen. "I interrupted your conversation, madam, but I hope you do not want me to go away."

"No, indeed, my dear," Lady Clendenen assured her. "Mayhap you can help me persuade Adela that she need not return at once to the Highlands."

"But why should she?"

Adela said, "I must accompany Ardelve, of course. He will be buried at home, and his home is mine too now, after all."

"Is it?" Sidony frowned. "Must you go soon?"

"Of course, I must. He is—was—my husband."

"As to that," Lady Clendenen said, "I wonder if that need be so. Forgive my plain speaking again, Adela, but I did see you and Ardelve step into the solar before you joined the rest of us at table. You were alone there, were you not?"

"Quite alone, madam. Why?"

"Did he . . . that is, did the two of you . . . ? Oh, mercy, I'll just say it. Is it possible that the two of you consummated your marriage then?"

"In Countess Isabella's *solar*?" The words came out in a near shriek.

Lady Clendenen's lips twitched. "I suppose not."

Sidony looked from one to the other. "No one would dare do such a thing in the countess's solar with half the world outside the door, madam."

"I had to ask the question," Lady Clendenen said. "Sithee, we were talking earlier of the settlements, Adela, and that subject may be troubling you. I can assure you,

the important ones would not be affected by an annulment now."

"Annulment?" Adela stared at her. "I couldn't. What
would people say?"

"Nothing when they learn that I support the idea,"
Lady Clendenen said. "Especially when they understand
that Ardelve arranged for such a possibility from the
start. His death before the two of you had children was always a risk. None of us gets to choose his own time,
Adela, and he wanted to be sure you were secure. Do you
know his son, Fergus?"

"I met him once," Adela said. "He is just a year or so
older than I am."

"Yes, and he will marry this year himself," Lady Clendenen said. "You would be most uncomfortable living
with him and his bride. Fergus would attempt to be civil,
as I know you would, but you would still be a stranger in
their midst."

"I could always move back to Chalamine," Adela said.

"Do you want to go from being a bride back to being
your father's daughter in your father's house?"

Sidony said quietly, "Would that not be somewhat the
same thing, Adela? Forgive me, Lady Clendenen, but
Sorcha did say you were reluctant to marry our father if
you had to share the management of his household with
his daughters."

"This has naught to do with me," Lady Clendenen
said, clearly taking no offense at Sidony's words. "You
are five-and-twenty, Adela, a woman grown. You have
had the barest taste of marriage—only an hour of it! You
need not seek annulment if the thought troubles you, but
if you do not use the money he left you to secure your

proper place amongst Scottish nobility, I'll tell you what will happen. Do you want to dwindle into an unhappy dependent of your father or your stepson?"

"Madam, even if I could do as you suggest, you cannot mean for me to shrug Ardelve off as if he'd meant nothing to me. I won't do that."

"Aye, 'twould be most unseemly. But to wallow in your widowhood with no more to your relationship than an hour-long, arranged marriage would be more so."

Adela gasped. But before she could find words to express her outrage, the door opened again and Sorcha entered with Isobel. Finding cushions for themselves, they sat on the floor, big with news from the great hall, where word of Ardelve's death, once known, had spread quickly.

Sorcha said indignantly, "One horrid man actually said that Adela must be suffering from some dreadful curse."

"Insolence!" Sidony exclaimed. "Who dared say such a thing?"

"Some arrogant courtier," Isobel said. "He said it is plain from her abduction, and now this tragedy, that God never intends Adela to marry."

They shared more anecdotes from the feast hall before Sorcha said, "You've barely spoken, Adela. Ardelve's death was a dreadful shock, but surely it is not only grief that has silenced you. What's troubling you so?"

Adela shook her head, but Lady Clendenen said, "I fear I took the opportunity before the rest of you arrived for some plain speaking."

When the others exchanged bewildered looks, she added with a smile. "I said nothing dreadful, I promise. I merely pointed out to Adela that she has choices to make and suggested she consider carefully what she means to do next."

Her ladyship explained, and the conversation took its course once again without assistance from Adela. Her sisters were happy to discuss what she should do, although all three seemed to agree that her future looked bleak.

"But if she truly has money of her own now . . . " Sorcha began thoughtfully.

"Aye, sure, that will make things easier," Isobel said. "And you can always stay here at Roslin with Michael and me, Adela."

"I'm sure you could stay with Sorcha and Hugo at Hawthornden, too, if you'd rather," Sidony said.

"As to that," Sorcha said, biting her lip, "I do not know that we will be at Hawthornden much longer. Sir Edward has said Hugo should go with Donald of the Isles when Donald leaves court to return home, and I mean to go with him. I have things to collect from Chalamine, and Sir Edward suggested that we might spend some time at Dunclathy on our way back, to see that all is in order there. We plan to be away most of the spring and summer."

"But Adela could stay at Hawthornden even without you, could she not?" Sidony persisted.

"If she wants to, I suppose she can. I'll ask Hugo."

"She has other options," Lady Clendenen said. "Besides a generous financial settlement, Ardelve left her a house in Stirling, to use for her lifetime. Or, if she likes, she can stay with me in Edinburgh. I'd enjoy her company."

"Thank you, my lady," Adela said. "However . . . "

"Pray, don't say that you will not," Isobel cut in swiftly, and soon the others were discussing her among themselves again as if she were not there.

Adela shut her ears to it all, staring into the flickering firelight, until Sidony said abruptly, "What do *you* want, Adela?"

For perhaps the first time in her life, Adela did not hesitate to say exactly what she was thinking: "I want you all to go away and leave me alone."

Sidony's eyes widened. "But—"

"I don't want to live in Edinburgh or Stirling, or in any town. Nor do I want to impose myself on you or Sorcha, Isobel. I'll do my duty to Ardelve, and then I will go home. But all I want now is peace, so go away, all of you, and let me be!"

A moment later, the door clicked shut behind them and she had her wish.

At first, she was grateful, but it was not long before her thoughts and emotions began to plague her. What had happened too many times before was happening again. Unfair though she knew it to be, she was angry with Ardelve for dying, just as she had been angry when her mother had died, and her sister Mariota.

A voice in her head suggested that she should depend on nothing and no one. People could not control the Fates. Certainly, she could not. The voice in her mind seemed so loud that she began to wonder if she were going mad.

Why had she told them so rudely to leave? What would they think of her?

The iron control she had developed had slipped away

without warning, and the result was as she had so often feared. She had to regain her composure and keep it, because what might happen if she lost it altogether did not bear thinking about.

Deciding she might relax if she lay down on the bed, she did so without even taking off her dress. No sooner did she shut her eyes than she fell asleep.

A nightmare wakened her. She did not recall details, only that she had been frightened witless as usual and felt as if she were choking. She had suffered from bad dreams since her abduction, but this time her necklace had tightened round her throat as she slept. So, at least, she told herself as she straightened it, the choking sensation was understandable.

The room was dark, the embers on the hearth barely aglow. She had no idea how long she had slept. But if her sisters had left her alone for hours, the chance that they would do so much longer was small. On the thought, she got up, relieved herself in the chamber pot, found the hooded lavender velvet cloak that Isobel had given her, and flung it on as she hurried to the door.

Opening it cautiously, she peeked out, found the landing reassuringly empty, and fled up the winding stairs to the narrow door onto the ramparts. Praying the fog had not dispersed and that Hugo had removed all the men to guard approaches from the glen, she quietly opened the door and stepped onto the wall walk.

Shutting the door behind her with no more sound than a metallic click as the latch fell into place, she felt as if she had shut out the world. The eerie black silence of the fog-shrouded ramparts engulfed her, banishing the discomfiting sense she had had since Ardelve's death of being swallowed up by well-wishers, critics, and fools.

The result of this peace, to her surprise, was a wave of gusty sobs that wracked her until she pressed hard against the stone wall, seeking comfort from its solidity in the black mist. No one would seek her here, she assured herself as she wiped tears with her sleeve and began to relax again. She should savor the quiet.

The air felt damp and chilly on her cheeks, but she did not care. The velvet cloak was warm, and its sable-trimmed hood protected her hair from the mist. The chilly, damp air was refreshing, but thoughts of what lay ahead still plagued her.

Although she had declared that she would do her duty, she did not want to accompany a corpse all the way to the Highlands. Such a journey could take a fortnight, and although days were still cool, no corpse could remain fresh for long.

A scraping sound, as of a boot on the wall walk, startled her.

"Who's there?"

A male voice, deep and unfamiliar, said, "Do not be frightened, my lady. There is naught in this darkness to harm you."

Chapter 3

The deep, disembodied voice sounded educated, soothing, even sensuous. Adela's tension increased nonetheless. "But who are you?" she demanded.

"Just a man, my lady, who finds the sound of a young woman's sobs distressing. Is there naught I can do to help you put things right?"

"No, sir, nothing," she said, embarrassed that he had heard her crying.

"Will you not tell me what has distressed you so, Lady Adela?"

"Faith, you know who I am?" Her embarrassment increased. Even in the chilly dampness she felt her cheeks burn at the thought that he had witnessed her uncharacteristic and most unladylike display of emotion.

"I recognized your voice," he said. "In view of what happened, I should say that you have cause for tears. But, clearly, yours was no ordinary arranged marriage if you care so much for your loss that you fled here to indulge your sorrow."

A suspicion stirred as to who he must be, for only one man other than Ardelve had shown interest in her that day. But surely guests at Roslin did not usually wander about the castle by themselves, let alone all the way up to its ramparts.

"Pray, sir, tell me your name?" she asked.

"My name is not important," he said. "Indeed, 'tis better that you continue to think of me as just a friendly voice in the darkness."

"Are you a friend of the Sinclair family?" she asked.

"Aye, a good friend."

"I wondered, because strangers do not normally come up here alone."

"I suppose not," he agreed. "However, tonight even the so-careful Sinclairs would scarcely expect an enemy to take a stroll around the wall-walk. Hugo Robison is famous for his ability to protect this castle."

"Sir Michael Sinclair, as well," Adela said, knowing that Michael served as master of Roslin when Henry was not in residence.

"Aye, but you change the subject, my lady. I was told you scarcely knew your husband. Do you indeed grieve so deeply for him, or for another cause?"

"In truth, I do not know why I was weeping," she admitted. In the silence that followed, she tried to sort through her thoughts and feelings, then added, "'Tis more likely that I was crying because I can *not* weep for Ardelve."

"I don't understand," he said. "If you cry but cannot cry for him, then for whom were you crying?"

"You make it sound like a bard's riddle," she said.

"The truth is simpler. You see, this morning I had no feelings at all. It seemed very odd, because a woman ought to be happy on her wedding day, don't you think?"

"Were you sad?"

"I felt nothing."

"Why do you think that was?"

"Faith, sir, I don't know. I do not know why I am talking to you when common sense tells me I should not even be here. Yet I am saying things I would not normally say to anyone, and I have no idea why. If I could see, I think I would have fled immediately upon hearing you speak. I'd never have entered into this absurd conversation with you."

"You may certainly return to your chamber if that is what you want to do," he said, still in that same calm, soothing tone. His voice was having an unusual effect on her, for it seemed to touch something deep inside, warming her in a way that was unusual but seemed desirable. She wanted the sensation to continue.

"At least you do not order me to go," she said. "Most men I know would say that I should return at once and lock my door. They would scold and insist that I ought not to stand here talking to you as if I knew you."

"You are perfectly safe talking to me," he said.

"You may say so," she said. "But I doubt Sir Hugo would agree."

"Hugo's opinion in such a case matters not one whit to me."

More certain than ever of his identity, and amused that he would dare to defy Hugo, she allowed herself a near smile. "I doubt you would say that to his face."

"Perhaps not," he agreed, and she heard a smile in his voice.

She was silent, and a moment later, he said, "I know about your abduction, of course. That must have been a terrifying ordeal."

"It was not pleasant," she said. "He snatched me right off the kirk steps at my wedding. The priest had just asked if anyone objected to our union when four men rode out of the woods nearby. Everyone thought they were just tardy wedding guests, except they wore masks and rode right to the steps, and their leader—"

"Waldron of Edgelaw."

"Aye, he rode right up to me. I thought he had a message, so I stepped forward. He just scooped me off my feet and rode off with me."

"Horrifying," he murmured.

"Aye, but he did not harm me. Nor do I believe he ever would have."

"I am sure you knew him better than I, my lady."

A certain sharpness in his tone made her stiffen. "I know only that I had no real cause to fear him," she said, firmly suppressing the irritating memory of how much the menacing Waldron had terrified her—especially in the beginning.

"I don't know that I've heard an explanation of *why* he abducted you," he said. "Did he ever supply a reason for such insolence?"

"He said it was vengeance for wrongs done to him and to the Kirk," she said. "I own, I never understood that, and I . . . I do not like talking about it, so if you . . . "

"Forgive me," he said as she sought words to explain. "I should not have probed into so personal a matter. 'Tis a failing of mine that I can never seem to keep my curiosity in check when something, or someone, interests me."

The comment stirred again that mild, twitching sense of humor. "You should meet my sister Isobel, sir. Your curiosity can be as nothing to hers. She asked so many questions that I finally lost my temper, or as near as made no difference."

As soon as she said them, she wished she could take back the words. He was too easy to talk to, and she did not want to admit Isobel had plagued her until she had spoken more sharply to her than to anyone else since arriving at Roslin.

"Living with the memories must be difficult," he said.

A flood of memories, mixed and jumbled pictures and emotions, spewed through her mind before she said curtly, "I saw him hang a man."

The words leaped out before she knew she was going to say them. Others had asked what she remembered, but the memories had eluded her. Had anyone asked her what stirred her to tell him about that, of all things, she could not have said. The man's power to make her speak seemed well nigh devilish. But one could not unsay things, as much as one would like to.

Her words hovered between them, making her stomach clench.

He let the silence continue until she ached to demand that he tell her what he was thinking. But to do such a thing was beyond her. She could not recall any time in her life that she had made that demand of anyone but an erring servant or a younger sister. Even then, the reason for asking had been a desire to know what either Sorcha or Isobel—for it was most likely one or the other—could have been thinking to fling herself into the mischief that had earned her a scolding.

Just when Adela began to think she could not bear the silence another moment, he said, "What a shocking thing to see. Why did he do it?"

She had not let herself think about the reason before. For that matter, she had scarcely let herself think about any part of her ordeal. But without hesitation she said, "He did it to punish the man but also, I think, to frighten me. He wanted to show me what he was capable of, to make sure I would obey him unquestioningly."

"Some men do try to rule by fear, and Waldron was a villain, so likely you're right about him," he said. "Had the man he hanged done aught to deserve hanging?"

She shivered, her mind as black a fog as that which surrounded them.

Her companion was apparently content to remain silent, but this time the silence was no comfort. Images formed unbidden in her mind until she shivered again. Giving herself a shake, she said, "H-he told me he would help me. He said all I need do was . . . " She drew a shuddering breath, but still he did not speak. At last, in a rush, she said, "He wanted me to kiss him first. He was horrid!"

"Then, truly, he deserved to hang," he said firmly. "You need concern yourself with such vermin as that one no longer, my lady. The man was no better than your abductor. Both richly deserved their fates."

"What do you know of Waldron's fate?" she asked, aware that only a few knew the truth of it.

This time his silence held a different quality, and she felt instinctively that she had surprised him. But his words, when he spoke, came as calmly as ever, "I suppose I know what most do, that he has not been seen anywhere since your rescue and is sure to be dead. Hugo and the Sinclair brothers are capable men."

Adela did not reply. She wanted him to say more but only because his voice was so calm, so reassuring. He made her feel as if she could tell him anything. As the thought crossed her mind, she heard Hugo's voice in her head, or Sorcha's, reminding her that she was being foolish to trust a man she could not see, a man she would not recognize if she met him the very next day.

She would know his voice, though. She was certain she need only hear him speak again to recognize him anywhere. Her suspicion that she already knew his identity was stronger than ever, but not strong enough to tell him so—not yet. However, one thing did remain to set straight before their conversation ended.

"You are wrong about my abductor," she said. "He was not evil in the way that you and others insist he was. He did dreadful, evil things, but he was only a man with strong convictions whose beliefs differed greatly from ours."

"You are kinder to his memory than he deserves," he replied.

His voice was as calm as it had been all along, but she sensed something in it now that warned her not to debate that point with him. Still, no one else had come to know Waldron of Edgelaw's thoughts and beliefs as she had. She did not think she was just being kind.

"'Tis he who was kind to me, sir, in many ways. He talked to me, said I was a good listener, and I think he truly did believe the things he told me."

"Did you think he needed someone to listen?"

"Aye, perhaps."

"So he needed you."

That was, she realized, exactly what Waldron had made her think. "He may have wanted me to think so," she said as she thought about that. "But then, he just set me free as if I had meant nothing to him, even as a hostage."

"Did you *want* to mean something to him?"

"No!"

He did not speak, but she could feel his disbelief as if it were a solid mass in the air between them.

"He was horrid! He was—"

"Evil?"

Feeling anger stir, she shut her mouth tight and inhaled. Releasing the breath, carefully calm and controlled, she said, "You twist my words, sir. That is unkind."

"Perhaps so," he said equably. "We can talk more about this another time if you like, but I suspect you must be growing chilly up here."

"I hadn't noticed," she admitted, feeling as if he had let the wind out of her sails by so easily accepting her rebuke. Gamely, she added, "But now I do feel the cold, and in any event, I must not stay any longer. I am grateful for my brief time of freedom, but someone will doubtless be looking for me by now."

"Do you think so?" he asked. "I should imagine that at this hour everyone must believe you to be sound asleep."

"Is it so late? I confess I have no idea what the hour is."

"They finished serving the late supper over an hour ago," he said. "The entertainment was in full force when I left, and probably still is, but most of the ladies had retired. We'll doubtless soon hear the chapel bell toll Nocturnes."

"Midnight! Mercy, I had no idea I'd slept so long."

"You should be thankful. That you were able to rest is good."

"Aye, but I must go. It would not do to stay up now only to exhaust myself tomorrow. They are bound to plague me again about what I should do next—all of them. I shall want my wits about me when they do."

"Who is daring to plague you?"

Realizing that once again she had simply spoken her thoughts to him, she bit her lower lip in vexation. Really, he was a dangerous acquaintance. She should not be talking of such things with anyone and certainly not with a man who refused even to tell her his name.

Since she had learned enough to know his continued silence meant he would await her reply, she said, "I should not complain. I know they do it only because they care about me. They worry that I'll make some dreadful mistake."

"Nevertheless, it is early in the day to be plaguing you about what you should or should not do next," he said. "Tell them to go and boil their heads."

"Is that what you do, sir, when people plague you?" she asked.

"Not always," he admitted. "But unless I owe duty, loyalty, or particular respect to the person offering me unwanted advice, I have been known to do that."

She sighed. "I think it would be wonderful to be able to speak one's mind to people who flit about one like anxious gadflies, but I cannot do it."

"I thought all the Macleod sisters spoke their minds," he said.

"Then, you must have heard tales about Isobel and Sorcha, rather than about the other five of us," she said dryly.

"True," he said. "But neither of them seems at all meek."

"I do not think I am meek either," Adela said. "I do try

to be tactful, though, rather than outspoken, unless I am truly vexed. I did finally ask everyone to leave me alone today, but only because I was still suffering the shock of Ardelve's death, and was so tired I could not think. Even so, I was as surprised as I'm sure my sisters and Lady Clendenen were when I snapped at them."

"Did they go away?"

"Aye, they did."

"Well, then."

When he said no more, she decided she would be wise to bid him goodnight before she admitted anything worse to him or someone else wandered up to the wall walk. It would not be a good thing for anyone to find her there alone with him—not that she believed for a moment that he would allow that to happen.

From what she already knew of him, he would be more likely to be as smoke in the dense fog, making no sound to betray his presence.

"Do you mean to stay up here?" she asked at last.

"I think that would be the wisest course, don't you?"

"I would like to know who you are."

"I'm glad you feel that way," he said. "I am also glad that we had this talk. I have much admired your courage."

"I have no courage, sir. I did only what I had to do. I tell you frankly that, even though I now believe I had little cause to fear Waldron of Edgelaw, I was terrified the whole while and for a good while afterward."

"But, my lady, that is the very essence of courage, is it not?"

"What is?"

"To do what must be done despite one's terrors. To act sensibly in a crisis is admirable. That you remain sensitive to others' needs and motives argues that you are kind, as well. I would like to know you better, to become your friend."

Adela stood very still, scarcely aware that her breathing had stopped until she felt the ache in her chest. She tried to remember if anyone had ever said such things to her before. She did not think anyone believed her to be unkind or to *lack* courage or sense, but she could not recall anyone ever defining her in such a way, certainly not as firmly as he had.

Nor could she recall anyone declaring that he would like to be her friend. She had friends at home, to be sure, but few from her own station in life and no one she could think of with whom she could share the thoughts in her head as she had with this man on this very strange night. She did not know what to say to him.

Then, and again without thought, the words came easily.

"I'd like that, but how can I be friends with a man whose name I don't know?"

"'Tis a rare challenge, but I believe you are equal to it. For now, though, you had better use that good sense of yours and take yourself off to bed."

"Aye, I should." But her reluctance to leave only grew stronger.

"We will meet again, I promise," he said. "Until then, know that whenever you need a friend, I am yours to command."

"A strange thing to offer, sir, when I should not know how to summon you."

"You need only let it be known that you need a friend, lass."

His words were perhaps apocryphal but nonetheless

soothing to ears that more frequently heard criticism, carping, and unwanted advice.

Quietly, wanting nothing to destroy the momentary sense of deep peace he had given her, she said, "Goodnight, sir."

"Sleep well, my friend," he murmured.

Feeling her way back to the door to the stairs, she opened it carefully, half expecting to come face to face with a demand to know what the devil she was doing there. What would follow depended, of course, upon who had found her. But the worst that could come of it was a scolding, and now that she was a married lady, she mused, only her husband truly had the right to scold her.

With another sigh, she realized that with Ardelve dead, any number of people would be willing to step into his position as her guardian. Therefore, it would be best if she could return to her bedchamber without meeting a soul.

As she went downstairs, she strained her ears not only for noise below but for any above her on the stairway. But she heard nothing.

Having never explored the wall walk, she did not know how many access points it had, but she was as sure as she could be that it had more than one. And doubtless the man on the ramparts knew all the others.

The voice in the back of her head continued to insist that she knew who he was, that he had to be the handsome stranger who had shown such interest in her, the man Lady Clendenen claimed to be her distant kinsman, Etienne de Gredin.

As Adela approached her own chamber, she wondered why she had not taxed him with that suspicion. It had been so easy to talk with him about anything else, so easy to say whatever came into her head. Yet she had not given him the slightest hint that she suspected his identity.

She was reaching for the latch on her door, it struck her that Lady Clendenen had said that her cousin had come from France. But the man in the fog had spoken as an educated Scotsman. He was not a Highlander, though. Or, if he was, he'd spent more time in the Lowlands than at home. But then, Lady Clendenen had said naught to indicate that his first language was French or that he was, himself. If she remembered correctly, her ladyship had said only that his antecedents were French.

Having reassured herself, Adela lifted the latch and pushed open her door to find cressets lighted, as well as a low-burning fire.

The trim, redheaded maidservant who had looked after her since her arrival at Roslin jumped up from a stool by the hearth. "Och, me ladyship," she exclaimed. "I thought mayhap ye'd gone to the garderobe tower, but ye were gone so long!"

"Aye, but I am back now, Kenna," Adela said calmly.

"I'd been looking in now and again to see did ye want supper or aught else."

"Just bed now, but thank you."

"I laid out your shift, and there be warm water in the ewer."

As Adela moved to attend her nightly ablutions, she thought back to the man on the ramparts and knew she was looking forward to meeting Lady Clendenen's cousin with much more eagerness than any so-recent widow had a right to feel.

Adela's erstwhile companion, having opened the stairway door again and listened to her soft footsteps descending, waited until he could be certain she had reached her room in safety. With watchers everywhere, both inside the castle and out, she would come to no harm if she did meet someone. Whether she realized it or not, even if she reached her room in solitude, at least a few would know by morning, if not before, that she had been wandering about.

If they were already concerned about her state of mind, as well they should be, considering all she'd been through in past weeks, her midnight rambling might cause more stir than he thought it warranted. She would recover from her trials faster, God knew, if the well-meaning womenfolk would give her some peace.

He had known before today that she was a beauty. But seeing her earlier in her form-clinging velvet wedding gown with her honey-gold hair streaming in thick waves down her back had stunned him to speechlessness. Her full, soft breasts had thrust hard against the plush golden velvet, fairly clamoring to fill a man's eager hands. His body had stirred instantly in response and stirred now at the memory.

At the time, one of his men had suggested that perhaps he ought to close his mouth before something flew in that he'd liefer not swallow, which had recalled him rather sharply to his wits. He remembered that moment uneasily now.

The Macleod sisters were all renowned beauties, but when people at Roslin spoke of them, they spoke first of the beautiful lady Isobel, who had married Sir Michael Sinclair, and next of Hugo's wife, the lady Sorcha. She was just as lovely as Isobel, but more often they spoke of her daring and her way of putting her chin in the air whenever someone suggested she should not do something she wanted to do.

A few spoke of their younger sister, the lady Sidony, but she was more elusive, less likely to draw notice. Moreover, Sidony was Sorcha's opposite in temperament, having always, they said, followed her lead in whatever they did.

If he had favored one over the others, it had been Hugo's lady, Sorcha, but he could not deny that something about the lady Adela had attracted him the first time he'd laid eyes on her, the previous summer at the installation of Prince Henry of Orkney. In the midst of the chaos attending that event, she had remained calm and in control of herself—except when she had cast a basin of water over Hugo's head. Michael had described that event to him in gleeful detail.

He just wished he had been with them at the time to witness that splendid moment himself, for with that one act, she had endeared herself to him forever, if only for blunting some of Hugo's impudence. Later, he had seen her only after her abduction, injured, shabby, and bewildered. But now . . .

Shutting the stairway door and turning back to the parapet, he shook his head at himself. He was at least seven kinds of a fool for even thinking about her, about any of them, for that matter. Such women were not for the man he had become.

Without land of his own or prospects for acquiring any, he had naught to offer her. Land, after all, a man either inherited, received as a royal reward, or acquired in a marriage settlement. But his father would leave him nothing, the present royal family was more likely to take land than to grant it, and in any marriage with land involved, the lass's father would expect her chosen mate to bring something equivalent to the marriage.

He could offer a wife only his knightly skills and his belief that the past nine years had taught him to master his volatile temper—nearly always. Nine years before, when he'd offered his services to the Sinclairs and Hugo, he had done so as a simple serving knight, without thought or concern for aught but his immediate future. And for nine years, the life had suited him. He had been content. But now . . .

He remained standing in that impenetrable darkness for a long while, hands braced on the damp parapet as he listened to rushing water far below and wrestled with his thoughts and memories. At last, realizing the fog had penetrated his heavy cloak and would soon soak him to the skin, Sir Robert Logan heaved a sigh, gave a last thought to what might have been, and took himself off to bed.

Chapter 4

Adela awoke to soft footsteps in her bedchamber, followed by the familiar scrape of a hearth shovel. Pushing the bed curtain aside, she peeped out to see Kenna crouched by the banked embers, coaxing tinder and kindling to flame.

The girl glanced at her, saying, "Good morning, your ladyship. I hope ye dinna mind me being late. But as ye were awake till such an hour, I thought I'd let ye sleep a wee bit longer. Still, the countess said ye'd want to be up to greet anyone as might want to pay respects to Lord Ardelve."

"I do," Adela said, throwing back the covers. One had to perform some duties whether one wanted to or not. Moreover, she had learned that one should view the countess's statements as commands rather than suggestions.

At least she felt rested, and for once, she had suffered none of the nightmares that had plagued her since her abduction. They had begun when she was under Waldron's control, which made sense. That they had continued af-

terward made no sense, because she was safe and would
be safe as long as she stayed at Roslin.

Roslin Castle was one of the strongest fortresses in the
country, boasting a high curtain wall and strong gates.
Perched on a clifftop promontory thrusting into a sharp
curve of the deep gorge cut by the turbulent river North
Esk, it was nearly unassailable for even the most determined enemy.

The river flowed almost all the way around the south-
facing promontory, leaving only a narrow, terrifying land
bridge to connect it to a treacherous, heavily wooded land
mass to its north. From there, a narrow cart track dipped
down to follow the river's western bank north to Edinburgh or south to the head of Roslin Glen. Another,
higher road reached by fording the river below the castle
followed the eastern ridge and was the better of the two.

Reminding herself again that she was safe, Adela put
all thought of the nightmares out of her head. Moving
quickly in the chilly room, she performed her morning
ablutions, then accepted Kenna's help to dress in a simple,
becoming tunic and skirt of soft, moss green cameline.

"Ye'll need a proper headdress today," Kenna said as
she brushed Adela's hair.

Adela agreed. Both Isabella and Lady Clendenen
would expect her to behave as a married lady—a widowed lady—and as such, she could not go about as she
preferred, with only a short veil to cover her hair.

"Just plait it, Kenna," she said. "But first brush it back
off my brow. I'll wear the plain white caul and the matching silk veil that Lady Isobel gave me."

Most of the clothing she wore at Roslin had come
from the generous Isobel, because Adela's abductor had

taken her from the Highlands with no more than the blue wedding dress and linen shift she had worn the first time she had tried to marry Ardelve. Thanks to the countess and the countess's seamstress, she did have her golden velvet wedding dress and one other, a fine tawny silk gown with bands of colorful embroidery to decorate its hem, deep neckline, and the edge of each sleeve.

Ten minutes later, heading to the great hall to break her fast at the high table, she warned herself that it might take effort to maintain her resolve and remain civil. Thus, she hesitated on the threshold when she saw that Isabella, Lady Clendenen, Isobel, Sorcha, and Sidony had all lingered at the table, chatting together.

She knew they had likely been discussing her, deciding amongst themselves just what she should do. None seemed to notice her right away, though, so she drew a breath to steady her nerves and moved quietly toward them.

Except for two gillies dismantling the last of the trestles in the lower hall, no men were present. But as she neared the dais, her father entered the lower hall from the stairway in the southeast corner that led to the main entrance a half-floor below.

"Hold there, lass," he said in his loud, blustery way, bringing conversation at the high table to a halt. "I want a word wi' ye."

"Aye, sir," she said. Turning to face him, she was aware that every eye at the high table had turned their way. She knew, too, that every ear strained now to hear what he would say to her.

Macleod was a large, robust man with a large, robust voice and an unpredictable temper. But he smiled and put a hand on her shoulder as he said, "I'm pleased to see ye up and about. Ye mustna shut yourself away."

"I've no intention of doing that, sir," she said, keeping her voice low despite the surge of annoyance she felt when she realized that he must have discussed her with Lady Clendenen. "I know my duty, Father," she added clearly.

"Aye, ye do," he agreed. "'Tis one o' your most admirable traits. By my troth, lass, I ken fine that I can depend on ye to do as ye ought."

"I hope so, sir, although I own that I do not know yet what that may be. Mayhap you, too, have advice for me."

When he glanced at the high table, fidgeting, she knew exactly what he would say and nearly sighed in her vexation when the prediction proved true.

"Bless ye, lass," he said. "Ye ought to stay right here at Roslin wi' your sisters and . . . and others ye can trust to ha' your best interest at heart."

"Indeed, sir, do you not think Ardelve's family may take offense if I do not accompany his body home? Surely, they'll expect me to."

"Sakes, they dinna ken that the man be dead, so they'll expect nowt o' ye."

Exerting patience as she so often had to do to avoid rousing his temper, she said, "They'll learn of his death soon enough, because word of such things travels faster than coffins do. Will they not expect me to accompany his funeral train?"

"Ealga—that is to say, Lady Clendenen—will attend to them if they do expect such," he said, glancing again at the high table. "She'll send her own message, telling Fergus she's invited ye to stay wi' her."

Adela fought a familiar urge to agree to whatever he

said, if only to end the discussion. But she knew she could not submit so easily, not if she was to hold her own against them all. Right or wrong, if she was not to lose what freedom she had, she had to choose for herself the course her life would take.

Therefore, deciding that she might as well make her case to the others as she made it to him, she said in a tone that would reach the dais, "I am grateful for Lady Clendenen's invitation, Father, but much as I appreciate everyone's advice, I will decide for myself what to do."

The heavy frown returned. "D'ye think that's wise, lass? Ye shouldna reject the opportunity her ladyship be offering ye."

Deciding to emphasize what she hoped would prove her strongest weapon, she said, "I am a married lady, sir, a widow, and I have resources of my own now, or I will have them soon. Surely, I have the right to decide this matter for myself."

"Resources? What resources?"

"Lady Clendenen said Ardelve settled money on me, enough so I can live independently. You agreed to those settlements, sir. Is that not so?"

Macleod's frown grew more ominous. "She shouldna ha' told ye such stuff!"

"Mercy, is it not true then?"

"Och, aye, it be true enough, but ye're nobbut a lass, Adela, and ye ha' nae business to be thinking o' living independently. What can ye ken o' such a life? I'll deal wi' your gelt for ye, my lass, or if ye dinna trust your own father with it, and choose instead to make your home at Loch Alsh, as *is* your right, I expect yon Fergus will be capable enough o' looking after your gelt for ye."

Stiffening, she looked him in the eye but lowered her voice again as she said, "I can think of no one I would trust more than you to look after my affairs, sir. I know you to be a most careful manager."

"Aye, sure," he said in his normal tone and looking less belligerent. "But if ye dinna want to live at Chalamine . . . " He paused meaningfully.

"I warrant you'd even welcome me home, despite having made it plain to me that Lady Clendenen will not marry you until you have married off your daughters. She meant me in particular, you know," she added, lowering her voice even more. "She certainly knows Sidony well enough to be sure *she* would never interfere with the management of your household."

"Aye, that's true," Macleod acknowledged. "That lass couldna make a decision an her life depended on it."

"Nor would I intentionally interfere with Lady Clendenen," Adela added, nearly whispering. "But I do understand her concern, because I cannot promise never to suggest she try another way of doing things. Not after so many years of running that household according to my own wishes, and yours."

"Aye, well, two women trying to control a household can be a wretched business," he said with a shudder. "I remember how it were wi' my mother and yours. Hoots, but until your uncle took your gran to live wi' him on the Isle o' Lewis, 'twere a dreadful arrangement! Me mam had a temper on her, and although yours were a gentler lass, mine could stir coals wi' a tree stump."

Feeling her cheeks redden at the realization that no one could have any doubt now what course her side of the conversation had taken, she raised her voice again to say,

"I don't think for a moment that Lady Clendenen would stir coals, sir. She simply wants to believe her household will be her own. Pray, try to understand, though, that I must think about this. I want to understand my position, and I will appreciate advice from anyone who offers it. But do please recall that I, too, am accustomed to running a household. I don't want to dwindle into . . . "

She hesitated, reluctant to speak the words that hovered on the tip of her tongue lest she anger him, but to her surprise, he smiled.

"Ye dinna want to become like your Aunt Euphemia," he said bluntly. "Sakes, lass, ye couldna do that an ye tried."

"But I think I could," Adela said. "Only think, sir, when Aunt Euphemia lived with us, she barely opened her mouth for fear of angering you and being turned out although you are her own brother and would never have done such a thing. And *she* does not like to manage things. But I do. I'd feel suffocated if I had to live with anyone who expected me to be always meek and submissive."

"But women *should* be meek and submissive," Macleod said.

"Perhaps some should," a new voice chimed in. "But, thankfully, most noblewomen of my acquaintance are rarely either."

Adela, facing Macleod, had briefly forgotten their interested but still silent audience. Although it was Isabella who had spoken, the surge of heat in her cheeks resulted from fear of what Lady Clendenen must be thinking. How, she wondered, could she face her again?

However, Macleod, typically, had paid the women at the high table no heed whatsoever until the interruption. He turned now, his heavy frown back in place until he realized who had spoken. Then, hastily, he bobbed a semblance of a bow.

"Good morning, madam," he said politely to Countess Isabella. "I ken fine that a woman o' your rank doesna submit easily to anyone but her king. However, I hope ye'll no be putting such notions in my lass's head as will set her against them wi' authority over her."

"Our Adela has too much sense to fly in the face of true authority, my dear Macleod," Isabella said. "But do stay the rest of your conversation until she has broken her fast. She scarcely ate a bite yesterday and must be well nigh starving.

"Moreover," she added when he hesitated, grimacing, "we are all of a single mind with you, you know. So we can help you persuade her. And you will both be more comfortable if you sit at the table with us," she added as a clincher.

"Ye'll do as ye're bid, Adela," Macleod muttered. Then, in a louder tone, he thanked the countess and put a hand on Adela's shoulder as if to turn her himself.

Knowing she had no choice but to obey the countess's summons, she was already turning, but the first person to catch her eye was not Isabella but Lady Clendenen. Her eyes were atwinkle, and she was smiling as warmly as if she had not heard a word of what Adela had said.

Adela expelled a sigh of relief, hoping she had not said anything to truly offend her. Lady Clendenen had never behaved any way but kindly toward her. Perhaps she truly did take a motherly interest. Reluctant to trust her own judgment on that score, Adela fingered the gold chain necklace she rarely took off as she went with Macleod to join the others at the high table.

Feeling her way carefully in the conversation that ensued, she made no effort at first to join in. When two gillies came running, Isabella sent one to the kitchen to fetch hot food for Adela and the other to the buttery to fetch ale for Macleod. The conversation continued while Adela ate, and although the other ladies agreed that she should heed their advice, they did not seem to agree with each other.

Sorcha said, "You are a fool if you insist on traveling all the way to Loch Alsh when you do not have to, Adela. To travel with a corpse—"

"Pray, Sorcha, don't be horrid," Sidony pleaded. "This must all be hard for her to bear, although I should not want to travel with a dead person, myself," she added with a shudder. "You don't *want* to, do you, Adela?"

Applied to in such a way, and quite unable to snub her youngest sister, Adela said, "Duty is often unpleasant, Sidony. But one must do it nonetheless."

"Have some ale, dear," Isabella suggested. "Ivor is behind you with the jug."

"Thank you, madam," Adela said, nodding to the gillie and shifting aside to let him fill her mug. She had no taste for ale at breakfast, but it was easier to accept it than to debate the point with Isabella.

Conversation continued to flow around her, but although she had told Macleod she welcomed advice, she let it flow unstaunched until Lady Clendenen said flatly, "Widowhood is not for the young or the faint of heart, dearest. I was in my fortieth year when poor Clendenen went. At first, even for me, life was bleak."

Despite herself, Adela listened.

"More than one warned me that people would think it scandalous if I lived alone in Clendenen House. Most insisted that duty to my husband required me to stay with a respectable kinsman, which meant moving in with Cousin

Ardelve or my brother. But both lived far from town, so instead, when a friend invited me to stay with her and her husband in North Berwick, I did. However, after a month's unbearable solitude there, I leaped at an invitation to accompany other friends to a house party in Linlithgow."

"Really?" Sidony said, smiling. "A party?"

"Aye, and I'd do the same again," Lady Clendenen said. "While it is true that some people, mostly here in the Lowlands, believe as the Roman Kirk teaches that one should observe what the Kirk calls a proper period of mourning, many more—certainly in the Borders and Highlands—believe in getting on with life whilst one has a life to get on with. My North Berwick friends are the first sort, I'm afraid."

"Hence, the solitude," Sorcha said dryly.

"Just so. But I believe that our time here is too short to waste it in mourning. So when the King removed to Edinburgh from Stirling a month later, I politely ignored my friends' renewed invitations and warnings and returned to Clendenen House. Life progressed thereafter with much more liveliness and gaiety."

"I dinna believe in long mourning, either," Macleod said. "But nowt could harm ye whilst ye stayed wi' friends, and ye were older and wiser than my lass here. Thank God, she has no house to be staying in by herself as ye did."

Lady Clendenen's twinkling gaze met Adela's solemn one.

"Do I not have the use of a house, sir, in Stirling?" Adela asked quietly.

A glance at Lady Clendenen revealed that her ladyship had shifted her gaze guiltily to Macleod, but he was glowering at Adela and did not appear to notice.

"Who told ye that?" he demanded. But he clearly figured it out for himself before the words had left his tongue, because he shot a furious look at her ladyship.

"I did," Lady Clendenen said, meeting that look. "I thought she should know."

Adela returned her attention to her breakfast as Macleod's temper erupted.

Her ladyship replied placidly, Isabella smiled, and Sorcha and Isobel soon joined in the fray. Clearly the latter two, at least, agreed that Lady Clendenen had made a grave error in mentioning the house in Stirling, but Adela was grateful for the knowledge. She wondered what else lay hidden in Ardelve's settlements.

She wondered, too, what her companion on the ramparts would think of the debate. Suddenly, she wished she could tell him about it, because she had confidence that, one way or another, he would help her decide the best course for herself.

The longer she sat there, half listening to the continuing debate over what she should do, the more persuaded she became that she did not want to return to Loch Alsh or to Chalamine if she truly did not have to go. One's duty was important, to be sure, but if everyone at the table agreed that she owed none to Ardelve's corpse, she found it hard to believe that he would feel otherwise or expect her to do so.

He had understood that she had feelings and ideas of her own, and he had also seemed to respect them. That he would insist that any widow—however recent—should accompany a deteriorating corpse on a long journey to a house she had never seen and, once there, should seek the hospitality of a stepson she had met only once seemed difficult if not impossible to imagine.

At that precise moment, Sir Hugo entered the hall from the main stairway with several of his men. Clearly surprised to find so many still at the table, he paused to bid them all good morning.

"Has the fog cleared yet?" Isabella asked him.

"Nay, madam, it still lies thick in the glen. Even so, Sir Edward and most of our other remaining guests have declared their intention to leave after the midday meal. I'll send two of our lads with each party to see them safely on their way."

"A good notion," Isabella said. "Thank you, Hugo."

He nodded, then glanced at Adela and smiled at Sorcha before turning away with his men toward the northwest stairs.

Seeing him reminded Adela of Sidony's suggestion that she might stay at Hawthornden Castle. That would give her privacy and a chance to think clearly.

Hawthornden lay a mile from Roslin. Her memory of it was vague, since she had gone there only the one time with Isobel, Sidony, and the countess to pay a bride visit, and thus had seen little of it, but she did recall that it sat above the River Esk on a high, sheer cliff. She knew that Hugo's men-at-arms had used it for themselves until he took Sorcha there, but it had seemed comfortable, even so.

Glancing at Sorcha, she wondered if her sister had broached the notion to Hugo. It being clearly not a good time to ask her, Adela wondered how long she would have to wait until they could speak privately.

On the other hand, Hugo was here now.

Deciding the time had come to take some action of her own, Adela waited only a few minutes longer before quietly excusing herself.

"I'll walk upstairs with you," Isobel said, rising.

"I'll go, too," Sorcha said.

Adela was certain she had kept her expression neutral, but she was aware of a shrewd glance from Isabella before the countess said lightly, "Don't run away yet, Sorcha, nor you, Sidony. I want to show you both some fabric that arrived yesterday from Paris, France. Come with me now. I left it in the solar."

Adela breathed a sigh of relief.

"Are we plaguing you so much?" Isobel asked as they stepped off the dais.

Guiltily, Adela shook her head. "I know everyone means well," she said. "It's just that I'm not used to so many people around all the time. I can scarcely think."

"You mean you're not used to so many trying to tell you what to do."

"Aye, that's it," she admitted. "Moreover, so much has happened that I want time to sort it out for myself before I decide what to do."

"I understand," Isobel said with a grin. "I never listened to anyone else until Michael came along. I listen to him because he listens to me. Father never did."

Adela gave her a straight look. "Are you trying to tell me you never heeded anything Hector said to you? Because, if you are—"

"You wouldn't believe me," Isobel said with a laugh. "And quite right, too. They don't call our sister's husband Hector the Ferocious for no reason, but he suits Cristina perfectly, which just goes to show that we don't always know best. She certainly never imagined that her marriage to him would be a good one, but it is."

"So now you're trying to tell me that I should listen to Father, as she did?"

Isobel sobered. "Not just Father, Adela. I agree you'd be unwise to return straightaway to the Highlands if you have to cast yourself on the hospitality of the new Lord Ardelve. We scarcely know Fergus, but Lady Clendenen tells me he is marrying soon, and she doubts his bride will welcome you even if he does. She is dreadfully homely, Lady Clendenen says."

"Ardelve said the same," Adela said, remembering. "He also told me she is an heiress, which recommended her highly to him as a wife for Fergus."

"Aye, well, the Macleod sisters have made good marriages, too."

"I'm beginning to believe I'm not meant to marry," Adela said as they crossed the stair hall. "Only look at what has happened each time I've tried."

Isobel grimaced. "Sakes, Adela, you are always the sensible one. Only think what you would say to Sidony or to me if we were to say such a thing."

"I know," Adela said, catching up her skirts in one hand and lightly touching the stone wall with the other as they went up the winding stairway. "Odd how one's advice to others so frequently differs from one's own behavior, is it not?"

Isobel's laughter echoed in the stairwell. "I'll leave you here," she said when they reached the first landing. "I want to see to my wee laddie, and Isabella expects me to return soon to bid our guests farewell. She said to tell you that you need not dine with everyone at midday unless you want to. Most will not expect to see you."

"Then I'll stay away," Adela said gratefully.

"Mayhap we can talk this afternoon," Isobel said. "I promise I'll not offer advice unless you request it, but if you'd like to talk just to sort your thoughts, I'd be happy to listen."

Thanking her without promising anything, Adela went on up the stairs past her own chamber to the next level, where the little chamber was that Hugo used when he stayed at Roslin. It faced another room across the stone landing one level below the doorway to the ramparts.

When Hugo had lived at Roslin before his marriage, the chamber had served as his bedchamber. Now, he used it as an office of sorts, and since he had headed that way and had not returned through the hall, she hoped to find him there.

That portion of the stairway was usually dark. But enough pale gray light spilled down the stairs to tell her that a door must be open above her. Since she still had some distance to go before reaching the door to the ramparts and wall walk, hope stirred that the door to Sir Hugo's chamber was open. If so, he was there.

As the thought formed, she heard men's voices, oddly distorted as they wafted through the stone stairwell. She recognized Hugo's at once.

She could not tell what he was saying at first. But two steps more and his voice grew clear just as he said, ". . . murdered, and not just Sir Ian but Will, too."

She heard a murmur, and as it occurred to her that she had chosen a poor time to approach Hugo, the other said gruffly with a thick Borders accent, "Then I trow ye mun be thinking we'll ha' to put an end to Einar Logan, as weel."

"I'm afraid so," Hugo agreed, his voice sounding nearer.

Chapter 5

Shocked and scarcely able to believe her ears, Adela stood stock still, remembering the familiar-looking, bearded henchman who had helped Hugo after Ardelve's collapse. She had forgotten about him, and not for the first time, either, now that she came to think about it. Einar Logan was one of the men who had helped rescue her after her abduction.

Indeed, except for Hugo and Sorcha, he had done more than anyone.

To be sure, at the time, she had seen him for only half a minute before Waldron had felled him with an arrow. But in the aftermath, she had heard Einar's name mentioned several times and knew he was captain of Hugo's fighting tail.

Thankfully, his jack-of-plate had protected him from serious injury from the arrow, but she had been hurt that day, too. And by the time she had recovered from her injuries, Ardelve, Macleod, and the countess had arranged her wedding.

What with preparing for it and being unable even to think about her ordeal, she had forgotten Einar Logan.

She realized, to her chagrin, that she had never even thanked him for what he had done. Certainly, she could not let anything bad happen to him now.

She wanted to hear more, but the door above shut with a snap, and she could no longer hear their voices. A part of her wanted to dash up the stairs, throw open that door, and demand to know what Hugo was thinking to betray a man she knew must be his chief and most loyal henchman. Put an end to Einar Logan, indeed!

A more familiar part of her shrank from such a confrontation. For one thing, she could not imagine Hugo responding well to her outrage. He would just tell her that his business was none of hers and refuse to discuss Einar Logan with her.

Even if he were willing to listen, he was unlikely to do so if she barged in while the other man was with him. Nor would it help if one of Hugo's men-at-arms caught her in the stairway just below that closed door with nowhere else that she might logically be going.

Making her way quietly back down to her chamber, she whisked herself inside and threw the bolt to ensure privacy so she could think. No sooner had she done so, however, than the best course of action announced itself. Minutes later she had flung on her lavender cloak and was hurrying downstairs.

It occurred to her before she reached the hall that she could find Sorcha and tell her what she had heard. Sorcha knew Einar much better than she did, because as captain of Hugo's fighting tail, he accompanied them wherever they went.

But Sorcha would insist that they confront Hugo. Tempers would flare, and heaven knew the trouble that would stir for everyone concerned. Adela shuddered at the image that leaped to her mind. It was just the sort of scene she abhorred. A wiser scheme, as she had already decided, was to find Einar and warn him herself.

Hurrying across the hall, empty now except for lads raking rushes to remove debris from the previous day's meals before setting up trestles for the midday dinner, she went down the southeast stairs to the castle's main entrance. Inside the entry alcove, the huge iron yett stood open, latched against the wall. So although the porter was nowhere to be seen, it was a simple matter for her to open the great door and hurry down the steps to the cobbled courtyard, still damp and heavy with mist.

Drawing her cloak closely around her, she crossed to the stables below the lantern tower on the northeast curtain wall, where she summoned a gillie and explained that she wanted to speak with Einar Logan.

"I dinna ken where he be, me lady," the lad said, scratching a mop of brown hair. "I'll look for him, though. Will I send him inside to ye when I find him?"

Her plan had been so clear, so simple, so easily accomplished that it had not occurred to her that Hugo's captain might not be available. But she could not leave such a message, asking him to meet her or to seek her inside the castle.

"That is not necessary," she said to the helpful gillie. "'Tis only that I've not yet had a chance to thank him for a service he did me. I'll do it another time."

Dismissing the lad and returning to the hall as quickly as she had left, she feared at any moment to encounter Macleod, Hugo, or one of her sisters. Glancing at the door to the countess's solar as she hurried across the hall, she realized there were less escapable hazards as well.

Gaining the stairway, she felt a measure of relief. She had no idea how many guests still lingered due to the fog, but she had seen only a few. Perhaps others were either dressing or supervising their packing to depart. Two chattering, unknown servants hurried down the stairs past her, giving credence to such possibilities.

Thrusting open her bedchamber door, she found Kenna inside smoothing the coverlet. She had fed the fire, as well, and it crackled cheerfully.

"Lady Isobel sent me, m'lady, to see if ye'd like to take your dinner wi' herself and the bairn," Kenna said as Adela moved to warm her hands at the fire.

"Thank her for me," Adela said. "But tell her I mean to rest. I doubt I'll be hungry again before suppertime."

"Aye, I'll tell her," Kenna said, turning toward the still open door.

"Stay a moment," Adela said. "Do you know Einar Logan?"

"Aye, sure," Kenna said, widening her eyes. "He's a friend o' me brothers."

Adela hesitated, uncertain what to say, but words came with surprising ease. "Will you tell him I'm grateful for all he did to help me, and that I'd like to return that service in a small measure?" Then, lowering her voice, she added, "I . . . I overheard something he ought to know, Kenna. Doubtless I make too much of words innocently spoken, but do tell him I'd like to speak with him."

Kenna had stepped closer when Adela had lowered her voice, but turned back to shut the door firmly before saying with a frown, "D'ye no think ye ought to tell Sir Hugo what ye heard, m'lady? He'd soon sort it out, ye ken."

Adela was anything but an accomplished liar. However, she had no intention of confiding more to the young maidservant than what she had already said. Nor would she admit that she could not go to Hugo without further endangering Einar.

She dared not repeat what she'd heard, either, because she did not know Kenna well enough to trust her. She did not think she knew anyone well enough to trust them with such information, but Einar deserved to know.

Therefore, she said, "I would have gone to Sir Hugo, but I only heard two voices echoing in the stairwell. When I looked, no one was there."

That, she decided, was near enough to the truth to salve her conscience.

"Aye, well, I'll tell Einar ye would speak wi' him, and if I canna find him, I'll tell me brothers," Kenna said. "I've nae need to tell them ye said aught else, m'lady," she added reassuringly. "I've only to say ye want to speak wi' Einar."

"Thank you," Adela said, as much in gratitude for the girl's discretion as for her agreement to carry the message. "Sithee, he acted as my friend, and I need friends now more than ever before. I don't want anything bad to happen to him."

"Aye, he's a good man, is Einar Logan," Kenna agreed. "Me brothers say that though there be bigger men about, there be none that be as good wi' a sword."

Her soft smile as she turned away made Adela wonder if the lass had an interest in Einar Logan beyond that of doing a kindness for her brothers' friend.

When she left, Adela bolted her door again and was able to rest long enough that, by the time someone rapped, she knew the midday meal must be long over. Noting the dim light outside the window, she realized it might even be suppertime.

"Adela, are you there?"

Recognizing Sorcha's voice as the rapping continued, and recalling that she had shot the bolt again, Adela got up hastily and opened the door.

"Sakes!" Sorcha exclaimed as she entered. "Why did you bolt it?"

"Because people seem to think I enjoy their company so much that they can just walk in and out at will. I wanted to rest a little and think," Adela said.

"Are you angry with us?" Sorcha demanded. "I know it must seem as if we have all been pelting you with advice when what you must want more than anything is to keep yourself to yourself. But I agree with Lady Clendenen that—"

"I know you agree with her," Adela said dryly. "You told me so at length whilst I was breaking my fast this morning."

"I didn't think you were listening then."

"Well, I was. But you, of all people, should realize that I am not accustomed to so many people being so interested in what I choose to do. I might be more receptive," she added, "if any of you seemed interested in *discussing* things rather than flinging advice at me and commanding me to accept it. Doubtless, the countess will be the next one to order what I must do."

"Aye, she may," Sorcha said. "But you are wrong in thinking she'll be next, because Father sent me to fetch you. They'll be serving supper soon, but Lady Clendenen persuaded Father to summon you now."

"Mercy, why should she?"

"I don't know," Sorcha said. "She was most mysterious."

"Who else means to sup with us?"

"Just the family. At least, that was my understanding, so you need not change your clothes. But do wash your face and tidy your hair."

Adela obeyed, and if her sister's understanding proved faulty, it was not Sorcha's fault that, in Lady Clendenen's view, the family was evidently more extensive than either of them knew.

When they entered the hall, it appeared as if, besides servants and men-at-arms gathering at two trestle tables in the lower hall—shorter than those for the wedding feast—only Hugo, Sir Michael, and Macleod were there. But as Sorcha and Adela approached the dais, the door to the ladies' solar opened, and Isabella emerged with Lady Clendenen, Isobel, and Sidony.

Following Sidony was the handsome, green-eyed chevalier de Gredin.

Adela's heart began to pound hard, stopping her in her tracks. "What is he doing here?" she asked Sorcha.

"I don't know," Sorcha said, stopping beside her. "He is Lady Clendenen's cousin, the chevalier—"

"I know who he is," Adela said, feeling heat in her cheeks as she remembered her encounter on the ramparts.

"Lady Clendenen told me yesterday that he is a kinsman of hers, but his title is French."

"I know little about him," Sorcha said. "No one has presented him to me, but he must be staying with her at her house in Edinburgh. I'll wager he is still here because she did not want him to have to return alone in the fog."

"I suppose not," Adela said, noting that the gentleman was looking at her, his gaze as intense as it had been the day before.

"Why is he staring at you like that?" Sorcha demanded, frowning. "I've a good mind to ask Hugo to speak—"

"Nay, don't trouble Hugo," Adela said. "He will not approach me here."

She wanted to stare back, to see if she could detect any indication that he, too, was thinking about the meeting on the ramparts, but she dared not. Her conscience pricked her at the thought, reminding her that whether she had known her husband as a husband or not, she was nonetheless a widow.

She had been in Ardelve's presence so few times that she might count them on the fingers of one hand. Still, she ought not to be thinking of another man little more than twenty-four hours after his death. What manner of woman was she that she even felt tempted to do such a thing? Perhaps . . .

She glanced at Sorcha, who said quietly, "What is it? You look . . . I don't know how to describe it. But something is wrong, Adela. Tell me."

Adela bit her lip. Of her six sisters, Sorcha was the most difficult to snub. Isobel's curiosity was nearly as great, but Sorcha was more aggressive in her determination to satisfy hers. She was also more likely to say exactly what she thought, though, and Adela wanted reassurance—or affirmation.

"Do you think it possible that a series of horrible events might drive a person mad?" she asked her.

Any one of her other sisters would have told her not to be silly. But Sorcha regarded her seriously without saying a word. She was silent so long that a chill shot up Adela's spine.

"Is that what you think?" Sorcha asked at last. "Is that why you have been so solemn and silent since your rescue? Do you fear you are going mad?"

Adela swallowed, realizing that she had wanted her sister to tell her instantly that she was doing no such thing. "I don't know," she said. "Sometimes—"

"Do forgive us for interrupting you, Adela, my dear, and you, too, Sorcha," Lady Clendenen said, appearing beside them as if a wizard had conjured her out of thin air. "But Countess Isabella grows impatient for her supper, and I want to present my cousin to you both before we all sit down at the table."

Having focused all her thoughts on trying to explain her worry to Sorcha, Adela stared blankly at the plump little woman before collecting her wits enough to say, "You need not seek forgiveness for such a cause, madam."

"Indeed, not," Sorcha agreed. "We are eager to meet your cousin."

"As eager as he is to meet both of you," the handsome young man said with a charming smile, a twinkle in his eyes, and a noticeable French accent.

"I'm glad you do not mind," Lady Clendenen said.

"Pray, allow me to present him properly. He is the chevalier Etienne de Gredin, although I don't know if I can bring myself to say anything complimentary to recommend him to you. He has been plaguing me to present him to you since his arrival here yesterday."

The gentleman bowed, holding Adela's gaze.

"Has he, indeed?" Sorcha said. "Then I wonder why he absented himself so soon after we dined today. I vow, I was in your company most of the afternoon, madam. You might have presented him to me had he been at hand."

"You unmask me, Lady Robison," the gentleman said, grinning at her as he straightened. "I confess to you, I accepted an invitation to go hawking."

"In the fog?"

"*Mais oui.* Doubtless you will not credit it, but the worst of that fog ends at the ridge top or as near as makes no difference to a goshawk. Goshawks, you see, unlike most birds of prey, are excellent hunters in wooded areas."

Adela stood silent, trying to match his light, accented voice to the deeper, decidedly firmer, unaccented one she had heard in the darkness the previous night.

Although she had been certain she would recognize that voice wherever she heard it again, she could detect no likeness. But if the man on the castle ramparts had not been Etienne de Gredin, who else could he possibly have been? Perhaps the chevalier was simply more adept at disguising his voice than anyone might expect.

"Have I said something to offend you, Lady Ardelve?" he asked gently.

Driven by uncustomary curiosity, Adela said, "Doubtless you will think such a question unmannerly, sir, but her ladyship indicated that you were not French by birth. So I *was* wondering about your title and . . . and your accent . . . " She hesitated, fearing she was truly crossing the line between politeness and the lack of it.

He flashed his charming smile again, saying, "*Mais non, madame*, my title was given me when I was a child attending my father at the French court. My unfortunate accent is no more than a result of habit and a recent visit to Paris. Does it distress you? I confess—I who perhaps should not—that the ladies of his grace's court find it most charming. I regret that you do not, because one desires to make a good impression with the so-famously-beautiful Macleod sisters. If it annoys you," he added archly, "I shall exert myself to speak as a proper Scotsman does."

"Sakes, sir, mind your manners," Sorcha said before Adela could reply. "My sister is not yet two days a widow. Would you dare to flirt with her?"

Instantly remorseful, he said, "Lady Ardelve, I implore you to forgive me. I am desolate to think my thoughtlessness may have caused you pain. I desired no more than to see you smile and perhaps to offer you simple friendship. I meant no offense to you either, Lady Robison. Have I stepped beyond all forgiveness?"

"No, of course not," Adela said, noting his reference to friendship but observing Hugo's approach with relief nonetheless. Impulsively, she said, "A person needs friends, sir. I hope you will become one of ours."

"To be sure, I will if you will but smile at me now and assure me, both of you, that you have forgiven me."

"Pray, do not be absurd, sir," Sorcha said. "It would

take more than unintentional rudeness to put you beyond forgiveness. But I hope you do not mean to tease my sister for smiles merely to please yourself."

"I won't, but if you need a friend, Lady Adela, I am yours to command."

He would clearly have said more, but Hugo joined them, saying with a sharp look at de Gredin, "The countess sent me to conduct you all to the table so they can begin to serve."

"Where's Henry?" Sorcha asked him.

"Gone back to Edinburgh with everyone else," Hugo said. "Since the King returned, Henry has been enjoying himself at court too much to want to stay here for long. But come now or I'll have my aunt handing me my head in my lap."

Sorcha chuckled, tucked her hand in the crook of his arm, and with a rueful smile said to Adela, "I suppose we should go. We'll talk more later if you like."

"We're going back to Hawthornden in the morning," Hugo said. "I hope you mean to visit us again before we leave for the Isles next week."

Her thoughts jumped to Einar Logan and the dreadful fate Hugo and the unseen man had planned for him. A vague nod of assent was all she could manage without revealing her knowledge to Hugo. But they had reached the dais, making it natural for her to look away from him as she stepped onto it.

Before good manners could force her to turn back to expand upon the nod, Isabella said, "I hope you had a good rest this afternoon, Adela, my dear, and have a hearty appetite now."

"Aye, madam," she said politely as she moved to take

the place Isobel indicated by her. Lady Clendenen followed, taking her place at Adela's left with Sidony beyond. Adela noted with relief that Hugo had stopped beside Sir Michael, who in Henry's absence sat next to the countess.

Macleod was beside Hugo with de Gredin beyond him.

Adela's gaze rested thoughtfully on de Gredin. Surely, he had spoken as he had, and with the French accent, hoping to keep his identity secret a little longer. He had said he wanted to be her friend, had he not? Nevertheless, her doubt lingered.

Isabella's minstrels played throughout the meal, but she had arranged no further entertainment, so Adela asked to be excused directly after supper.

The countess expressed a hope that she would join her and the other ladies for a short time in her solar. But she made no objection when Adela thanked her but said that she would prefer to go straight to bed.

"Run along then, my dear," Isabella said with a warm smile. "Sleep well."

Making her escape without further ado, Adela noticed as she left the dais that the chevalier smiled at her, but she hoped he did not mean to follow. Sorcha was not the only one who would think a private talk between them unseemly. Adela thought the same, although she had to admit, at least to herself, that she had not felt any such discomfort on the ramparts.

She could not decide what she thought of de Gredin. He seemed reassuringly at ease with himself tonight. Even when he had drawn Sorcha's censure, he had recovered swiftly and with grace. Adela thought she could like him as a friend, but friendships between men and women who were not kin to each other were so rare that she could not call any to mind. Perhaps after Lady Clendenen married Macleod, the kinship would then be such that friendship between them could follow.

She realized that she was still thinking of him as the man she had met on the ramparts, despite her inability to detect similarity in the two voices. But logically, they had to be the same man if only because no one else remained at Roslin who could be the man on the ramparts.

And surely, he must still be at Roslin, because he had told her she could summon him easily if she needed him.

She went to her bedchamber, hoping her sisters would not feel compelled to follow. She was not usually one to seek solitude so often—certainly not as often as she had since her abduction. To converse politely with near strangers was a strain now, rather than the rare treat it was at Chalamine.

Even to converse with people she knew well took effort now. She suddenly recalled that she had told Sorcha about the strange fear of madness she had recently experienced. If Sorcha recalled their discussion, and recalled that Lady Clendenen and the chevalier had interrupted them, she might come in search of her.

Entering her bedchamber, she stirred up the fire and added fuel from the hearth basket to warm hands grown chilly again in the stone stairwell. The water in the basin was cold, too, and Kenna would not bring hot until she came to help her prepare for bed. Pulling a stool close to the hearth, Adela sat and held her hands out to the warmth as she gazed into the fire and tried to think.

The flames danced and flickered. Although they did

little to move her thoughts in any sensible direction, they were both comforting and mesmerizing. She was still staring into them, her mind nearly blank, when the click of the latch startled her so much that she nearly tumbled off the stool.

Turning, expecting to see Sorcha, she beheld Kenna instead.

"Faith, is it time to go to bed already?"

"Nay, m'lady," Kenna said, shutting the door carefully behind her, then moving toward Adela with one hand extended. "I've brought ye a message."

"A message? From whom?"

"Me brother Tam said to ask nae questions, so I brought it straight up to ye."

"Prithee, do not mention this to any of my sisters, then. Mayhap it is from Einar Logan, if you were able to get my message to him."

"Nay, mistress, for I doubt he can read or write, nae more than me brothers, or I m'self. When I asked them what it said, Tam said I should swallow me curiosity and remember me place."

Adela shook her head at herself, realizing it ought to have occurred to her that a man in Einar's position would be unlikely to read or write. A moment later, as she read the message, she was grateful that Kenna could not read either.

I'm told you need a friend. Go to the chapel when it is empty midway between Compline and Nocturne. Leave a candle lit near the archway if you are alone. Then kneel at the altar and wait. You'll be quite safe.

The message bore no signature, but Adela needed none. He had said to let him know if she needed a friend, and she remembered saying something of the sort to Kenna, who must have repeated it to her brothers. Clearly, people at Roslin discussed each other just as people in the Highlands did. And word had reached him just as he had said it would.

Recalling the chevalier's offer of friendship, she wondered if he might have meant to reassure her that he had received her message. But it was still hard to merge thought of him with her memory of the voice on the ramparts.

Even if they were the same, and despite his having realized she might be reluctant to visit the chapel alone after dark and taken pains to tell her she would be safe, she hesitated to go. It was one thing to visit the ramparts once on a night black with dense fog, and with fair certainty that Hugo would leave no guards there. It was quite another to cross the open courtyard an hour and a half before midnight to visit the chapel. She was not even sure it would be open.

That it would be highly improper for her to meet him there did not trouble her. Had he intended to betray her trust, he might easily have done so the previous night. She had trusted him instinctively and would continue to do so unless he gave her cause to change her mind. Nothing dreadful could happen in the chapel. The courtyard would not be deserted. She need only shout.

It occurred to her then that she might meet Hugo, Michael, or her father. Not one of them would view her solitary presence outside with approval.

She looked at Kenna and said matter-of-factly, "I want

to go to the chapel later. I have neglected my evening prayers of late, and although I do not want to attend Compline with the family, I do want to make my peace with God privately after they have returned from the service. Will you accompany me as far as the courtyard and await my return, so that I need not go alone?"

"Aye, sure, m'lady. And I'll no say nowt about it, neither."

"Thank you," Adela said, grimacing as she realized that she might as well have asked Kenna to help her sneak out to the chapel to meet the person who had sent the message. Clearly, she ought to have warned her "friend" that she was not wise in the ways of subterfuge.

"I'm thinking I should go lay out Lady Isobel's night things first, whilst I can," Kenna said thoughtfully. "She willna mind an I tell her ye want me later, especially if Sir Michael comes upstairs wi' her as he often does. But I should tell her I'll be wi' ye, and I dinna want to shirk me regular duties unless I must."

"Mercy, no," Adela said. "I don't want you to either, and it must be all of two hours and more before the chapel will be empty. Attend to all your chores, Kenna, and return when you can. I'll wait for you."

It was considerably more than two hours, but Adela did not complain. The chamber was peaceful, the fire cheerful, and when Kenna returned, she said, "I went to the kitchen, m'lady, and watched from the postern door until everyone left the chapel. If we wait a bit longer, we can be sure it will be empty o' the priest and all. I'm thinking ye'll be less likely to meet anyone an we return the same way."

Since it would not have occurred to Adela to go by

way of the kitchen, she was grateful for the suggestion. It would considerably diminish the likelihood of meeting anyone who would instantly send her back to her bedchamber.

Twenty minutes later, she and Kenna slipped through the kitchen unseen by anyone except a woman kneading dough for the morrow's manchet loaves and a lad tending the fire for her. Outside, torches lit the yard, but the chapel lay only a short distance from the postern door. She saw that she could reach the east-facing entrance without showing herself longer than a minute or two.

"Shall I wait here, m'lady?"

"Aye," Adela said, deciding that even if Kenna chanced to see him enter the chapel, he would have taken good care to render himself unrecognizable to her.

Doing her best to look as if what she was doing were ordinary, she strode to the chapel door. Half expecting to find it locked, she felt mixed relief and unease when the latch lifted easily and the door swung inward.

Shutting it after herself in the small entryway, she noted a dim orange glow emanating from the chapel proper through its arched entrance. On a shelf inside the archway, she found a candle already alight. A tinderbox sat beside it, making her wonder if he had somehow arranged to spare her the necessity of lighting one herself, or if it was normal practice at Roslin to leave a candle burning there.

Whatever the cause, thanks to the lighted candle, the place seemed to welcome her. She walked to the altar with assurance, realizing that if she knelt on a prayer stool there, she would have her back to the entrance.

That he trusted her to wait for him so made her think

again about Sorcha and Isobel, neither of whom would merit such trust. Their curiosity was too powerful. But his trust was sufficient for her. She would await him as he had requested.

She did not wait long. Without a sound to warn her, the candle went out, and blackness enveloped her again. She remembered from her wedding that the chapel boasted no windows. Wax candles and cressets had lighted it even then, at midday.

His voice was as deep, firm, and comforting as it had been the night before. "Have no fear," he said. "It is only I."

Chapter 6

After extinguishing the lone candle, Rob still felt her presence like a warm breeze in the chapel. He heard the faint rustle of movement as she turned his way.

"What happened to your French accent?" she asked a bit stiffly.

He hesitated, uncertain how to reply.

"As you see, I . . . I have guessed who you are," she added.

"Have you?"

"Aye, but you need not fear me, either. And although I do *not* approve of secrets or clandestine behavior, I did want to seek your advice. Therefore, for the present, I shall acquit you of any ill intent in concealing your identity."

"Will you?" Still feeling his way, he added, "Forgive me, but I am not certain I understand what you are saying, Lady Adela."

"Will you deny that you have affected a French accent, sir?"

Although tempted to deny it categorically, he did not want to lie to her unless it became necessary. So he said, "I will admit that from time to time I have found it useful to affect such an accent, and others, for that matter."

"I knew it!" Her tone was lighter, less strained than before.

"What did you know?" he asked.

"Your identity, of course. I am not a fool, sir. You did give yourself away to me, you know—straightaway."

"Did I?"

"You must know that you did. I own that had you not stared at me so conspicuously in the chapel and afterward, I'd never have guessed. And then, flirting as you did tonight . . . You sounded completely different, that's all."

Realizing that his hands had clenched at the thought that someone had been staring at her, had even dared to flirt with her, he forced himself to relax and let the irritating thought go. Evenly, he said, "You expressed need of a friend today, my lady. And, too, you expressed concern for another man."

"I did," she admitted, surprising him. He'd half expected a coy demand to know if he were jealous, but as quickly as the thought formed, he berated himself.

She had given him no cause to expect such a reaction from her. Indeed, she had revealed little of herself other than her simple trust that he meant her no harm and a confidence or two. He was tempted to warn her that such innocent trust could be dangerous, but aware of her history, he feared such a warning might frighten her.

It was more important to discover how much she had

overheard, so he said instead, "What happened, exactly, to make you feel so concerned for him?"

"I . . . I heard two others talking. They said it was time to put an end to him. He did me a particular service, so I don't want harm to come to him, but I cannot imagine what you could do to help him. You do not even know him, do you?"

"I know who he is," he said, realizing as he did that he was sinking deeper into the pit of his deceit. But he had to know what he was dealing with and what she meant to do about Einar Logan. "Who were the men you overheard talking?"

"I don't know," she said hastily. "I just heard voices in a stairwell."

He could hear the lie in her voice and would have discerned it even had he not known the truth. Still, it was good to know that, although she disapproved of secrets, she would protect those for whom she cared. She had not recognized his voice, but surely she had recognized Hugo's.

With nothing to gain by letting her know he had detected the lie, he said, "What else did the men say?"

"One said someone had died. Nay, that two had died. That is . . . " She hesitated, evidently trying to recall all that she had heard. At last, with an audible sigh, she said, "Truly, I am not certain. He did say someone had died— Sir Ian, I think—but the only name I knew was Einar Logan."

"What else did they say about him?"

"That was all. I heard a thud, as of a door shutting, then nothing more."

"So you saw no one."

"Nay, and I did not try to go nearer, either."

So she wanted him to believe she did not know exactly where the two men had been. Well, he would not press her on that, either. He had no need.

"You were wise to keep your distance," he said. "Was that the reason you let it be known you needed a friend, or was there some other cause?"

She was silent for so long that he thought he would have to coax any further information from her. But at last she said, "I should not bring my trials to you."

"A friend is always willing to listen."

When still she hesitated, he wondered what had happened to put her off. She had trusted him the night before. That she had, had laid an unexpected burden on him, a burden that grew heavier now. Exerting patience, he waited.

"It is nothing to make a song about," she said as if she spoke to herself. Drawing another audible breath, she said, "I know they care about me, but everyone still plagues me so with advice that I cannot think. I'd hoped that discussing the matter with you might help, but I have no right—"

"Don't trouble yourself about rights. I am wholly at your service. I will not claim to offer good advice, but I am an excellent listener if you want to talk."

"I'd like that," she said. "I've found it easy to talk with you. Only I cannot stay long. Lady Isobel's maidservant, Kenna, accompanied me to the postern door and waits there for my return. I don't want her to have to explain herself to anyone."

"Doubtless the lass can think of something to say that won't give you away."

"Then I'll tell you. I'd expected I'd have to go home with Ardelve's body, you see, but Lady Clendenen said that would be unwise. My sisters agree, as does my father. Still, I fear people will think it is my duty to go, even to assert my right to stay there with his son. I don't want to live with a man I don't know. He may be my son by marriage, but he is only a year or two older than I am."

"Did Ardelve provide otherwise for you?"

"Aye, and generously if what Lady Clendenen told me is true. I'll have money enough to support myself and the lifetime use of a house in Stirling."

"Lady Clendenen has been busy," he said dryly.

"I am not surprised that *you* should think so. I warrant you know her much better than I do."

He let that pass, saying only, "I wonder why she is sticking her oar so deeply into your water."

"She has said she will not marry my father until he has got rid of his last daughter. She would not be pleased if I were to return to Chalamine."

"Mayhap she only wants to see you happy."

"That is possible, but she has been . . . " She stopped, then said, "I should not say this to *you*, of course, but it is just so easy to tell you things that I will anyway. She has given me cause to believe she has already selected one whom she believes would make me a good husband. I'm certain that must be why she invited me to stay with her at her house in Edinburgh."

"I see." He did not, but it sounded like the sort of nonsensical thing lassies often said, and he did not want to lose sight of her primary concern. "If you truly want my advice," he went on, "I think you'd be wise to accept her invitation. If Ardelve arranged an income for you, you've no need to apply to his son to support you. That *would* be uncomfortable. Nor need you seek a new husband. In fact, I'd counsel you strongly to avoid that course until you are sure you are ready for it."

"I understand why you would support her ladyship's invitation. At least, I think I do," she said. "'Tis why I hesitated to discuss that with you."

"I think you must explain that to me more clearly," he said, utterly baffled.

"I want to trust you," she said. "Indeed, I am persuaded that you mean me no harm, but you *were* flirting with me earlier, and . . . "

Nearly interrupting her to set her straight, he bit down hard on his lower lip to prevent any inadvertent sound.

". . . and, in truth, I do not know why you *should* flirt when we scarcely know each other and . . . and in my present circumstances."

Forcing calm into his voice, he said, "Before we continue this conversation, my lady, I must ask you to tell me exactly who you think I am."

"But . . . " This time her hesitation was of shorter duration before she said on a note of relief, "Oh, I see how it is. You think I may be wrong, that I believe you are someone you are not. I feared that might be the case until you explained about the different accents you have used. It did not occur to me till then that you might have reason to conceal your identity other than to make yourself mysterious and thus more interesting to me. That was foolish, for I do recall that your father—"

"My father?" The words were out before he knew he would speak them.

"Aye, for your cousin told me—"

"Lady Adela, please, just tell me who you think I am."

"I beg your pardon. You must think me a dafty, because I'm chattering away like a clap-dish. I promise you, I do not often do so, but I already fear I may be going mad. There now, you see how easily I speak my mind to you, and that is another thing I don't often do. So if I am wrong in my belief as to your identity, I shall be certain that I *have* lost my wits."

Her voice wavered, and realizing that she truly did fear such a happening, he felt like the lowest worm in Christendom to have manipulated their conversation to that end. Although he could not see her, the picture of her in his mind was clear.

She was small and slender, almost fragile looking. And doubtless she wore the solemn, sad look that had dimmed her glow since her abduction and rescue.

That mental picture made him wish he had the right to walk up and put his arms around her, to hold her tight, because she sounded as if a hug might help. But he had no right to do that, so he waited, despite suspecting that she would soon begin to fear he had tired of what she called her chattering.

"I'm sorry," she said in a small voice, instantly confirming that thought. "I suppose I'm afraid to say the name aloud lest I do discover I'm wrong. But if you are not the chevalier de Gredin, I do not know who in the world you can be."

He would have given anything then to be able to utter the strongest epithet he knew, but he could not. Moreover, every word of his training warned him to admit nothing in haste or without thinking the whole situation through carefully first.

And since he could not tell her the whole truth, in any
event, until he knew exactly what course he would take,
he would be safer to admit nothing at all.

"Well?" she said with a hint of impatience.

To give himself time to let his thoughts sort themselves, he said gently, "I hope you will not voice that suspicion to anyone else."

"No, no, of course I won't!"

The relief in her voice told him she was certain now
that she was right in believing he was de Gredin, and it
did nothing to ease his guilt. Still he persevered, saying
firmly, "The chevalier de Gredin should *not* be flirting
with you. Nor should he be living under the same roof.
If you explain that to Lady Clendenen—not that she
should require explanation—I warrant he will remove to
some other abode to accommodate you. If you fear people may talk—and, given the least encouragement, they
will—you should avoid his company in all but the most
public settings."

"I . . . I see," she said. "I'll take care to avoid other
meetings. Doubtless there is more you are not telling me,
but I do think I can decide now what I shall do."

"Can you?" He tensed, hoping she had not decided to
accompany the body.

"I shall stay where someone honestly wants me to
stay."

"I'm glad," he said sincerely.

"Think you that if I need a friend again, I may count
on you?"

"Any time, lass. As long I have power to help, I will."

"Thank you," she said. "I should go now before Kenna
looks for me."

"Can you find your way to the door?"

"I think so. Do you want to leave first?"

"Nay, I'll linger yet a while. I'm near the archway. Will you feel more at ease if I move some distance away?"

"I . . . I don't mind if you stay where you are."

' "Then I will," he said. His body stirred suggestively at the thought of her walking so near him, and he wondered if he was the one who had lost his wits.

Adela had risen and turned to face the sound of his voice as soon as he had spoken, but in the silence now, after a step or two, she faltered in the darkness.

"Talk to me," she said. "I cannot see a thing, and I feel as if I could be walking in any direction."

"I'm here," he said. "Just walk toward me. There should be nothing in your path even if you veer a little one way or the other."

"I know. The floor is clear without all the kneeling stools out."

"I think you've made a wise decision," he said. "I don't know Lady Clendenen, although everyone knows her name, and many are kin to her. But—"

"I still don't know that I'll stay with her," she said, thinking she had better make that plain lest he believe later that she had deceived him. "She wants to take me to the royal court, and I am not—"

"Surely, you don't mean to stay at the house Ardelve left you in Stirling! I'd wager he never meant you to stay there alone—not until you were many years older than you are now, at all events."

"Nay, I've no wish to do that," she said. "But I may have another option."

"What?" His voice sounded as if he stood right in front of her now.

"I want to see if it truly is an option before I give it more thought," she said. "I need to talk to Sir Hugo."

"You must talk to him anyway, lass," he said gently as a large hand touched her shoulder in the darkness.

She stopped still, nearly unable to breathe. Raggedly, she said, "Why?"

"You must tell him what you overheard in the stairwell. He will know what to do about it. Einar Logan is the captain of his fighting tail, and Hugo can protect him more easily than anyone else can. You should have told him straightaway."

She did not want to tell him Hugo knew all about the conversation, but since she had realized that Hugo would arrange for her to speak to Einar Logan if she said she wanted to thank him, she said, "I'll talk to him."

"Good," he said without taking his hand from her shoulder.

She made no attempt to move away.

"You should not so easily trust men you do not know, lassie," he said, his voice sounding oddly gruff.

"I feel as if I do know you," she said. Her voice came from low in her throat, and her body tingled, feeling more alive than it had for weeks, perhaps forever.

"You don't, though," he said.

"'Tis strange, I know," she added. "But from the very first moment the other night on the ramparts—"

"Sakes, lass, that happened just last night."

"Did it? It seems longer than that. But since that moment I've felt as if I'd known you all my life."

"Have you?"

Warm fingers touched her left cheek, then moved gently to cup the side of her face. She licked her lips nervously but stood still.

Slight pressure against her cheek tilted her face upward. It seemed a perfectly natural thing to do, and the gentle touch of warm lips against hers felt natural, too. When the hand on her shoulder shifted to draw her nearer, she did not resist.

His lips pressed harder against hers, then broke away. But still he held her, saying quietly, "A while ago, you made me think you might need a hug."

In answer, she leaned closer and rested her cheek against his chest, realizing as she did that he wore a leather jack of some sort.

Her head fit under his chin without touching it. He was hard, his chest muscular. His arms as they eased around her seemed to draw her to safety.

She felt his heart beating, at first slowly and steadily, then faster. His embrace tightened for a moment before his hands moved to grip her shoulders and he said gruffly, "I'm a right scoundrel, lass. You seek safety and sanity; and instead you meet me. I fear you'll never forgive me for this."

"There is naught to forgive, for am I not safe with you?" she asked, feeling no less safe for his suggestion that she might not be. "Your flirting before distressed me because . . . Mercy, I don't know why, but it did. Mayhap 'twas because others were around, or because despite scarcely knowing Ardelve, I *am* his widow."

"Aye, but you're a Highlander, lass, and in my experience, Highlanders, like Borderers, set expediency ahead of others' notions of what's proper. The dead are dead and remain so, but the living continue to live and should do so."

"That's true, and it sounds perfectly sensible when you say it."

"Here is more sense, then, so heed me well," he said, his voice stern for once. "You are safe enough with me whilst others know naught about it. But this world is a dangerous place, as your recent experience proves. If the wrong people come to suspect a connection between us, you may find yourself in danger again."

"Is that why you pretend to be other than you are?"

He sighed. "Don't ask me to share my secrets with you, lass. Not only would it be unsafe for us both if you knew them, but I do not share them with anyone."

"I'd never betray you."

"I know you'd not mean to," he said, his voice gentle again. "But secrets are dangerous—at least, some are. And the only way to be sure of keeping one is not to share it with anyone. You've admitted yourself that you hate secrets. I'd be a beast to burden you with mine."

She felt as if her own words had betrayed her. Was this what curiosity did to one? She had always, in the past, felt superior to Isobel and Sorcha in that respect, as if their burning curiosity about everything were somehow an offense against good manners. But now, with him, her curiosity seemed reasonable, and his unwillingness to confide his secrets a personal affront.

She wanted to tell him as much, but her recent ability to speak frankly with him had vanished, making way for more customary reticence. She would not lower herself to pry into what was so clearly his business. That his shutting her out hurt seemed of less importance than her own need to understand why she should feel so strongly that she had a right to know what he refused to tell her.

Gathering her dignity, she said, "I should go now. Kenna will be growing impatient, and it would not do for her to come here in search of me."

"No," he said, giving her shoulder a gentle squeeze before releasing her. "I'm glad you have decided not to return to the Highlands."

"I, too," she murmured. "Goodnight."

As she moved past him into the entryway, less dark now than before, thanks to a slit of light round the door and the courtyard torches, she felt his gaze on her.

Just as she reached to lift the latch, he spoke once more. "Stay well away from de Gredin, lassie."

She did not answer. It was all she could do not to look back to see if she could make out any of his features in the ambient torchlight.

She was certain he would not allow that to happen. But the diversion kept her from wondering until she was crossing the yard how he expected her to avoid him if she were to stay with Lady Clendenen. Even if he moved out, they would be bound to meet socially, especially if both of them went to court.

Standing at the door of the chapel with the door held open
a crack, Rob watched Adela cross the courtyard to the patient Kenna. He could easily guess what she was thinking
and cursed himself again for having put her and himself—however unintentionally—in the position in which
they now found themselves.

Unlike Adela, he had always liked having a secret or
two. He knew his grandfather had tested him more than
once—probably more times than he knew—before en-
trusting him with portions, at least, of his two most prized
secrets. He recalled the conversation that had ensued
when Sir Walter revealed the first one.

"I've learned ye can keep your mouth shut when ye
must, laddie," Sir Walter had said. "So I've summat to tell
ye and summat I mean to ask o' ye."

Puffed with importance, thirteen-year-old Rob had
waited with breathless anticipation to learn what it was
his grandfather wanted him to do. Enlightenment had
hardly seemed worth the effort.

"Ye're strong and quick on your feet, lad, as I were
and me own father afore me. Your father took his
physique from his mother's kin and never were much
good wi' a sword, but ye display the Logan skill already.
Your father said he'd foster ye wi' the Douglas, but I'm
thinking I'll send ye to Dunclathy instead. Ye'll ha' to
work gey hard, but the reward will be worth the effort."

"Dunclathy?" He'd never heard of such a place, or
such a person, if it were a person. And he'd looked forward to learning to fight with the Earl of Douglas.

Their family ties to the Douglas were strong and had
been so since that long ago time when Rob's great-
grandfather and his brother, and Sir James Douglas, had

died during their attempt to take the Bruce's heart to the Holy Land. Their ties to the Sinclairs were just as strong from that same connection to Sir William Sinclair.

"Ye'll learn swordsmanship at Dunclathy, as well as other knightly skills, and more," his grandfather had said. "Ye want to be a knight one day, d'ye no?"

Rob did. His desire to study swordsmanship and other fighting skills under the Earl of Douglas's command had stirred when he'd heard Douglas say he meant to be King of Scots, a goal the man pursued for some time before deciding it would suit his clan better to side with Robert the Steward, now Stewart. Douglas had called the Steward a peaceful man, one unlikely to challenge the Douglas power in the Borders, and his support had guaranteed the Steward's bid to become Robert II of Scotland.

A second reason had stirred Rob's ambition. The Douglas had a stunningly beautiful daughter. Then but thirteen and smitten, Rob secretly harbored dreams of a magnificent marriage even then.

"I'd thought to go wi' Douglas," he'd said boldly to his grandfather.

"'Tis a great honor, Rob, the greatest you can imagine, to go to Dunclathy. But ye must keep it to yourself. Speak nowt o' this and do as I bid ye."

"Aye, sir," Rob had said with a sigh, feeling much put upon but knowing he had little choice in such a matter unless his father objected. And that was most unlikely, because Sir Ian never set himself against Sir Walter.

However, when his older brother Will learned that Rob was not to serve under Douglas, he had taunted him until, angry and determined to defend himself, Rob had snapped that he was doing a good thing, a fine thing, and in fact, a far more important thing than going with Douglas, as witless Will was to do. What was more, he added, *he* knew a secret that Will would *never* know.

The result was yet another fight between the two, broken up by Sir Ian and reported to Sir Walter. It was the only time in Rob's memory that his grandfather had ever beaten him, but he had done so thoroughly, and Rob had never forgotten it. The lesson had stuck. And as far as he was concerned, it would stick until his dying day.

But as he watched Adela speak to Kenna, other hard-learned lessons taunted him. A knight never acted dishonorably. A knight did not practice deceit. A knight never abandoned or abused those in need or who were weaker than himself.

In the case of Lady Adela, Rob realized, he had done all those things. If he were ever going to put things right, he would have to begin by talking to Hugo.

He did not look forward to that conversation any more than he supposed Adela was looking forward to hers—which was to say, not one bit.

Chapter 7

Not one to put off unpleasant tasks, Rob went in search of Hugo. Learning that he was in the countess's solar, he sent Ivor in to fetch him with a message that he desired to speak to him about a private matter.

The gillie soon returned with Hugo, who raised his eyebrows at Rob and said, "What's amiss?"

Aware of Ivor's interest, Rob looked pointedly at the northwest stair archway. When Hugo nodded and led the way, he followed him up to his private chamber.

Inside, Rob took the precaution of shutting the door firmly behind them. Then he turned and said without preamble, "It's time now, I think."

Hugo regarded him with amusement. "I agree, although you did not think so earlier. Has it occurred to you that after so many years of ignoring your family and most of your connections you may have difficulty proving who you are?"

"Nay, why should I? I've not altered so much that a

few slight changes in my appearance won't right the matter. I'll need proper clothing, of course, and a good horse or two. But if you, Michael, Henry, and the countess acknowledge me . . . "

"My lady and I will depart for the Isles before you can be ready, but you're right. Henry's word alone should be enough. Won't you go home first?"

"Why? Until I've established myself, I'd likely encounter some difficulty or other there. For one thing, I've no idea who is in charge of the place. My father had only one brother, who is long deceased, and as the estate comprises most of the land between Holyrood Abbey and Leith Harbor, I'll wager that any number of other folks who have decided that I must be dead, too, may be about to proclaim themselves third baron Lestalric. I want to see who steps forward."

Hugo perched on the sturdy table he used to deal with the accounts. "Can't you guess who might?"

"The Douglas perhaps, on Lady Ellen's behalf, but I doubt he will challenge me or try to install his own people on Lestalric land. After Will's death, he's more likely to have had someone collect Ellen and escort her to him at Hermitage or Tantallon."

"Aye, he'll wait to see who shows interest before he acts. Who else?"

"Sakes, Hugo, Ealga Clendenen is doubtless kin of some sort to me. If she is, anyone who claims kinship with her could conjure up a claim to Lestalric."

"I was thinking more specifically," Hugo said. "The Stewarts, for example. One reason folks call them upstarts is that they have practically no land of their own outside of Carrick in Galloway."

"Except Stirling Castle and Edinburgh," Rob said dryly.

"Those are royal holdings they acquired with the crown," Hugo said. "The only reason they count them as Stewart is this rather new notion that the King's eldest son should inherit instead of the Scottish nobility choosing their King. His grace has more offspring than land, and several of his sons are determined to increase their own holdings. The Earl of Fife is one of them, and Lestalric lies less than two miles from Edinburgh. That makes it a grand seat for any prince with ambition to acquire great power. Fife makes no secret of wanting to be King of Scots."

"The Stewarts can have no legitimate claim to Lestalric, even so."

"I'm just saying that you may find yourself up against powerful interests."

Rob sighed. "My grandfather expected Will and Ellen to produce a litter of children, and I warrant it would disappoint him greatly that they didn't. He certainly never expected me to inherit. Nor did I. He'd have been gey wroth with me for leaving home when I did, though," he added, thinking affectionately of Sir Walter.

"One could scarcely blame him if he were, especially now," Hugo said.

"Aye," Rob agreed. "But I was young and angry, and I felt betrayed. Perhaps if I'd got along better with my father or Will, things would have been different, but I had little respect for either of them. I kept my surname because I'm proud of it, but I shed the rest, so I'd have no obvious connection to them and so they'd not easily find me if they searched."

"Or so that if they failed to search, you need not know and be hurt more by their lack of feeling," Hugo said shrewdly.

"Do you think that was it?" Rob asked.

"It doesn't matter now," Hugo said. "That was then. But when I told you they had died, you still seemed reluctant to change anything."

"Aye, well, I'd grown accustomed to my life here. I never trained to be a landowner, after all, never had any to worry me. And although I expect I might have traded on my grand Sinclair connections to find a rich wife . . ." He shrugged.

Hugo smiled. "What changed your mind?"

Rob eyed the larger man warily. "Do you suppose we might sit properly and talk like civilized men? I'd gladly stir up those embers and put a few sticks on them."

Indicating his agreement with a gesture, Hugo drew up a stool near the hearth and watched him as he dealt expertly with the fire.

Glancing up, Rob drew a deep breath. It was no secret that people had expected Hugo to marry Lady Adela before her abduction. But neither was it a secret that Hugo was as much in love with his wife as a man could be. Still . . .

"Out with it," Hugo said impatiently. "I won't eat you."

"I wish I could be sure of that," Rob said with a wry smile. "Sithee, I've just come from talking with your sister-by-marriage."

"Sidony?"

"Nay, but I ought to have recalled that you've several such here. 'Twas the lady Adela."

"I thought she went to bed an hour ago."

"We met in the chapel." When Hugo frowned, Rob added hastily, "I may as well begin at the beginning and confess the whole to you straightaway. I was on the ramparts in that fog last night, and she wandered up there. She was . . . " He paused, not wanting to betray her more than he had to, to explain himself. "She thought no one else would be there on such a black night and sought to be alone with her grief. Not wanting to frighten her, I spoke as I'm speaking to you now, and she confided things to me. I did not reveal my identity. For one thing, she seemed content to talk to a voice in the darkness and she needed to talk. For another . . . " He hesitated.

Hugo did not. "You didn't want to tell her who you are," he said grimly.

"I dared not, not without explaining everything else to her," Rob said. "I'll go to court, swear fealty to Old Bleary, and claim my heritage. When I see what comes of that, I'll know better what to do next."

"Someone is bound to recognize you from here, though, don't you think?"

Grateful that Hugo seemed disinclined, for the moment at least, to pursue details of his talk with Adela, Rob gave a last stab at the fire with the poker, pulled up a stool, and sat as he said, "I don't think so, not in the way you mean. I'm sure they *will* recognize me as Sir Robert of Lestalric, though. People see what they expect to see, and in court dress with an air of rank and wealth, I'll do well enough."

"Nevertheless, your appearance at court is likely to irritate anyone hoping to claim Lestalric for himself," Hugo said.

"Perhaps, but I can think of only one man likely to reveal his displeasure, and that's the chevalier de Gredin."

"Sakes, why would he?"

"If I'm not mistaken, he's taken strong interest in Lady Adela. And she told me that she means to accept Lady Clendenen's invitation to stay with her in town."

"I begin to think de Gredin is not the only one with an interest there."

"I want only to be her friend," Rob said. "She needs time to find herself, and I need time to get my feet on the ground at Lestalric. Anything more that may come of it lies in the future. But de Gredin seems intent on pursuing her."

"I own, I don't think much of the man," Hugo said.

"I've taken a strong aversion to him myself, for all that I ken nowt o' the slink," Rob added, lapsing into the accents that had become customary over the years.

"I'm beginning to wish I weren't about to leave for the west," Hugo said. "But now that the new Lord of the Isles has paid his respects to his grandsire, the King, he will soon return, and my lady and I are to go with him."

"Lady Sorcha is looking forward to the journey," Rob said with a smile.

"Because she can collect what she needs from Chalamine whilst we're about it," Hugo said. "However, not only would I like to watch you act the baron, but you may need me, especially as Henry will likewise be leaving soon, for Orkney."

"Michael will be here," Rob reminded him.

Hugo nodded. "Aye, and he'll do all he can, but something else occurred to me. What about Adela's reaction to the new baron? She's seen you, after all."

"Not clearly," Rob said. "Ladies don't notice knights who behave as simple men-at-arms, and you'll recall that even after I was on my feet again at Hawthornden, you kept me there until just a few days ago. She saw me only once the day we rescued her, briefly, at a distance. I doubt she recognized me when we were removing Ardelve's body from the dais."

"You're sure she didn't see you on the ramparts or in the chapel tonight?"

Rob shook his head. "I couldn't see my own hand in that black fog. And I put out the candle in the chapel tonight before she could get a glimpse of me there."

"So you scared the poor lass witless whilst she was at her prayers, did you?" Hugo said in a near growl.

"Nay, but the truth won't please you any better," Rob admitted. "I sent her a message to meet me there."

"The devil you did! By heaven . . ."

"Easy, Hugo," Rob said. "It isn't what you think." He had just begun to explain when the door opened without ceremony to reveal Sir Michael Sinclair.

Michael paused at the threshold when he saw the two of them. "What devilry are you two plotting?" he said.

"Shut the door," Hugo said. When Michael had obeyed, Hugo added with a grim smile, "Apparently Sir Robert of Lestalric has decided to claim his heritage."

"Has he?" Michael said, glancing at Rob. "Well, then, I warrant we'll enjoy the stir, because, if I know our Robbie, he'll create one."

"Oh, aye, I think so," Rob said. "After all, when one makes noise, folks generally don't wonder straightaway why he is making it."

"Just see that you don't draw the wrong sort of attention," Michael said. "I've just come to tell you, we've had word that the men who murdered your father and brother were not English—not part of the English army, at all events."

"Who provided this information?" Hugo asked.

"The Douglas," Michael said. "The English have been growing ever more daring again about crossing the border, and Sir Ian and Will were searching an area between Jed Forest and Carter Bar to confirm or deny rumors of a raiding party thereabouts. Douglas logically concluded that the raiders they sought found them first. However, of their own small party, only Sir Ian and Will were killed."

"What happened to the others?" Rob asked.

"Not even hurt," Michael said. "They saw four men in black, fully armed, wearing light mail. The few English they'd seen were all Borderers, they said, and wore jacks-o'-plate as our lot do. No similar incidents have occurred, Douglas said, and no one has seen the four raiders since."

Hugo said, "I don't like the sound of that, especially in view of what we were discussing earlier. You'll have to beware, Rob."

Rob grimaced. "If I must take my father's place and act the baron, I'll seek my fun where I can find it. I've no inclination yet to put up my sword."

To Michael, he said, "Tell Douglas when next you communicate with him that I'll need time to sort out my people before I'll have any notion how many I can spare him. I warrant my father was none too supportive of his border defenses. He'll have wanted to protect Lestalric, and he was not a man to recognize that supporting Douglas would more efficiently accomplish that."

Michael nodded. "The messenger did say Sir Ian provided only that small party. Douglas was irked with him for bringing so few, but apparently he joined Douglas only to decide if the threat warranted lending him any men at all."

"And Will rode with him?"

"Aye, your brother, as you know, was always eager to find the least taxing way to impress others with his prowess. He'd doubtless have returned to court full of exploits, sporting new finery and spewing tales to impress the lasses. But I should not speak ill of him now," Michael added with a look of apology.

"I'd as lief we not speak of him at all," Rob said. "I wish I could feel grief for either of them, but other than a sense of outrage at whoever dared to murder them, I feel nothing. There is one other thing I should discuss with you both, however," he added reluctantly.

Hugo and Michael were two of his three closest friends in the world. He trusted them completely, would trust either with his life or with his wife if he had one. But he'd never told either one what he needed to share with them now.

Both regarded him intently, and Hugo said, "I'm guessing this must be even more important than what you and I discussed before."

"Aye," Rob said. "It may have something to do with the Order—if not with what we found before, then with some item given into its care in similar fashion."

"You're speaking riddles," Michael complained. "Talk plainly."

"Wait," Hugo said, getting up and moving to the door.

He opened it, looked out on the stairwell, then shut it tight again and threw the bolt. "Now, what is it?"

"I need to talk to Henry, too," Rob said. "My grandfather Logan gave me information before he sent me to Dunclathy. But a key feature of what he knew lies elsewhere, and I'm thinking Henry may be of some help with it when I find it."

"Do you want him now?" Michael asked. "He's gone back to Edinburgh."

"Then I'll talk with him there," Rob said. "One thing about claiming my own is that I'll be able to approach him without drawing undue notice."

"What sort of information did your grandfather give you?" Hugo asked.

"He told me two things," Rob said. "The first was that I'd learn things at Dunclathy and become part of something there that was both secret and vitally important, something that I was never to talk about to anyone else."

"He was talking about the Order, of course," Michael said.

"Aye, but he did not say so. He was also cryptic about the other matter, saying only that he would leave information for me in a safe place, but I'm guessing it's most likely a map. He was already ailing when he sent me to your father for training, Hugo, and he feared he might die before he saw me again. He never trusted Will, who began as soon as he learned he was Master of Lestalric to care only about being heir to the barony and to seek his own advantage."

"Where is this item and what makes you think it's a map?" Michael asked.

"In troth, I may have created the notion of a map in

my own head," Rob said. "But Grandfather said I'd know all that I needed to know when the time came to look for it and would find the key in the most likely place for him to hide it at Lestalric. He said I'd learn then where it would lead me."

"How could he know all that?" Michael asked, drawing up a stool to sit on.

"He said I'd understand more as I came to know the Sinclair brothers better," Rob said. "That was when I learned we'd be training together. But when Sir Edward revealed that our heritage included the Knights Templar and all the duties the Order entailed, I began to think the secret must have to do with something the Order is guarding, as it guards the Templars' own treasure now. If that is true, it may be something my grandfather meant to entrust to the Templars or that someone else entrusted to my family because of its early connection to the Templars."

"Perhaps the Logans took possession of a second portion of the Templar treasure," Michael said. "We know it had to be larger than what we've discovered so far. Mayhap bits of it were scattered all over Scotland."

Rob shook his head. "I cannot say that you are wrong, but recall that in 1307, when the treasure ships arrived in the Isles, my family lived here in Lothian. And it was my great-grandfather and his brother, both Templars, who were close friends with Sir James Douglas and Sir William St. Clair."

"The English overran this area in those days," Hugo reminded him. "And they invaded twice more after the Bruce routed them. You cannot know whose aid your ancestors might have engaged, or who might have engaged theirs—or your grandfather's later, come to that."

"That's all true," Rob said. "I'm thinking this may be something different, though. Recall that the Order acted as bankers to the world, securing all manner of treasures for royal houses everywhere. Recall, too, that the Bruce was close friends with your ancestors and mine, as well as with Sir James Douglas, and that the greater part of the Order's archives are likewise missing."

Michael and Hugo looked at each other, and when Hugo raised his eyebrows, Michael said, "We know that the Order also guarded items for heads of state, and at least one chest full of maps and documents." To Rob, he said, "Your grandfather said you'd know when the time was right. Why do you think that time is now?"

Rob grimaced. "If aught happened to me, no one else would know what he'd said. That's been true all along, I expect, but never before did I see it so clearly, and the English seem bent now on a new invasion, so I decided that the men I trust most should know as much as I do about it. Also, someone seems eager to do away with the barons Lestalric," he added dryly. "Since I'm not ready to die yet . . ."

"Understandable," Michael said when he paused.

"Aye," Hugo said. "But you left out at least one detail, Rob."

"What's that?"

"Will's beautiful widow. I warrant the lady Ellen will be pleased to learn of your return. Had you not considered that?"

"Nay, truly, I had not," Rob said. Although his brother's widow had once been the love of his life, he had ceased thinking of her as such long ago, and had not thought of her at all until reminded of who might have interest in Lestalric. That she might be interested in him seemed unlikely now that she was a widow, too. Even for the daughter of Scotland's most powerful lord, it was no easy thing to lose a husband.

The three continued to discuss details of his departure, and a short time later he took his leave of them. Having accumulated but few belongings, he had little to pack and soon was fast asleep.

Rising early the next morning, he saddled his horse, said a few words to the stable lads, and left Roslin Castle behind him.

Waking later than usual, Adela dressed and broke her fast in the privacy of her bedchamber with a manchet loaf and an apple that Kenna brought to her, and asked the girl if her brothers had spoken yet with Einar Logan.

"Tam said I just wanted to flirt wi' the man m'self and he were no going to have Einar clout him one for putting him in the way o' a lovesick lass. But I'm no such thing, m'lady. I like Einar, but he's no interested in me. I ken that fine."

So, Adela went to the stable again. But the lad who had spoken with her before said Einar had gone.

"Left at dawn wi' a message to the Douglas from Sir Hugo," he said. "But he said to tell ye, ye needna thank him, m'lady. He were that glad to help ye."

"I see," Adela said, disappointed and more concerned about him than ever.

Thanking the lad, she went next in search of Sorcha,

only to learn her sister had not yet returned to Roslin from Hawthornden Castle.

"But Sir Hugo be here, me lady," the gillie added. "He'll be wi'— Och, nay, there he be now."

Following his gaze, she saw Hugo emerging from the countess's solar. She was reluctant to confront him, especially since her midnight comforter had insisted that she tell him all that she had overheard. Hugo would be angry, but she could not ignore what she knew. Accepting that she had no choice, she hurried to meet him.

"If you please, sir, I would speak with you," she said when they met.

"What is it, lass?" he asked.

She looked around, noting several gillies attending to their chores.

Hugo said, "Let us move close to the fire by the dais. I'll dismiss the lad there, so we may speak privately."

She would have preferred total privacy, but she doubted he would agree to such a request. He was more likely to deem it improper, so she nodded and went with him to the dais. Even without the privacy screens, if they spoke quietly, their voices should not carry to anyone else.

"Now, how may I be of service to you?" Hugo asked when they stood before the warm fire.

"I want to ask a boon, sir," Adela said, deciding she would be wise to ask him before discussing Einar. If Hugo agreed to let her stay at Hawthornden, he would not change his mind only because she managed to make him angry about something else.

He smiled. "Ask away. If it is in my power, I'll do what I can."

"Did Sorcha not ask you about Hawthornden?"

He shook his head. "What, exactly, was she to ask me?"

It was annoying that Sorcha had forgotten to ask, but perhaps she had been waiting for the right moment. But, bad timing or not, Adela had to ask him now.

"You see," she said, "everyone has been telling me I need not go home with Ardelve's body, but I hesitate to accept Lady Clendenen's invitation to stay with her in Edinburgh, because it does not seem right that I should go to court with her when I am so recently a widow. Yet she insists I should."

"I see naught amiss in such a plan, but you had better decide soon. Bodies don't keep overlong, sithee, so they mean to leave for Glasgow at midday today."

She winced at the image that leaped to mind but said, "I mean to stay, I think, but . . . " She drew breath, then said in a rush, "If you will let me, I'd like to stay at Hawthornden. You see, I'm not used to living with so many people. Roslin is teeming with them, and half of them spend three-quarters of their time telling me what I should think and what I should do. I'm longing for peace."

"I wish I could oblige you, Adela," he said.

"Please, sir, I would take a maidservant with me, and . . ."

"I'd provide all the servants you'd need if I could do it," he said. "The fact is I've already promised a friend of mine that he can stay there. He means to pay his respects to the King but prefers not to stay long in Edinburgh. Like yourself, he prefers a quieter place, so as we'll be leaving, I've offered him Hawthornden."

"I see." She bit her lower lip.

"Is there something else you would discuss with me?"

"Aye," she said, gathering herself. "What have you done with Einar Logan?"

His eyebrows shot upward. "As he is mine to command, I warrant I may do anything I like, within reason. Why do you ask?"

"I . . . I am concerned for his safety."

"Why?"

His sudden intensity disconcerted her. She saw no hint of guilt, only disquiet. Could she be wrong? Could the voice she'd heard be someone else's? Common sense said no, that she knew his voice well. And both men had been in his chamber.

"I looked for you yesterday to ask about Hawthornden, and I heard you," she said. "You were talking with a man, a Borderer, I think. He said you'd have to do away with Einar Logan and you agreed. And now Einar is gone, because I asked for him at the stable. I wanted to thank him for helping rescue me. I never have thanked him, you see, and I should have. Where is he, Hugo?"

"Did they not tell you when you asked for him?"

"They *said* he'd taken a message for you to the Douglas. Is that true?" She looked right at him, daring him to lie to her.

"I can tell you only that he is safe, lass, and in no danger from me or anyone I call friend. But you should know that listening at doors rarely supplies the listener with accurate information. What you heard was but a small piece of a conversation. The rest does not concern you, nor do I intend to explain it to you."

Squirming now, knowing he had every right to be

displeased with her, she said, "I believe you, sir. I do not think you would lie to me about such a thing."

"I would not," he said. "I must ask that you not discuss this matter with anyone else, though, including your sisters." He smiled then, adding, "I've no time for fratching just now, and if Sorcha didn't have my head for worrying you, she'd want it for making you fear for Einar's life."

She knew that for all his faults, he was a man of honor. "I'll say nothing, but you see that nothing bad happens to him. I suppose he'll go with you to the Isles."

He smiled warmly, the way she had seen him smile at her sister, and said, "You need not fear for him, lassie. We look after our own."

"I know," she said, relaxing, although she noted that he had ignored her supposition. "Is Lady Clendenen with the countess?"

"Aye, and that cousin of hers, as well. Although he says he'll be leaving today, the fog cleared enough yesterday afternoon for him to have left then."

"You don't like the chevalier de Gredin?"

He grimaced. "He's not a man I'd choose for a boon companion. I ken fine that he charms the ladies, though, so I'll say no more."

When they parted, she went to the solar, where she found Lady Clendenen with the countess, Sidony, Isobel, and the chevalier engaged in conversation.

"You are looking much better, dearling," Lady Clendenen said with an approving smile. "I vow, you have roses in your cheeks again."

"Thank you, madam, I feel more rested. I have come to tell you that if you still desire it, I shall be honored to accept your kind invitation."

Lady Clendenen exclaimed her delight, but Sidony's eyes had widened, and as soon as her ladyship paused to draw breath, she said, "But I thought you were set on re-turning with Ardelve's corpse, Adela. What changed your mind?"

"Her good sense," Isabella said. "You will of course be going to court, Adela, so we must put our heads to-gether and determine how best to provide you with all you'll need. You will want to leave us now, Chevalier," she added brusquely. "Such conversation can hold little interest for any man."

"I assure you, madame, I should be most honored to take part in such a discussion," he said, flashing his smile. "I have excellent taste in ladies' dress."

"Well, we don't want you," Isabella said bluntly. "Do run away now so we may talk of matters better discussed without a gentleman's assistance."

The merry look de Gredin threw Adela's way as he obeyed made her want to laugh, and since it was the first time in a fortnight that she had experienced such a feel-ing, it surprised her. That she had dared to challenge Hugo had also surprised her, but she had been so worried. Perhaps she was just learning to feel things again.

⁓

Rob had not ridden anywhere near the Earl of Douglas, nor did he intend to. Not only had Hugo's suggestion about Ellen's possible new interest in him shaken him more than he'd realized, but having arranged with Michael for his own message to reach Douglas, he intended to fix his attention firmly on what lay ahead of him.

Hugo had also suggested that he make whatever use he thought best of Hawthornden, but he had no intention of doing so until Hugo and his lady had gone. To go there now meant either taking Lady Sorcha into his confidence or suffering her anger later if he did not. Since he could not in good conscience ask her to keep secrets from her sister, he thought it best to go straight on to Edinburgh, to Henry.

Having managed large estates almost from puberty, Henry was an expert in matters that Rob knew little about. He would tell him all that he had told Hugo and Michael and would welcome his advice on nearly everything that affected Lestalric.

Perhaps Henry would even know what the devil to do about Ellen. It seemed unlikely that Douglas would expect him to support her at Lestalric, but she did have a right to such support if she demanded it. That thought was no comfort to him.

More importantly, though, Henry's knowledge of old maps might prove invaluable. Rob had thought often over the years of where his grandfather might have hidden the map, if it was a map, and he was fairly certain he knew.

But he had not been next or nigh Lestalric Castle in nine years, so it was possible that the hiding place he had known no longer existed.

Chapter 8

With donations from Isobel's wardrobe and even from Isabella's, it seemed to Adela that she would have clothing enough for a decade at court. Even so, it took nearly a fortnight before the countess and Lady Clendenen declared her ready to go.

Sorcha and Hugo had left for Glasgow days before, taking Macleod with them, so he and Hugo could help supervise preparations for the return of Donald, Lord of the Isles, to his own territory. Donald would meet them at Dumbarton at the end of the week, after he had taken formal leave of the King and the royal court.

To Adela's surprise, and a little to her dismay, the formidable countess had insisted on accompanying her to Edinburgh.

"I must bid Donald farewell," she said. "But I'll be staying at Sinclair House, of course, with Henry. He is always pleased to welcome me, or any other visitors."

Sir Michael had ordered a large contingent of men-at-arms to escort them. Lady Clendenen had multiple boxes and bags, and the countess traveled with her own servants, piles of personal baggage, and some of her favorite furniture. So they created a cavalcade that Adela thought might easily be mistaken for a royal procession.

The journey from Roslin was not long. As they topped the last rise, a broad plain spread before them with a large hill to the northeast, its craggy face making it resemble a sleeping lion.

"That is Arthur's Seat," Lady Clendenen told her. "That one to the west is Castle Hill. The royal burgh of Edinburgh lies right between them."

She went on to identify other hills, the blue waters of the Firth of Forth, and the distant coast of Fife beyond. But Adela's gaze had come to rest on Edinburgh Castle, gleaming in late afternoon sunlight. It sprawled across its own craggy hilltop, its curtain wall extending to the easternmost crags and down the hillside.

It looked, she thought, as a royal castle ought to look, forbidding and impregnable. That anyone could conquer it seemed impossible, but she knew the English had taken it on several occasions, King Edward I more than once. When he and his army had invaded the country the first time, they'd held the area from Edinburgh south for the better part of eighteen years and had taken the crown records, crown treasury, and Scotland's coronation stone back to England with them.

In 1335, her father had told her, the English had recaptured the Castle. They had not only occupied it but also refortified it. They had held it for nearly six years that time before the Scots reclaimed it. And now, they threatened to do it again.

As their cavalcade approached, the royal burgh looked enormous. Its roads were broader than any Adela had seen, even in Stirling. Houses lined each side. Their gardens, according to the countess, lay tucked away behind them.

Lady Clendenen said proudly, "If one counts the Canongate, the burgh boasts nearly four hundred houses now."

"Mercy," Adela exclaimed. "How many people are there?"

"Oh, nearly two thousand, I expect, if one counts the Castle folk and the abbey. Those spires straight ahead are St. Giles's Cathedral, which lies halfway betwixt the Castle and the abbey. That tall, single tower to the east is the abbey's."

"Holyrood Abbey?"

"Aye, of course, and you should know that inside the burgh, all the roads are called gates in the old Norse fashion. We'll enter along the Cowgate. My house and Sinclair House lie near each other on the Canongate, just west of the abbey."

Drawing a long breath, Adela said, "It is so good to smell the sea again."

"Aye, it is," Isabella said, smiling at her. "Edinburgh's harbor lies nearby at Leith, yonder to the northeast," she added with a gesture.

Lady Clendenen said with a sigh, "Your mentioning Leith makes me think of poor Baron Lestalric and his heir, killed so tragically. A dreadful thing, that was. I wonder who—or for that matter, how many—will claim that vast estate now."

With an edge to her voice, Isabella said, "I'd not be

surprised to find a royal prince amongst them. These days, his grace is easily persuaded to accept even weak arguments to claim lands for the Stewarts or for the Crown. If those arguments fail, it is only because they require the support of the Scottish Parliament. But the most ambitious of his sons seeks to control Parliament as well as the King."

"You mean Fife, of course," Lady Clendenen said. To Adela, she said, "No one likes him, because everyone knows he resents being a younger son and will do almost anything to gain enough power to win the throne. But surely, Isabella, there must be more legitimate claimants to Lestalric than any of that upstart Stewart lot."

Adela, inhaling deeply again of the refreshing sea air as the discussion continued without her, paid them scant heed. But as they moved toward the center of the burgh, she soon had so much to look at that she just stared. Horsedrawn and handdrawn carts moved everywhere. Many carried handsomely garbed passengers.

The Canongate, an extension of the royal burgh's high street, proved to be broader than the Cowgate, with large houses of stone and timber on either side.

"So many large houses!" Adela exclaimed as they turned east onto the Canongate. "Where do all the people who own them come from?"

"Merchants who use the harbor for shipping have to reside in Edinburgh," Isabella explained. "Because of that law, many such men have built houses here."

They parted with her at a big, south-facing stone house and, minutes later, Lady Clendenen pointed out her own house, as spacious as any, facing north.

A short time later, Adela found herself in a pleasant

chamber overlooking a large garden, with a cheerful maidservant to attend her. As she gazed out on a green lawn with budding flower borders, the door opened.

"Don't stand dreaming, my dear," her hostess said. "We must dress at once if we are not to be late."

"Late?"

"Aye, sure. Did you not hear us speaking earlier? We are to collect Isabella immediately after Vespers. We'll join the court for supper."

Dismayed, Adela struggled to smile and nod. She had not heard them. And having assumed they would need an invitation first, she had expected to have time to adjust to her new surroundings before plunging into life at the royal court.

The countess's arrival at Sinclair House caused a stir. Maidservants and gillies rushed to welcome her and then scurried to carry in all she had brought with her. But the initial tumult quickly eased.

Henry waited with Rob in the solar at the north end of the main hall, which occupied most of the second floor. When they heard her coming upstairs from the ground floor entryway, Henry stepped out to greet her. Waiting in the doorway, dressed more finely than ever before in his life, Rob watched their meeting warily.

"Madam, welcome," Henry said, moving to embrace the countess. Releasing her, he said, "I believe you are acquainted with Sir Robert of Lestalric."

Rob had been aware that her gaze had fixed on him as

she hugged Henry, but he could not tell from her expression what she was thinking.

She smiled then and said, "I would scarcely have recognized you, sir. I am glad that you mean to claim your rightful place at last."

"Thank you, madam," he said with heartfelt relief.

"You will excuse me, I know," she said. "I want to tidy myself and dress for court. Ealga and I mean to take supper at the Castle tonight. Adela, too," she added.

A moment later, she had disappeared up the stairs.

Rob looked at Henry, aware of a sudden, unsettling flutter of nerves.

"The time has come," Henry said. "I think you are ready."

"Aye," Rob said. "I hope so."

"Once we've established your identity, you can proceed with the next step."

"I just hope I'm right in thinking the key lies at Lestalric," Rob said. "The hiding place my grandfather showed me is the only place I know to look."

"So the next step is to ride to Lestalric and have a look," Henry said practically. "At least Lady Logan is not there. She is with her father."

"I'm glad of that," Rob said, realizing that Ellen had slipped from his mind again. Grimacing, he added, "But first I must make my bow at court, Henry."

"I warrant you'll make a grand impression there," Henry said, grinning.

"Aye, sure," Rob said, his thoughts shifting instantly back to Lady Adela. "I might if I don't find my head in my lap before midnight."

Lady Clendenen possessed an enclosed wagon, drawn by two horses, which she called a coach. Having lived her life in the Highlands with no roads, Adela had never seen one before but thought it must be a most convenient vehicle.

Her hostess insisted, however, that it was not just convenient but a necessity in Edinburgh, where inclement weather was the rule rather than the exception.

"It is too far to walk to the Castle, and too steep," she declared. "And on horseback, most days, one would be soaked through before one arrived."

So Adela and her ladyship climbed into the coach but without the chevalier de Gredin. He, apparently, had removed to other quarters. Adela had seen no sign of him at Clendenen House and did not think it fitting to ask about him.

The short ride to Sinclair House proved interesting, even amusing. But after Isabella and Prince Henry joined them in the rattling, jolting vehicle, its interior became too crowded for comfort. To make matters worse, the latter part of the journey, up the narrow, precipitous road to the Castle gate tower, proved more terrifying for Adela than any wild boat trip on heaving winter seas.

Fearing at any minute that coach, horses, and all might plunge off the road and down the steep embankment, she held her breath and sat as still as she could.

They arrived safely in the pebbled courtyard and walked to the Castle's noisy hall in an enormous four-story tower at the west end of the yard.

"This is David's Tower," Isabella said. "They finished

building it thirteen years ago. It contains the royal apartments as well as others for noble visitors."

"I've rooms here, myself," Henry said as they waited
for the lord chamberlain to announce them. "You ladies
must make use of them whenever you like. The weather
is sadly unreliable at this time of year."

"Just what I said about it myself," Lady Clendenen
told him. "And although they maintain that track well, I
do not trust any wheeled vehicle on it in a storm."

"Nor should you," Henry said, grinning at her as he
pushed a strand of fair hair back from his forehead and
adjusted his plumed hat. He was clearly eager to join the
merrymakers.

Adela listened to them talk but made no comment.
Not only could she think of nothing suitable to say about
her ride in the bone-jarring coach, but she was also trying
to take in all she saw and heard as they waited.

The air inside the hall was hazy with smoke from two
great fireplaces. Minstrels' music competed with the roar
of conversation, punctuated by bursts of laughter, barking
dogs, and once, a woman's scream. The din was appalling
to one unused to such gatherings. Players occupied the
central area, but acrobats were doing flips and hand-
springs through their midst. Their antics and a nearby dog
fight, apparently over scraps, spoiled whatever the players were attempting to portray.

Not that any of the uproar seemed to matter to anyone
else.

As far as Adela could tell, no one watched the players
or listened to the music. Some strolled about the perime-
ter. Others supped at two linen-draped boards extending
at right angles from the high table. Still others, mostly

men, sprawled near a fireplace. They seemed to be dicing, with mugs or goblets in their free hands.

The sound of a too-near trumpet blast startled her into
a sharp cry. Although she doubted that anyone else had
heard her, she looked nervously about as the noise diminished a degree or two, and the lord chamberlain roared,
"Your grace, I beg leave to present the Earl of Orkney, the
Countess of Strathearn and Caithness, Lady Clendenen of
Kintail, and Lady Ardelve of Loch Alsh and Glenelg."

As the women went forward with Henry to make their
curtsies, Adela peered through the haze, trying to decide
which man at the high table was King of Scots.

Beside her, in an undertone that barely carried to her
ears, Isabella said, "His grace is in the center, the elderly
man. Beside him on his right is MacDonald, second Lord
of the Isles. The next man is the Earl of Carrick, the
King's eldest son and heir to the throne of Scotland.
He is the kindest of his numerous family, but you would
be wise to keep your distance from all the King's sons.
They are ambitious, often dangerous men, most of whom
eat innocents like you."

"Do they, madam? Then I shall certainly take care,"
Adela said.

A moment later, she was making her deepest curtsy to
the King, although he seemed to take little notice. He
merely blinked his reddened eyes briefly in her direction
before turning away again.

"Our beloved King does not see well, I fear," a familiar voice said from behind. Turning her head as she rose
from her curtsy, she saw that Chevalier de Gredin had
joined them.

He flashed his charming smile, looking deep into her eyes. "Good evening."

Observing him with a renewed flicker of doubt, she wondered why he had ignored his own advice to keep distance between them. But as the thought crossed her mind, something about it struck her as wrong. She did not try to analyze the feeling, but she did not reject it. She said only, "Your accent has diminished."

"*Oui, madame*," he said. "You declared that my Frenchiness displeased you, and I mean to show you how amiable I am. I'm glad you came tonight. I feared you would not recover from the fatigue of your journey before tomorrow."

"Roslin is only seven miles away, sir," she said. "Moreover, the countess wanted to speak to Donald of the Isles before he departs for home."

"You are looking remarkably beautiful tonight," he said. "That gown is enchanting. Will you stroll with me, or do you desire to eat something first? The food is excellent here."

"We'll take supper first," Lady Clendenen said, cutting off the flow. "But you may join us at table, Etienne. Thank you for removing your belongings from Clendenen House as I asked. I'm sorry to have put you out, but it would have been most unsuitable for you to remain. Doubtless you have found acceptable quarters."

"*Bien sûr*," he said. "A friend managed to acquire a small apartment here in the Castle for me. I shall be nearly as comfortable as I was with you."

"Excellent, but I must warn you yet again not to be too particular in your attentions to Lady Ardelve. Few will condemn her for staying here in town with me or appearing at court, but she must still be careful about her behavior."

Having watched a woman plop herself in a man's lap, fling her arms around his neck, and kiss him soundly without anyone looking the least shocked, Adela wondered what her ladyship thought she might do to upset anyone accustomed to such a place. She hoped her companions would not want to stay long and that if they ever took advantage of Henry's invitation to use his apartments, it would not mean having to stay overnight in the Castle.

Her discomfort increased when they sat down to supper. The entertainment had grown wilder and noisier. Even the servants seemed to have taken too much to drink. But her companions were oblivious, or had become inured to such activities.

Lady Clendenen had placed de Gredin on her left with Adela on her right, so Adela did not have to contend with the chevalier's fulsome compliments. She liked him well enough but wished he were less effusive in so public a place.

Henry had disappeared into the crowd.

Isabella's calm dignity offered a measure of reassurance, but whenever anyone passed too near, Adela jumped like a nervous tabby. She nibbled bread and a slice of apple but felt no enthusiasm for the rest of her food.

When de Gredin offered again to escort her around the chamber, she glanced at Lady Clendenen, who said, "We would both enjoy a stroll, Etienne, thank you."

If he was disappointed that she meant to accompany

them, he was too much of a gentleman, or too intelligent, to say so.

Isabella was chatting with the woman on her other side but paused long enough to tell them to go without her. So Adela arose with her ladyship.

When de Gredin laughingly offered an arm to each, her ladyship immediately accepted the one offered to her. When Adela shook her head, the chevalier smiled his understanding, saying lightly, "I had forgotten you come from the Highlands, my lady. 'Tis generally much quieter there, *n'est ce pas?*"

"Aye, sir, it—" She broke off, starting violently again when the lord chamberlain's trumpeter blared another fanfare.

"Your grace," the chamberlain bellowed, "I beg leave to present Sir Robert Logan, third Baron Lestalric, who comes tonight to swear fealty to your grace."

The last portion of his announcement sounded unnaturally loud, because the chamber had fallen abruptly and astonishingly silent.

Looking to see what had caused such a phenomenon, Adela beheld a ruggedly handsome, broad-shouldered man with a tapered waist and powerful-looking, well-shaped legs. He was dressed in the height of fashion in a tight fitting, scarlet-velvet doublet, cross-laced with gold cording down the front. Its short "skirt" barely covered his hips. He wore a matching scarlet, white-plumed cap and parti-colored, red-and-black silk leather-soled hose with pointed toes.

The lace-edged sleeves of his doublet sported ornamental gold buttons from elbow to wrist where each fanned out to his knuckles. Around his hips, he wore a jeweled knightly girdle of gleaming gold links and an ornamental sword. His deeply dagged lavender silk mantle, buttoned to the right shoulder and thrown back, hung in graceful, fluttering folds down his back to his heels. It billowed as he strode forward. He swept his hat from his head as he knelt before the King of Scots.

"Sacrebleu! C'est paré des plumes du paon!"

Adela, hearing the muttered epithet, looked at de Gredin. His eyes had narrowed, and his jaw tightened until a muscle twitched low on his cheek.

"Is aught amiss?" she asked him. "I do not know that phrase."

"I said he's a damned peacock, that's all," de Gredin said. "The fellow makes a mockery of court fashion."

"Doesn't everyone dress finely?"

"Not like that."

To be sure, the gentleman's appearance represented the height of masculine fashion. She decided de Gredin was right. The effect was a bit overwhelming.

The newcomer straightened, looking directly at the King as he said in a flat but carrying voice, touched with a most unusual accent, "I regret that I have no handful of Lestalric dirt to cast at your feet, sire, but the House of Lestalric swears fealty to your grace and to the House of Stewart, now and forevermore."

The voice sounded familiar, but before Adela could identify it, the sight of the King of Scots emerging from his lethargy and leaning forward to peer at Sir Robert through narrowed, bloodshot eyes diverted her.

"Robbie, lad, is it truly yourself?" the King asked, his voice gravelly and uncertain. "We thought ye'd died years ago, lad."

"I trust you are not disappointed to see me still alive and hale, your grace. I vow I am not eager to plow myself six feet under yet, even to gratify you."

The King chuckled along with many others in the chamber. Then he beckoned the baron closer, apparently desiring to converse privately with him.

"Do you know him, Isabella?" Lady Clendenen asked as the countess joined them under cover of the increasing din of renewed, buzzing conversation. "He must be a kinsman of mine. Indeed, if he is who he says he is, he must be Lestalric's younger son, but I doubt I've ever laid eyes on him before. Have you, Etienne?"

"*Non*," de Gredin said. Then, apparently realizing she had expected more, he smiled ruefully and said, "I beg your pardon, cousin. I am a villain to be so curt to you, who have been so kind to me."

"Oh, aye, but we are all agog at this, after all."

"I do know Sir Robert," Isabella said. "That is to say, I remember him well. He took his training at Dunclathy in Strathearn, you see, with Sir Edward."

Adela looked at her. "Sir Edward Robison? Hugo's father?"

Isabella nodded, her gaze scanning the royal dais. They came to rest several seats from his grace on a man who rose abruptly.

He was tall and thin, and wore black velvet trimmed with gold lace. The only other colors on his person gleamed from the jeweled belt he wore low on his hips. His hair was nearly as dark as the velvet, his face long and lean, his features harsh, and the fingers of the hand he raised for silence were unusually long and slender.

"That is the Earl of Fife," Lady Clendenen said for

Adela's sake. "He's the King's second son and, some say, the real power behind the throne. They say he has had his eye on the crown of Scotland since he first learned of its existence. He has declared that all noble estates without obvious heirs should revert to the Crown."

"Forgive me, your grace," the Fife said smoothly, "but have we proof that this fellow is who he says he is? 'Tis not yet a fortnight since the second baron and his son died. Whence comes this dazzling fellow to present himself so quickly?"

"I will speak for Lestalric, your grace," Henry said, striding forward.

"Nae need, Henry," the King said. "Even I can see that he's the spit o' his late grandsire, the first baron, named so by the Bruce himself."

"Come, walk with me, Lady Adela," de Gredin said. "This mummery can hold little interest for you."

But Adela watched Sir Robert and the King. Their voices had hushed, but whatever Sir Robert said to the King must have amused him, for his grace laughed aloud. Henry had joined them, and his eyes were alight with laughter, too.

However, when de Gredin repeated his invitation to stroll, she collected herself and accepted politely, assuming Lady Clendenen would go with them. But her ladyship had either forgotten her intent or had decided Adela needed no protection from de Gredin, for she did not take her eyes from the high table.

Adela and the chevalier completed only one turn of the chamber, however, before Henry approached with the baron beside him and said, "Lady Ardelve, permit me to present my good friend Sir Robert of Lestalric."

Adela curtsied. "'Tis an honor, my lord."

"The honor is mine, Lady Ardelve," the baron said, sweeping off his plumed hat again and bowing as deeply as he had to the King.

Adela stiffened. Although he had spoken only six words in the flat, oddly accented tones he had employed before, any faint, lingering notion that de Gredin was the man she had met on the ramparts vanished. Her palms itched, her temper rose, and for the first time since her rescue, she felt truly deep emotion. Only her training and long-held fear of making a public spectacle of herself kept her from smacking the finely clad baron or snatching him baldheaded.

She was aware that Henry was watching her. She noted, too, the warily speculative glint in the baron's hazel eyes, turned almost golden in the reflected light of the myriad candles, cressets, and torches in the hall. His lashes were as long, thick, and dark as women so often wished theirs could be.

"De Gredin, I'd like a word with you, sir," Henry said. "My mother tells me you returned recently from France and are acquainted with the Duke of Anjou. I've a notion to visit there again this year, and I wondered if you might advise me."

De Gredin clearly wanted to linger, but he was no match for Henry's cheerful determination. Isabella had drawn Lady Clendenen aside, as well, Adela noted, although Henry had not yet formally presented the baron to either of them.

Thus, she was as alone with the baron as two people could be in the midst of a crowd when that familiar voice, its odd accent and flatness gone, murmured, "Will you walk with me, lass, or are you determined to murder me?"

"I'd prefer to murder you."

"That's what I feared."

"What is this deceitful game you are playing with me, sir?"

"Peace, my lady," he murmured. "We've a fascinated audience, who must all be wondering why you are flashing such fire at me. But if you will condescend to walk with me, one circuit of the room at least, mayhap when the noise increases, as I'm sure it soon will, we may speak more freely."

Realizing that nearly everyone in the room was watching them, Adela nodded with as much grace as she could muster and placed her hand on his outstretched forearm, noting as she did that although he wore a fine pearl pin on his hat and other jewels about his person, he wore only one rather plain ring on his left hand.

She said nothing to him until, as he had predicted, the noise level returned to its previous din. Then she muttered, "Someone is bound to ask why I looked at you so, although I swear I could not help myself. Whatever am I to say?"

He said ruefully, "I'd hoped my disguise, and my accent—"

"'Tis an absurd accent," she said. "What sort was it meant to be?"

"Orkney," he said. "Orknian? Sakes, I don't even know what such folk call themselves when they're from home. I've only heard their accent once, you see, when I . . . when I chanced to visit the Isle of Orkney last summer."

"For Prince Henry's installation?"

"Aye, that's it."

"I was there, too," she said.

"I ken that fine," he told her. "Twas the first time ever I saw you. I thought then that you were the most—"

"Don't, please," she interjected. "I am not accustomed to compliments from you, sir. Indeed, I am not accustomed to hearing them from anyone. Moreover, Chevalier de Gredin has already paid me more than my share tonight."

"We can discuss whether you deserve them another time," he said equably. "At the moment, I should like to know why you encourage that appalling fellow."

"I don't encourage him," she said, looking up at him.

He was gazing straight ahead, his lips thinned to a straight line. His profile was admirable and stirred another, different tickle of familiarity. But the fleeting sensation vanished before she could identify its cause.

He looked about to speak to her, but before he could, she said severely, "You must have guessed that I thought he was you. Faith, sir, I told you as much!"

"I'll forgive you almost anything, my lady, and I richly deserve your censure for deceiving you as I did. But learning that you had mistaken that rogue for the man you had met in the darkness . . . Well, it was a hard blow, I can tell you."

"Do you expect me to apologize?"

"Certainly not. Every fault is mine, whilst you remain the perfect woman."

Adela repressed an unexpected bubble of laughter. It would never do to forgive such deceit easily, no matter how she felt. Still, her mood had lightened, and the strain caused by the uproarious crowd had vanished. She said, "Have you known so many women that you can judge perfection, sir?"

"I have known my share," he said with a smile.

He had a nice smile, a contagious one. She almost smiled back, but something else occurred to her. "Did we perhaps meet at Orkney? You seem slightly familiar, but I do not recall that we met. I hope you are not offended."

"Nay, not at all," he said. "No one was kind enough to present me to you. I own, though, I'd have given anything to have seen you toss that basinful of holy water at Hugo's head."

"So you know Sir Hugo," she said, feeling fire in her cheeks at the thought of the scene he had described. That had *not* been her finest moment. She so rarely did such things, only when people pushed her too far.

"Aye, I know Hugo," he said. "And Michael Sinclair, too. We took our training together at Dunclathy."

"Training?"

"Aye," he said. "As with most lads of our rank and her-itage, we hungered to become proper knights and protect Scotland from the English, or indeed, invaders from any source. Hugo's father is an excellent teacher, albeit a gey stern one."

"I have met Sir Edward," Adela said. "He has always been kind to me."

"Aye, but just wait until he sees you with a sword in hand, or a lance. As he teaches you to wield either weapon properly, he will surely turn into an ogre."

Astonished at the image he'd introduced to her mind, she laughed aloud. "You are the most absurd man!"

"Am I? My comment seems to have been successful nonetheless."

"Successful?"

"Aye, for I wanted to see if I could make you laugh."

Feeling heat again, not just in her cheeks but throughout her body, she stared at him. "But why?"

"Because in all the time you have been at Roslin, lass, I don't believe you've laughed once. At all events, I have not seen you do so."

"But you never saw me," she protested. "We met only in the dark."

"One hesitates to contradict a lady, but I have seen you numerous times at Roslin. Moreover, when I saw you at Henry's installation, I distinctly recall your smiling more than once. And as you have a singularly entrancing—" Breaking off with an exaggerated clap to his forehead, he said, "Forgive me! Compliments again! They just spill out, but I do beg your pardon."

"Please, sir," she begged, struggling not to laugh again but failing. "You will be the one to draw attention to us this time, and truly, I should not be laughing with you like this. Recall that it has not yet been a fortnight since . . ."

"Since your husband died?" he said when she hesitated. "Laughing or not laughing won't change that, lass, any more than I can change anything in the case of my own father and brother."

Adela's breath caught in her throat.

"You!" she exclaimed more loudly than she had intended. Lowering her voice as much as she could, she said accusingly, "Mercy, I did not put it all together when I first heard your name, but two men dying . . . It was *you* with Sir Hugo—the conversation I overheard, the very one I told you about in the chapel."

"Aye, it was," he admitted. "But—"

"How *could* you?"

"I know I should have owned up to it at once, but at the time—"

"I don't mean that," she said, striving to control her growing fury. "I mean, how could you have decided so cold-bloodedly to put an end to poor Einar Logan? What did you do with him? After what I heard, and now this, I *don't* believe for an instant that he just went off somewhere on an errand for Hugo."

"You may murder me later if you still want to, my lady, but I beg you, hold your sword for the moment. Lady Clendenen is coming this way."

Adela followed his gaze and wanted to scream. Both Lady Clendenen and the chevalier were walking toward them.

Chapter 9

Rob did not know whether to curse Lady Clendenen, now beaming at them, or kiss her. What he did know was that he should kick himself for his stupidity in imagining that the lass would not recognize his voice straightaway.

His intention had been for Henry to present him to her in full view of an audience so fascinated by his entrance that everyone would think they had just met. And a fine entrance it had been, too, he told himself.

Having contrived his outfit with Henry's generous assistance and the aid of Henry's tailor, he had been very pleased with it. But perhaps because of that confidence, he had not given enough thought or credit to Lady Adela's intelligence. He had likewise underestimated her ability—even in the tumult of the royal court—to recognize a voice she had heard only in the darkness.

But to have made the comment about his father and Will without counting the cost had been a worse mistake. He knew he might well tell her everything in time, but he had hoped to choose that time. It had been foolish to assume he would have that luxury and truly dimwitted to think he could fool her for long.

She then astonished him again, for when Lady Clendenen and de Gredin reached them, she greeted them both warmly, as if she had not been ready to shred his face with her fingernails only ten seconds before.

"I hope we don't intrude, dear ones, and that you'll not be offended, my lord, if I treat you as one of my family," Lady Clendenen said. Without waiting for a reply, she went on, "I wanted to tell you that Isabella is talking with Donald of the Isles now. But she will soon be ready to depart. I thought you might like me to present you to her before then, my lord, to refresh her memory of you."

"I thank you for your kindness, madam," Rob said, affecting the flat, higher-pitched tone again, albeit softening the assumed accent and taking good care not to look at Adela. He felt instinctively that she would maintain her composure more easily if he did not catch her eye. He wondered, though, if either Lady Clendenen or the irritating de Gredin had noticed the increased color in her cheeks.

Glancing at the latter, he saw only that the insolent dog was gazing at her.

"Sakes, but I'm remiss in my duty, my lord," Lady Clendenen said. "I ought to have presented my cousin, Chevalier de Gredin, to you at once. Pray, forgive me."

Rob nodded when de Gredin looked at him, deciding to take an aloof tone with the slink rather than a friendly one. *See how he likes that*, he thought.

He did not trust the chevalier, but if he had had to explain his distrust, he knew he would be hard-pressed to provide a good reason. His instincts had served him excellently over the years, though. He would not ignore them now.

No sooner had de Gredin murmured a polite greeting than her ladyship said, "I warrant Etienne must be a cousin of sorts to you, too, sir, since you are both kin to me. In troth, I think every Scottish nobleman must be kin to every other one."

"Do you think so?" Rob asked. "I imagine not everyone would be so delighted to hear that as one might think."

Her eyes twinkled. "Indeed, you have the right of it, for I can promise you, I never mention to anyone that our poor Lady Ardelve's abductor was another cousin of mine. And only think how repugnant to have to admit kinship with the upstart—"

"Take care, madam," Rob interjected hastily as her ladyship's gaze drifted toward the royal dais. He grinned as if they shared a joke but said earnestly, "Say naught here that you do not want to hear repeated in every household in town."

"I fear that is most unfortunately so, cousin," de Gredin said, also smiling.

Her expression now rueful, Lady Clendenen turned to Adela and said, "They are right, my dear. I should not have said a word, but sometimes my tongue rattles like a clapdish. It does not do to offend folks with the powers of pit and gallows, though. And in this room, that includes half the men and more women than one might think."

"Mercy, madam," Adela said, flicking a glance at Rob. "You terrify me."

De Gredin said, "A royal court can be a dangerous

place for one who lacks experience with powerful men, my lady. However, my own experience with such people is great, and I am ever at your service. Do not hesitate to command me."

"Thank you, sir," she said, shooting another glance at Rob.

His usually glib tongue failed him. He would have liked to make a brilliant remark to impress her and disarm de Gredin. But before he could think of one, the latter said ruefully, "I fear my cousin exaggerates our relationship, Sir Robert. I am but distant kin to her, so I doubt I'd claim any connection to your family."

"Don't expect me to tell you," Rob said, recovering. "My father said I had no family pride. I do, of course. Who would not, given my ancestors' heroism at Bannockburn and afterward? Even so, one hesitates to boast of one's ancestors lest others expect one to act as they did. Don't you agree?"

De Gredin grinned. "I do see your point, sir. But to have won your spurs as young as I'm told you did, you must have proven yourself with a sword."

"The merest slicer," Rob said modestly with silent apologies to Sir Edward as he wondered who de Gredin's informant had been. "I'm told one must practice daily to remain skilled, and I've been away for years. Fell out of the habit, I'm afraid."

The smile this information elicited from de Gredin was a superior one, and seeing it, Rob congratulated himself. It would do no harm for de Gredin to believe himself the more skilled of the two with a weapon in hand—not, in any event, when the time came to test that skill, as Rob rather hoped it would.

Donald of the Isles took formal leave of his grandfather, the King, a short time later amidst great fanfare.

Since Donald habitually wore no hat when he came to court—a ploy learned from his father to avoid having to remove it in the King's presence—no part of that leave-taking ceremony suggested aught but that the two men were of equal stature. The elder was King of Scots, the younger King of the Isles.

That, as Adela knew, was how all Islesmen and Highlanders viewed Donald, whom they called MacDonald. There could be only one MacDonald at a time, but there were Stewarts aplenty, as many illegitimate as legitimate. Moreover, the King apparently took no notice of which was which.

All of his many offspring considered themselves of royal blood, entitled to royal privileges. However, not only were the Stewarts a younger clan than most in the Isles and elsewhere, but their surname derived from their hereditary position as royal stewards. The present King's father had served Robert the Bruce so, and the King himself had served the grandson who succeeded Bruce. When the latter died without issue, Robert the Steward inherited by Bruce's own order, his claim sustained by the Scottish Parliament if not by most Scottish nobility. He had reigned now for nine years and had consistently proven himself a better Steward than King.

What Adela had seen of his court so far did not speak well of the vast family. Nonetheless, she reserved her opinion, knowing her elder sister, Cristina, was well acquainted with the King's daughter, Princess Margaret

Stewart, widow of the first Lord of the Isles and mother of the present one. And Cristina liked the princess.

Adela watched MacDonald's entourage gather around him and parade from the room, but if her opinion of the Stewarts sank more when the princes at the high table went back to their dicing and drinking before MacDonald had left the hall, every other part of her remained intensely aware of Sir Robert of Lestalric.

He stood silently not two paces away with the equally silent Lady Clendenen and de Gredin flanking him.

Although Adela dared not look at him, she sensed that he was as powerfully aware of her as she was of him. Energy flowed between them and had done so from the moment Lady Clendenen and de Gredin had interrupted their conversation at so ill-chosen a moment. Adela found the strain of having to greet them politely and continue to behave in a civil manner nearly unbearable when what she wanted to do was to drag Sir Robert of Lestalric outside by an ear and have it out with him.

That thought, flitting through her mind, nearly made her smile, but she wondered at herself, too, because the thought was alien, the sort of thing that might occur to someone else but never to the woman she had become in the past weeks. It reminded her of angry moments in the past with Sorcha, a past that seemed eons before her abduction. At least, it had seemed so during recent weeks.

She had been in control of a large household and of herself in that long ago time, easily able to control her younger sister Sidony, nearly always able to manage their father, and even to guide if not always control the headstrong Sorcha. But of late, she had felt as if she controlled no portion of her life or of herself.

How the change had occurred she could not have said, but her reaction to Sir Robert's deceit—indeed, to the man himself—had been more like the old Adela. As for the energy surging through her, urging her to take him to task and hinting that she would thoroughly enjoy doing so, that was energy she had not felt under any circumstance for years, if ever. So strong was it that she had scarcely noticed Lady Clendenen's mention of Waldron. Her ladyship might have spoken of anyone at all.

"Doubtless this gathering will grow rowdier now that Donald has gone," Isabella said, rejoining them as the last man in the parade of Islesmen left the hall. "I mean to leave, as well, but Henry has offered to arrange an escort for me if you want to remain, Ealga, so—"

"Mercy, no," Lady Clendenen said with a laugh. "The only folks who should linger are those who want to drink and carouse with Fife and his cronies. Those women yonder amongst the players are already behaving in a manner that I find unnerving." Turning to Sir Robert, she said, "As much as I wish we need not say goodnight so soon after making your acquaintance, sir, I believe we must do so before Lady Ardelve encounters any of the worst offenders."

"I, too, mean to depart, madam," Sir Robert said. "Henry has offered me a bed at Sinclair House tonight, and his people know me, so if he does not mean—"

"He will go, too," Isabella said. "He said he hopes to converse with you before you retire, since you mean to go early in the morning."

"Oh, no," Lady Clendenen protested. "You must not leave Edinburgh before we come to know you better, sir. I'd hoped you would do me the honor to dine with Lady

Ardelve and me tomorrow before we return here for the evening festivities."

Certain that the baron had no intention of leaving, Adela felt no surprise when he said mildly, "Nay, my lady. I go only to attend to duties of my new position. I've not seen Lestalric for nearly a decade, you see, so I mean to have a look at the place tomorrow."

"Then, mayhap you would deign to take supper with us at Clendenen House," she said hopefully. Glancing at her cousin, she said, "De Gredin, I include you in my invitation, too. You gentlemen will do as you like afterward, of course. I prefer to enjoy the court at suppertime or earlier. To my mind, the activities grow less enjoyable afterward. But we need not come here every day."

Isabella smiled at Adela and said, "I believe you have not visited Holyrood Abbey, my dear. You should make a point of seeing it whilst you are here."

Adela wondered at the apparent non sequitur, but Sir Robert said, "Aye, you should, Lady Ardelve. Lestalric lies not far from the abbey. Perhaps we can arrange a riding party if Lady Clendenen or the countess would condescend to lend us an air of respectability. Indeed, I'd be delighted if you all would join me."

De Gredin chuckled. "Take care, my lord, for I'll wager they think you mean tomorrow. And they may well expect that invitation to include me, although I doubt that was your intent."

"You malign me, *monsieur*," the baron said instantly. "I'd be honored if everyone joined me tomorrow. Such a party would vastly improve a day I had expected to be filled with duty and despair. I fear Lestalric, once a fine property, may have been neglected in past years. I'm told my brother stayed there when the royal court was in Edinburgh, but my father preferred Logan House."

"*Logan* House?" Adela said, looking sharply at him.

"Aye, my lady," he said with a wary look that she knew was for her alone. "'Tis my family's fortalice in the Pentland Hills."

"Then Logan is your surname?"

"Aye, and so the lord chamberlain did announce me." He watched her intently now.

"I recall that," Adela said. "At the time, though, I did not realize—"

But Isabella interrupted to say, "Do I understand, sir, that you are inviting us all to ride with you to Lestalric and perhaps to the abbey tomorrow?"

He smiled. "To be sure, Countess, if would please you."

"I shall have to take it under consideration," she said with an answering gleam of humor. "I'd intended to stay only a day or two to see Donald. And as he is departing for Glasgow in the morning, to take ship to Isla, I had nearly decided to return to Roslin tomorrow."

"Faith, Isabella," Lady Clendenen protested. "You've just arrived! Moreover, you brought enough baggage for a month!"

"Aye, I did, but I mean to spend more time here after Henry returns to Orkney. I brought much of what I'll need then this time. Our Isobel does not mean to leave Roslin whilst her bairn is so small, though, and I want to spend time with them, too. I warrant you'll all get on well enough without me."

"What would *you* like to do, Lady Ardelve?" Sir Robert

asked, surprising her. She had been wondering only if the others would decide to go with him or not.

When her startled gaze met his warm one, Adela knew she was blushing. "I expect I'll do whatever the others choose," she said, hoping she sounded cool but not as if her words dripped icicles. "I am her ladyship's guest, after all."

"We shall be delighted to go with you, sir," Lady Clendenen said instantly.

When his lips twitched, Adela's earlier anger stirred and she wrenched her gaze away from his lest she reveal it to the others and create one of those dreadfully uncomfortable moments she loathed so much when others created them.

"Perhaps I should fetch Henry now," Sir Robert said.

"Quite unnecessary," Isabella said. "Henry walked outside with MacDonald's entourage. He said he would call up Lady Clendenen's coach and meet us at the gate tower. How did you come here tonight, Lestalric?"

Adela glanced back at him the moment his attention shifted to the countess. She thought she saw his look of amusement return, and he continued to affect the silly accent he had been using as he said, "I rode my horse, Countess. I don't trust contraptions like her ladyship's coach. Enough to rattle one's teeth from one's head, I should think. What think you, de Gredin?"

"As I've rooms here in the Castle, I need not think of coaches at all," de Gredin said, smiling. "But, as to comfort, I am in full agreement with you."

"Will you walk out with us then, sir?" Sir Robert asked. "I doubt I can provide escort for three such enticing females by myself. More likely, I shall be overwhelmed by eager swains determined to cut me out."

"I'll go with you, and willingly," de Gredin said.

"How kind you are, my dear chevalier," Isabella said. "Will you lend me the support of your arm? I find some of the passageways here quite treacherous underfoot. Do not you find them so, Ealga? Mayhap you should take his other arm. Adela will not mind walking with Lestalric."

De Gredin had turned toward Adela, but he held out his arm at once for the countess. If a cloud of disappointment flitted across his brow as she offered the other one to Lady Clendenen, he recovered speedily.

"Don't glower at me, lass," Sir Robert murmured in his normal accent as the other three preceded them from the hall. "Some caperwitted dafty will draw his sword to protect you, and I'll have to slay him."

"I'll glower if I want to," she muttered back. "If I have to pretend to be in charity with you much longer, sir, I shall lose my temper completely."

"And doubtless will feel much better for the losing of it," he said. "Watch your step here. It's one of the uneven bits that annoy the countess. If you won't take my arm, at least do me the courtesy of remaining upright until you are safe inside her ladyship's coach. Consider my reputation as a cavalier."

Seeing nothing to gain by trying to explain why losing her temper would not make her feel better, she said instead, tersely, "What happened to Einar Logan?"

"I'll tell you all I can of what you want to know, but not here and not now," he said firmly. "If you will resist persuading the countess or Lady Clendenen to forbid our outing tomorrow, I will contrive a way to speak privately with you then. Mayhap we can arrange enough time for a full explanation."

"But you did say that Logan is your family name."

"You ken fine that I did," he said, looking into her eyes.

"Is Einar Logan a kinsman?"

"Most Logans are kinsmen to each other, lass, but I'll answer your questions tomorrow as well as I can. For now, recall that this castle has ears everywhere. I do not make a gift of my private affairs to just anyone."

"I must know one more thing, sir."

"What is it?"

"Is Einar still alive?"

He hesitated, then said, "Aye, and that's all I'll say about that now."

She wanted to ask why he had hesitated, but although the annoying voice in her head insisted it was an indication that he had lied to her, she could not make herself believe it. She had known liars—not many, to be sure, for most Highland folk, noble or not, disdained lies. They would occasionally equivocate, though, and she had the distinct impression that he was equivocating now.

But evasion was not lying. And although his behavior gave her furiously to think, she no longer feared for Einar's safety. Not only had Hugo said he was safe, but now Sir Robert had said he was alive. So he was, for the moment at least.

Outside, in the torchlit, misty dampness of the inner courtyard, they found the coach and Henry. To her surprise, he waited not only with Lestalric's horse but with another for himself.

"Borrowed it from the royal stable," he said with one

of his happy grins. "Your coach is a handsome vehicle, Ealga, but my backside is bruised from my shoulders to my knees. And my head still aches from a clout against the roof."

"You talk a deal of nonsense, sir," Lady Clendenen said roundly. "You were wearing your hat, so if anything got clouted it was not your handsome head. By all means, though, ride with Lestalric. That will leave more room for us."

They bade goodnight to de Gredin and climbed into the coach, where Adela found herself much more comfortably seated than before between the countess and her hostess. The two older women chatted amiably, leaving her alone with her thoughts and a tingling awareness of Lestalric riding only yards away.

Once Rob and Henry were mounted, Rob let him lead the conversation, which he did easily, discussing members of the royal court and the apparent rapid deterioration of the King's mental and physical faculties.

"I'm glad he recognized you," Henry said as they passed through the gate into the tunnel beneath the tower and the heavy iron portcullis that guarded it.

"Do you think I look so much like my grandfather?" Rob asked.

"Sakes, I barely remember him," Henry said. "Only met him once unless we count visits he must have made to Roslin when I was a child. But I don't recall those. Your father visited more often, but he never came after you left home."

"I warrant he feared you'd want to know why I'd left," Rob said. "He'd not have liked explaining that, I think. Not to you or to Sir Edward."

"He'd have known we'd side with you, all of us at Roslin," Henry agreed. "He must have guessed we'd hear your side of it, too."

They were silent for a while after that. But when the coach had drawn a short distance ahead, Rob said, "I invited them all to make up a riding party tomorrow when I visit Lestalric. We may stop at Holyrood, too."

"An excellent notion," Henry said. "It will provide a measure of protection for you without endangering them if you do have enemies about looking to put you in your grave. Do you want me to go along?"

"In troth, I'd as lief no one go with me but Lady Ardelve."

Henry glanced sharply at him. "Like that, is it?"

"Sakes, I don't even know what dangers lie ahead," Rob said. "I cannot deny that she attracts me as no lass has before, but I need to get my feet on the ground at Lestalric before I do aught else. So I'm not going to make the poor lass an offer she's certainly not eager to receive from any man right now. She's had a blow—nay, two heavy blows! First, the damnable abduction and your cousin Waldron terrifying her all the way from the Highlands to Lothian. Then Ardelve falling over dead beside her. Has it occurred to you that his death may be questionable?"

"Are you asking if I think someone murdered the man?"

"I expect I am. Someone murdered my father and

Will, did they not? What if a connection exists somehow betwixt their deaths and Ardelve's?"

"Such as what?"

Rob shrugged. "I don't know. He was only here because of Adela. What if they connected her abduction to Waldron's search for the treasure and wanted to prevent her from returning to the Highlands before they could question her?"

"That's possible, but with Waldron dead, I cannot think who such an enemy might be. No one outside the Order and my family knows that the treasure exists."

"Not so," Rob said. "Waldron knew, and when we rescued Adela, the glen was alive with our men and his. Most of them can't know what we have, but they must guess we have something to protect. And, thanks to my ready tongue years ago and Will's penchant for boasting, I'd wager that a number of people know the Logans guard a secret. What if someone thinks we all know the same one?"

Henry grimaced. "I'd meant to ride to Roslin before I leave for the north, as I'm sure my mother will expect if she does go home soon," he said. "But perhaps I'll put that off and ride with you when you go to Hawthornden. I'll wager you're right in thinking that's the most likely place for your grandfather to have concealed whatever it is. I can easily get to my maps from there, too, if we need them."

"Are they at Roslin?" Rob asked.

"Aye, a good many from the chest are. Have I ever shown them to you?"

"Nay, ye ken fine I've got nowt to do wi' old maps and

such, me lord," Rob said in the accent he had favored during his self-exile.

Henry chuckled. "You made a fine serving knight, my friend. I like my comforts too much to have ever done what you did, but you seemed to enjoy it."

"Most of the time," Rob said with a wry smile. "I like the life, and Hugo was easier on me than Sir Edward was on any of us at Dunclathy."

"Tell me more about this business with Adela," Henry said a moment later. "If you don't mean to offer for the lass, what are your intentions?"

"Presently, I hope to reassure her," Rob said. "But to do that, I'll need time alone with her without risk of interruption. The devil of it is how to contrive that without further endangering her reputation. Her abduction did enough damage without my making it worse."

"Aye," Henry said. "I noticed a few black looks cast her way tonight. I know Mother urged her to accept Ealga Clendenen's invitation, but this may be dangerous territory for her. What with that unholy litter of Stewarts clawing at each other for status if not power, and with Fife determined to rule them all despite Carrick's being rightful heir, the ground is riddled with pitfalls for the unwary."

"True," Rob said. "But I can do nowt about that. Also, Henry, she's a bit peevish on the subject of Einar Logan."

Henry choked back a laugh. "Why would she be?"

Rob lifted his chin. "She says she's grateful for his assistance in rescuing her, and—" He remembered his resolution not to betray her, then recalled as well that he'd told her to tell Hugo what she had overheard. Certain she must have done so, he said, "She heard me tell Hugo we'd have to put an end to the fellow."

Henry laughed.

"You may think it's funny," Rob said with a sigh. "But I promise you the lady Adela does not. Nor, I'm sure, will she find it amusing to hear the truth."

"You mean to tell her, then."

"I do," Rob said. "May heaven aid me."

Henry frowned, then said, "I have so far found the Macleod sisters to be completely trustworthy, and I have no reason to believe otherwise of Adela. If anything, she is steadier of temperament and certainly less likely than either Isobel or Sorcha to act impulsively. But have you considered that by appearing to develop an interest in her you might be marking her as a target for your enemies?"

"That did occur to me," Rob admitted. "But I don't know how to prevent that, Henry, and I've promised to be as frank with her as I can be."

"I see. Then I'll say no more about it."

Rob wished he could believe him, but having a pretty clear notion of what Henry was thinking and not at all sure he was wrong, he said nothing.

Chapter 10

⁓

In the coach, Adela listened as the countess and her hostess chatted about the evening. Wondering if she would join the expedition the next day, she told herself it would serve Lestalric right if she feigned a headache and stayed home.

She knew she would do no such thing, though. Meeting him had made life enjoyable again, and more stimulating to her senses than it had ever been before.

As the coach drew to a halt in front of Sinclair House, the countess said, "I hope you mean to take advantage of Lestalric's invitation, dearling. The abbey is remarkable, and Lestalric Castle boasts a fine view of the Firth and Leith Harbor."

"I'm sure it will be an interesting day, madam," Adela said.

"Then we're going," Lady Clendenen said happily. "You are making a stir, my dear. Not in town a full day yet and two eligible suitors. 'Tis an excellent start."

Embarrassed but knowing she meant only to be kind, Adela said, "I hope you will not put that notion into either of their heads."

"Oh, but I need not do any such thing, because—"

"Have mercy, Ealga," Isabella said with a laugh as a gillie flung open the coach door and she prepared to descend. "Her husband is not yet buried! For now, my dear Adela, I suggest you think of nothing but getting a good night's sleep."

"Thank you, madam," Adela said, sincerely grateful for the intervention.

Lady Clendenen said no more about suitors during the short drive to her house or after they went inside. But her beaming smile revealed her delight in Adela's success, so Adela was glad to retire. The cheerful maidservant helped her prepare for bed, and once under the covers she had thoughts only for the day ahead.

It seemed as if she had no sooner shut her eyes than she was tossing on a windswept sea in a boatful of people she knew one minute who were strangers the next. As larger and larger waves crashed around them, the others vanished one by one until she was all alone in a terrifying, much smaller boat.

A distant wave seemed to grow larger and larger the nearer it came until it loomed as high as a castle's curtain wall and began to break directly over her, certain to drown her and crush the wee boat she was in. She awoke then, sitting bolt upright and shaking, to find herself alone in the dark bedchamber.

Getting up, she went to the window, pushed the curtain aside, and gazed out at misty moonlight gleaming on the garden below until her pounding heartbeat slowed to normal. Then, returning to bed, she slept soundly until the maid woke her with a cheery demand to know what she wanted to wear for the fine day's outing.

~~~

Not long after Adela and Lady Clendenen had broken their fast in her ladyship's sunny solar, a gillie informed them that Sir Robert, the countess, and the Earl of Orkney had arrived. They went downstairs to the spacious hall to greet them.

Isabella had chosen a riding dress of russet kersey in a simple style similar to Adela's moss-green one. But both men looked nearly as grand as they had at court. Henry wore an emerald-green cape trimmed with sable and Lestalric a doublet of purple so dark it looked black until a sunbeam from a nearby window struck it.

His eyes, which had looked golden in the amber glow of candles and firelight, were light brownish hazel by daylight. As he bowed to Lady Clendenen, Adela decided his dark lashes would still be the envy of any woman.

"Where is Etienne?" Lady Clendenen asked after she'd greeted her guests.

"The chevalier sent his apologies for the delay," Henry said. "He hopes to join us at Holyrood but assures us that if he misses us, he'll find us along the way."

Adela, watching Lestalric, saw his lips tighten. Then he turned toward her and smiled. "'Tis a fine, bright morning, is it not?"

She agreed, and they did not tarry but went right outside, where they found their horses awaiting them, plus an escort of six men-at-arms that Henry had provided.

The morning was bright but chilly, and Adela was glad the snug-fitting tunic she wore over her full skirts would keep her warm.

The horse her hostess had provided for her was a fine gray gelding bearing the plain man's saddle that Adela and her sisters preferred. Isabella's saddle was similar, because both women rode astride. Macleod had taught all his daughters to ride, and Adela had begun riding astride when she learned to walk.

In contrast, Lady Clendenen's liver-colored mare sported a large, boxy, sheepskin-lined lady's saddle. "My Gussy is a good, trustworthy lass, and her gait is as smooth as a mare's can be," she said, eyeing the flat leather saddles with strong disapproval. "But I want more than a mane and a rein to cling to when I ride."

Lestalric rode a spirited bay with dark mane and stockings, and Henry a black.

Adela soon discovered that Lady Clendenen's notion of riding was more like a stately royal progress than anything akin to exercise for horse or rider. But the public road was no place for exercise, and it was only a short ride to the abbey.

"Do you know the origin of the name Holyrood?" Henry asked Adela.

"It relates to the cross on which Christ died, does it not?"

"Aye, but David I, who built the abbey, named it to honor a piece of the Holy Rood contained in a small, ebony-inlaid, golden casket that his mother brought to Scotland when she married his father. 'Twas called the Black Rood of Scotland, and it became the most sacred of our nation's emblems."

"Until it was snatched from David II by his English captors at the battle of Neville's Cross," Lestalric said lightly as they rode into the abbey kirkyard.

Henry chuckled. "One does wonder why any sensible King of Scots would carry so valued a relic into battle."

The imposing abbey façade with its deeply recessed doorway loomed ahead of them. On its north side, its great square tower stretched skyward.

"It's beautiful," Adela said, certain it was the largest kirk she'd ever seen.

"Would you like to see the interior?" Lestalric asked.

She hesitated, wondering if he thought they could talk privately there. It did not seem a proper place for it if he truly did mean to confide in her.

Lady Clendenen settled the matter, saying indignantly, "Mercy, sir, would you have us dismount when we've just got settled?"

"'Tis too splendid a morning to waste indoors," Isabella said. "There are at least two fine stretches of country on the track to Lestalric and Leith village."

Lestalric guided his horse alongside Adela's as they rode along the rounded arcade on the kirkyard's north wall.

She said, "Is Leith where your home lies?"

"The castle sits yonder on that hilltop, a mile north of the abbey," he said with a smile. "Leith village lies another mile beyond."

"Aye, and 'tis a quaint place," Henry said. "How much of Lestalric do you want to see today, Rob? As I recall, it extends east from Leith to Portobello."

Lestalric protested that he had no intention of dragging everyone over the whole estate, but Lady Clendenen looked perplexed. "Does the land beyond the abbey not belong to the Kirk? I thought they owned even the village of Leith."

Henry said, "They don't own it, but they draw their rents from North Leith, the portion across the river. The fishermen there provide fish for the Kirk's many fast days and maintain the abbey's fishing boats and other vessels. South Leith and the land east of it comprise the barony of Lestalric."

Isabella said curiously, "Other vessels?"

Lestalric chuckled. "The abbot's ferry was my favorite. I warrant it's still the only practical way to get from this side of the river to North Leith."

"Aye," Henry said with a grimace. "The abbot makes a fine living from that ferry, too, because Edinburgh's only safe harbor is the one at North Leith. All merchants' ships and others, including mine, harbor there."

Isabella declaring that she thought Adela had seen enough of the abbey for one day, they rode through the gates and turned north. In minutes they were in open country, and soon the castle they sought loomed ahead on a craggy outcropping that overlooked a long oval loch just east of it.

Tilled fields, lush woodland, and open moors spread in every direction. Adela sighed with pleasure at the sight.

"Shall we let these beasts stretch their legs, mayhap as far as the woods hugging the base of the outcropping?" Lestalric murmured beside her.

She glanced at him hopefully. "Dare we? Won't they object?"

"I doubt it," he said. "Henry is enjoying himself, and

he knows the way. With luck, the countess will keep her ladyship entertained as they plod along."

She glanced back to find the countess watching her as she chatted with Henry and Lady Clendenen. When their eyes met, Isabella nodded.

Rob saw the exchange and heaped blessings on the countess. He could do nothing to slow the pace of the group as a whole, but if he had not misread the signs, Isabella would exert herself as much as Henry would to let him try to explain himself to Adela. He'd feared at any moment to see de Gredin bearing down on them, but they'd seen no sign of him yet, and Rob hoped he would stay away.

Accordingly, when Adela turned back to him with her eyes shining and her smooth cheeks pink from the chilly fresh air, he gave his horse a touch of spur. As the bay increased its pace, Adela's gray kept up easily. When she leaned forward, clearly intending to push ahead of him, he let her extend her lead for a minute or two before urging the bay to catch up with her.

The track was firm, the footing for the horses excellent, and he soon saw that her skill matched that of any other horsewoman he knew. He had expected no less, for he had seen two of her sisters ride and knew both to be fine horsewomen, too.

He exerted himself then, thundering after her to let the horses decide the race. When his pulled ahead, he grinned at her and slowed again, delighted to see her smile as she reined in beside him. The woods still lay some distance ahead.

"May we talk now, sir?" she asked, sobering.

He nearly told her to keep smiling, that she possessed a beautiful, warm smile that she ought to share often. But memory of her condemnation of fulsome compliments the previous night stopped the words before they left his tongue. Instead he said, "I am willing to talk, but do not be surprised if that fellow de Gredin should suddenly pop up from behind a bush to interrupt us."

"He is a kind, charming man," she said, giving him a look. Disconcertingly, she added, "I must remind myself of that often, because if I do not, I tend to think of *him* as the one who deceived me. And that is unfair, as *he* did nothing of the sort."

He gave her a look of his own then and saw her lips twitch, which nearly undid him. He had not suspected that she even had a sense of humor, let alone that it could surface at such a time. Before, she had stirred only a strong desire in him to protect her and another, more intense but elusive emotion that he had not defined.

There was lust, of course. He could not deny that, not after his body had responded instantly and so unexpectedly to her nearness in the chapel and again the first time he'd walked with her at the royal court. It fairly hummed now in simple enjoyment of being alone with her. But there was more, a new and different hunger that he wanted to explore.

First, he had to respond sensibly to her questions and still leave his honor and his oath to the Order intact. Hoping he sounded only as if he were remembering his promise to be frank, he said, "What would you like to know?"

"First, about Einar. You admitted that he is your kinsman, and he did me a significant service. I want to know what has become of him."

"He has risen above his proper station in life," Rob said, suddenly fearful of what she would say when he told her the truth but knowing he had to tell her. It was not a matter of trusting her not to tell anyone else, the cynical voice in his mind muttered. She could tell the world if she chose. What mattered was what she would think of the choice he had made and the fact that he had deceived her.

He wanted to trust her to understand what he had done and to learn to trust him again despite his deception, because she had touched him as no one had before. She answered that unexpected, indefinable hunger in him that he had forgotten he could feel until their meeting on Roslin's ramparts had brought it to life again.

She remained silent, regarding him soberly.

He had the distinct impression that had she been standing, instead of on horseback, she would have tapped her foot with impatience. He met her gaze.

"Do you mean to explain that odd remark about Einar, sir?"

He sighed. "I've imagined this moment, my lady, over and over. But in my imagining, I am always more adept at explaining myself."

"You need only speak the truth," she said. "Where is he?"

"He stands—that is, he sits astride the horse next to yours."

Wide-eyed, she gaped at him but recovered swiftly. "What are you saying?" she demanded. "Do you take me for a dafty? You cannot mean *you* are *he*!"

"That is exactly what I mean."

"But how can you be? Einar Logan is a simple man-at-arms."

"Nay, lass, a serving knight," Rob said with a wry smile. "'Tis a small difference, I grant you, but an important one. It was a nonetheless humbling experience, but in the beginning, I thought I needed humbling."

"Why?"

"Because, despite all my training, I'd let them goad me into losing my temper. It was always unpredictable, but I thought I'd mastered it."

"Have you mastered it now?"

"I hope so."

"And you have risen to be captain of Hugo's fighting tail now."

He smiled. "Aye, I rose quickly. I'm proud of that."

She did not respond to his smile. Her cheeks and eyes were brighter than ever. "You are very glib, sir," she said. "But I simply don't believe you. Einar Logan is a rough Borderer who speaks like a ruffian. I've heard him."

"I canna say nowt agin ye," he said in Einar's accents. "That be plain fact."

"Mercy," she said, then frowned again. "But Einar had a beard."

He said nothing, then nearly smiled when she grimaced. "One needs no more than a razor to alter that."

"And a steady hand," he agreed. "In troth, I let Henry's man shave me. He is a more skillful barber than I shall ever be."

"And no one recognized you? Not as Sir Robert before or as Einar now?"

"Logans abound in the Borders," he said. "Even into the Highlands, although they call themselves MacLennans there. I'd only to admit I was kin to the baron. If folks got a notion he'd spread his seed far afield, who was I to correct them?"

"But did your father never know where you were? Or your brother?"

"Nay," Rob said. "I doubt either gave me a thought after I rode away."

"Och, poor laddie," she exclaimed impulsively, reaching toward him.

"I'm no cause for pity," he said more sharply than he had intended. Then he was immediately sorry when she jerked back her hand. Gently, he said, "To be fair, lass, after my mother died, the relationship between the three of us suffered greatly. They'd scarcely set eyes on me for four years before the day I returned and left again."

"You fostered at Dunclathy, then, with Hugo and Michael."

"Aye, and Henry, too," he said. "He was older and kept his distance at first, for he wore his rank heavily then. He'd been head of his family for years before I trained with him. His father died in battle when Henry was only thirteen."

"What was it like, your training?"

"Much the same as any other lad's, I expect. Boring stuff for females but interesting to us. And we practiced the art of chivalry when Sir Edward's daughters visited. Lady Robison died years before I went there."

"I find it hard to imagine that Hugo's sisters did not know you."

He winced inwardly at certain memories but said, "The wee ones, Kate and Meg, were but six and seven when I went to Dunclathy. Moreover, since their mother had died by then, they fostered with kinsmen. I doubt they were more than nine and ten the last time I saw them before I won my spurs."

"I see." She paused. "Did not someone tell me Hugo has a third sister?"

"Aye, the lady Elizabeth, but she married soon after I arrived. I seldom saw her there, and I promise you, she never spared a look later for a mere serving knight."

They had reached the woods leading up the east end of the outcropping to the castle above. Lestalric Castle had been a fortress in its day, Rob knew, but after his years of experience at Dunclathy, Roslin, and other more solidly fortified places, his view of it now simply explained how easily the English had occupied it a half century before, and why, having done so, they'd used it only to store supplies.

Glancing over his shoulder to see the rest of their party still far behind, he said, "We'd better wait here. Isabella will support our talking together if we stay in view, but I doubt she'd be happy if we went on to the castle alone."

"If you want to ride on to see the place, I'll wait for them," she said.

"Nay, lass, I only contrived this outing so we might talk. What else would you know of me?"

Adela hesitated. There was so much she wanted to know, because his revelations thus far had astonished her. She had seen little of Einar Logan, but she had formed a clear impression of the man.

For one thing, he had seemed smaller than Lestalric. As the thought formed, the sight of the approaching party with Henry's men-at-arms riding tactfully behind them reminded her that the Sinclair men and Hugo surrounded themselves with large, powerful henchmen of Nordic ancestry like their own. Amidst Borderers, Sir Robert would appear abnormally tall and broad. Amidst Highlanders, who mixed Celtic traits with Nordic ones, he would appear a bit taller than the average, albeit no match for truly large men like her sister Cristina's husband, Hector the Ferocious.

But amidst Hugo's men, Sir Robert might easily have seemed smaller.

The silence between them felt comfortable. But although he seemed inclined to be patient, the rest of their party had closed a third of the distance between them.

Realizing that if she wanted to ask him anything more, she had better do so at once, she said, "Why did you do it? Why did you become *Einar* Logan?"

When he hesitated, she wanted to kick herself. What a thing to ask when it was most likely the one question he did not want to answer. What could the reason be but something he was ashamed of or felt deeply remorseful about?

Then he said ruefully, "I lost my temper. I'd arrived at midday, proud of winning my spurs, and we talked of battles and such whilst we dined. Then my father demanded information I could not give him. We disagreed, and Will entered the fray. That just made me angrier, but we'd never been ten minutes in the same room without fratching." He paused, clearly reluctant to continue. "My father said then that I was a damned disappointment to him and not worth anything, so I left."

"It was a dreadful thing for him to say!"

"Aye, well, I swore he'd never see me again. I kept my word, too, but that was pride more than anything else. I went to Hugo and Michael at Roslin because they'd always felt more like my family than my father or Will did. But I wasn't family, of course, and had nowt of my own. I told them I wanted to earn my way, and I didn't want anyone calling me Sir Anything whilst I did. My new knighthood had lost its luster, you see. But Hugo's lads knew me for a knight and felt insolent calling me Rob so I told them I'd had a falling out with my family and did not want my father or brother to find me. I suggested they call me Einar Logan and treat me as one of themselves. 'Twas a good Norse name from my mother's family."

She cocked her head to one side, regarding him with narrowing eyes. "Did you really *not* want your family to find you?"

He smiled wryly. "You remind me of Hugo. He suggested that I didn't want to know if they *didn't* try to find me. In troth, I don't think it matters much now what my reasons were then. The others are almost here," he added, nodding toward the approaching riders. "We'll talk more when we can, because I want to know about you, too. You should know, though, that nothing I did reflects badly on me now. I've paid my penance for the things I regret, and—" He broke off.

"What?" she asked. She looked toward the others, half expecting to see that de Gredin had arrived, or that something else had occurred to annoy him.

When she looked back, he seemed rueful. "I may be

wrong about paying full penance," he said. "It occurs to me that mayhap I have not."

Adela wanted to shake him but could not. Not only was he too far away, and much too large for shaking, but the others were now much too near.

~

Rob saw the spark of anger but could think of nothing to say that would not ignite it to flame. As he had spoken the words, he realized they might prove false.

For all he knew, the cause of his father's and brother's murders lay at his door. If someone *was* trying to eliminate the Logans of Lestalric, might the reason not be an attempt to acquire what they believed the Logans guarded? Was it possible that what she called the beginning, the boyish taunt he had flung at Will years ago, had bloomed over time into something greater? Or was he turning a seed into an oak tree?

The others joined them moments later, and they continued through the woods and up to the castle gate. Rob had only to identify himself before it swung open, and they entered the small, square courtyard that he remembered from visits to his grandfather. The castle's constable emerged from the gate tower to welcome him.

"Ye'll be remembering Tam Geddes, lad," the man said bluffly as he glanced at Henry and the half dozen men-at-arms that had ridden in behind them. "One o' me lads did hear in town that ye was back and would be a-coming today. I'm that glad to see ye. I wager ye'll be wanting to make a good many changes, will ye no?"

"Oh, I expect I'll look into things," Rob said as he

looked around. The yard looked tidy enough, but he could see that the place was poorly maintained. Still, he did not want to give much away before finding a clear path. "I can see that you might want to furbish up a few things," he said. "But I expect you know more about that sort of thing than I do, Tam Geddes."

"Aye, well, ye've no been next or nigh the place in years, and your da were content enough whenever he were here," Geddes said. "Young Will were more interested in spending Sir Ian's gelt on fine clothes to impress the lassies in Stirling or at the Castle when the royal court were in residence there."

"I'll want to see your accounts before I leave Edinburgh," Rob said. "But I'll be in town a few more days, so I'll look them over next time I come. No need to keep the ladies dangling about today whilst we talk."

"Nay, sir," the man said with another glance at Henry, who looked truly splendid in his fine cape. And splendidly vacuous, too, Rob thought.

He remembered Tam Geddes as a gillie from his youth, and he thought the man seemed nervous. He detected no extraordinary relief in him at learning he need not yet share his accounts, but neither did he read any enthusiasm for change.

They dismounted and walked to the main entrance and into the great hall, where clearly a number of men had been living for at least a fortnight without benefit of servants to clear up after them. The place was as untidy as if they had simply cast their belongings everywhere.

"How long has Lady Logan been away?" Rob asked Geddes.

Frowning, he said, "I expect it'll be nigh two months

now. She went to stay wi' her lady mother when Sir Ian and our Will rode to join the Douglas."

Rob decided that if he wanted to live comfortably at Lestalric, he'd have to institute a number of changes. But to his chagrin, he hardly knew where to begin.

Henry said blandly that he was looking forward to seeing more of the place. But Isabella and Lady Clendenen both declined to examine the upper regions.

"Faith, I feel as if I'm still in that saddle, fearing I'll be pitched to the ground any minute," Lady Clendenen said. "I mean to sit still until I must move again."

Glancing at Henry, who nodded, Rob said, "We'll be a few moments then, if you don't mind waiting. Mayhap Tam Geddes can find you something to drink."

"Aye, sir, I'll find summat," the man said, still clearly nervous.

Adela said, "I'd like to go with you, Sir Robert. Countess Isabella said Lestalric boasts some splendid views of the Firth."

"It does," Rob admitted, ignoring the twinkle in Henry's eyes. With no polite way to deny her request, he said, "We'll go this way, my lady."

He led them up the main stairway to the next floor, then along a corridor on which several chambers opened, to the last. Entering, he found Sir Ian's bedchamber, which had been Sir Walter's before him, as untidy as the hall had been. "Sakes!" he exclaimed. "Have the men been sleeping here, too?"

Adela had followed him in. "This mess is not mere untidiness sir," she said. "That kist appears to have been purposefully turned upside down."

"She's right, Rob," Henry said from the chamber next

door. "This one looks the same. Everything's upended. They've even taken the bed apart."

"Someone has searched the place," Rob said, feeling his temper stir, and dismay as well. "Lass, watch the stairway. If anyone comes, greet them loudly enough for us to hear."

She obeyed without question, and he moved swiftly to the wood-framed bed against the wall. It boasted two posts, a carved tester, and rich red velvet curtains, but he was interested only in the wood panels at its head.

Feeling along the bottom edge of an unadorned flat panel between two carved ones, he located the long, slender wedge at its base, holding it in place. Easing it out, he removed the panel and reached into the shallow space behind it, finding a narrow roll of vellum. Removing it, he unrolled it, glanced at it, rolled it again, and slipped it up his sleeve. Then he replaced the panel and its wedge and went to find Henry sorting through things in the next room. "Let's go," Rob said.

"Did you find what you were looking for?" Henry asked.

"I hope so," Rob replied, glancing at Adela near the stairs. "But I'm afraid it's only half a map. Look here." He stepped into the room and opened the map. "What do you think?"

"It does look incomplete," Henry agreed. "That one side looks neatly cut, despite being all curves. But what will please you is that I'm nearly certain I've got something similar amongst my maps from the chest."

Adela knew now that she had been fooling herself by believing she lacked curiosity. She had been curious about Lestalric from the first moment they'd met, and curious about his castle from the moment they had entered it. Now, as she stood gazing out one of the corridor windows with her ears aprick for the slightest sound from the stairway, she was dying to know what he'd found.

She thought she had heard him say it was a map, but she was not sure. Both men had spoken, and were still speaking, only in murmurs.

Isabella was right about the view of the Firth of Forth, though. She could see what must be Leith Harbor to her left in the distance. But her thoughts were not on the view. Having managed a household with untidy sisters and a father who cast his belongings thither and yon, she had seen at a glance, even before she had seen the bedchambers, that someone had searched Lestalric's great hall.

But Lestalric had asked no questions. His intent from the first, she thought, had been to get upstairs. Hearing the two men coming, she turned.

"I think I'm going to be asking a few more questions, Sir Robert," she said.

"Aye, well, I've a few to ask myself," he said grimly.

❧

But confronting Geddes in the hall, Rob said mildly, "Those rooms abovestairs are a bit of a shambles. Who's been in Sir Ian's chamber?"

The man's face reddened. "Ha' mercy, me lord. 'Twas none o' us here! They came a sennight ago wi' a royal banner flying. When they said the laird were dead and the estates likely to revert to the King, I didna dare deny them entrance."

"I trust you will find the courage to deny them if they come again."

"Aye, sir, I will."

"Good. I shall want the place cleaned up before I return. You may hire as many men as you need and more men-at-arms to safeguard the castle, as well. If you cannot see to it quickly, I expect I shall have to look for a new constable."

"Mayhap hiring a housekeeper would be wise, sir," Adela said. "It does not appear as if one has tended the place for some time."

"I warrant you can see to that as well, can you not?" he said to Geddes.

"Aye, sir. I'll do what I can, but it'll take a good bit o' gelt, that will."

Henry said with the bland disinterest he had shown earlier, "If you require funds, sirrah, send those you hire to Sinclair House in the Canongate, where Sir Robert presently resides. He will attend to their recompense there."

"Aye, my lord," Geddes said, turning back to Rob. "I'll do as ye bid, sir."

Rob said lightly, "I shall rely upon you, Tam Geddes."

"But must I send the lads into town to get their gelt? Ye could let me attend to it for ye," he suggested. "'Twould be more convenient for the lads, ye ken."

With effort, Rob avoided looking at Henry as he said with every affectation in play, "But 'tis more convenient for *me* to do it at Sinclair House."

"Sakes, I guess it *will* be more convenient," he said afterward as he and Henry followed the women down the slope toward the woods at its base. "What the devil was that about, Henry? I didn't think about the money, but if you can tell me how I'm to pay all those men before I know what rents Lestalric collects and—"

"I'll pay them," Henry said, cutting in without apology. "And before I leave for the north, I'll arrange for you to draw on my funds here if you need them. Don't stiffen up like that, Rob. You were wise back there not to set Geddes on his guard. But if you cannot see by the state of the lands we've ridden through to get here and all we see right now that your rents here must be enormous, I certainly can."

Rob frowned. "You know that I've had training in managing what finances come my way. We all did, because a man cannot plan for battle without knowing how to assess his resources and pay for his men's needs. But I ken little of rents. I can see that the land is in better trim than the castle, but I assumed that Geddes had passed the rents on to my father or Will and that they'd spent it all on finery."

"That may well be the case," Henry acknowledged. "But you'd have to be a fool not to inspect his accounts. I'd remind you that someone has already stuck a finger in your affairs. And that means your father and brother may not have been the only ones to whom Geddes paid the rents. If I may presume a step more . . . "

"As many as you like," Rob said as they entered the shady woodland. "Much as I'd prefer not to be beholden to you in such an enormous way—"

"I'll get it all back," Henry said. "But you'd do well to

let me set my man of affairs onto Geddes with a few of my men-at-arms to back his efforts. You'll know then that you're getting a full accounting. If you can be content to trust my chap as much as I do, I think you'll find him satisfactory."

"Sakes, Henry, I'd have to be daft to refuse such an offer," Rob said sincerely. "Will he mind trying to impart some of his knowledge to me?"

"Not a bit," Henry said with a reminiscent smile. "Only think what it must have been like for him to try to train a thirteen-year-old who was angry at the Fates for taking his father and cocksure of himself and his rank besides."

"Were you ever like that?" Rob asked innocently. "I don't recall it."

"Wise of you to forget," Henry said with a grin.

Rob was laughing aloud when the arrow struck.

Chapter 11

⁓

Having fallen back to let Isabella and Lady Clendenen ride two abreast ahead of her on the narrow track, Adela heard a sudden shout and gasped when she turned to see Lestalric pitching headfirst from his saddle.

Only Henry's swift action saved him from falling between their horses, into the path of the horses and men behind them.

"Two of you lads, to the countess!" Henry shouted.

Somehow, one-handed, he caught Lestalric's doublet shoulder. But Adela saw that he'd grabbed only cloth. And as Henry fought to control two unsettled horses and assist a struggling Lestalric trying to right himself, the cloth began to rip where the arrow had pierced it. Seeing this all in a blink, she wheeled the gray and kicked it hard, forcing it nearer until she could catch the cheek-piece of the bay's bridle.

Holding it firmly, praying the animal would not panic,

she spoke soothingly, steadying it effectively until Lestalric suddenly jerked himself away from Henry.

"Don't fight him, you fool!" she snapped. When his horse tried to rear again, she added hastily but in the soothing tone she had used before, "I can see the arrowhead and it looks to be sharply barbed, my lord. Be still, or you may injure yourself more. Good laddie," she murmured to the horse as it calmed.

"I know I hurt you then, Rob, but the lass is right," Henry said. "I'll take more care, but we must get you off your horse to have a good look at that wound."

"Get the women to safety first," Lestalric growled as he let Henry help him ease back onto his saddle properly. He sounded angry but whether at himself for revealing his pain or at the archer, Adela did not know.

"We're not going anywhere," she told him. "As you can see, two of Henry's men-at-arms are already protecting the countess and Lady Clendenen, and have moved them out of the line of fire. Surely, we're safer here with Henry's men than if we tried to ride on without them."

"Aye, she's right again, Rob," Henry said with a sweeping look around. "Your brain is muddled, lad. So listen to her unless you want a good clout."

"Spare me, Henry. This damn thing hurts like fire."

"I see that," Henry said, gesturing for one of his men to dismount and help him.

"He's bleeding badly, sir," Adela said. "We need to get that arrow out and the wound bound up as quickly as we can."

"Aye, but I'm thinking I might send a couple of my lads—"

"Listen," Adela said sharply. "Riders!"

Exchanging a glance with Lestalric, Henry signed to two other men. One turned his horse deeper into the woods. The other rode toward the newcomers.

A moment later, a shout came from the latter. "A score or more, m'lord, bearing a royal banner and that o' the Earl o' Fife!"

Henry frowned, but Adela said, "Thank heaven! Now all will be well."

Rob said quickly, "How badly am I bleeding, Henry? I can't see the wound."

"Badly enough to ruin your pretty doublet," Henry said. "But at least that dark velvet will prevent anyone's noticing from a distance."

"Please, sir, get him off his horse," Adela pleaded. "We must tend his wound."

"It may be more important to hide it," Rob said. "Are you wearing a cambric underskirt or shift, lass?"

She frowned, making him wonder if she would object. But to his relief, she caught his meaning quickly and began tearing strips of cambric from her underskirt.

"Use those to bind me up," he said. "Henry, my doublet may be dark, but the bandage will show. I'll need that splendid cape you're wearing."

"Sakes, you insolent pup, you'll be like to leak all over it," Henry said as he whisked off the cape and laid it ready across his saddlebow.

"Never mind that," Rob said, reaching into his left sleeve and extracting the narrow roll of vellum. "Take this, lass, and shove it inside your bodice for me."

"Men," Adela muttered as she held her strips, steadied her horse, and awkwardly slipped the vellum through the lacing of her tunic without asking what it was. "You know I cannot just wrap a bandage round it. That arrow must come out."

"Henry, see if you can do it without rendering me unconscious," Rob said.

"Sakes, sir," she protested. "He cannot pull it out from where he is!"

"He must," Rob said. "I'd as lief they not know I'm injured until we know why they're here. Let them believe the arrow missed me."

"I doubt the person who shot it will believe that," Adela said.

Henry did not waste time arguing but said, "Shut your eyes and try to relax, Rob. I've got to push the damned barb through to cut it off."

"Don't worry about neatness," Rob said. "Just break it off when you can get a grip and try not to leave any splinters in me. And for the love of God, Henry, do it fast. Their hoofbeats have slowed. They're nearing the woods."

He noted that Lady Clendenen and Isabella had ridden back onto the path. Like Adela, they believed all was safe with a royal party approaching. At least neither was a prattler. They would take their cues from him or from Henry.

He was not at all sure they were safe. And he knew that Henry—who understood much more than he did about the politics and intrigue rife within the royal circle—found no reassurance in knowing Fife was there.

Adela saw that Henry knew what he was doing when he pushed the shaft of the arrow through the wound until the barb was well past the exit area. But the speed with which he did it astonished her.

Calling to the man who had dismounted to help him, he held the long shaft firmly as the other gripped the barb end in one gloved fist and snapped it off.

She heard Lestalric gasp, but he remained conscious without visible effort.

Dexterously, Henry extracted the shaft and reached for one of the wide strips of cambric Adela held out. By the time he had deftly bound it around Lestalric's shoulder and upper arm, she had realized something else from the way the arrow had pierced his left shoulder and emerged through the back of his upper left arm.

"It came from above," she said. "Back there, from those trees."

"Aye," Henry said. "Tie that knot tight. I'll throw my cape over his shoulders as you do. We've time for no more, so don't get blood on your sleeve."

His voice was calm, as was Lestalric's. "Get rid of that thing," the latter said to the man who held the barb. "Stow the shaft, too, but shove it into the ground under a bush if you can. And make haste, man. They're upon us."

A moment later, they were. But before Adela recognized anyone in the royal party, Isabella said in a clear voice, "Why, Ealga, look. 'Tis your charming cousin, the chevalier de Gredin, and the Earl of Fife."

Adela was further amazed then to see Henry take from one of his men an arrow that looked like the one they had just broken. He held it and was still gazing raptly at it when the first riders in the royal party joined them.

"Your skirt, lass," Lestalric said urgently.

With as casual a gesture as she could quickly manage, she smoothed the overskirt off her knee, where she had gathered it to tear strips from her underskirt. Then she turned the gray to face the newcomers but kept it near Lestalric's horse.

Lestalric looked pale, she thought, but he was otherwise in full command of himself. He had looped his reins loosely around his left hand and chose that moment to pluck a bit of leaf off the borrowed cape with his right.

"We are glad to see you, my lord," Isabella said as the Earl of Fife approached her without bothering to doff his plumed hat.

He nodded, saying, "Good day, madam. Did you meet with trouble here?"

"How astute you are, my lord!" Lady Clendenen exclaimed, clutching a hand to her breast. "I vow, I have never been so glad to see anyone. My poor heart is still pounding. Someone was shooting arrows at us!"

"How dreadful," Fife said, shifting his haughty gaze to Lestalric. "I hope no one suffered injury."

Raising the arrow he held so the others could see it, Henry said, "We are glad to reassure you, sir. The archer's aim most fortunately went amiss. I trust, though, that such mischief does not occur often hereabouts."

"Not often," Fife said, turning back to Lestalric. "I was told you had not yet visited these estates. Had you mentioned your intent to come today, I'd have warned you we'd had reports of trouble here."

"Sakes, then I wish I'd announced it to the whole court," Lestalric said in the disingenuous manner he had employed the previous evening and with Geddes.

Adela noted, however, that his absurd accent was less obvious with Fife.

Fife replied, "'Tis fortunate that I asked de Gredin here to meet with me this morning to discuss his recent visit to France. We are looking to seek aid from the Auld Alliance if the English continue to provoke us."

"An excellent notion," Lestalric said. "One heartily commends it."

"At all events," Fife said with a cynical look, "when de Gredin said he was to join your expedition, I suggested we come along lest you encounter such rogues. He did not know your party had increased its numbers so."

"Doubtless I ought to have discussed our plan with you first, my lord," Lestalric said. "I fear I am not well versed yet in all my duties."

Adela detected a satirical note in his voice and feared Fife would hear it too, so she was almost glad to hear a shout from the woods behind them.

Henry and his men all stiffened as one and looked that way, but Fife said smoothly, "I took the liberty of sending a few of my lads to search for those rogues I mentioned. I'll wager they've treed your murderous archer for you."

Believing as Adela did that the archer had shot from a treetop and must have fled at once, and recalling that one of Henry's men had slipped in amidst the trees earlier, she hoped he was not the one they had found. She dared not glance at Henry though, lest Fife and the others suspect she knew more than they did. She sensed intense aware-ness in Lestalric, too, more than he had displayed before.

They heard approaching riders, and a moment later, two emerged from the woods. "We got him, me lord," one announced to Fife. "He jumped from his tree and were fleeing wi' his bow, but we took him down."

"What have you done with the fellow?" Henry asked mildly. "I own, I should like to ask him what the devil he meant by shooting at us."

The henchman glanced at his master before he said, "He'll tell ye nowt, me lord. The devil hisself ha' got his hooves in him now, and I warrant auld Clootie willna send him to trouble ye again."

"But why would such a person want to shoot at us?" Lestalric asked with uncharacteristic plaintiveness.

Fife shrugged. "Mayhap because Sir Ian neglected his people. Doubtless that will change now if you mean to take things in hand. But until you arrived so unexpectedly, the King feared he would have to take this place in hand himself."

"I am pleased to spare his grace the trouble," Lestalric said. "But although I am learning a great deal, to be sure, I believe we are keeping you from important duties, my lord Fife. Thank you most heartily for your timely assistance."

Fife nodded, then said, "Shall we see you at the Castle tonight?"

Adela stiffened but managed to avoid shooting a minatory look at Lestalric.

"Oh, aye, I expect so," he said to her profound annoyance. "I found it most entertaining last evening and look forward to repeating the experience."

Having been certain he would make an excuse to absent himself, she had to exert herself not to contradict him outright.

Fife and his men departed moments later, leaving de Gredin to exclaim at what a near miss everyone had had.

"Lady Adela, it must have terrified you out of your wits, especially after your unfortunate experience a few weeks ago."

"'Tis kind of you to concern yourself," Adela said as she urged her horse forward to meet him so he would ride no closer to Lestalric. "I am sorry you missed the earlier part of our expedition. It has been a splendid day."

When two of Henry's men fell in behind them, she knew his thoughts had matched hers. So she encouraged de Gredin to flirt with her, responding coyly to his comments and acquitting herself well, she thought, for someone whose experience in such behavior was nonexistent.

De Gredin's interest in every word she said provided novelty for one whose father dismissed female conversation. The attention proved heady until she realized his questions had moved from casual to more pointed ones about Lestalric Castle.

"I suppose you and the other ladies were left kicking your heels whilst Lestalric examined every inch of his new possession," he said archly.

"Mercy, sir, we scarcely saw more than the hall," she declared. "If Lestalric and Orkney did more than poke their heads up that musty stairwell, I'd be surprised, for the place reeks of men, dogs, and moldy rushes. I vow, we all longed for fresh air. Highlanders are much tidier."

"I'd heard the place had become a mess," he said with a chuckle. "I warrant our new baron has much work ahead. I hope you will not think me unkind if I say he does not seem likely to be a capable landowner."

Her mouth half open to insist that Lestalric was capable of anything he set his mind to do, she recognized the pitfall. Smiling innocently instead, she said, "I'm sure I do not know if it is kind or unkind, sir. I barely know Sir Robert."

"Oh, indeed, I thought it looked as if you, he, and Orkney had your heads together like old friends."

"Oh, but I do know Orkney, of course," she said. "He is, after all, my sister's brother-by-marriage. As you know, I was staying with Countess Isabella at Roslin before I came to town. But as to Sir Robert, I did not even know he existed until his grace's lord chamberlain announced his arrival to the entire court."

And that, she told herself virtuously, was perfectly true.

Remembering how fervently she had assured Lestalric that she loathed secrets, she told herself that she still hated them, but she hated villainy more. And she was coming to think she had met with villainy again. Whether de Gredin was knowingly part of it all or not, she would have to tread warily with him.

＊　＊　＊

Rob gritted his teeth as he watched the lass ride ahead with de Gredin, and only a portion of the accompanying grimace was for his pain. Every step the horse took stirred jolts of agony, and if it was not the pure agony he had experienced as Henry and his man removed the arrow, neither was it the mere ache of a flesh wound. His whole shoulder and upper arm hurt, and he could barely grip the reins. Even moving his right arm hurt, which seemed decidedly unfair. Fortunately, his mount needed little direction even when Henry signed to him to fall back a little.

One of Henry's lads passed them as Henry muttered, "Damn de Gredin! I don't trust any man who keeps company with Fife, Rob, and no more should you. His only interest is acquiring power. The only reason his brother Carrick is alive is that everyone would believe Fife responsible even if another plague killed him."

"A good many folk would agree with Fife, though, that Carrick is the wrong man to be the next King of Scots," Rob said.

"Aye, sure. I'm one, and so are you and any other man who kens aught of soldiering or leadership. At the right time, Carrick might make a fine King of Scots. But not with England still trying to conquer Scotland, nor with the greedy, bickering royal family we have. They all want more power, more land, more everything, if only to spit in the eye of everyone who ever called the Stewarts upstarts."

"Enough, Henry, I'll beware of Fife. But how do you think his men knew, without a word of communication betwixt us, where that devilish archer was?"

"We'll find out," Henry said, looking over his shoulder. "As you doubtless saw, I sent one of my lads to have a look. He's coming up behind us now."

The horseman, who had managed to ease his mount up so quietly that Rob had not heard him, drew in beside Henry and said, "They went for him as if they'd a leading string on him, m'lord. Someone must ha' told him to stay put, for he were still in his tree and came down when he saw them. I'd concealed m'self when I heard them coming. And when I saw what they was about, I kept still as death, I can tell ye. I kent fine they'd leave nae witness did they see one."

Rob said, "You believe they knew him, then?"

"Och, aye, for he wore the same all-black livery they do till they stripped his body and dressed it in a ragged jack and breeks. I heard one say his lordship would be spitting fire over the business but that he should ha' sent a better marksman."

"So Fife sent the archer," Rob said. "I wonder what he hoped to accomplish."

"Thank you," Henry said, dismissing his man. "I'm wondering," he added a moment later. "Suppose that marksman did exactly what Fife asked of him?"

"By just wounding me, you mean?"

"Aye, for the search tells us someone knows something is missing," Henry said. "To have done that, they must believe it to be of great value. They must likewise believe the Logans have it or ken its whereabouts. And—"

"And a Logan has just visited Lestalric," Rob said. "You think they hoped I'd collect whatever it is they've searched for, and expected to be able to collect it when they appeared so fortuitously to aid me. So Fife, whose men all wear black as he does himself, and as the murderers did, must be involved in all that has happened."

"Aye," Henry said. "Never mind how that archer got to his perch. Think about *when* he must have done it. De Gredin could as easily have told Fife last night about your expedition, you know. And as I did not decide to accompany you until this morning—nor did my mother—the size of our party surprised them."

Rob nodded.

Gently, Henry added, "Your friend Tam Geddes may be in it, too."

"Perhaps," Rob admitted. "My instinct says no, and in any event, the rest of Lestalric should be with me. For all my father's faults, Grandfather was popular, and there is a long tradition here of loyalty to my family."

"Are you really going to join the royal court tonight?"

"I must," Rob said. "But I think we shall have to decline Lady Clendenen's invitation to dine. I can move everything, so I don't think that damned arrow did any permanent damage, but I doubt I can manage to eat with any grace."

"I'll tell my mother," Henry said. "She's a witch when it comes to healing, so she may know some way to aid you. And you can stop glowering at Adela," he added with a grin. "She is only doing what she can to protect you."

Rob turned his glare on Henry, but Henry only laughed.

A moment later, Rob said, "I'm sure Fife is in it. As haughty as he is, I can think of no reason but guilty knowledge to have sent his men into the woods as he did. He also explained rather too much about how he came to be here this morning."

"Aye," Henry agreed. "'Tis uncharacteristic, that. Still, I doubt he expects us to worry him. You were right to act the halfwit, Rob. As Sir Edward often said, to gain advantage in a battle, even of wits, if one is able, one should appear unable."

"And if one is *dis*abled," Rob said dryly, thinking of the painful evening that lay ahead, "one must appear able."

⌐◡⌐

Adela would have liked to tell Lestalric just what she thought of his intent to attend the royal court that evening, but she had no opportunity. Not only did she feel obliged to let de Gredin ride with her on the return trip, but he soon dashed any hope that he might have forgotten Lady Clendenen's invitation to dine with them.

"I look forward to another excellent meal," he said as they neared the house. "In my opinion, her ladyship's cook is one of the finest in Edinburgh."

"I thought you preferred the food at the Castle," Adela said, smiling but wishing the devil would fly away with the man.

"It is admirable," he said. "But the company is not nearly as admirable."

Lightly, she said, "I trust both will live up to your expectations today."

"They cannot help but do so," he said, reaching to give her hand a squeeze.

Stiffening but managing to keep her tone light, she said, "Pray, do not do that. The countess will disapprove."

"She is not looking," he said, squeezing her hand again.

Adela gave him the same look she had often directed at an annoying sister.

With a sigh, he pulled back his hand. "You are cruel, *madame.*"

A prickling sense told her Lestalric was watching, and she had no doubt that he would soon demand to know what she thought she was doing to encourage the man to such liberties. To her surprise, the thought stimulated her. Let him scold, she told herself. She had some things to say to him, too.

But at Clendenen House, when Lady Clendenen said she hoped they all still meant to stay and dine, the countess said, "I've a fearsome headache, Ealga. If we are to visit the court tonight, I must rest first. Indeed, I am surprised you do not feel the same. After such a terrifying adventure, I vow, the day has exhausted me!"

Adela glanced at de Gredin but saw no indication that he realized how unusual it was for the energetic countess to admit weakness. He said only that he hoped she would quickly recover and that he was sure Henry meant to stay.

"Nay, I must decline, for I've a number of tasks yet to attend before I leave for the north," Henry said. "I'm taking Lestalric, too, Ealga. I regret depriving you of his company, but he wants advice about changes he means to make at Lestalric. And this may be the only time I can oblige him."

"Do not concern yourself, sir," Lady Clendenen said. "Adela and our dear Etienne will keep me entertained."

Watching as de Gredin dismounted to aid the gillie assisting her ladyship from her cumbersome saddle, Adela did not realize that Lestalric had moved his mount to the offside of hers until his bay snorted, startling her.

"Sakes, lass," he murmured. "You leap like a scalded cat, and not for the first time, either. I've never known your like before."

"You startled me," she said, reaching into her bodice for the roll of vellum he'd given her. As she gave it to him, she said, "Are you really going tonight?"

"Aye," he said, slipping the roll up his sleeve. "And I hope you will, too."

"I'm sure we will," she said. "But I think you must be mad."

He began to shrug, clearly thought better of it, and said, "If we are to talk of madness, what were you about to let that scoundrel put his hand on you?"

She lifted her chin. "It can be no concern of yours if I did, my lord."

"You may hope," he said. "But I do not speak from jealousy, lass. I have no thought of trying to enmesh you in my tangled affairs, only a hope that I may keep you from doing anything foolish before I untangle them. 'Tis one thing for a young widow to visit the royal court with two powerful kinswomen as chaperones. It is another to encourage the liberties of a slithersome coof like de Gredin."

"Slithersome coof?"

"Aye, and when you say I've no right to speak, recall that you invited my concern on Roslin's ramparts when you confided in a man who was no more to you than a voice in the darkness."

His words shook her, reminding her that had the arrow struck true it would have stilled that comforting voice forever. Her throat ached at the thought, but she raised her chin. "I suppose it was foolish to be so trusting of such a voice."

"Nay, lass, nowt o' the sort," he said, smiling so warmly that she felt it to her bones and the ache vanished. "I never meant that, and you know it," he added. "I meant only that something binds us. It is as easy for me to talk with you as for you to talk to me. I don't understand why, and I know it may not be easy for you to trust me now that I've admitted deceiving you. But I do hope to know you better." He paused to draw breath, wincing. "I want to be friends, nothing more—not yet."

"I'd like that," she said impulsively, nearly reaching a hand to him as she did. Realizing he would have to move his injured shoulder to take it, she pulled it back again.

Then, lest he make too much of such a reaction, she said firmly, "But do not think a growing friendship gives you leave to criticize me, sir."

"I'm not criticizing *you*, lass, only that jackanapes de Gredin. But see that you don't allow him to entertain her ladyship by making sheep's eyes at you."

Shaking her head at him, Adela jumped again when Henry said from behind her, "Allow me to assist you down, lass. Lestalric is presently useless in such a case, of course. And my mother must be longing for her nap."

Hiding a smile and taking care not to look at Lestalric, who doubtless knew the countess's habits as well as she did, Adela accepted Henry's aid to dismount.

"Let me escort you inside, Lady Adela," de Gredin said, approaching her.

Feeling the prickling sense of Lestalric's disapproval again, she smiled brilliantly at the chevalier and took his arm.

Lady Clendenen beamed, but the supper that followed was tedious. De Gredin talked of nothing but Sinclairs and Lestalric. Her ladyship's replies were glib enough to tell Adela that someone, probably the countess, had warned her to guard her tongue, but recalling that de Gredin was her ladyship's cousin, Adela knew it must be hard for the gregarious woman not to tell him everything she knew. By the time the meal ended, her ladyship looked as mentally drained as Adela felt.

As Lady Clendenen arose from her chair at last, she said, "This has been a pleasure, Etienne, but you must leave us now if we are to look our finest at his grace's court tonight. I, for one, want a bath." When he had gone, she confided to Adela, "Such unnatural discretion is difficult for me. Most unfair, too, I think, for Isabella to insist we not tell dearest Etienne what really occurred. He would not tell another soul if we asked him to keep it to himself."

"Can you be sure of that, madam? You said we must all be wary of Fife, did you not? The chevalier seemed quite friendly with him."

"Faith, he can scarcely appear otherwise! Fife is no one to annoy, my dear." But she seemed much struck and said no more then in defense of de Gredin.

Adela could not congratulate herself, however, because she suspected that her ladyship's own words had had more to do with that look than anything Adela had said. In any event, her ladyship proved correct in predicting that they would need all the time they had at their disposal to prepare for the night ahead.

When Lady Clendenen's coach drew up at Sinclair House two hours later, they found that Henry and Lestalric would also travel to the Castle in a wheeled vehicle. Henry's was an elegant two-wheeled, one-horse tilt-cart with a seat at the front for its driver. Henry said he was showing it off for Lestalric's benefit.

"I just got it," he confided as he helped the countess enter the coach. "But it won't take more than two in any comfort, so Mother will ride with you."

"How is he?" Lady Clendenen asked Isabella, nodding toward Lestalric.

"He'll do," the countess said confidently. "It struck

hard but slid along the shoulder bone and out his upper arm. Painful, to be sure, but not crippling."

"Excellent," her ladyship said. "Then he need only rest it and let it heal."

But no sooner did the lord chamberlain announce Lestalric's name than a beautiful, dark-haired young woman flew out of the crowd toward him.

He stopped, staring at her, and thus made no effort to protect himself from the onslaught as she flung her arms around him and hugged him hard.

Rob gasped at the wave of pain that threatened to over-whelm him but collected his wits quickly, putting his right hand on the young woman's shoulder and pulling away as if to get a better look at her features. Not that he needed one. Even after nearly a decade, he recognized her easily.

"Lady Ellen?" he said, blinking as if he could not be-lieve it.

"Aye, Robbie, 'tis I, indeed!" she replied gaily.

"What are you doing here?"

"I came with my parents," she said, gesturing vaguely toward the high table.

Catching a whiff of spirits, he suspected she had had more wine or whisky to drink than was good for her and hoped it had dulled her senses enough that she had failed to realize she'd hurt him.

Reassuming his witless demeanor, he said languidly, "I vow, madam, you do not look a day older than when I last saw you. But forgive me. In my astonishment, I forgot my manners. Allow me to present you to the Countess of Strathearn and Caithness. Madame, this is Lady Ellen, my brother's widow."

Lady Ellen turned to Isabella and, with the slight curtsy of one earl's daughter to another, said, "We have met before, but I am honored, madam."

"I, too, my dear," Isabella said. "I know you are likewise acquainted with Ealga Clendenen, but I must present our dearest Lady Ardelve. She has also suffered the recent, tragic loss of her husband."

"Och, aye, I've heard much of you, Lady Ardelve," Ellen said, nodding. "I must add, though, that I don't believe *any* of the horrid things people are saying about what your dreadful abductor did to you. As for poisoning your husband, well, I promise you, I don't believe a word of that, either!"

Chapter 12

Although her lips had already parted to respond to Lady Ellen Logan's greeting, Adela froze at the airy disclaimer, unable to believe what she had heard. Her first inclination was to ask her ladyship to repeat her words, but she did not.

Instead, taking an extra breath to let her emotions settle, she said, "How pleasant to meet you, madam. Pray accept my sympathy for your great loss."

"I hope you are mistaken about those rumors, Ellen," Isabella said sternly.

"But I'm not, madam," Lady Ellen said, surprised. "In troth, they say the horrid man who stole her ladyship from her wedding also stole her maidenhood. They say, too, that when Ardelve discovered the theft, he threatened to return her to her father in disgrace. To avoid that fate and to keep her marriage settlements, they say, she poisoned the poor man at their wedding feast."

"At Roslin?" Isabella's tone had turned icy.

Feeling dizzy, Adela swayed, but a firm hand at her elbow steadied her.

"Who are these insolent rumormongers?" Lestalric demanded.

"I vow, I do not know," Ellen said. "Sithee, it is just what one hears."

Collecting herself as his steadying hand left her elbow, Adela said with careful dignity, "You are kind to have warned me, madam. I thank you."

"You need not," Lady Ellen said, turning as she did to Lestalric and saying in her artless way, "But come and talk with me now, Robbie. You may escort me back to my lady mother, on the dais. I yearn to hear about all that you have done since you went away. You can imagine my astonishment at learning you were here. I am truly sorry to have missed your grand entrance. They say you created a great stir. Until that moment, everyone had thought you must be dead."

"You give me too much credit, madam," he said. "I doubt that 'everyone' had held any thought of me whatsoever all these years since I left home."

"Faith, Robbie, art angry with me for marrying Will? You must know that even had I not wanted him, my father would have forbidden me to marry you."

"Ah, but you see, you did want him—or all that he could provide for you."

"I'd have had to be mad to marry a man with naught," she said, smiling winsomely. "You'd not have wanted to marry a madwoman, would you, Robbie? In any event, now we can put everything right in a trice, as we are both free to do as we will. So come and walk with me. The countess will excuse us."

Adela's palm had begun to itch midway through her ladyship's discourse, but she said nothing, merely shifting her gaze to Lestalric.

He was looking at Lady Ellen, and Adela saw a muscle twitch in his jaw. But his tone was the languid one he had used before as he said, "Sakes, madam, you cannot want everyone here to see you parading about with someone of such low estate as myself. I will spare you my company and provide you with a Norse prince instead. If you will be so kind, Orkney," he added, turning toward Henry.

"Aye, sure, and with pleasure," Henry said, extending his arm to her. Then he rather blunted any delight she might feel at having the wealthiest man in the room escort her by adding, "I want to talk with your father, in any event, lass."

"What a thing to say!" Adela exclaimed when the two had walked away.

"That he wants to talk with Douglas?" Isabella said with a smile.

"She means those awful rumors," Lady Clendenen said fretfully. "Etienne did say some unfortunate murmuring had begun. But he did not suggest anything as horrid as this."

"I don't mean what Henry said or what Lady Ellen said to me," Adela said angrily, unable to believe for a moment that anyone could imagine she had poisoned Ardelve in front of a hall full of noble wedding guests. "I meant the heartless way she spoke to Robert. I wanted to slap her. How dare she!"

The words were out before she knew she would say

them, and when she saw the gleam of amusement in his eyes, she wished she could take them back.

He said, "Countess, with your permission I would like to walk with her ladyship and explain that she has no need to defend me from Lady Ellen or her ilk."

Lady Clendenen said, "My lord, you must not be so particular in your attentions to her—not now, at all events. If such rumors as Ellen repeated are flying about the court, we must all be circumspect."

Isabella returned his smile, saying, "You, sir, should make your inten—" She stopped, her gaze shifting to a point beyond him.

Lady Clendenen, following her gaze, immediately swept a deep curtsy, thus giving Adela small warning before she turned.

"Good evening, Countess, ladies," the Earl of Fife said mildly. "I'm relieved to see that you have all recovered from your terrifying ordeal."

"Thank you for your concern, my lord," Lady Clendenen said, rising as Adela made her curtsy. "Thank you again for your timely arrival today."

He nodded, then said to Adela, "We of the court have heard troublesome rumors, madam, that his grace would like me to look into further."

"Indeed, sir?" Adela stiffened, lifting her chin.

Lestalric said, "If you want to converse with her ladyship, Fife, you must await your turn. I promised his grace I would bring her to converse with him this evening, and would do so in good time. Where, pray, shall we find you afterward?"

"Never fear, Lestalric, I'll find you," Fife said. Turning back to Adela, he said, "You will learn, madam, that being a lawful nation, we punish women who poison their husbands, and most severely. Moreover, if you have come to court in the hope of persuading some other poor devil to marry you, you will find that no man here has the slightest interest in taking Ardelve's place."

Adela's fingers curled into her palms, and a hot retort sprang to her lips, forcing her to press them tightly together as Lestalric said in his most languid manner, "You are wrong, Fife. I wager most men here tonight would count themselves honored to win her ladyship's hand. I would, certainly."

Fife sneered. "Then you are a greater fool than I thought. No man of sense or intelligence wants a wife who is likely to poison him."

"Aye, sure, some prefer women who bring them earldoms," Lestalric said. "But come, my lady. We must not keep his grace waiting."

He extended his arm, but Adela waited until the earl turned on his heel and strode away. Then, she said, "How did you dare say that to him? Did he not get his first earldom by marrying Margaret, Countess of Menteith in her own right, and his second by arranging to inherit it from his brother's widow, the Countess of Fife?"

He smiled. "How is it you ken so much about such things, lass?"

"My father talks of news he hears from the mendicant friars," she said. "And before my aunt Euphemia went to live with my sister Cristina, she often explained how noble families were related to each other. But you do not answer my question."

"Fife was haughty, pretending a certainty he cannot feel," Lestalric said. "I thought it wise to push him off his pace by stirring his anger. Madam," he added, turning to Isabella, "I shall take Lady Adela to speak briefly with his grace. They appear to be clearing space for a ring dance, so mayhap you will find that the noise of this place has stirred another headache. Also, if you see Henry, pray tell him I want him. I mean to get her ladyship away before Fife tries to stop us."

"Do you think he would dare arrest her here?" Isabella asked. "We Sinclairs wield considerable power ourselves, after all."

"Aye, but in Midlothian more than in Edinburgh," he said, abandoning his languid manner. "Edinburgh has become his ground, madam. If we must do battle, 'twould be best to fight on our own ground, where we have greater resources."

"What of Lestalric Castle?" Adela asked. "Should you not protect it?"

"Henry's man of affairs has already gone there with a force of men-at-arms to take command," he told her. "Moreover, the estate's great size and value does much to protect it. Don't forget that the King of Scots has no royal army for Fife to muster. Fife has only his own people and those of other nobles he can persuade to support him. Presently, he is playing the concerned son and brother, fretting at his father's weakness and his brother's inability to lead. But many powerful lords have discerned his true nature. They'll not oppose him as long as he continues in this role, but if it begins to appear that he means to take noble estates by force, that will quickly change. He is too astute not to know that, but he could create a great deal of trouble for you, lass, merely by pretending to believe these foul rumors."

"Go with him, Adela," Isabella said. "Ealga, you and I will find Henry."

Adela put her hand obediently on Lestalric's outstretched arm, but she was by no means persuaded that Fife truly threatened her. "Surely, no one can believe I poisoned Ardelve," she said to him as they wended their way to the royal dais. "How could I have done any such thing?"

"It does not matter what anyone else believes," he murmured, bending his head close so she could hear him without others doing so. "All that matters is such weakness as Fife imagines he can exploit to his benefit. Your father left with Donald of the Isles. Everyone here knows Henry means likewise to depart for the north, and Isabella for Roslin. However, if Fife believed your sole protector would then be Lady Clendenen, he may have got a step or two ahead of himself."

"But why would the Earl of Fife have any interest in me?"

"In troth, I thought I was his target," he said. "More accurately, that Lestalric is. He seeks to acquire land, but I also suspect he's heard rumors of a secret some believe my family keeps. Indeed, now I wonder if more than that may be at stake."

A merrymaker jostled them, and she heard Lestalric gasp. When she looked at him, he still wore the vacuous expression he had affected, but his face was pale.

"Why do you want Henry?" she asked quietly.

"We are vulnerable in Edinburgh and greatly outnumbered," he said. "I'll feel safer if we can put some ground between this town and ourselves."

"Robbie, there you are!"

A grimace creased his face, but he collected himself to say with a smile, "Lady Ellen, you must forgive us. We are—"

Cutting in without apology, she said, "I *shan't* forgive you. The ring is forming and I want to dance with you. Lady Adela will not mind." Without affording Adela time to respond, she added, "Indeed, you must both come. It will be fun!"

"Nay, then, my lady, we cannot. His grace has sent for us, but here— De Gredin, how fortunate!"

"Good evening, Lestalric," the chevalier said, beaming. "You will not think it fortunate at all, I know, because I have come to beg Lady Adela to let me escort her into the ring dance."

"Then you are just the man we want," Lestalric said with an answering beam. "First, I must make you known to Lady Logan, the Douglas's youngest daughter and recent widow of my brother. She desires to join the dancers, but his grace has summoned us to the high table. So I would count it a great favor if you would lend her your escort in my stead."

"An honor, to be sure, but prithee, my lady," de Gredin added, bowing to Adela, "do not be so cruel as to refuse to dance with me later. We'll make a fine pair, garbed in tawny silk as we are," he added, smoothing his embroidered doublet.

Adela smiled politely but left it to Lestalric to promise faithfully that they would join the dancing as soon as his grace excused them.

As they extricated themselves from the other two, Adela said rather tartly, "You are the most accomplished liar, sir. I hope you do not make a habit of it."

"Behold me all integrity where you are concerned, lass," he said with one of his warmest smiles. "I warrant you would see through any lie I tried to tell you in a blink. At all events, I have no wish to tell you lies. Now come, for the only sure way to win this skirmish is to do so before Fife realizes we know we're in a battle."

To her further astonishment, he took her straight to the high table, where the King, looking more bleary than usual, sat beside the Earl of Carrick. Both men looked as if they wanted only to retire to their beds.

"Your grace," Lestalric said, "I've brought Lady Ardelve, as you requested."

If it came as a surprise to the King of Scots that he wanted to extend his acquaintance with Adela, she saw no sign of it.

He peered myopically at her as she swept him a curtsy, then said, "I know you, madam." Motioning for her to rise, he tilted his head in a thoughtful way and added, "I thought so last evening, and now I am sure of it. We have met before."

"One does not like to contradict your grace," Adela said. "But—"

Beside him, the Earl of Carrick—lean-faced, fair, and scholarly looking—interjected gently, "Lady Ardelve is one of the famous Macleod beauties, sire. You met her sister Cristina at Ardtornish soon after she married Hector Reaganach."

"Aye, that's it," the King said. "You look just like her, lass."

Lestalric said, "Forgive me, your grace, but we would ask your leave to retire. Isabella, Countess of Strathearn and Caithness, who is with us tonight, is feeling unwell. With your permission, we would take her home."

"Aye, sure," the King said, nodding. "'Tis good to see you here, Robbie lad."

"Thank you, your grace. Come, madam."

Moments later, they were but two amongst many in the noisy throng, for the lower tables had vanished and the dancing had begun in earnest.

"Quickly now," Lestalric said. "Fife won't expect us to try to leave until his grace retires, but I'd not give his grace more than ten minutes now before he does. I want to be outside the gates before then."

She did not argue, especially as she could see that he was in greater pain than before and knew there would be more jostling as they made their way to the nearest doorway. Soon she had no idea where they were in the vast interior maze of David's tower, but Lestalric had either been there before and knew his way or possessed an unerring sense of direction, for in minutes they came to a heavy, narrow door that opened onto the inner bailey. Walking swiftly and silently downhill and through an archway, they found Henry and the others waiting with the vehicles.

Henry said, "I can protect her if we can get her to Sinclair House. They'll look for her, though, either there or at Ealga's. Sakes, they may be waiting already."

"If they are, we'll go to the abbey," Lestalric said. "Even at Sinclair House, you can protect her only as long as she stays inside and they stay out."

"You have a plan," Henry said, eyeing him shrewdly.

"Half a plan," Lestalric said, glancing at Adela. "We'll take your tilt-cart, Henry, for it is not well known yet. Tell your man to drive past your house if I signal him or if he sees any sign of Fife's people. In either event, he is to drive straight into the sanctuary part of the abbey kirkyard."

Adela was surprised when neither Isabella nor Lady Clendenen objected to her riding with Lestalric in Henry's cart. The intimacy of its close interior made her unusually aware of him. She could smell the light, pleasant scent of rosemary or something akin to it either wafting from his clothing or his skin. As they passed beneath the heavy iron portcullis, she asked how his shoulder felt, expecting him to say, as most men of her acquaintance would, that he was fine.

Instead, he said, "It hurts like the devil. But Isabella smoothed one of her potions on it earlier and gave me something to drink that eased the pain until people began crashing into me. I'll do, though, and I've something important to say to you, so listen carefully, lass."

"What is it?" she asked, astonished again at how easy it was to be with him and talk with him, as if they had grown up together and had always talked so. To be sure, he had deceived her and she loathed deceit, but even with what little she knew about him, she had already acquitted him of any malice in what he had done.

He was silent for a long moment, clearly gathering his thoughts. Then, with a glance at the driver, he said quietly, "I've been thinking there must be more to this business than we know, that somehow you have become part of it. I can imagine no other reason for the accusations made against you tonight or for the rumors about you that pervade the court."

"His grace did not mention them."

"I doubt he knows. 'Tis Fife who controls the King rather than the King who controls Scotland. Fife holds no office that allows it, but that does not stop him, and his grace seems weaker each time we see him. Naught will change when Carrick takes the throne, either, because Fife will rule him as easily. Do you know Fife will be the coroner—the man who crowns Carrick—when his grace dies?"

"How can that be?"

"Because it has long been the right of the MacDuff of Fife to set the crown on the King of Scots' head. And whilst Fife is not a MacDuff, he claims the right of coroner through his marriage to the last MacDuff's wife. We're nearing St. Giles now," he added. "Sinclair House lies just beyond, so try not to let anyone near us see your face. I doubt that Fife's men will look twice at this cart, since it would be unlikely to carry any man and woman who are not married."

"Why are we going to the abbey?"

He took a deep breath, his gaze still fixed on the passing scenery outside the coach. "If Fife means to make trouble for you, I can think of only one reason for it. He hopes to get to someone or something else through you."

"To you?"

"To me or to the Sinclairs," he said. "As Lady Clendenen said, I have shown an interest in you. Anyone can tell that we have a bond between us greater than that of a man and woman who apparently met so recently. Even if that were not so, everyone seems to know about your recent ordeals."

"My abduction and Ardelve's death, you mean. But what of it?"

"It makes you more vulnerable, lass," he said gently. "A man like Fife would see that vulnerability and know that those who care about you would exert themselves to protect you. They might even reveal all they know to do so."

"I . . . I see."

She didn't, though, not until he said, "Waldron of Edgelaw may have shared his thoughts with others of his ilk, or with someone whose power he hoped might aid him. If he did not, his successor or successors may have done so."

The pieces fell into place. "So they may be after the treasure," she said.

Rob had not been sure that she had ever heard about the treasure or that, if she had, she had remembered it after recovering from her ordeal. But he dared not discuss it now, with the driver so near.

As he had half expected, men awaited them outside Sinclair House, but it was as much to give himself time to think as for any other reason that he leaned forward and said firmly, "Drive on, man."

The horses picked up the pace as he told her glibly about the waiting men.

"Are we truly going to seek sanctuary at the abbey?" she asked.

"We'll see what transpires," he said. "I do have another idea, though."

"What?"

"It is no longer safe here for you," he said. "So you

must make another choice for yourself. The same possibilities exist. You can go home to your father's house, seek asylum with your good-son at Loch Alsh, or you may choose to remain at Roslin with the countess, Michael, and Isobel."

"Or?" she said with an anticipatory look that told him she knew he had something else in mind and was curious to know what it was.

"Or you could marry me and let me protect you," he said more calmly than he had imagined he could say the words. An imp in his mind muttered that at least it should divert her from thoughts of the treasure.

Silence fell again, but heavy tension filled the air between them. In the dim glow of ambient torchlight from torches outside the houses lining the Canongate, he could see her chewing her lower lip.

Gently, he said, "Well?"

"Mercy, sir, you cannot mean that." Her voice sounded loud, and hoarse.

His heart pounded. "I always mean what I say."

"But so soon! You hardly know me, and my husband . . . "

"Ardelve is dead and cannot protect you. I am alive and I can."

"But others can, too, and you cannot possibly *want* to marry me."

His throat tightened as he realized that he did want her, more than he had ever wanted anything in his life—except, possibly, as a lad, his knighthood. He'd thought, all those years ago, that losing Ellen Douglas had devastated him, but he realized now that it was not the losing but the manner in which he had lost her.

Until that day, he had believed his father cared enough

about him to take pride in his knighthood even if Will would not. That Sir Ian, aware that he wanted Ellen, could so callously arrange to marry Will to her instead had felt like base betrayal. That they could taunt him with that decision, even suggest that Sir Ian might change his mind if Rob would part with his secrets had only made it worse.

Able to say none of that to Adela but knowing he must say something or she would certainly believe he didn't want her, he said, "More to the point, lass, could you find it in yourself to want to marry me?"

She was silent.

Her profile was lovely but stiff and strained. He wanted to see her face, her expression, to judge what she might be thinking.

"Adela? Prithee, lass, look at me."

She turned then, looked straight into his eyes as if she studied him, as if she would peer into his soul.

He gazed back more confidently. She had not rejected his suggestion outright. Perhaps . . .

"I do not know what you may have heard about me," she said.

"I ken fine that those rumors are false," he said.

"Not about the rumors, about me. My sisters talk, I know, because . . . well, because they do, that's all. I know they believed—" She stopped. "Nay, what they believed of me was true, and I should not make it sound as if it were not."

"What was true?"

"That I married Ardelve for comfort and expediency,"

she said, licking her lips. "Moreover, I ken fine that you would rather marry Lady Ellen."

He grinned, glad he could speak the unvarnished truth to her, and said with deep sincerity, "Not if every other woman in the world were to vanish overnight."

A gurgle of laughter escaped her. "What a thing to say!"

He put his right hand over her left. "Lass, truly, you should learn that I rarely say things I do not mean. But we are nearing the abbey gates. As you have not said you do *not* want to marry me, may I at least hope that you will?"

"Mercy, sir, if we are to speak plainly, I married Ardelve because I was tired of managing my father's household, tired of trying to manage sisters who flouted my authority. Sorcha never even acknowledged that I had any! *And* because my father wanted to marry Lady Clendenen, who had sworn she would not set foot in the place until I *had* married. So I accepted him because he offered me a comfortable home and promised he would require little of me in return."

"But I would require much in return," he said, still gazing into her eyes.

"Would you?"

"I would."

Her pupils were so large that her eyes looked black with gold flecks from reflected torchlight. She licked her lips again, making his body leap in response.

"Then if you really mean it, I think I will say yes," she said.

"You won't mind if our wedding is a hasty one?"

This time her smile was wry, and as the cart came to a

stop in the kirkyard, she said, "I'm not good at weddings, sir, so the hastier, the better."

The Earl of Fife was annoyed and in no mood for confrontation. But the man who had brought the lady Adela to his attention had come to him in the Spartan chamber he used to conduct business at the Castle and dared to question his actions.

Having silenced him with an angry command, Fife said, "I told you not to come to me unless I sent for you, Chevalier. To be seen together like this would do neither of us any good."

"Doubtless you are right, my lord," de Gredin said, eyeing him warily. "But I do not understand this course you have set."

"It is not for you to understand my actions, sirrah," Fife retorted coldly.

"I had no objection to your ordering Lestalric shot," de Gredin said. "Faith, I'd not have cared if you'd killed him. But what can you hope to gain by accusing the lady Adela of poisoning Ardelve? I thought we had agreed that our best course was for me to win her confidence. I shall do so, I assure you, for even Cousin Ealga seems inclined to support such an endeavor."

"Your cousin Ealga is so distant a kinswoman that you cannot hope to influence her more than the Countess Isabella can, and I've seen no indication that Isabella favors you," Fife snapped. "My methods will gain the information we seek far more swiftly."

"But we both know perfectly well that her ladyship did not poison Ardelve," de Gredin protested.

"Others will have suspected as much straightaway, however," Fife assured him. "I merely took advantage of human nature by whispering the possibility into an ear or two. As to evidence, you can supply that with your testimony."

"I suppose you have reason to believe I'd testify if it became necessary."

Fife sneered. "We both seek the same goal, do we not, *mon ami*?"

Chapter 13

~

Lestalric explained as he handed Adela from Henry's tilt-cart that they had passed the points marking the beginning of the portion of the abbey kirkyard lawfully designated as sanctuary.

"So even if Fife comes after us, we're safe enough for now," he added.

"Will I wait here for ye, m'lord?" the driver asked.

"Drive round to the east side of the abbey, out of sight of the Canongate," he said. "We'll send for you when we want you."

Nodding, the man urged the horse forward, and as the cart rattled away over the cobblestones, Adela accepted Lestalric's right arm and they turned toward the abbey. Before they had taken more than a few steps, one of the monks came hurrying toward them, his long black, hooded gown and white cassock flapping around his legs as he walked.

"Who art thou, sir?" he asked in a quiet but carrying voice.

"Sir Robert of Lestalric," he said. "Prithee, send for the abbot at once. I would have speech with him."

Without argument, the monk turned to precede them inside.

"Mercy," Adela said as they followed him, "I did not think they would welcome us so easily."

"My family is held in high regard here," Lestalric said. "Holyrood Abbey stands today only because, when Edward of England took Edinburgh Castle in 1296, and all lands south of the Firth including those of the abbey, a Lestalric priest who had become abbot here swore a solemn oath of fealty to him. He thus secured the safety of the abbey and its lands."

"The English destroyed Scone Abbey during their occupation then, did they not?" Adela asked as they approached the imposing entrance to the abbey kirk.

"Aye, and threatened or destroyed other abbeys, as well," he said, nodding to the monk, who held the door for them to enter the candlelit vestibule.

"Wait here, my lord," the monk said quietly. "I will fetch my lord abbot."

"I warrant some would think your Lestalric abbot ought to have been more loyal to Scotland," Adela said as the man passed her and walked toward the transept, where another monk was just rising from his devotions. "Many men died defying the English then to win our freedom."

"Aye, but an abbot's first duty is to his abbey, lass. Many of those who stood against the English, including the original de Lestalric family, forfeited everything. Edward I seized their lands and castles for his own use. Don't forget, the English stayed here for many years. Abbot Adam did his duty when he saved Holyrood."

"Aye, he did, and for that we must all be grateful," declared a booming voice from the front of the kirk. A large, plump, elderly man in the same black-and-white Augustinian habit as the monk's strode forward, and Adela realized he was the one she had seen at his prayers. "I am abbot here, my son. My baillie, Brother Joseph, tells me you are Sir Robert of Lestalric. Indeed, I can see as much for myself, as you are the image of Sir Walter. But Brother Joseph says you have need of me."

"Aye, my lord, but I should warn you that aiding us may anger the Earl of Fife. I do not want harm to come to you or others of the abbey."

"I believe I can manage the lofty earl," the abbot said with a look of distaste. "His lordship declares himself a religious man. . . . but I must not be uncharitable. Tell me instead how I may serve you."

"We want to marry, my lord abbot, at once and without banns. I am prepared to make a generous gift to the abbey if such a gift would be suitable and if you will not object to waiting until I learn more about my newly inherited holdings."

"We never reject alms, my son, but no Lestalric need offer gelt in exchange for favor here. I expect you are both free to wed and have need for haste, also that you prefer not to resort to such ancient customs as marriage by declaration."

"We are both free, and in this instance, I believe having the seal of the Kirk and your blessing, if possible, would be preferable," Lestalric said.

"Then I will do as you ask," the abbot said. "Brother Joseph, fetch one of the other brothers, so the pair of you can bear witness. Stay, though, as it is close upon the hour of Nocturnes, ask the others to lend us their presence, as well."

The monks arrived swiftly, and as they took their places on the left side of the transept, the abbot led Adela and Lestalric up the arcaded right-hand side aisle to the small transept chapel at the end of it. He began the service in front of the altar there with a brief benediction, asking God's blessing on all present, then adding, "Does any man here object to this union?"

Adela held her breath.

Then, as he started to speak the first words of the rite, just as she dared to breathe again, she heard Lestalric, beside her, say, "Hold one moment yet, sir."

Surprised, the abbot broke off to look at him. "What is it, my son?"

Lestalric turned to face her. "Art sure, lass?"

She smiled, thinking how much his coming into her life had improved it already, how he had made her feel things again, had made life itself appealing again. "Aye," she said softly but nonetheless firmly. "I'm sure."

Without further delay, Sir Robert promised to take her as his wife for all time forward, "to have and to hold, for fairer, for fouler, for better, for worse, for richer, for poorer, in sickness and in health, till death do us depart, if Holy Kirk it will ordain."

"Have you a ring, my son?" the abbot asked then.

"Aye," he said, pulling the plain gold band from the little finger of his left hand. "'Twas my grandmother's," he said as he slipped it on Adela's finger.

She recited her vows then, which were the same as his except that, as his wife, she also promised to be meek and obedient in bed and at board. As she repeated those words, she remembered wondering at Roslin what Sorcha had thought of such a vow and if Hugo expected her temperamental sister to abide by it.

As she knelt beside Lestalric to receive the abbot's blessing, she believed she would have no trouble abiding by her vows. Lestalric seemed even-tempered, even mild by comparison with men such as Sir Hugo or Hector the Ferocious. It felt right and good to be marrying a man less likely to provoke her to any extreme behavior.

"You may rise and face the witnesses," the abbot said, smiling at them and declaring as they obeyed, "It gives me pleasure to present to you Sir Robert and Lady Logan of Lestalric, now man and wife. You may kiss your bride, my son."

As Lestalric bestowed a gentle kiss on Adela's lips, a familiar voice echoed from the rear of the nave.

"I vow, Rob, I did not expect this," Henry said as he strode toward them. "May one with some small responsibility for Lady Adela's welfare ask how you persuaded her to this mad course?"

Adela smiled. "Are you displeased with us, sir?"

"Not when I see you smile like that, lass," he said. "I had begun to fear we'd not see that smile again. But are you truly content with this?"

"Aye, sir, although I don't doubt that Sir Hugo and Sorcha will also think 'tis madness that drives me."

"My mother may wonder about your sanity, as well."

"Mercy, do you think so?" She had not considered

what the countess's reaction might be. "Will she be vexed?"

"We'll just have to wait and see," Henry said.

"Don't torment her," Lestalric said. "I've a strong notion your mother will approve. Did you think to bring horses, Henry?"

"Nay, for despite what you see I am not really here at all," Henry said.

"You are but a shadow representing yourself; is that it?"

"Just so," Henry said. "When we saw the men waiting at Sinclair House, my mother insisted that we stop to discover what reason they might give for such insolence. When their captain said Fife desired to question Lady Clendenen's guest further about certain matters, Mother declared with great haughtiness that Adela had suffered a severe indisposition. Being in my mother's charge and mine, as much as Lady Clendenen's, she told him, Adela had retired with his grace's consent to my rooms at the Castle and is not to be disturbed until at least midday tomorrow."

"Excellent," Lestalric said. "But will it serve, do you think?"

"We must hope it does until at least midday tomorrow."

"Mercy," Adela exclaimed, trying to ignore a shiver of fear. "What will happen when they cannot find me?"

"Doubtless, my mother will demand an explanation and accuse Fife of spiriting you away," Henry said, glancing at the fascinated abbot. "You won't repeat any of this, I hope, my lord abbot."

"I shall treat all you say as if said under the seal of the confessional."

"Just so you don't whisper a word of it to Fife," Henry said.

"Nay then, I would not!"

"But we'll need at least two horses," Lestalric said.

"Aye," Henry said. "But I'm thinking you'd better borrow them from the abbot here. Not only do I prefer not to show myself again tonight but I mean to send my mother home to Roslin tomorrow with a large mounted escort. With luck, Fife and his minions will not have any notion of what became of you two."

"You'll be traveling with the countess, of course."

"I want to discuss that with you," Henry said. "I slipped over here by crossing the back gardens until I reached the abbey grounds, from which only a hedgerow separates those on the Clendenen House side of the Canongate. No one saw me, but you should know that Fife's men tried to gain entry to Sinclair House."

"Doubtless they failed."

"Aye, but they did try."

"What of Clendenen House? Did they try that as well?"

"Apparently not. I doubt they'd expect to find anything there," Henry said. "You have been staying with me, after all, and if they are seeking the same thing they searched for at Lestalric, I doubt they'd expect you to trust Adela or Ealga with any secret you'd refused to entrust to your father or Will."

He smiled at Adela, then chuckled when she rolled her eyes.

"Anything that important, I'd keep on my person,"

Lestalric said. "But we are missing something, Henry. Fife did not try to arrest me. He wants Adela."

"Mayhap he seeks to use her to get to you."

"But why? To his knowledge, we've barely met. Even seeing us all together at Lestalric is hardly reason enough to suspect any closer relationship than that. But think of what he knows about Adela."

"Still," Henry said, "they searched Lestalric and tried to search my house."

The abbot said apologetically, "It is nearly time to ring the bell for Nocturnes, my sons. If you do not mean to linger for the service . . . "

Lestalric shook his head. "We ken fine that it is not your practice to include outsiders, my lord. But if you could lend me a pair of horses and allow us to depart southward through your grounds, we'd be grateful."

"South? Then you do not go to Lestalric Castle."

"Nay, Lestalric is not yet prepared for my bride. I will take her where I know I can keep her safe."

"You are welcome to the steeds," the abbot said. "Mayhap you would likewise accept a guide to see you safely through the abbey woods until you are south of Arthur's Seat. The area from here to where the ground begins to rise is marshy, because our drainage is poor. But you'll want to avoid the main roads for the first few miles. I collect that you also mean to make for Roslin."

"We would be most grateful for a guide, my lord," Lestalric said, without denying the suggested destination.

There were documents to sign, with Henry and Brother Joseph signing as witnesses to the wedding. When they'd finished, Lestalric thanked the abbot again.

"Brother Joseph will take you to the stables and provide you with a knowledgeable guide," the abbot said, extending a hand to him. "Go with God then, the pair of you. We hope to see you again when all is safe."

Outside, gathering mist formed a gauzy veil through which the full moon overhead glowed dimly. As they followed Brother Joseph to the stables, the abbey bell began loudly to toll the midnight hour of Nocturnes, startling Adela nearly out of her skin. Beside her, Lestalric put a calming hand on her shoulder.

"'Tis to be hoped this mist does not thicken," Henry said when the bell's tolling ceased. "Mayhap you should take torches as well as a guide."

"We'll be fine," Lestalric said. But when Brother Joseph left them to roust out a gillie, he said in an undertone, "What is your plan, Henry? I know you must be chafing to leave for the north, but—"

"That's what I wanted to discuss with you. But first, the countess sent this." Henry handed him a flask and a small jar. "Decoction of willow bark in the flask," he said. "The jar contains more of that salve she smeared on your wound."

Lestalric opened the flask and drank before saying, "Are you not leaving?"

"I've sent orders to my captain to take my ship to St. Andrews for a few days. I told him the countess requires my escort back to Roslin, so I'm hoping to save time afterward by having him attend to a matter for me in St. Andrews now. But I likewise told him that if anyone should inquire into my whereabouts, he is to say I am aboard ship. So, if Fife looks into my activities, he will believe me safely on my way to Orkney or Caithness."

"But if you escort Isabella—"

"I mean to do so, but I'll dress as one of her retainers with helmet and jack. Our people know me, of course, but none will betray me. I'll join you after I see her home. Here is our man returning," he added in a warning tone. "I'll go back the way I came, then bid Ealga farewell and escort Mother to Sinclair House before appearing to depart for my ship. That should settle them nicely if they're watching."

"Mercy, I forgot about Ealga!" Adela exclaimed. "I cannot just ride off—"

"Doucely, lass," Lestalric interjected, nodding toward Brother Joseph. "Henry will make your excuses to her ladyship."

"But there can *be* no excuse for such a departure," Adela said, controlling her tone with effort. "She has been so kind to me. To go in such a rude manner—"

This time it was Henry who interrupted, saying, "Rob is right, Adela. I'll say all that is necessary, and Ealga will understand. I do not think you realize how much danger you may be in. Obey your husband, lass."

She glowered at him, fighting to guard her tongue.

To her increasing fury, he chuckled. "The very picture of Sorcha," he murmured provocatively.

"Aye," Lestalric agreed. "And Lady Isobel, for that matter."

Much as Adela would have liked to slap them both, she could not. Moreover, the picture they had given her of her demeanor made her lips twitch.

Her husband put his right arm around her shoulders then, pulled her close and kissed her on the forehead. His lips were warm, his arm likewise, and she sighed.

Nevertheless, she said, "I pray you, Henry, do not just offer her meaningless excuses. Tell her I am abject in my apologies for treating her so badly and look forward to seeing her as soon as possible to make those apologies in person."

"I'll tell her everything that is proper, lass, I promise. Now, here is your eager escort, so I must bid you both farewell."

Lestalric said ruefully, "Before you do, Henry, I should tell you that your tilt-cart with its driver and pony are waiting patiently for us behind the abbey. I told him we would send for him when we wanted him, but we don't want him, and I haven't a notion what to do with him. Do you?"

"Aye, I'll ask them to put him up here and stable the cart until it's safe to collect it. I shan't need it, and the less anyone sees of it now, the better. I'll deal with that after I've seen you off."

Both horses were equipped with men's saddles, but as the gillie held the sleek bay mare he had brought Adela, and Henry lifted her to the saddle, Lestalric said, "You are scarce costumed for riding, lady wife. I know you deplore the use of a woman's saddle, but are those skirts full enough to let you sit properly astride?"

"I can make them so if you men will turn your backs long enough," she said.

They did, and although the doing was awkward, since it entailed pulling up her shift, once it was rucked under her hips, her outer skirts were full enough to let her straddle the mare. She wore silk and her favorite lavender velvet cloak, so she knew she would be warm enough even if the air grew colder.

When she declared herself ready, Lestalric mounted his horse with less effort than one might have expected, considering his injury. Then, following their young guide out of the stable and around to the back of the abbey with Henry striding alongside to deal with his driver, they soon bade them farewell and were off.

The moon was still bright enough to show them the narrow muddy track the gillie followed through the abbey woods, which skirted a long, narrow loch extending much of the half-mile distance to the base of Arthur's Seat.

Trees grew to the lochside with the path wending its way a dozen feet from its bank, but the moonlight reflected from the mirrorlike surface of the water and provided sufficient light for them to see their way.

Eventually, they came to the foot of Arthur's Seat, and Adela gazed up at the hill the people of Edinburgh fondly called their sleeping lion.

Their guide urged them toward the hill's western end, and fifteen minutes later, he said, "There be the road ye want yonder, me lord. D'ye ken your way?"

"Aye, lad, I do," Lestalric said, extracting a few coins from his purse to give him. "Thank you for your aid."

Stammering his own thanks, the lad bade them goodnight and turned back toward the abbey.

Adela was alone for the first time with her new husband.

Rob gazed at her, sitting so serenely and easily on the bay mare. She had pushed her hood back. Now she reached up and began to pull pins from her caul.

"You might want to leave that on, lass," he said. "It could turn much colder before we reach our destination." He knew the lad might still be within earshot and did not want to mention where they were going.

Not that Fife would have trouble following if he discovered they'd headed south. He'd assume what the abbot had assumed and take the track toward Roslin, and, doing so, he would easily find them. Still, they had a head start, and Rob could see no reason to make anyone a gift of the information.

Adela was still pulling pins from the caul. How many did women use, he wondered, to hold the things in place? She was watching him, and when he frowned in his musing, she said, "I'm taking it off because it will give me a headache. It is one thing to wear a formal caul whilst one is dining or dancing, although I'd probably have pulled it off if we had joined the ring dances."

"Are you warm enough?" he asked, thinking she looked deliciously cool, almost silvery with her hair freed of its confines, spilling in a sheet down her back and looking almost white in the moonlight. He wanted to stroke it.

Just the thought of touching her stirred him, making him wish they could gallop the horses all the way to Hawthornden. But not only would such speed be impossibly foolhardy, it would be painful as well. Isabella's potion had worked its magic, but he was not sure it would keep doing so if he tested it in such a way.

As it was, he hoped he would be able to claim his bride when they arrived.

She smiled and said, "I shall do, sir. You need not

coddle me. Our Highland weather is harsher than any I have met since I left there."

"Then let us not tarry," he said. "I look forward to a warm bed at the end of this journey." *And more than that, pray God*, he added silently.

She sobered, giving him a direct look. "You have not asked me," she said.

"Asked you what?"

"If I am . . . that is to say whether Waldron of Edgelaw took—"

"Sakes, lass, I thought I'd made it plain that I harbor no doubts. If you would have it plainer, let me say that in the very unlikely event that I should discover you are no longer a maiden, I'll own myself astonished and assume Ardelve somehow found sufficient time betwixt the ceremony and the feast to demand his husbandly rights. Either that or you suffered injury somehow through your love of frequent riding. Sithee, I have heard of such occurring."

She smiled again, this time more shyly. "I do not think I have ever been so injured, my lord."

"You may call me Rob, you know."

"Not Robbie?"

He grimaced. "I cannot imagine that you would want to call me so, but you may choose, lass. Call me what you will. I would be friends with my wife."

"Were you friends with Lady Ellen?"

"I do not want to talk about Lady Ellen on my wedding night," he said.

She gave him a narrow-eyed look, but he was growing accustomed to the way she sometimes seemed to peer right into the depths of him, and he gazed steadily back.

He was not sure he could easily manage so steady a gaze had his conscience not been clear. But on the subject of Lady Ellen, it was as clear as a conscience could be. If he never saw the woman again, he would be content.

She nodded. "You did not ask, but you should know that Ardelve never touched me either. As you may have noted, we did spend some time alone in the countess's solar, but that was so he could tell me he had no intention of demanding his husbandly rights, as you say, until I was ready for him to do so."

She gazed limpidly at him, clearly awaiting his reaction.

He grinned. "Art hoping I'll make the same declaration? Because I'll tell you to your head I won't do any such thing. We've little more than five miles to travel, but at the end of those five miles . . . "

He watched her, still grinning, letting her fill in the rest for herself.

Adela could not have explained why she told him what Ardelve had said to her. Perhaps it was only that she found it easy to say what she liked to him. But it had seemed right to tell him, even to tease him a little and hear what he would say.

She had not expected his reply to stir feelings that she had experienced only once before. It was as if he had touched her—nay, as if he had kissed her again and not in the gentle way he had kissed her earlier in the abbey kirk, but thoroughly, as he had kissed her the night they met in the chapel at Roslin.

She fell silent then, thinking about what lay ahead—and not far ahead, only five miles. He seemed content to be silent, too.

She wondered when he would tell her about the map, for although she had not looked at it, she was sure that was what she had concealed for him in her bodice. He had trusted her with it, so it had not occurred to her to look. But she hoped he would tell her all about it and would do so before long.

The track they followed was wide enough for them to ride two abreast, and although the misty veil still occluded the moon, the night remained pleasant.

The air was still, the horses' hoofbeats dull and steady. Crickets chirped and frogs croaked. These sounds, punctuated with the occasional night bird's cry or fox's bark, filled the night with the music she loved best.

Without warning, he said, "Tell me more about what happened."

She did not have to ask what he meant, for she knew. And although she had scarcely spoken a word about her abduction to anyone, she hesitated only a moment before saying, "I told you how they came for me in Glenelg, that they rode right up to the kirk porch. 'Tis where we wed in the Highlands, sithee, not inside the kirk. I was beside Ardelve when Waldron snatched me up and rode away with me."

After that, it was easy this time to tell him more. He rarely asked questions, just let her relate her tale in the way she found comfortable. As she talked, she remembered details that she had not thought about since they had happened.

"He never hurt me," she said, then shivered, remembering. "He did slap me once, quite hard, before I learned to take care how I spoke to him."

"Did he?"

Only two words, but she shivered again at his tone, thinking it was as well that Waldron of Edgelaw was already dead.

"That was just the first day," she said. "He never struck me again."

"But he hanged someone right in front of you. You told me that. You must have been frightened witless the whole time you were with him. Do you still think he was not truly evil?"

"I know he was," she said. "'Tis odd, but since meeting you, I remember that time more clearly. Near the end of my time with him, I did come to realize he was evil. He believed the things he said, but perhaps if I'd been with him longer . . . "

"It was a gey long time, lass, just two days shy of a fortnight."

"You know exactly?"

"Aye," he said. "It was not so long ago, after all."

"No." She bit her lower lip, suppressing a flurry of unwelcome thoughts.

"Are you afraid something like it might happen again?" His voice was calm, matter-of-fact, as if they discussed something ordinary.

When she did not answer straightaway, he added, "What did you think at first when Fife and his men came upon us today?"

She shivered again.

He reached for her and clearly did so without thinking, because his horse was to her right, his reins in his right hand. So he reached with his left.

"Damnation," he muttered.

"I'd nearly forgotten your wound," she said. "It seems to be mending much faster than I'd thought possible."

"Isabella is a witch with her potions," he said, smiling. "Sir William Sinclair traveled a great deal. He made a collection of potions and their recipes, as his father and grandfather had before him, and Isabella has long studied them. She gave me a decoction of willow bark in wine to drink for the pain and to avoid fever, and smeared some sort of salve on the wound. But she warned me to clean it well and put more salve on it when we change the wrapping."

"Do you think she would be willing to teach me some of what she knows?"

"Aye, and willingly," he said. "But let us talk more about you. It frightened you when Fife came upon us, did it not, even with Henry's men there?"

"I don't trust Fife."

"Nor should you," he said. "But I'm thinking it will do you no harm to learn some things I can teach you, ways you can protect yourself in the future. You must still be wary, of course, because women are always more vulnerable than men. But no woman is helpless, lass, as you learned for yourself. You handled yourself well. You stayed calm whilst you were with Waldron. Despite being frightened, you retained your ability to think and to act. Most men would not have done as well."

His words warmed her and stirred a sense of her old pride. She turned to thank him, but he was looking straight ahead. As she turned, he smiled.

Following his gaze, she saw a tall, square tower ahead, the pale moonlight turning its gray stones to silver. She could see portions of the river North Esk far below, flowing at the base of the high, sheer cliff atop which the castle perched.

"That's Hawthornden," he said. "Welcome to your new home, lass, at least until we can move into our own."

Chapter 14

The entrance to Hawthornden Castle was a tall archway boasting stout double gates. But when Lestalric whistled and shouted his name, the gates opened swiftly for them. As he and Adela rode into a small, flagged, torchlit courtyard dominated by the great, square keep, he pointed out the stable, bakehouse, and carpenter's shop, three small stone buildings that abutted the curtain wall.

Fearing that Lestalric—or Rob, as she would try to call him privately now—must be in pain again, she watched as he dismounted. But he did so without using his left hand, so she could not judge how much his wound was hurting him.

Compared to Roslin or Chalamine, Hawthornden was small, but when they entered the keep, she saw that the architecture inside was similar to Roslin's.

The hall, located directly off a half-landing, was much smaller than Roslin's, and the rushes on its floor gave off an odor that told her they needed replacing as much as those at Lestalric did. Her first inclination was to blame Sorcha for the lack of care, but recalling that her sister had been resident there for only a month before departing again for the Highlands, she knew blaming her would be unfair. Sorcha and Hugo had stayed at Hawthornden only at night, too, returning to Roslin every day.

A number of men were sleeping on the hall floor, but when several stirred and began to get up, Rob signed to them to stay where they were and guided her back to the stairwell. On the next landing, he pushed open a door to a shadowy chamber that seemed at first glance to be full of curtained bed. With the door fully open, she saw that the room was larger than it first appeared.

Crossing it, Rob threw back the shutters on a tall window to let in the pale light of a moon much lower now in the western sky than when they had left the abbey. "Come," he said quietly. "Look at the view."

Shutting the door behind her, she obeyed, passing the large bed extending along most of the wall to her right, its foot end toward the window. It still seemed overlarge for the room, but when she went to stand by him and gaze out on the moonlit landscape before her, she forgot about the bed.

"How beautiful."

They had followed the wooded track along the eastern rim of the gorge, rather than the cart trail that followed the river's course through its depths, and she had seen during her journey to Edinburgh that the west side of the river was not as steep or as high as the eastern side. From the castle, she could see Roslin, more than a mile to her left up the glen. And she could look straight down to the river, too, which had not been possible from the track, since it ran through dense woodland some distance from the cliff edge.

She stood to his right, and when his arm slipped around her shoulders, she turned to him willingly and raised her lips to meet his. His were warm and touched hers lightly, but then his arm gripped tighter and his lips pressed harder, opening slightly as his free hand eased up between his body and hers to brush over her left breast, stirring nerves to life in the nipple, making her gasp. But the hand did not linger. Warm fingers touched her chin.

As if it were a signal, his right hand shifted to cup the back of her head, and his kisses grew more demanding. His tongue pressed between her lips, and when she parted them, it slid inside to explore the interior of her mouth. Astonished, since no one had ever kissed her so before, she stiffened and would have pulled back but for his hand at the back of her head. Then his body pressed hard along the length of hers, and new feelings awakened in her, making her forget her surprise. Moaning softly, she leaned into him and touched her tongue to his.

The fingers touching her chin moved to the ties of her cloak, tugging briefly until the sable-trimmed lavender velvet hushed to the floor at her feet.

"Doesn't your shoulder hurt?" she murmured.

"Aye, but some things are worth the pain," he murmured back before his lips possessed hers again.

Her tawny-silk surcoat followed swiftly, then her front-laced kirtle and underskirt, leaving her in her linen shift, heavily wrinkled, she was sure, from riding with it rucked round her hips. The only other things she still wore were the gold chain necklace her mother had given her, and the ring from her husband.

Trying to smooth the worst of the wrinkles from the shift, she said, "Have you undressed women often, sir? You seem most adept at the business."

His eyes twinkled. "I vow, 'tis no more than male instinct."

"You once claimed to be all integrity," she said sternly, raising her eyebrows. "But I suspect falsehood in those words."

"Doubtless *that* is no more than male instinct, too," he said with a grin. "Deriving from the strongest of all male instincts, that of survival."

"So now I must guess when you are honest with me and when you are not?"

"Nay, lass, you'll know. Do you doubt that?"

She looked narrowly at him for a long moment, but he met the look easily.

"No," she said. "I believe I will know."

"Good," he said, kissing her again lightly. "We've more important things to do than to fratch about words or about things that should remain in the past."

~⌐

Sakes, but he would have to watch his step! How foolish to point out how easily she would know if he were lying!

Although he had told her the only way to keep a secret was never to share it, in troth, the only way was never to let anyone know one *had* a secret. She already knew he harbored at least one, and doubtless she suspected he kept others.

When she had mentioned the treasure earlier, he had diverted her by proposing that they marry. How smug he

had been then to believe marriage would make no difference, that her unusual lack of curiosity and disdain for secrets would let him keep his easily. But he could hardly
count on that if the subject of the treasure arose again
now that she knew she could discern a falsehood.

And what about the map?

She had held it in her hand, had concealed it for him,
and had returned it without a murmur. To be sure, others
had surrounded them at the time, and events of the
evening had doubtless pushed it from her mind. But he
could not keep diverting her. Not if she could read him
merely by narrowing her beautiful eyes.

His attention diverted when he touched her cool skin
and realized that, in her shift and so near the window, she
must be chilly. Yet there remained the not insignificant
matter of removing his own clothing before they could
both get into bed. Ignoring the continuing ache in his
shoulder, he gently rubbed both hands up and down her
bare arms, then indulged himself by kissing her more.

The skin of her upper arms was soft to his touch and
silky smooth. Her hair smelled of dried lavender and
rosemary, her skin of something similar but lighter, more
herbal. He pulled her close again and nuzzled her neck,
easing her necklace aside so her could kiss her there,
making her giggle as a child might when he did.

"Art ticklish, lassie?"

"Aye, there . . . and other places, too."

"I shall have to explore them all," he said soberly.

"Will you?" Her eyes were wide, their pupils huge and
black.

He kissed her lips again. "I'll need help undressing.

Shall I waken one of the lads to aid me so you can get into bed and stay warm, or—"

"You undressed me, my lord. Surely, I should have the same pleasure."

He grinned. "Please yourself, sweetheart. I begin to think this marriage may have been a wiser decision than I knew, providing me with a beautiful handmaiden."

"Mayhap you should keep a still tongue in your head, sir," she said with a slight edge to her tone. "Recall that if you irk me, you may cause me to forget your injury for one brief, unhappy moment."

"I was teasing, lass."

She frowned as if her thoughts had turned inward. "I'm not a good subject for teasing, I think. But strangely, just tonight I realized I had spoken teasingly to you. That is unusual, too. I am generally of a more sober disposition."

"Laughter is good for the soul, but mayhap we both should beware. My temper has got me into trouble more than once, although over the years I *have* learned to control it much better than I did as a lad. Still, if you are venturing into the art of teasing at such a late date, don't forget to trust your instincts and be sure I am of a mind to laugh. I'll promise to do the same."

She nodded, then said, "Should we not clean and tend your wound whilst you have your shirt off?"

"Nay, for I'm sure it will just need tending again later," he said. "But come now, you must be freezing. At least put on your cloak over your shift."

"It will only get in the way," she said. "The air is just cool, not cold."

He tried to keep his hands off her, to let her unlace

his doublet and hose quickly, so she could get into bed. It seemed impossible, but despite her assurance, he saw gooseflesh on her upper arms as she knelt and freed his hose lacing from the eyelet holes on the underside of his doublet. After that, he did naught to delay her.

The rest came off quickly with the exception of his doublet and shirt, both of which she eased away from his wound so slowly that his patience nearly expired before both were off. He was ready for her by then, pain or no pain.

"Is that the same bed Sorcha and Hugo sleep in?" she asked as he pulled back the coverlet and quilt and gestured for her to climb in.

"Aye, do you mind? Hugo won't."

"Nor will Sorcha, I'm sure, but it does seem strange to be in their bed," she said as she climbed in and shifted to the far side.

"It would seem stranger, and far less comfortable, to be in the one Hugo provided for me whilst I lived here with them."

"Mercy, did he give you an uncomfortable one?"

"Recall my position at the time, lass. Even as a captain, I slept on one of those straw pallets in the hall with the others."

"It is hard to think of you as Einar Logan," she said as he got in beside her. "When I think about him, all I remember is his beard."

"No beard now," he said as he moved carefully toward her. "I may be somewhat clumsy, though. Take off your shift for me. I want to look at you."

Obeying, she said, "I don't know how you will manage."

He shook his head at her as he said, "Sakes, I've fought battles with worse injuries and scarcely noticed them. But stop talking, sweetheart. It has been a long day, and we both need to sleep at least a few hours tonight."

So saying, he moved over her, leaning on his right elbow and thus blocking much of the moonlight from the window, although there was still enough to glint on her simple necklace. He would buy her a jeweled one, he decided as he cupped one soft breast. He stroked it gently, then moved to stroke her ribs and belly before shifting to the breast again, teasing the nipple, then bending to lick and taste it. Little shivers fluttered across the silky skin beneath his hand as he did.

Easing himself up, he claimed her lips, his body already pulsing for her and beginning to ache elsewhere than his shoulder.

"Will it hurt?" she asked.

"Aye, probably," he said, adding with a smile, "or so I'm told. But if we go slowly, mayhap it will not."

"I don't know what to do."

"You need do nothing this time, sweetheart. Just relax and don't jump out of your skin if something I do should startle you."

Smiling, she said, "I never used to do that." Her words ended in a gasp when he began sucking the nipple he had tasted earlier.

He teased her body and stroked her from her breasts to her belly and lower, getting her used to his touch until he began to fear he could wait no longer. Easing his hand to the fork of her legs, suppressing all thought of the sharpening pain in his shoulder, he gently parted her nether lips and eased a finger inside her.

She was tight but moist and ready for him. Still he spent a few minutes letting her get used to his fingers, hoping that by doing so he would ease the way enough so that she could more easily endure the pain his penetration would cause.

Adela marveled at the feelings his lightest touch stirred. Nerves she had not known she possessed had come to life, and the sensations fascinated and delighted her. Had anyone told her she could feel this way with any man, let alone one she had known for only days, she would never have believed them. But so it was, for she had felt from the beginning as if she had known him forever, as if by his voice alone he were familiar to her and beloved.

Common sense told her such a thing was impossible, that no one could know another person well without a long, close relationship to develop kinship. She had never had that with a male before. She had no brothers and no male cousins to whom she could speak so freely. But she had felt kinship with Rob from the start, and something more, a bond that she had never felt with anyone before.

His hands felt as if they belonged on her body, stroking her, making her gasp with delight. And when his fingers penetrated her, she gasped again. As he eased himself atop her and fitted himself inside, she felt a frisson of fear, but it passed. She felt a dull ache then. But he was still for a few moments, and the ache passed, too. He began to move again, slowly, rhythmically, and her mind filled with the feelings he stirred until all awareness of anything but his movements and her feelings ceased.

She savored each moment, focusing on each new sensation until he began to move faster and faster, plunging deeper with each stroke. She felt pain again, but it did not seem to matter as much as the thought that he might be giving her a child at that moment. His child and her own, to love and to cherish.

Soon he was moving so quickly and so powerfully that she feared he must be hurting himself badly. But instinct and desire banded together to suppress that fear, and Adela savored the moment.

When he collapsed atop her, they both lay still for several long moments before he murmured, "Can you still breathe, sweetheart?"

"Aye, well enough. How is your shoulder?"

"I feel nothing. I'm numb." He raised himself up and looked into her eyes, and he was smiling.

She smiled back. "I felt many things, new and wonderful things," she said.

"That was only a beginning," he said. "There is much more I can teach you."

He got up then and poured water into the basin from the ewer on the washstand, and soaked a cloth to help her clean herself.

"I'll help you, too," she said. "Where is the countess's salve?"

"In that pouch I was carrying," he said. "I set it somewhere."

He found it, and after she had dealt with his wound, they got back into the bed, where he slid his good arm under her shoulders and drew her close again, holding her comfortably so until she slept.

She rode peacefully beneath a big golden sun in a clear azure sky, her mount a snow-white beast with a lovely, silken mane and tail, her saddle so comfortable it was as if she floated on pillows, rocking gently, ever so gently, the way one did in a small boat on a calm sea. But as she became aware of the boat and realized she was not on horseback at all, the boat began to rock faster, then wildly.

The sky was no longer azure, no longer clear. Clouds swiftly gathered, including a huge black one that enveloped her as the sea heaved and water rushed into the boat, threatening to drown her. She was cold to the bone and all alone, abandoned again. A cruel, taunting voice in her head said she always would be.

Everything was black and wet and cold, and silent, although before the silence she had not been aware of any noise other than that awful voice in her head and before it, birds perhaps, singing in the sunlight, or water lapping at the boat.

Now, all was silence and darkness. She was sinking downward, underwater, plunging ever deeper. But she could breathe as easily as if water were air.

Then light again, a bright beam from an unknown source that illuminated a brassbound chest. As she stared in awe, the lid opened, revealing great treasure—rubies and pearls, gold and silver, piled high and spilling from the chest.

Hands in black gloves reached around the lid to lift a long strand of pearls and a handful of glittering rubies. When the strand of pearls coiled upward and changed into a coal-black snake with slitted green eyes, she felt fear deeper than any she had ever known, chilling her as if ice had filled her veins.

Then Waldron of Edgelaw, all in black, huge and menacing, stepped from behind the chest and wrapped the snake around her neck.

Adela screamed . . .

. . . and awoke, sitting bolt upright in bed, still screaming, naked and cold, clutching the gold chain necklace she had forgotten to take off the night before.

A shadow loomed over her, making her jump again. But it was only Rob, moving swiftly toward the bed, dim twilight from the window outlining him.

"What is it?" he demanded gruffly. "What happened?"

"A . . . a horrid dream," she said, hating the quaver in her voice. "I have them sometimes."

"Sakes," he said. "I leave you for no more than a minute to relieve myself, and you have a nightmare. What happened in it?"

She hesitated, and when heavy rapping sounded on the door, she jumped.

"Be aught amiss, me lord?" a man shouted.

"Nay, my lady wife just suffered a nightmare," Rob told him.

"Come now, tell me," he urged, putting his arm around her and drawing her close as the man's footsteps retreated down the stairs. "It will sound silly when you put it in words. I know of no better way to exorcise such demons."

The warmth of his body against hers was comforting, and she leaned into him and helped him draw the coverlet over them both.

"I was cold," she said.

"Foolish lass, I pulled the covers over you when I got up, but you pushed them off again." Then, more firmly, he said, "Tell me about this dream of yours."

"I meant I was cold in the dream," she said, and described it. When she mentioned the treasure chest, she felt him stiffen. "Waldron stood behind it," she said. "At first I did not see him, only hands playing with rubies and pearls. But then he stepped from behind the chest, and the long strand of pearls he held coiled into a snake. He . . . he wrapped it around my neck." She shuddered.

He was silent for a moment, then said, "Common sense tells me that our talk on the way here stirred thoughts of that devil in your mind and mixed him in with other things you may have thought. Then, when your necklace got tangled . . . "

"Aye, I suppose that is all it was," she said doubtfully, reluctant to remind him of how much it had frightened her, lest he think less of her.

"That *is* all it is," he said confidently. "You're safe now, sweetheart. I won't let anything bad happen to you."

"No one should make such a promise," she said. "People die, or things happen to prevent them from keeping such promises." Then, for the first time in a conversation with him, she wished she had not spoken her thought aloud. Half to herself, she murmured, "Mayhap it means he is coming back again."

"He can't, lass. Surely you know he's dead."

"Ardelve told me he drowned," she said. "But I never saw him dead."

"Nor did anyone else," he admitted.

She stared at him. "Mercy, sir! Then I would remind

you that Waldron has been thought dead before and come back. Why should he not do so again?"

~~~~

Damnation!

Rob wanted to kick himself for revealing that detail. They had purposely told Ardelve only that Waldron had drowned, not how and certainly not where.

Recalling what she had said before she began talking about Waldron, he said ruefully, "You are right to take me to task, sweetheart, on two heads. I wanted to ease your fright, and I have done the reverse. And some of the secrets I hold are things I begin to believe you should know."

"You trusted me at Lestalric when the Earl of Fife came," she said, her tone making it clear that she was displeased with him. "I trusted you, too. I have not even asked you what you gave me."

"Aye," he agreed. "But trust is not always such a simple matter. Some secrets must remain secret. I have sworn an oath to that, and I will not break it. This business of Waldron, however, is not of itself one such as that."

"Are you certain he drowned?"

"Aye," he said. "But I remember that Hugo told me afterward that you recalled little about the day we rescued you. Do you remember the cavern?"

"Aye," she said. "I remember the chests, too, and talk of treasure. And, too, Waldron told me he served God and was seeking a treasure taken from Holy Kirk."

The room was gray now with the light of approaching dawn as it spread over the landscape outside.

Ignoring the treasure, he said, "Waldron drowned in the cavern's lake. He went under, and the devil claimed his own, because he never surfaced again. Hugo and I built a raft and searched every inch of that lake shore. In most places, the cavern wall is sheer, impossible to grip even if one were not severely injured, and he was nearly dead before he went in. Other places, one might climb out but not go anywhere, only sit on a narrow ledge or out-cropping. And, too, that underground lake is very deep and very cold, not likely to return its dead to the surface."

To his surprise, she nodded. "'Tis like the sea round the Isles," she said. "That water is so cold that bodies just sink and stay sunk, even in the sounds."

Her head rested in the hollow of his good shoulder, and hugging her closer, he kissed her hair, breathing in the scent of it and feeling himself stir again.

Doubting that she would be as interested in the state of his libido as he was, and knowing he had at least one more apology to make, he strove to ignore his eager, apparently sex-driven body as he said, "I should not have made it sound as if I believed your nightmare to be of small account. The experience you had with Waldron is bound to stay with you for a long while. I wouldn't be surprised to learn that your jumpy nature results from that, too. Your nightmares certainly do."

"I think they do, although it seems silly for them still to plague me so long afterward, when I am perfectly safe again."

"There is a rule in warfare," he said. "If one suffers great defeat, especially if a commander loses many men, that commander and his surviving men must train even harder than his new recruits. They must sharpen their skills and strive to learn new, even more difficult ones."

"I'd think such survivors prove just by surviving that they know what they are doing."

"Aye, sure," he said. "They may be the finest soldiers in the land. Even so, each saw close comrades killed, mayhap even stood beside one cut down by a weapon that could easily have killed him instead. Learning new skills rebuilds and strengthens one's confidence, and confidence does more than any skill to aid a man fighting a battle. I'm thinking it ought to do the same thing for a woman."

"Mercy, would you train me for battle?"

Suppressing his too-ready sense of humor, Rob kept his tone serious as he said, "There is more than one way to do battle, sweetheart. It is early yet. Do you want to sleep a little longer, or are you too fully awake now for that?"

"I am wide awake, so if you want to get up . . . "

He chuckled. "Part of me is likewise wide awake, standing up in fact and causing me some small suffering. Mayhap we can do something to ease that first."

"What can I do?"

"I'll show you," he said.

Adela's second lesson proved even more pleasant than the first. Afterward, her husband being willing to help her find and don her discarded clothing, she was in full charity with him when he left her to finish her ablutions while he found a manservant to tend his wound and ordered food for their breakfast.

That she was wearing her tawny silk dress from the night before reminded her again of her abduction, when she had worn one dress for days. Recalling that Isobel had sent clothing to Hawthornden for Sorcha, who likewise had arrived at Roslin with little of her own to wear, Adela decided that after breakfast she would search until she had found more suitable clothing for such an untidy place.

Mentally making lists of where she would begin the task of setting Hawthornden to rights, she hurried downstairs to find her husband, shirtless, on the hall dais, having his wound tended by a burly young man-at-arms as gillies prepared the linen-draped table nearby for their breakfast.

"My lady," Lestalric said, "I would present Archie Tayt to you. Be kind to him. His uncle is an influential burgess in Edinburgh. Make your bow, lad."

Smiling at the "lad," who, like most of Sir Hugo's men, stood more than head and shoulders taller than she was, Adela responded to a twinkle in his blue eyes as she greeted him by adding for her husband's benefit, "Indeed, my lord, and I hope I should be kind to him even if he had no uncle."

"And *I* hope not too kind," he warned with a teasing look.

Stifling the retort that sprang unbidden to her lips, she said, "How does his wound look, Archie?"

"It's fine," Rob said, grimacing as Archie returned to smearing salve on it.

"I was asking Archie Tayt," Adela said, moving closer

as Archie shot her a look of near anguish, telling her as plainly as words that he feared saying something that might anger her husband. "Never mind," she said. "I'll look for myself."

Rob said in a long-suffering way, "Sakes, Archie, you see what I've done?"

"Aye, me lord, ye've married yourself a good woman, ye have. Likely she'll make a gey fine mother for your bairns."

"True enough," Rob said. "But *I* don't require mothering."

"Aye, well that be . . . "

"Thank you, Archie," Adela said. "Stand aside now, if you will, and let me see how it progresses. I have seen it thus far only by moonlight. Stand still, sir," she added as Archie made way for her and Rob started to turn toward her.

"Well, lass," he said a moment later. "What do you think?"

"I think you were singularly fortunate for a second time, sir. You mend with commendable speed."

"'Tis nobbut the countess's potions," he said. "Many of us have had cause over the years to be grateful for her skill. Cover it up now, Archie, and I'll thank you not to be telling every man and rascal that my wife leads me by the nose."

"I'd no do that, m'lord, nae for nowt," Archie said earnestly.

Rob thanked him, adding, "Don't forget that other matter I asked you to attend for me."

"Nay, then, sir, I willna forget."

"What did you ask him to do?" Adela asked as they sat down at the table.

"To find a wee item I've a mind to give my wife as a bride gift."

"What?"

"You've become gey curious all of a sudden." He grinned at her. "Well, I'm not telling, so eat your breakfast. And don't give me that look, either. I have already decided to let you slap me after we eat, so save your ire for that."

Chapter 15

Adela barely spoke to her husband as they broke their fast, afraid he would continue to tease her about her increasing curiosity. She certainly could not deny it. Had it not leaped in response to his promised gift, it would have done so after his astonishing declaration that he expected her to slap him. She could not imagine striking him—not without far more provocation than he had provided.

He had stirred her ire more than once, but naught that was slapworthy, even had she been a woman inclined to slapping large men.

Sakes, she thought, she had never even slapped Hugo. And he had offered her ten times the provocation that Robert had.

Curiosity continued to burn in her, giving her to understand better than ever before her more curious sisters' impatience to satisfy theirs. But at last he ate the last bite of his bread, swallowed the last few drops of his ale, and stood up.

"You'll need suitable clothes," he said. "You don't want to spoil that gown."

"I thought about that earlier," she said. "Sorcha may have left things here, things Isobel lent her. But if Sorcha wore Isobel's clothes, I can, too."

"Let's go see," he said. "There's a kist with a few items in it upstairs. I ought to have thought of that this morning, but I had other things on my mind."

She felt a rush of flames to her cheeks at the memory of what had diverted him. But he said no more about it, and she let him hurry her upstairs.

They found two garments in the kist that she thought would fit her.

Accepting his help, she donned the plainer one, a simple blue kirtle with red silk front lacing. As she tied the embroidered girdle that went with it low on her hips, she glanced at him to judge his reaction.

"Very becoming," he said. "I hope you don't mind if it gets dirty."

"Why should it?"

"You'll see. Come with me." He led her back downstairs and out to the courtyard. "To do this properly I'd take you out on that grassy hillside yonder. But until I know what danger may come our way, we'll stay here in the yard."

Determined not to give him more reason to tease her by demanding further information, she followed meekly until they reached the farthest corner of the courtyard, where two pairs of men were wrestling.

Setting the four to new tasks without explanation, Rob faced her and said, "Now, lass, do as you have been yearning to do and slap me as hard as you can."

The invitation was tempting to say the least, but she said with dignity, "I don't slap people, sir, however irritated with them I may be."

"No? I'll wager you would happily have done so when I warned you not to be too kind to Archie Tayt this morning. For that matter, where is the woman who snapped that I was a fool after the arrow struck, the one who swore she wanted to slap the lady Ellen . . . that is, Lady Logan?"

"I should not have said that about her," Adela said. "It was wrong of me, and if you want me to apologize, I will do so."

"Nay, for that lass wants slapping. I hope she suited Will as a wife, for I can tell you that she would *not* have suited me."

"You are unfair, sir," she said, wondering even as she did why she was defending Lady Ellen. "Mayhap she would have behaved differently had your father and hers allowed you to wed when the two of you wanted to."

"Sakes, I'm not sure now that she ever wanted me, for I had naught to offer her. And as you heard, she counts her worth high. Looking back, I'd not be astonished to learn that Will was the one she wanted from the start."

"Did you not love her?"

He frowned. "Whatever I may have thought then, I doubt that I did."

"But you must have cared greatly to have left home over it as you did."

"You make too much of it all. I was hot for the notion and lusty for the lass, so when she took my brother instead of me, it stung my pride, that's all. I'm more than content with the wife I have. Now, slap me."

It was more than tempting, nearly irresistible. But Adela couldn't do it.

⌐～

Rob watched her closely. The last thing he wanted was to drop his guard with her, not because he feared her strength but because he feared her remorse if she managed through his own carelessness to clout him a hard one. He wanted to teach her a lesson, not earn another one himself.

It hadn't dawned on her yet that every man-jack in the place knew him well. But it soon would, and he did not want it to happen because they all burst into laughter at him for letting a woman knock him silly.

She was still gaping at him as if he were daft, so he said, "Come now. Just pretend that I'm Ellen and give me a good smack."

"I am not going to slap you. Even if I were the sort who would, I certainly won't do it here in front of your men—or Hugo's, since they are probably his."

"Aye, but they need not concern you, for you won't be able to hit me. That's what I want to prove to you. Now, give it a try."

"So you do this to mock me," she said, bristling. "To make me look foolish."

"To teach you. They'll all see that if you do not. Now, do as I bid you."

She rewarded him with that increasingly familiar, narrow look.

He met it soberly. Then he put his hands on his hips and spread his legs, bracing himself, wondering as he did if he would have to make her truly angry before he would be able to teach her.

She looked around the yard and must have gained confidence from seeing the men occupied with their tasks. None seemed to be paying the two of them any heed—not any that she would discern, at all events.

She raised her hand at last and took an open-handed swing at him.

He blocked it easily, catching her slender wrist gently in his right hand and holding it. "Try again," he said, releasing her. "Swing harder."

Three times more she repeated the same action, each time with the same result. And each time he issued the same grim command to try again. The fourth time, she gritted her teeth, and hope stirred. Her determination—or frustration—was increasing, but once more he caught her wrist easily with his right hand.

"Harder, woman. Have you no muscles in those wee arms of yours?"

She grimaced, drew her arm back as far as she could, and let fly.

Catching her hand again, he said provocatively, "Ellen could hit harder."

"I suppose you know that for a fact," she snapped, suddenly rushing at him, flailing with both hands and striking hard enough that when he caught both wrists he feared she might have bruised the one he held in his right hand.

Rubbing the area gently with his thumb, he said nonetheless sternly, "You won't do it, not that way, but at least now you see that you cannot defend yourself by reacting impulsively, without forethought."

"If this is supposed to make me more confident, I fail to see how," she said grimly, jerking her hand from his grasp and rubbing the wrist herself.

He rested his hands on her shoulders. "What will build your confidence," he said, "is learning skills that will nearly always work, where your smaller size may even prove helpful."

"Like what?"

"First, you need to consider the advantages you have," he said, still holding her close and looking into her eyes.

"Mercy, sir, I have none that protected me against Waldron."

"You're wrong, lass. As I told you last night, you did well against him. The proof is that you are here with me today and he is dead."

She shrugged. "Not through anything I did."

"Aye, perhaps, but from what I heard before and what you've told me since, I know you did not panic. You remained calm and able to talk sensibly with him."

"He talked to me rather than I to him," she said.

"He'd not have done that had you been the hysterical female I'll warrant he expected you to be. Sithee, I knew him. He was a villain to his black soul, a brutal man who believed that he acted in God's name and God supported all he did."

"I know, but—"

"We are not going to talk of Waldron now," he said. "I mean to teach you that you have weapons you've already proven you can use successfully. You are sensible, Adela, and you retain your common sense in situations where many women—and men, too—would abandon theirs."

"But how can common sense prevent such a thing from happening again?"

"You'll not be so trusting of strangers. Recall that you stepped toward him, despite his being masked and riding through your wedding guests to reach you."

"Aye, but I thought he must be . . . someone we knew."

"I ken fine what you thought," he said. "But the best way to defend yourself against attack is to avoid putting yourself in the way of it. If something looks wrong to you, trust yourself. Don't persuade yourself that it isn't wrong; just avoid the situation. For one thing, don't ever let yourself be alone where you may invite attack. Don't ride or walk alone anywhere, especially now."

"I wouldn't," she said.

"Good." He released her and stood facing her, his hands on his hips again. "Now think of me as the enemy. What do you see?"

She smiled wryly. "I see my husband looking arrogant and sure of himself."

"Most men who mean harm to you will look so," he said. "They have only to see you to assume you're weaker than they are and thus defenseless against them."

"In most cases, they would be right."

"In most cases, that will be your first weapon against them," he countered. "You *want* your enemy to think you defenseless, to believe he is in control. If you don't see him coming and cannot run or hide, you need to be able to surprise him. So let him see what he expects to see whilst you give yourself a moment to evaluate the situation, to clear your thinking. The key is to act as soon as possible after you sense a threat but not so hastily that you defeat yourself. The action you take may prove to be as simple as leaving the room. If you've given no indication that you sense a threat, your enemy may well assume that you'll return."

"And if he doesn't?"

"We'll discuss that later. How to surprise him is the first thing to think about. What can you do that he won't expect? For this first lesson, I want you to think why you might want to slap someone—not me, but a man you suspect means you harm."

"To make him stop," she said, frowning. "But if he truly means me harm, he would just slap me back, or worse."

"Aye, so slapping won't aid you much. You want to do something more useful, something that stops him long enough for you to obey the first rule, which is to get away. You need to hurt him, lass, and you cannot pause to wonder if you should. If you feel threatened, it's his own damn fault and you have every right to defend yourself. You must do it, and you must mean it."

She nodded, but he doubted that she believed him. She was tenderhearted, always a strong disadvantage in battle.

"You strike where he is weakest," he went on. "You strike hard and not with just your open hand."

"With a fist?" Clearly, she could not imagine it.

"Show me your hand," he said, holding his out.

She obeyed, displaying long slender fingers and neat, well-shaped nails.

"Make it stiff, like this," he said, showing her, his hand straight, his fingers pressed together. Then he touched his fingertips to her throat and pressed gently.

She pulled away quickly. "That hurts!"

"Aye, it is one place you can be sure to hurt him if you strike hard enough, especially with your nails. His eyes and nose are good targets, too. But the surest way a woman can hurt a man is by kicking, kneeing, or striking him here in the cods," he said, touching himself. "If you strike hard enough, you'll incapacitate him long enough to escape, especially if he's not well-trained in fighting or is relaxed and believes you don't threaten him. We'll try that first," he said. "I'll show you."

"It would be easier if I were to practice such things in lad's clothing, would it not?" she said as he moved her into position.

"You need to learn to manage in skirts, sweetheart. The chance that you'll meet an enemy whilst wearing male clothing is small. But if you've learned to deal with your skirts, you'll manage well no matter what you're wearing. Strike fast," he said. "And if you can grip his shoulders as you lift your knee or foot, you'll steady yourself and pull him toward you, so you'll do even more damage. But after you strike, don't linger to study the result. Always remember the first rule, and when you can, run as if the devil himself were after you."

She nodded, sober now and paying close heed. "What else?"

"That is sufficient for a first lesson," he said. "We'll practice the things I've shown you for a while now. Tomorrow I'll teach you more, but I want you to practice the things you learn, just as my men-at-arms would."

"Every day?"

"Aye," he said. "It does no good for me just to tell you what you should do. You must try it over and over until you feel sure you'll remember. There is one thing that will help you, though, with every skill I teach you," he added. "Watch your opponent's eyes, not his hands or feet, or even his weapon if he holds one. His eyes will tell you more about his intentions than anything else will."

Adela had listened carefully and was grateful for his teaching, although she doubted she would ever have recourse to such tactics or that they would help her if she did. That she might successfully defend herself against a man determined to do her harm seemed absurd. But the fact that Rob thought she could was oddly endearing, and that he would take time to teach her even more so.

"Come now," he said. "I'll show you over Hawthornden later. You should know your own ground well. And as we'll stay here until I can be sure Lestalric is safe for us, unless Hugo returns unexpectedly and we're forced to remove—"

"Why forced?" she asked. "Do you think Hugo would turn us out?"

"Sakes," he protested. "To think I congratulated myself only yesterday on having married a woman who so delightfully lacked curiosity!"

"I don't mean to pry," she protested. "Indeed, I don't know why I am so curious about things now. I never used to be."

He smiled then and put his arm around her. "Sweetheart, don't apologize for being normal. Does it not occur to you that you may have had little cause to display curiosity before leaving the Highlands? From all I've heard, you spent most of your time managing your father's household and looking after your sisters. Until you left, there must have been little to stir curiosity, but the fact is that the more we learn the more we find to arouse it. As to Hugo, all I meant was that I'd prefer more privacy than we'll have if they return. The preference is selfish, too, because it is my duty to see to Lestalric. But my inclination is to let Henry's man of affairs set everything in order there whilst I stay here and learn more about my wife."

"What about Lady Ellen?"

His smile disappeared. "What about her?"

"Is it not her right to live at Lestalric, as it was mine to live at Loch Alsh with Ardelve's son? Lady Ellen has made no secret of wanting you. Might she not resist leaving the castle? It has been her home, after all, for many years."

"Aye, but she is with her mother now, and even if she had contemplated such a plan, I doubt the Douglas would allow it. Moreover, when she learns that I have married, she'll look elsewhere soon enough."

"Will she?"

"Aye, sure. She won't want long for a husband. Unless I misread him, your friend de Gredin looked to be taking an interest in her. Now, come, try to strike me again. Stay, though," he said, looking beyond her. "I've a better notion."

She turned and saw Archie Tayt striding toward them. "Surely, you don't mean for me to do any of those things you suggested to him!"

"I mean for you to try," he said, adding casually, "I doubt you will succeed. Although if you truly want to, I suspect you could."

She wanted to show him she was perfectly capable of

doing the things he had taught her, but she was reluctant to hurt Archie. "He is not my enemy," she said.

"Nay, but he is well trained. If any lass managed to strike him, he'd deserve flogging, but I'd like you to see how close you can come to success even with a trained man-at-arms. Sakes, if you do hit him, I'll give you your present at once and I won't order him punished, although his pride will suffer."

Archie approached, carrying a small cloth bundle.

"Is that what I asked you to find for me?" Rob asked.

"Aye, sir," Archie replied.

"Good, toss it to me and just stand there for a moment." Eyeing him warily, Archie obeyed.

As he tucked the bundle under his arm, Rob said, "I've been teaching my lady wife some things about defending herself. I want her to try to slap you."

Glancing at Adela, then back at Rob, Archie Tayt looked horrified.

Rob chuckled and said, "Don't fear her, Arch. She's nobbut a wee lassock."

"Aye, sure, but I dinna want her to slap me."

Rob shrugged. "Then don't let her."

Adela saw him smile at Archie and realized he expected her to fail. Pride welled in her along with a touch of anger and grim determination to prove him wrong. He was so arrogant sometimes, so sure about everything that it made her itch to show him he was not the only one who could teach lessons.

She approached Archie with a reassuring smile, looking into his eyes. The poor man, as large as he was, was clearly nervous and kept glancing at Rob as if seeking guidance as to exactly how Rob wanted him to act.

Without looking away from Archie's blue eyes, Adela made her expression rueful. "Are you sure you don't mind, Archie?" she asked in a small voice.

He shook his head, but she saw him swallow hard.

"It should not matter to you if he does mind," Rob said sternly. "You just think about what I taught you and see if you can get close enough to make him alter his opinion a wee bit about how weak women are."

"Do you think women are weak, Archie?" she asked gently.

"Aye, mistress, I ken fine that they are, because . . . "

She drew her arm back the way she had the first time she'd tried to slap Rob.

". . . well, they be but lassies and no as strong as—"

His words ended in a sharp cry, for although he had been watching her eyes, he flicked a glance at Rob as she raised her hand. She had anticipated such a glance, and before his gaze darted back to her, she stiffened her rising hand and abruptly shifted direction to stab hard instead at the target between his legs.

He had pulled his head back, clearly believing he could easily make her miss his face. But at the last second he saw her true intent and jerked up his left knee to counter it. She had been too quick, though, and her hand slid over the knee, striking him higher than she had intended but making him gasp and cry out nonetheless.

Reacting even as the cry escaped him, he caught her shoulders, holding her arm's length away from him.

Adela stiffened at being grabbed so, but one look at his anxious face assured her that he sought only to protect himself from further injury.

Rob burst out laughing so hard that he doubled over, hands on his knees.

Temper rising, Adela grasped Archie's big hands and firmly removed them, then turned and strode purposefully toward her husband.

He sensed her approach and looked up, grinning widely, still gasping, tears of hilarity streaming down his cheeks.

Without breaking stride, she put her hands on both of his shoulders and shoved as hard as she could. He dropped the bundle and grabbed for her, but she easily eluded him, and he landed hard on his backside on the dusty cobbles.

"That's for making Archie the goat of your daft game," she said fiercely. "You should think shame to yourself for taking such callous advantage of him."

A large but gentle hand on her arm made her look away from Rob to find Archie looming over her, looking more unsettled than ever. "Please, m'lady," he said as his gaze flicked unhappily toward Rob. "Dinna be wroth wi' him to defend me. He's no a man wha' takes kindly to such."

Rob was on his feet with the little bundle he'd dropped in his left hand. "Stand away from my lady, Archie," he said as he moved toward them.

Seeing the look of angry intent on his face, Adela stepped backward.

"Here, man," Archie protested. "What d'ye mean to do to her?"

"I've a few more things to teach her," Rob said grimly, reaching for her.

Adela stepped back again. "Don't touch me," she snapped.

"Too late for that," he said, wrapping his right arm around her waist and lifting her off her feet. "Archie, tell those lads yonder to stop laughing and get back to their chores. And, whilst you're at it, thank your Maker that I promised her ladyship I'd not punish you if she managed to slip anything past your guard."

Archie nodded, and Adela, thus reminded that Archie might still be in some peril, stopped kicking, tried to get a breath, and prayed that Rob would not drop her.

He carried her thus one-armed up the steps to the castle's main entrance. One of the men having the presence of mind to run ahead and open the door for them, Rob strode in and stopped on the landing, kicking the door shut behind them before he set her on her feet.

"Upstairs," he said curtly.

"What are you going to do?"

"Go," he said, smacking her on the backside.

Grimacing, she snatched up her skirts and hurried upstairs ahead of him to the bedchamber they'd shared. Pushing the door open, she turned to face him.

"I only did what you—"

He was grinning at her, his eyes alight with laughter and something else that changed any anxiety she felt to a tingling that spread through her entire body.

"Come here," he said, his voice low in his throat.

She hesitated. "I thought you were furious. You had every reason to be. I don't know what possessed me. I swear to you, I almost *never* do things like that. And in front of your men! Mercy, I would not blame you if you—"

"You must learn to obey when I speak to you, madam wife," he said, catching her arm and pulling her close, then capturing her lips with his. His right hand moved to the red silk lacing of her kirtle as his tongue plunged into her mouth.

Moments later, they were naked on the bed, writhing together, enjoying passion that Adela had not known could exist, passion that seemed only to increase with every touch and movement.

"Ah, lass, you do things to me I did not know women could do to men," he said as he rolled atop her and moved a hand to the fork of her legs, using his fingers to ignite fire there.

"I'm not doing anything," she said, arching against him. "You . . . " She cried out as the fingers plunged into her, then moaned when they left her and gasped as, in place of them, he began to insert his—

Hammering on the door startled them both, and Rob muttered a curse that made Adela gasp again before he shouted, "What the devil do you want?"

"Beg pardon, sir, but Prince Henry of Orkney be below, and he says ye must come gey quick. He said to tell ye there's been murder done and they may be a-coming for ye straightaway."

"Mercy!" Adela exclaimed. "What can have happened now?"

Grimly, Rob said, "Did one of you brainless louts tell Orkney I was occupied, doubtless beating my wife?"

Silence.

"Just as I thought. Go back and tell him I said he should go boil his head."

"But, sir—"

"Go!" Rob roared.

Cheeks aflame as she imagined having to face Henry after sending him such a message for such a reason, Adela protested. "We cannot keep him waiting whilst we stay here like this!"

"Aye, sure we can," Rob said, resuming where he had stopped.

"But what if he meant what he said? What if someone really *has* been killed? What if—"

Silencing her the best way he knew how, Rob pressed his lips to hers and his hand to one breast. Teasing the nipple as he plundered her mouth, he eased himself inside her. He was throbbing, his body more eager than ever for her. His shoulder ached, both from his ignominious fall and the exercise, but he did not care a whit.

She responded then, stroking his back and buttocks, kissing him passionately, arching to meet him as he thrust into her. He moved slowly, then faster, until he could feel himself nearly there, almost . . . almost . . .

"Robert! Damnation, man, this is no time for idling. I must talk with you!"

Groaning, Rob collapsed atop his wife, muttering imprecations. "So help me," he said. "If someone is *not* dead, Henry soon will be."

Chapter 16

With a sigh of resignation, Rob rolled off Adela and when she got up and headed for the washstand, he watched her as he shouted, "Go downstairs, Henry, and order food for us. I'm starving. We'll be along shortly."

Henry began to protest but broke off, apparently realizing he had done all he could and that there might be good reason for the delay.

Adela poured water into the basin from the ewer and began washing her hands and face while Rob collected their clothing. As she turned to take her shift from him, a thought struck him that made him chuckle.

"What?"

"I was thinking about Archie," he said, taking her place at the washstand. "The look on his face—aye, *and* yours. In troth, lass, I never thought you'd do it. I knew you could if I could persuade you to try in earnest. But I thought it would take much longer before you'd act so decisively. By heaven, though, you used what you'd learned and you did it well. The only criticism I'd have would be for your disrespectful treatment of your husband afterward."

"You made me angry, laughing at him like that," she said as she pulled the shift over her head and smoothed it into place.

"Aye, and doubtless I'll make you angry again, often. But I hope you don't mean to make a practice of tilting me onto my backside in front of all the lads."

She looked rueful. "I expect they all knew you as Einar Logan."

"Aye, they did," he said, pulling on his breeks as she donned her kirtle and tied the laces. "Some did not always treat me with the respect I thought I deserved, either, although I'd come to Hugo determined to learn humility. Not knowing then, any more than *I* did, that they dealt with a future baron, some of them went right out of their way to humble me."

"It must have been difficult for you," she said.

"Difficult" did not come close to it. "Not much worse than when I began training at Dunclathy," he said. "I must not have learned as much as I'd hoped, though, because when they began laughing after you pitched me to the cobbles, the old temper surged right up again. I failed to see any humor in the situation until I was halfway up the stairs watching your skirts twitching so invitingly ahead of me."

He leaned against the bed and pulled on his boots with one hand.

"Did all of them at Roslin or Hawthornden know you before you became Einar?" she asked as she tied the embroidered girdle low on her hips and carefully overlapped its long ends to hang properly.

"Nay, only Hugo's own men, because most of the others here are Sinclair men," he said. "They serve Henry or the countess. I'd visited Roslin before, of course, but only as a lad or in Sir Edward's fighting tail. A few of Sir Edward's men from Dunclathy knew me well enough to have recognized me even after I'd grown Einar's beard, but I kept out of their way. To everyone else, I became Einar Logan, known for things I did well and teased for other things, as most men are. I soon came to be one of Hugo's closest captains, though, because we'd so many things in common. With no land or men of my own, life seemed good with him, sithee."

Adela was not sure that she did see, but as he reached for his shirt, she remembered his wound and demanded to see if it had suffered in his fall or during their more recent activities.

This time he did not object, and she saw that although it still looked angry, it seemed free of incipient putrefaction.

"You certainly are moving more freely," she said.

He grinned. "Aye, lassie, you provide excellent motivation. In truth, the wound, though painful, is not as bad as the one before when the arrow pierced my jack o' plate and went straight in. That wound kept trying to close up, wanting to fester, so someone had to keep opening it to let it clear."

She grimaced at the image.

"'Twas no pleasant experience, that," he said. "This

one, being open at both ends, behaves better, and moving about is good for it. So I can scarcely lay blame to it for letting my lass overset me as she did. You learn fast, sweetheart."

She smiled, pleased with herself. The satisfaction his approval engendered was delightfully new to her. She was far more accustomed to criticism or being taken for granted.

"Sakes, that reminds me," he said as he laced his shirt. "What did I do with that wee packet Archie gave me?"

"It's there on the floor," she said, pointing. "What is it?"

He picked it up and handed it to her. "See for yourself," he said.

She unwrapped it to find a short, leather-handled dirk in a leather sheath.

"I wanted you to have something to defend yourself," he said. "I'll show you how to use it later. First, let me show you how to wear the sheath." With a grin he told her to raise her skirts, then strapped the sheath snugly above her knee. "Your sister Isobel has one just like it," he said.

"It feels strange," she said, unsure how she felt about carrying a weapon.

"You'll get used to it," he said. "Now let's find Henry and eat. Afterward we'll all have a thorough look round. There is much here I want to show you."

In the hall, they found a grim-looking Henry supervising the serving of their overdue midday repast. As gillies scurried around the high table, Henry glanced appraisingly at Adela. When she smiled, his expression remained somber.

She shot a questioning look at Rob, but he gave a

slight shake of his head, so she did not comment on Henry's mood.

Rob said, "You made good time, Henry."

"Better than I'd expected, given the countess's usual traveling habits. She was eager to return to her new grandson. I've brought all your clothing, too."

They thanked him, Adela fervently, and the three continued to chat desultorily as they took their places at the table.

When they had ascertained that they had all they needed, Rob dismissed the servants and said, "Let's have it, Henry. What's amiss?"

"Did you think I was jesting with you?"

"Sakes, then, is it true? Is someone dead—murdered?"

"In troth, I do not know the whole. I own, I exaggerated because your man said you ..." Hesitating, he glanced at Adela, then added glibly, "But what I heard as we were leaving town was that someone attacked de Gredin late last night as he walked back up to the Castle from town, and that he lay near death. I did not stay to learn more, thinking it more important to get my mother safely back to Roslin."

"Why was the chevalier in town?" Adela asked. "We left him at the Castle."

"Apparently, he was attempting to call on you," Henry said. "He went to Clendenen House whilst the countess was still with Ealga, but they sent him away, saying you had retired and it was too late for callers, in any event."

"It was certainly late," Rob said.

"Aye, but their wee lie may somewhat complicate matters," Henry said.

"How so?"

"I sent one of my lads to learn what he could before he followed us to Roslin. He caught up to us just as we reached home and told me de Gredin had managed to say you were the one who had attacked him."

"When am I supposed to have done that?" Rob asked.

"Aye, well, that's the rub for them, isn't it?" Henry said. "Sithee, he says he knows the time exactly, because the abbey bell had just begun ringing Nocturnes. He said he could have counted all twelve strokes whilst his attacker beat him."

Adela said, "But we were in the abbey kirk then."

"We were approaching the stables when the tolling began," Rob said. "You jumped a foot, remember? Where did this supposed attack take place, Henry?"

"In the High Street just past St. Giles."

"Then I think we can clear my name easily enough."

"Aye, if you get the chance," Henry said. "The abbot can speak for you, but it won't help if you're dead before then. Of course, he may be Fife's man. If so—"

"Nay, he's not, for he called Fife the lofty earl," Rob said.

"Aye, he did," Adela agreed. "He said he was a religious man, too."

"Well, the lofty earl is apparently setting it about that no one can be sure that you are, in fact, Sir Robert of Lestalric," Henry said. "He has said that since no one knows where you've been the past nine years, you might even be an English spy."

"But the King recognized him," Adela reminded them both.

Henry shrugged. "Fife will say the King is too senile

to know what he is saying, that he heard the name and saw what he expected to see."

"The abbot recognized me, too," Rob said. "In any event, we'll deal with all that if we have to. For now . . ." He hesitated, then said, "Henry, was your man able to learn if de Gredin was truly injured or how serious his condition is?"

"He knows only what he heard at the Castle," Henry said. "According to Fife's people there, de Gredin was grievously wounded and may not survive."

"I'd guess his survival depends on how Fife judges the value of his sudden death against that of his continued existence," Rob said.

"Aye, but you can see why the countess and Ealga having told de Gredin that Adela had already retired to bed may create a problem."

"Easily explained," Rob said. "We need only say they did not want him to cause a scene at the abbey. Considering his attentions to my lass, they might well have thought he would create one if he learned why we had gone there."

"Then someone had better relay that tale to Ealga, because I did not tell them you had married Adela," Henry said. "I thought it best to keep that to ourselves until we knew where we stood all round. I did think it best to tell my mother about your wedding before we reached Roslin, however," he added.

Adela looked at Rob again and was surprised to see his eyes twinkling. "I'm almost afraid to ask," he said to Henry. "What did she say?"

"That she knew how it would be from the first and wishes you both happy."

"Sakes," Adela exclaimed with a surge of relief. "I hope my father reacts as well when he learns what we've done. I don't even want to imagine what Ardelve's people will think when they hear of it."

"I'll wager that no one will complain," Henry said. "Ardelve's son will be glad not to have to concern himself with a widowed stepmother his own age that he barely knows. And Macleod has only to learn who Rob is to be content."

"If I'm still amongst the living," Rob said with a frown. "Whatever Fife may be up to, Henry, we must act speedily on the other matter we've discussed."

Adela looked from one man to the other, then said stiffly, "If it is something you cannot discuss with me, sir, pray send me away. To speak so in front of me suggests that you do not trust me. I thought you did. I thought—"

"Enough, lass," Rob said. "We cannot discuss it here in the hall, but in troth there are subjects that I cannot discuss with you. I told you so. Recall that I said—"

"Not here, Rob," Henry said. "Let us adjourn to the wee chamber Hugo uses here to deal with accounts and such. It'll be snug, but no one will overhear us there."

"Aye, sure, but I did promise my lady that I would show her Hawthornden," Rob said, looking warily now at Adela.

As well he might, she thought, wondering at herself yet again. She was as willing to do battle with him now as she had been with Sorcha or her other sisters. She did not feel the need even to be tactful with him, except as a matter of civility—for as long as civility between them might last. The thought of fighting with him having somehow become stimulating rather than frightening, she eyed him grimly, unfazed by his own narrowing, suddenly stern gaze.

Henry, watching, said provocatively, "I believe Adela should come with us."

"Henry!" Rob shot an astonished look at him.

"The wee chamber, Robert," Henry said with a smile. "We'll have that chat first, and then we'll take her round the place together."

Adela turned to her husband, saw the grim look return to his face, and lifted her chin. When Henry indicated that she should precede them, she smiled at him.

Feeling his temper rise again as he followed Henry and Adela, Rob reminded himself that his anger was his own to control, that he need only exert himself, and that doubtless Henry was testing him.

Surely, Henry did not intend to reveal any secrets of the Order to Adela. Not, he assured himself, that his lass was not trustworthy, because she was—as trustworthy as any person could be. He simply was not a man who believed in sharing true secrets with anyone. If one got lazy, it became too easy to share them inadvertently even if one had never before been in the habit of sharing them at all.

Emotions entered too easily into such matters. And sometimes plain, ordinary conversation wandered into territory rife with pitfalls for the unwary.

The devil of it was not only that she knew the secrets existed but that she had seen evidence of at least two of them. Although Waldron apparently had not mentioned the Templars to her, he had told her he sought the treasure they guarded to "return it to Holy Kirk." And Rob himself had handed her his map. So she could put much together with what she already knew. That thought gave him pause as he followed the other two up the winding stairway to the cell-like chamber where Hugo kept his Hawthornden accounts.

By the time he entered the chamber, Henry had perched himself on Hugo's stool by the table that filled most of the room and Adela had moved into the corner farthest from the door. He listened to be sure no one else was in the stairwell, then shut the door behind him.

"Well?" Henry said, raising his eyebrows.

"You're right, I suppose," Rob said, noting the flash of surprise on Adela's face. He saw something else, too, relief and something warmer—mayhap gratitude. "I don't like it, though," he added almost curtly, still looking at her. "The more who share a secret the more likely it is that it will cease to *be* a secret."

"Aye, but you realize that two of her sisters already know," Henry said. "Moreover, it is nearly impossible to keep such things from someone who lives with you and comes to know your every thought and mood. But being able to trust that person is an excellent thing, something to strive for in a marriage, not to fight against. And, too . . ." Henry paused, looking at Adela.

She gazed solemnly back. When his gaze shifted to Rob, hers followed.

Rob said, "He's reminding me that you already know more than you should."

"Do I?" she said, regarding him intently.

Henry said, "I have found the Macleod sisters to be

both intelligent and persistent. She will learn more on her own, and sooner rather than later."

"And she might give something away without knowing the dangers that exist." Rob sighed. "I'd already decided to show her Hawthornden and ways to protect herself here. I own, I'd like to tell her more about my grandfather, too, and show her where he and his cronies hid in the old days. That could easily lead to trouble if she does not comprehend why she must keep silent about it."

"I wish you would both stop talking about me as if I were not here," Adela said tartly. "Does all this talk relate to the map you found at Lestalric, Robert?"

"Aye," Rob said, wondering how she'd guessed it was a map and wishing she would not call him Robert. People only did so when they were vexed with him. "Did you find what you sought at Roslin, Henry?"

"I did," Henry said, reaching into his doublet and extracting a rolled piece of vellum that looked much like Rob's own. "Do you still have yours with you?"

"In my boot," Rob said, bending to tug off the right one.

As he put his boot back on, Henry spread his own portion on the table and held it until Rob had done likewise. The curvy edges of the two fit together neatly.

"What do you think?" Henry asked doubtfully. "It seems to be little more than a webbing of lines and symbols."

~⁓

Adela moved closer to help hold the two pieces in place and saw that Henry was right. If it was a map, it was the oddest she had ever seen, because it looked like a child's drawing with lines going every which way. The only recognizable bits were symbols, two that looked like plant sprigs—one with a flower, one without—a sword, an arrow pointing north, and other less easily identifiable things.

"What are those?" she asked, pointing to the two plants.

As one, Rob said, "Furze," and Henry said, "Whin."

"They look similar but for the flower on Henry's half," she said.

"Aye," Henry said. "'Tis the same plant. Whin is the Norse word for furze."

"Both are nobbut plain gorse," Rob said. "The flowered one on Henry's is the way my grandfather drew our heraldic plant badge."

"The one on Rob's is how my great-grandfather drew whin," Henry said.

Adela frowned. "Was that so each would know who had the other half?"

"Who can tell?" Rob said. "Sithee, one rarely sees them as symbols. I only told Henry about mine because . . ." He stopped, grimaced, and looked at Henry.

"Because he kens fine that I have a strong interest in maps and have recently come into possession of a good many old ones," Henry said.

Adela caught his gaze and held it. "So, once again, we come to the treasure."

⁓

Rob watched Henry to see how he would react to that too-wise gaze of hers, but Henry just smiled lazily. "Aye," he said. "We do."

Still uncomfortable with the broader topic, Rob said, "This map has nowt to do with treasure, lass, and we can sort out that tale between us two another time. For now, it is more important to learn where this map will take us."

"But don't you know what lies hidden?"

"Nay, but I *have* been thinking about that," he said.

"Speculation does less good than discovering where the map takes us and seeing with our own eyes what we find there," Henry said.

Forestalling Adela's next question, knowing she would ask what he expected the map to reveal, Rob said, "The one place we know to which both our families have a strong connection is Hawthornden."

"It was part of the original barony awarded to my ancestor Sir William Sinclair when he arrived in Britain with the Conqueror," Henry said.

"Then later, during the English invasion of 1335," Rob went on, "my grandfather and others who refused to submit to Edward III took shelter in caves hereabouts and raided English supplies until we sent all the English home again. So we suspect the map refers to something hidden here or hereabouts."

Adela had been studying the tangle of lines on the map as he spoke. Without looking up, she said, "Then could these lines indicate a route from cave to cave, or are most of them huge caverns like the one near the upper end of Roslin Glen?"

The silence that followed made her look up, first at Rob, then Henry.

Rob looked pensive, but Henry met her gaze with his usual lazy smile. "How much do you remember about that place?" he asked.

She thought for a moment. "I couldn't find it if I tried," she said. "I was frightened when we went in because it was so black inside, but Sorcha found a torch and lit it. We were in a passageway that soon opened into an immense cavern. I remember the lake, but not much that happened after that."

"That isn't important now, in any event," Rob said. "That cavern you saw is one of hundreds that litter this area, but most are much smaller. Only Wallace's cave is well known, because William Wallace once hid there. Others are known to a few, and doubtless others lie undiscovered. But we'll all have to give some thought to this map, so come now, and we'll look round the castle. We can start here and show you everything from its ramparts to its pit."

Adela was annoyed that he was still clearly determined to say as little as possible, despite Henry's willingness to be more candid. But she kept her irritation to herself if only because seeing the whole castle would tell her exactly what needed doing to put the place in order. True to their word, Henry and Rob showed her every chamber from the crenellated ramparts down to the great chamber below the cliff top where, eyes twinkling, they pointed out the sally port to her.

Rob opened the wooden door, stepped aside, and said, "Have a look, lass."

Disoriented from descending the spiral stairway, she was amazed to see that the sally port opened onto the cliff face. They were a dozen feet below the clifftop, and even had they been able to climb up, they were right below the sheer keep wall.

"What use is it?" she asked. "There is no trail up or down. And one would have to be a fool to leap from here down to the river."

"That rope coiled on the wall beside it is tied to the iron ring it hangs on, and the ring is driven into the stone," Rob said. "One heaves the whole coil out, then slides down to the water. 'Tis only for emergencies, of course, enemies within or a siege. I doubt anyone has used it except lads testing its strength and wanting a swim. But you should know of it in the event you ever need such knowledge."

"Those caverns you mentioned, can one reach them from here?"

He nodded. "Some of them. The way down lies yonder, beyond the pit."

She shuddered as they passed the pit, the entrance to which was no more than a rough hole in the wall barely wide enough to admit a man's shoulders. The other side was deep and sheer. Once inside, the only way out would be if someone threw a rope down and the prisoner were still strong enough to climb out.

The door Rob opened was set into the rock wall. Before he pulled it open, she had seen no indication of its presence. It swung open silently and with apparent ease. In the meantime, Henry lit a torch. Handing a second, unlighted one to Rob, he led the way with his into the narrow passageway beyond the door.

The air there was dank and still, and Adela found nothing appealing about it. Before they had gone far, she was longing for fresh air and sunshine.

After a while, a second passageway split away to the right from the first one.

"What do you think, Henry?" Rob asked.

"I've not been down here in years, Rob. Did you explore at all when you were here before?"

Rob nodded. "I did take a look whilst I was recovering after Waldron's arrow got me," he said. "It was my first time alone inside this castle. So, although I was under Hugo's orders to do naught but rest, it seemed a good opportunity to see if I could learn more about my grandfather's time here."

"And?"

"Well, I learned nowt to say this is the area to which the map refers," he said. "But I didn't have the map, and I saw nowt to say this is *not* the right place, either."

"If the square drawn north—or what looks to be north—of the tangle of lines is supposed to be Hawthornden, we should follow the right-hand passage," Henry said. "That is, if we're meant to follow my half to start, and if the line that seems to lead to the sword is the one we want to follow. Most of the symbols seem randomly placed, but the sword stands out and it does mark the end of a line."

"Sakes, Henry," Rob said. "If neither of us knows what we're doing down here, we ought to study the map more closely before we start wandering about. We may need to await Hugo's return. He must know these tunnels better than we do."

"But if he knows them so well," Adela said thoughtfully, "would he not long since have found what you seek?"

"Aye, sure, if he'd had cause to look for it," Rob said. "But I'll wager whatever it is lies well hidden unless one knows the approximate place of concealment and how to recognize some sign of its presence."

"Aye," Henry agreed, smiling. "We'll have to tell you about when Mich—"

"Later," Rob said. "For now, we should return and plan more carefully how to go about this search. If we can find it quickly, well and good. Otherwise, we'll await Hugo's return."

"But what about Fife? If he comes . . . " Henry left the rest for them to fill in.

"We'll just have to deal with him if he does," Rob said. "But these passages twist and turn about on one another like a devilish maze. If we keep going without any clear understanding of our path, we could wander for days."

Just the thought sent a chill up Adela's spine, and she was glad when Henry agreed to return to the castle. Once there, he insisted that he and Rob each make a fair copy of the whole map.

"If we conceal the original bits as before and study the copies, we can cast them on the nearest fire if need be."

Rob agreed, and Adela left them in Hugo's chamber to attend to that task and went back to the bedchamber she shared with Rob to tidy herself.

Copying their maps was quickly done and proved useful, because there did seem to be a clear path to the sword on Rob's half from the square they were hoping was Hawthornden on Henry's half. Following that course underground by torchlight might prove to be another matter, though, Rob thought.

Bidding farewell to Henry with a promise to meet again on the morrow after both had studied their copies, Rob went in search of Adela and found her standing at the window in their bedchamber, looking out on the western view.

She turned when he entered and said, "Did you ask Henry to stay to supper?"

"Aye, but he wanted to get back, doubtless to put away his maps and tidy himself. I certainly need a wash," he added, moving to pour water into the basin.

"Tell me more about your grandfather," she said.

Willingly, he related several tales of his grandfather's raids on the English, the last of which made her laugh aloud. When she did, he hugged her, and matters progressed satisfactorily for them both from that point.

Afterward, he showed her the copy he had made of the map, and they studied it together but decided at last that, without clearer landmarks, the task of following such a map was going to prove nearly impossible.

The next day when Henry returned while they were breaking their fast in the great hall, Rob suggested warily that the two men might explore more ground together in less time than the three of them would together.

Adela's lips tightened but she said nothing. Henry, perusing the platters and bowls on the table, ignored the porridge and helped himself to a manchet loaf, a mug of ale, and one of three mutton cutlets on a platter. He, too, said not a word.

"What is it, lass?" Rob asked, knowing full well but hoping she would tell him it was nothing and urge them to go without her.

Instead, and without any regard for Henry's presence, she stood to face him and said angrily, "What *is* it? You know perfectly well what it is, my lord."

His own temper stirred. "*Do* I?"

"Aye, sure you do!"

Henry ate placidly, as if he were alone.

Knowing he had overreacted, Rob said more gently, "Adela, lass, this is—"

"Don't 'Adela, lass' me," she retorted. "One minute you pretend to trust me, the next you want only to keep your precious secrets from me. I vow, sir, I should find it easier if you told me nothing at all."

"Aye, well, mayhap I should," he snapped. "Recall that you are my wife and owe me obedience, madam. I'll decide what I will tell you and what I will not. In the meantime, since you yearn to set this castle to rights, you may start today."

"May I, indeed?" she demanded furiously, leaning toward him, hands on her hips. "Then you won't mind if I begin right here!" So saying, she snatched up the bowl still half full of porridge and heaved it at him, following even as he ducked the bowl by heaving a platter after it that still contained two cutlets.

"Here now," Henry protested. "That's very good mutton."

"Leave us, Henry," Rob ordered.

Henry raised his eyebrows. "Sakes, Rob, I own this place."

"Then we'll leave you to your food. I would speak privately with my wife."

"You do that," Henry advised. "Then find out what your people have done to this mutton. I like it very much."

"'Tis no more than rosemary cast on the fire as it cooks, sir," Adela said.

"Never mind that," Rob snarled. "You come with me."

Adela followed him from the hall, filled with remorse. He had provoked her, to be sure, but she had been wrong to throw things. She could only be grateful that neither the bowl nor the platter had struck him. He did have a splatter of porridge and a spot on his jerkin that looked like grease from the mutton, however.

Doubtless she deserved whatever he meant to do to her, and she was sure that this time, he would not be laughing when they reached their bedchamber.

He stopped on the landing outside its door and turned to face her. His expression was solemn. "You should not have done that."

"No, sir, but you must decide if you can trust me or not. As it is, I never know what to expect, and my anger has increased bit by bit until . . . "

"I know it is difficult," he said when she paused. "But some matters are more important than others, more secret, and the trouble is that they all connect in some way or other. It is like pulling a thread and having the whole garment unravel."

"You say that, but Henry clearly thinks I should know more than I do."

"I am not Henry. And I don't like things thrown at my head."

"I *am* sorry for that," she said sincerely. "I did not know I would throw those things until I did. Truly, I have done such a thing only once before in my life, and I am *not* proud of it. It was a dreadful thing to have done."

He put a hand to her shoulder and pulled her closer,

kissing her lightly on the lips. Then he said, "I'll forgive you, I expect, but don't do it again."

Relieved, she said, "Then I may go with you?"

"Nay, sweetheart, this time we'll go alone. We don't know what we'll find, and I'll worry less about you if you are here, safe. I'll tell you if we find anything."

Knowing he was punishing her and aware that she deserved punishment, she nodded. She could do nothing in any event to change his mind.

Chapter 17

For two days Rob and Henry explored together while Adela organized the servants and began a thorough cleaning of the castle from top to bottom. She also persuaded Archie Tayt to help her practice the skills Rob had taught her, and show her how to hold her new dirk and wield it to some effect. Rob's attitude was affable, but his mind was on the search, and she decided that if she wanted him to trust her, she had to trust him to keep his word if they found anything.

But at the end of the second day, with still no sign of riders from Edinburgh or anything resembling a sword in the caverns beneath the castle, and with Henry's ship returning to Leith in two days to fetch him, the men had reached an impasse.

"I can give it one more day," Henry said as they took supper with Adela at the high table. "But if we don't find it, Rob, you'll have to wait for Hugo."

Rob agreed, and later after Henry had ridden back to

Roslin, he and Adela went upstairs to their bedchamber. As they were preparing for bed, she said, "Are you still angry with me?"

"Nay, sweetheart. We both gave way to our tempers."

"Then may I make a copy of your map to study for myself?"

He hesitated, doubting she would see anything that he and Henry had missed.

"Sakes, do you think I'd let anything happen to it? I loathe secrets, sir, but I'd never betray one of yours."

"I know," he said. *Not willingly, at all events.* "You are certainly as capable as I am of finding a fire to throw it on if anyone should try to take it from you."

Still reluctant, despite knowing that she was as unlikely as Henry, Michael, or Hugo to betray him, he fetched paper, quill, and ink for her and watched as she carefully reproduced the fair copy he had made.

She was nearly finished when she said, "What is this bit here, sir? I can't make out your drawing."

He looked. "I remember those odd lines. I suspected they were naught but a flaw in the vellum, but they are on my half of the map. Let's have another look."

Moments later, she said, "I don't think that's a flaw. Might it be a waterfall?"

He frowned, his gaze fixed on three obscure wavy lines on his original half-map. "The ink is faded," he said. "Moreover, the grain in the vellum may have deceived me, but I think you may be right."

"Are there any waterfalls in the caves under Hawthornden?"

He shook his head. "Not any that I know about. But several falls spill into the glen, and I'm certain that entrances to other caves exist, too. One thing has plagued me about this the whole time we've been searching."

"What?"

"The size . . . " He grimaced, then gave his head a shake to clear it. *But it just showed how easily one could slip.* "I own, lass, I still don't want to tell you all that I've been thinking," he admitted. "I'd like to say I've good reason for that other than my dislike of sharing secrets, but I'll admit that enters into it."

She sighed. "You said 'the size,' so I expect you meant the size of the object you think the map may lead us to is of a size that makes it unlikely to be in the caverns we've seen. Why won't you just tell me what you think it is?"

"Because I'm likely wrong," he said. "I may have taken details heard over a period of years and added a childish hope to come to my conclusion. If that is what happened, I'll look a proper dafty, and the Sinclairs will never let me forget it. I've told you some of it. Perhaps if I tell you more, you'll come to the same conclusion."

"You haven't told me about the treasure," she said. "What is it, exactly, and where did it come from?"

"Get into bed," he said, kissing her cheek. "I'll put out the other candles."

Leaving one lighted taper on the stand by the bed, he climbed in beside her, plumped pillows behind them both, then lay back, slipping his good arm around her.

⌒

Adela waited patiently as he settled himself, but then he hesitated again until her impatience stirred and she wanted to urge him to get on with it. She held her tongue, though, and at last he said, "Have you heard of the Knights Templar?"

"Aye, sure," she said, striving to gather her wits. "They existed during the Crusades, did they not? They protected pilgrims traveling to the Holy Land, and the King of Jerusalem housed them in his own palace over King Solomon's temple. My aunt Euphemia used to tell us stories about them when I was small. But what have Templars to do with you or with the treasure that Waldron sought?"

"The treasure belongs to the Templars. The whole story is too long to tell tonight, but for two hundred years they were the world's bankers. They guarded valuable items and lent money to nobles and heads of state. In 1307, King Philip of France, having borrowed vast sums from them, decided he did not want to repay what he owed. In a single night's raid, he arrested many Templars in France and tried to seize their Paris treasury. But most of the Templars escaped, taking all their ships and the treasure with them. At least a portion of that treasure came here to Scotland."

"But that was long ago," she said. "What is your part in this tale?"

"My training is that of a Scottish Knight Templar," Rob said. "Like my grandfather and great-grandfather before me—and like Hugo, Michael, and Henry, too. Sithee, the Sinclairs were among the guardians of the treasure from the outset."

"Was your father not a Templar as well, then?"

"He was not suited to the life, my grandfather said. Moreover, my father had no brothers to inherit if aught happened to him. Protecting our heritage and Lestalric was more important, Grandfather said. My brother Will did not please him either," Rob added. "Will was boastful and lazy. My grandfather said my father fed Will's pride but not his brain, with unhappy result."

"But your grandfather was proud of you," Adela said.

Dryly, he said, "I have my faults, too, as you will agree. As to what my grandfather thought . . . Sithee, I was for training with the Douglas. He is the finest commander of our time and more powerful in many ways than the King. So when Grandfather told me I was to go to Dunclathy instead, I was disappointed. He explained what an honor it was to go and said I would learn secrets I must never tell. He also said he'd entrust me with one secret that only he and one other knew."

"He told you about the map."

"Not the map, only that he had hidden something important for me to find one day. He gave me a strong hint where to look for it and promised to explain more at a later time. Only that time never came, because he died soon after I left for Dunclathy. I believed when I left home that he'd put it off because I'd taunted Will, and I wondered for a long time afterward if I'd ever know what it was."

"You taunted your older brother?"

"Aye, I told him I was doing something he'd never be allowed to do and that I knew something he'd never know. It wasn't much, I thought, just words flung in anger, but we got into a fight. My father stopped it. Then he told my grandfather what I'd said, and my grandfather soon had the whole tale out of me."

"Was he angry?"

Rob winced. "He'd never raised a hand to me before then, but he flogged me till I feared I'd have no skin left and told me that things said in confidence were not playthings to be flung in anger, that if he was ever to trust me further, I'd have to prove myself worthy. I swore to him I'd never disappoint him again, but he died before I could win back his trust. I made a second vow then that I'd strive never to act again in any way that would disappoint him."

"I see," Adela said. "That does explain your reluctance to part with secrets. You told me before that the day you left for good your father demanded information that you could not give him. Was that what it was?"

"Aye," he said.

"And then your brother really angered you. I do understand that. No one can make me angrier than my sisters can—except you, perhaps," she added thoughtfully.

He chuckled, pulling her closer. "They both angered me, sweetheart, but the reason won't please you. Art sure you want to know?"

She sighed, remembering. "Lady Ellen."

"Aye, I'd made no secret of my interest in her, and my father learned of it. When I returned home that day, I thought he'd be proud of me for earning my spurs, but he demanded to know what I'd meant by those taunts I'd flung at Will. He asked what secrets my grandfather had told me. I'd never mentioned that he'd told me anything, but my father guessed somehow that he had. He wanted to know them so badly that, although Douglas had already accepted Will to be Ellen's husband, my father suggested that he'd ask him to take me instead. All I had to do was to share my secret with him so he could offer it to Douglas in exchange for Ellen."

Aching for what he must have felt at such betrayal,

she said only, "Did your father know that your grandfather had flogged you for that taunt?"

"Aye," he said. "Oh, I see where your thoughts led you. Very likely you're right, too. If that flogging impressed me, it must have impressed my father, too. And he may have felt as resentful as Will did, or worse. He was Sir Walter's only son, after all. I admit, I didn't give much thought to his feelings."

"Even so," she said, "I cannot imagine, from what you've told me, just what it is that you think you know about what the map may reveal. Should I know more about the Templars and their treasure, or more about your grandfather?"

"Since you ken fine that I'd liefer say no more about either, I'll not gnaw that bone again. Most likely, all you need know is that the conversation with my father took place shortly before the present King was crowned. Father seemed to think I might know something that could add to the splendor of that occasion."

Adela nibbled her lower lip thoughtfully, then looked at him, waiting until he turned to meet her gaze. Then she said quietly, "Only one object leaps to mind that both relates to a coronation and might be secretly hidden."

"Aye," Rob said. "Bear in mind, sweetheart, that I've no knowledge of what stirred my father to think I might know aught of such, and no reason other than his questions for my conclusion. Doubtless 'tis nobbut more bairn's yearning."

"Was your father an imaginative man?"

"Nay, but rumors have run through the kingdom for the better part of a century, since the Coronation Stone got carted off to London with Edward I."

She nodded, relieved to know they were thinking the same thing. "My aunt said she could never believe loyal Scots would allow such a thing to happen, that surely someone had done something to stop it, especially as they'd been warned he meant to take it. But he did take it, she said, and then afterward he still razed Scone Abbey to the ground."

"Aye," he said. "But he razed it two years later, and they say he did it because he'd learned that the stone he had taken was not the true Stone of Destiny."

"Yet the English still claim to have the real one."

"Aye, and mayhap they do." He snuggled closer. "But this is all imagining, lass. We'll not know the truth unless we find where that map leads. I'll ride to Roslin early and tell Henry and Michael what we think about that odd symbol. If the scale of the map means anything, and if you are right about the waterfall, it cannot be far away, because it must lie somewhere between here and Roslin."

"I want to go with you."

"Aye, I ken fine that you do, but I want you to stay here."

"But—"

"Hear me before you eat me, lass. I agree that you deserve to be with us when we find it, and I give you my word, if we find any opening near a waterfall, we'll come to fetch you. But I don't want to have to fret about your safety if Fife comes upon us whilst we're looking. If he comes here, the lads can bar the gates and tell him to seek me at Roslin. In any event, if he shows his face hereabouts, we'll have warning and come back straightaway."

"Then why can I not go with you and come back with you?"

"Don't argue with me, sweetheart," he murmured, kissing her forehead and then the tip of her nose. "I don't want to fratch with you tonight."

His hands were moving over her body, and although she knew he was learning how easily he could arouse her and thus divert her, she had no objection.

She could always fight with him later.

⁓

They made love and talked of other things, made love again, talked again briefly, and then a comfortable silence fell for a time before Rob thought of something else to say to her. But as he opened his mouth, he realized that the pattern of her breathing had changed to the deep, even rhythm of sleep.

He lay there, listening to her breathe and thinking how pleasant it was to have someone he could talk to, even argue with, as easily as he did with Hugo and Michael but about things he would never discuss with either man. He barely remembered his mother, and he had no sisters, so he had always assumed that he knew little about women. Heaven knew, Countess Isabella terrified him.

He had met Hugo's three sisters and thought Eliza, the eldest, much like Isabella in temperament but haughtier. He liked the younger ones well enough, but had rarely spoken to them. The lady Sorcha amused him because, although she clearly loved Hugo with all her heart, she treated him as if he were her own size instead of twice as large and twice as temperamental.

And Hugo, who could be as fierce and stern as anyone Rob had ever known, regarded his wife one moment as he might a precious jewel, and the next with much the same mixed fear, astonishment, and exasperation that one might accord a wild, unpredictable creature from the land of myths.

The lady Isobel, Sir Michael's wife, was cheerful and pleasant, and Rob liked her very much, but he could never think of anything to say to her. And Lady Sidony was practically unknown to him. But Adela was different from all of them.

He had been as surprised as anyone when he had declared that he wanted to marry her. But the words had spilled forth. And once said, they had sounded natural and right. The ceremony, too, had been right, and he had felt no regrets since. As he lay there, holding her, he felt more contented than he could recall ever feeling before. Until he had met her, contentment had been something other people talked about, not something Rob Logan even understood. Now he thought he could.

But Adela's difference, whatever it was that set her apart from everyone else, was something he could not identify. Whatever it was, it had made him feel at ease with her from the outset, as if he had known her all his life. Possible reasons teased him, but none explained what he felt for her.

One minute he was lying with her in his arms, and in what seemed the very next, dawn's gray light awakened him. Adela lay curled beside him, one fist under her chin, a smile playing on her lips. No nightmare had wakened her for three nights now, but he doubted she had seen the last of them. Such things took time, he knew, but he could keep her safe. And in safety she would find peace again.

Her lips twitched, and he wondered what she was

dreaming. Whatever it was, she was enjoying it, so he watched silently, unwilling to disturb her. When the tip of her tongue appeared between her lips, his body stirred, and he wished she would waken. As the wish formed in his mind, her eyes opened and she smiled.

"Good morning," she murmured.

Needing no further invitation, he replied with a kiss, and matters progressed quickly until he had slaked his thirst for her. Afterward, he dressed quickly and bade her farewell, repeating his promise to fetch her if they found an opening by a waterfall. Taking only a fresh manchet from the kitchen to munch as he rode, knowing there would be food aplenty at Roslin, he was soon on his way.

As expected, he found Henry and Michael up and at the table. Accepting an invitation to join them, he made a good meal but lost no time in letting them know that he had things to discuss. Accordingly, they soon adjourned to the solar.

"Pull up that table yonder, Michael," Rob said. "I want to show you both something. Henry, do you have your fair copy of the whole map?"

"Aye," Henry said, extracting it from his doublet as Michael dragged the table into place and they each found stools. Michael and Rob sat facing each other with Henry on Rob's right between them.

When Henry opened his map, Rob saw that he had not copied the three lines that had caught Adela's attention.

"Look here," he said, pointing to them on his own fair copy. "What do you think that might be?"

Henry peered at it. "I remember that. I thought it was a flaw in the vellum, but I suppose it could be some sort of symbol."

"Adela thinks it might be a waterfall," Rob said.

"It's on your half," Henry said.

"I brought my original, too," Rob said, bending to take off his boot. He laid his map on the table by Henry's fair copy and watched as the other two examined them.

Michael turned Rob's original half toward himself, and Henry turned the fair copy the same way, saying he wanted to be sure he had missed nothing else. Rob glanced from one to the other, and felt a sudden prickling sensation.

His first, instinctive reaction was to say nothing, to think more, to be sure, and then perhaps to look into this new possibility by himself before sharing it.

Michael said quietly, "What is it, Rob? You've seen something."

Feeling a flush of heat in his cheeks, he realized that both men were watching him and that neither looked annoyed. Henry seemed amused.

"I'm not certain," he said. "But turn that bit of my original map so that it lies exactly lengthwise between us, Michael, with the cut side to your left."

"What are you seeing?" Henry demanded, frowning at the map.

Rob said, "Because of the symbol pointing north on your bit, we've assumed that you had the top half, Henry, and I the lower half."

"Aye, sure, but that much is obvious."

"What if the north symbol means nowt? What if the sword points north?"

The other two stared at him for a long moment before both shifted their eyes to the map. Michael saw it first. "If that is so, the map is cut along the river Esk, and not alongside the castle as we thought. Do the caverns extend east across the river?"

"Perhaps," Rob said. "But recall Adela's waterfall . . . here." He pointed. "Note the only line approaching it begins on my half of the map and extends only as far as those three small wavy lines before it hooks right, to the north. I don't think the division itself marks the river. The river is the line we first thought was the route to the sword. See how it curves in here, just south of the castle?"

"By the Rood, I think you're right," Henry said. "Moreover, I think I know where that might be. It is not so much a waterfall, more of a trickle most of the time, but the cliff has eroded there into what amounts to a wee side glen now."

"I know the place," Rob said. "But I've never seen a waterfall there."

"You can see it after a heavy snowfall and a fast thaw," Henry said. "But come with me now. I'll show you."

"Are you going to come, too, Michael?" Rob asked.

"Nay, I've things to do here today, and I promised my lass I'd spend time with her. I know that place, though. I doubt it can be what you seek, Rob."

"We won't know until we look," Henry said.

Rob's heart was pounding. Despite Michael's pessimism, he felt sure that Henry was right. The pieces seemed to be falling into place at last.

⌒

Throughout the morning, Adela busied herself with chores. Archie Tayt had found two young women to help her, and Rob had told her to call in as many gillies and men-at-arms as she needed. So with Archie to act as her chief assistant, she was getting on famously.

During the previous two days, while Rob and Henry had explored the caves beneath the castle, she and her helpers had tidied the upper floors and raked all the old rushes from the hall. Now she was replacing them. The two maidservants had mixed rosemary and other herbs with clean, dry rushes collected from tenants whose business it was to dry them in the rafters of their crofts or cottages, and two gillies were distributing them carefully from threshold to threshold.

"Don't pile those too high," Adela warned one lad who was raking them into place. "We don't want straw spilling over the threshold onto the stairs."

"Aye, mistress." But even as he spoke, he moved away from the doorway, and Archie hurried in, his pleasant features creased in a heavy frown.

"Mistress, there be dunamany horsemen coming, five score at least."

"A hundred men? From what direction?"

"North," he said. "They be riding fast and nearly upon us."

"But who can they be?" Even as she asked the question, she knew it must be the Earl of Fife. Other than the Sinclairs, the Earl of Douglas or—and most unlikely—the King himself, few noblemen rode with such large tails.

"Tell them to bar the gates, Archie," she said quickly, recalling Rob's instructions. "If the riders stop here, have our men say that Sir Robert has ridden to Roslin and they should seek him there."

"Aye, m'lady, I'll tell them," he said, turning on his heel and hurrying away.

Noting that all work in the hall had stopped and that her four helpers were regarding her nervously, Adela said, "Back to work, all of you. I mean to finish our cleaning today so we can move on to other tasks I have in mind to furbish this place up. When Sir Hugo and his lady return, I want the results to make them stare."

Three turned back to their work, but one lad hesitated, looking more nervous than before.

"What is it?" she asked.

"What if they get in?" he asked.

She raised her chin. "If they do, we will greet them with civility and welcome them to Hawthornden in Prince Henry's name, of course. We are not barbarians here, whatever they may be."

He nodded and returned to his raking. Although she was glad that her words seemed to give him more confidence, they had done nothing to ease her own concerns. It was all very well for Rob to say he would hear in good time if Fife were on the move, and would return at once. But as she had no idea where he and Henry were and realized they could be wandering around in tunnels and passageways underground, his words brought no comfort to her now.

She told herself she had no cause to worry, because the men had barred the gates and Fife would ride on to Roslin where the Sinclairs would deal with him. But her confidence had evaporated. The waiting would be easier, she thought, if she could just see what was happening outside the wall.

Remembering Rob saying that one should know one's own ground, she wished she had taken time to explore the ramparts more carefully. Doubtless there was a vantage point there from which one could overlook the main entrance.

On that thought, she gathered her skirts and began to hurry to the stairway, but as she reached it, the main door on the landing below banged open and running feet came up the stairs. Recognizing steps of one man, she stopped to wait for him.

"M'lady," the gasping lad said, "Archie Tayt did say to tell ye it be me lord o' Fife, but he's no riding wi' just his own banner, mistress. Them devils be riding under the royal banner, Archie says."

"I don't care what flags they wave," Adela snapped. "Don't let them in."

"Aye, sure, but that makes for a wee difficulty, Archie says. It be treason, he says, to defy a royal command."

"But surely his grace the King has not ridden here from Edinburgh," Adela said. "And it cannot be a royal command unless he is with them."

"D'ye think Archie should tell that to the Earl o' Fife, m'lady? The earl thinks he *is* King, Archie says, and he wouldna hesitate to level the charge against Prince Henry, all his commanders, and every man wha' obeys them. Archie says—"

"Tell them to admit the earl if he insists on it," Adela interjected.

She was thoroughly sick of hearing what Archie had said, but they had underestimated Fife and she could do nothing about that now.

Even if Hawthornden's gates were strong enough to withstand determined effort to breach them, she dared not put Henry or Rob in the path of a charge of treason. Not when she was certain that Fife would delight in hanging Rob, even if he lacked enough courage to hang Henry.

"We need not admit them all," she added. "Tell Archie Tayt that if the earl insists on seeing for himself that Sir Robert is absent, he may do so, but that his lady is here alone and would prefer that most of his men remain outside the gate."

"Sakes, mistress," the lad said, his eyes widening. "D'ye think ye should—"

"Go," she said, pointing back down the stairs. "And hurry!"

But as he obeyed her, she heard the familiar sounds of arriving horsemen—hoofbeats, male voices, and the squeak and clink of harness—and she knew it was too late to stop Fife had she tried. One hundred riders could not possibly all fit in the courtyard, but they would easily prevent the gates from being shut.

Recalling Rob's orders to avoid any dangerous confrontation that she could avoid, her first inclination was to turn and run. But one look at the four frightened faces of her helpers dissuaded her.

"All of you, leave the hall at once," she said. "If you know a way to leave the castle without meeting those riders, do so."

No one stirred, and she realized they probably knew nothing about the sally port and that even if they did, most if not all four would be afraid to use it.

"Just go upstairs," she said. "I will speak to his lordship when he comes."

"M'lady, ye shouldna do that," the same lad who had spoken up earlier said. "The Earl o' Fife be a gey wicked man, they say."

"Don't argue with me. Just go."

Mentally sorting through the options she had, she could think of only one that might afford her any chance to escape.

Hearing boots on the stone steps, she straightened her shoulders, drew a deep breath to steady her nerves, and prepared to act the proper hostess.

The first person up the stairs was Fife himself, his hand on the hilt of his sword, the weapon half out of its scabbard.

"Faith, my lord, you've no need of weapons here," she said, curtsying. "Did our people not inform you that Lestalric is at Roslin today?"

His gaze swept the hall before narrowing and coming to rest on her. Smoothly and without so much as a polite nod, he said, "Art here alone, lass?"

The wave of fear and nausea that surged through her then told her that, whether she had thought so at the time or not, her abduction had indeed taught her to recognize evil when she was in its presence. Standing by Fife, she knew she might well be in the presence of the devil himself.

"Lady Adela?"

Forcing her gaze from the earl, she saw that he had not come alone.

The chevalier de Gredin, his smile as charming as ever and showing no sign of injury, stepped across the threshold into the hall.

Chapter 18

R ob stood beside Henry and looked skeptically up the steep north slope of what at best he'd have defined as a lushly verdant, narrow, quarter-mile slice into the west bank of the river North Esk's gorge. From the top of the glen's innermost point spilled what Henry insisted must be Adela's waterfall, if indeed the symbol she had pointed out was meant to be one.

"It is still spring, Henry," Rob protested. "If this thin rivulet is as heavy as it gets, I don't see how—"

"Don't scoff," Henry said. "I have seen it tumbling, sending froth and spray into the air. And, more to the point, this flow never dries up. That of any other likely nearby stream does. Just look at those great slabs of rock yonder, too. If I wanted to conceal a cavern entrance . . ."

Rob saw what he meant. The three slabs, all taller than he and Henry, stood upright, looking at first glance as if precariously balanced. But closer examination revealed that all three stood solidly unmovable. They would need the shovels and other equipment they'd brought.

They had left the horses on the narrow fishermen's track along the west bank of the river, and had walked into the trackless glen, following its barely noticeable watercourse. Had Henry not known where to go, Rob doubted he would have found the place for days. Trees near its opening formed a canopy thick enough to obscure the size and depth of the glen, and dense shrubbery clustered at the base of the trees. Thus, the whole looked and smelled like an ordinary patch of damp, herbal-scented woodland. The western side of the gorge was not as steep or as sheer as the eastern side, but it was still impressively precipitous.

As Rob stood frowning at the three rock slabs, Henry chuckled. "Sakes," he said, "did you expect them to topple at your touch? If your grandfather helped hide something here, it was forty to forty-five years ago, when he and his friends were capering about, harrying unsuspecting English invaders. Anything so easily tipped would be lying flat by now, the hiding place revealed to anyone who looked here."

"Aye," Rob said absently, still eyeing the rocks speculatively.

"I did not ask before what you think lies hidden here, knowing how you feel about secrets," Henry said. "But unless you think you can send me away if we do find an opening here, you may as well confide your thoughts to me now."

Rob had realized that he must do so and had been expecting the request if not an outright command. Nevertheless, still fearing his suspicion was wishful thinking, he told Henry only what he had told Adela about the long-ago confrontation at Lestalric. But Henry was as quick as she had been to follow his thinking.

"Sakes," he exclaimed, "you cannot believe the Stone has been sitting here ever since Edward I invaded Scotland!"

"Nay, but I do think they might have moved it here later," Rob said. "The likeliest time would have been during the 1335 invasion, when they realized Edward's grandson meant to try again to conquer Scotland and find the real Stone."

"So you believe Edward I knew he had the wrong one."

"Aye," Rob said. "Why return and take Scone Abbey apart if he did not? Doubtless loyalists expected more such depredations when Edward III came."

"Would it not have been foolish to move the Stone right into his path?"

"'Twas scarcely in his path here in the gorge," Rob protested. "The road to Edinburgh from the Borders lies miles east of here, through Selkirk."

"But just to bring the Stone south of the Firth would have been foolish."

"Without knowing the circumstances, who can judge anything as foolish?"

While they continued this mild debate, Rob began examining the edges of the three slabs closely, brushing dirt away from the central stone that seemed to hold the others in place. Dirt clogged all the crevices, and plants had taken root.

"I'll fetch the shovels," he said.

"I'll go with you, because we might as well bring the

torches and ropes, too," Henry said. "We may need them, and I'd as lief no curious fisherman wonder why our ponies carry shovels and torch sticks, be they ever so well disguised."

Since the only disguise was plain canvas wrapping, Rob agreed that the sooner the implements were out of sight, the better. Silently, he followed Henry along the narrow, barely trickling stream bed they had used before. Both men wore daggers and carried their swords in scabbards on belts slung across their backs.

A quarter-hour later they returned, and ten minutes after that, Rob said, "Look here, Henry. I think this must be a hand grip of some sort along this side."

Making an effort to appear undisturbed by the calculating way the Earl of Fife looked at her, Adela said in surprise to de Gredin, "Did we not hear that you had suffered grievous injury, sir?"

"In troth, my lady, I thought myself sped to God's waiting arms," he said.

"He's fortunate to have recovered quickly," Fife said. "Where is Lestalric?"

"Surely, the men on the gate told you he is at Roslin, my lord."

"They said as much, to be sure. But if you ken the news from Edinburgh, I'll wager he does, too. He must know he will have to answer for his crime."

"What crime?"

"Sakes, woman, you must know he's the one who attacked de Gredin, doubtless out of jealousy for his attentions to you, and your unseemly flirtation with him. I fear you'll find that women of your ilk are not welcome in the royal burgh."

"Women of my ilk?"

Hearing the chill in her voice, she reminded herself to tread lightly. She had strapped her new dirk in its sheath to her leg, but it could not help her against Fife. Striving for calm, she said, "I know not what you mean by such words, sir."

He sneered. "Do you not? How, then, do you come to be living here with Lestalric? Or am I mistaken, and does some other lady—an older kinswoman of yours, perhaps—reside here with the two of you?"

He terrified her, yet she could still think clearly. It occurred to her as she was about to tell him she and Rob had married that it might be wiser to affect blank, innocent astonishment instead, especially with de Gredin there. If the chevalier cared for her, he might prove more useful if he did not learn his cause was hopeless.

So, instead of uttering the words that sprang to her lips, she widened her eyes and said, "No other female is here save a pair of maidservants, my lord. Do you think I require a chaperone whilst in *your* presence?"

Hearing a hastily muffled sound, she suspected she had tickled de Gredin's sense of humor but hoped he would not display it to the earl. She doubted that Fife had a sense of humor.

He said, "Don't be impertinent, lass. When do you expect Lestalric's return?"

"Mercy, it is not for me to expect him, sir. He will return when he returns and no earlier. He may arrive at any moment, but if you want to see him sooner, you should ride toward Roslin and meet him on the way."

"I warrant we'll see him soon enough," Fife said. "Meantime, I must ask you to ride back to town with us."

A chill shot up her spine, but she managed to retain the blank look, hoping he would think her witless. "I . . . I do not understand, sir. Why should I ride anywhere with you? Indeed, how can you expect such a thing?"

"Do you forget so quickly, lass, the accusations laid against you? You ought to remember them, particularly as your dear Lestalric even suggested he might consider marrying you because of them. As if a wedding could save you," he added snidely. "That he later realized he had no need to sacrifice himself to enjoy your evident charms must have been a grave disappointment."

"I do not understand what you are saying," Adela said, although she did indeed understand and burned with anger at the insult. But she had learned much about concealing her feelings during years of managing her father's household, and even more during her abduction. Although she hid her anger, she knew she could not continue to pretend she did not know he thought them as yet unmarried.

"What do you not understand?" he asked with another sneer.

With calm civility, she said, "I don't understand how you came to think that Sir Robert and I did not marry."

For the first time since his entrance, he hesitated. But then his eyes narrowed and he said, "Don't try to cozen me, lass. Lestalric would never be so foolish as to wed a woman about to hang for murder."

A scream of fury welled up in her but she stifled it

ruthlessly to say, "Again you mistake me for another sort of woman, sir. I have killed no one."

"Do you deny that Lord Ardelve died of poisoning?"

"I do not know if he was poisoned or not," she said honestly. "He collapsed against Countess Isabella after sipping wine. He and I were both in plain view of the entire company from the time we entered the hall. I gave him naught, nor poured his wine. Gillies served us."

"What about the time you spent with him in the ladies' solar, alone?"

"Faith, my lord," she said, nettled and not caring if he detected her displeasure now. "Did you set spies to watch me my whole wedding day?"

"Don't challenge me. I set no spies, but I did hear from those who were there that they saw you go into the solar with him and stay for some time. They likewise reported that you showed none of the joy of a bride when you returned. As Ardelve likewise remained stoic, the rumors of his anger over the unfortunate result of your abduction must be true."

"I fear your informants are merely evil-minded men, sir."

"Nonetheless, you will come with us now for questioning. Lestalric can follow as he will and answer to the King's justice when he does."

"Faith, if you believe we never married, what makes you think he'll follow?"

"I don't care if he does. I can hang him and forfeit his so-called claim to the Lestalric barony without having to prove that he conspired with you in Ardelve's murder or that he tried to kill de Gredin. The fact is that I mean to question you, Lady Adela, most thoroughly, about several subjects.

Ardelve is the least of them. And to that end, by the King's royal command, I declare that you are under arrest."

Another chill flew up her spine, and she knew she dared not let herself guess what his methods of thoroughly questioning a woman might entail. Straightening her shoulders and taking a measure of reassurance from the dirk under her skirts, but more from her own unusual lack of budding panic, she said, "If you act at the King's command, sir, I shall naturally obey. Doubtless, before we depart, you will let me fetch my cloak . . . and visit the . . . the . . . "

Satisfied to feel heat in her cheeks and know she was blushing, she paused.

Fife frowned, but when de Gredin said with a touch of impatience, "*Mon Dieu*, my lord, if you desire me to accompany her . . . "

Fife shook his head. "I have a hundred men at the gate, lass, so there is no way for you to escape. You would be unwise, nonetheless, to keep me waiting."

"Thank you, my lord. One appreciates your chivalry," she said with the same wide-eyed look she had assumed before.

He nodded regally and stood aside to let her pass him and go up the stairs.

As soon as she rounded the first corner, she picked up her skirts and ran lightly to the next floor, then across it as fast as she could go, to the narrow service stairs in the northwest corner. From there, she hurried down to the lowest level.

Racing to the sally port, she unbarred it and heaved it open. Ignoring the wave of dizziness that struck when she looked out, she struggled to lift the heavy coil of rope from its place on the wall and, moving carefully but listening for any sound on the stairs, she put it on the floor and shoved it out the door.

Standing again, she held onto the door frame and looked out to see that the rope easily reached the river. But the water was flowing swiftly, its strong current pulling the rope end with it. If she lost her grip and fell, she would be swept along in that current. At the thought, the dizziness struck again in a wave that made her grip the door frame harder. Shutting her eyes to the view, she drew a long, deep breath and stepped back to recover her equilibrium.

Easing her way back without looking down, she gripped the rope in her right hand, trying to imagine stepping out and climbing—or, more likely, sliding—down to the river. Doubtless, its water was still nearly as icy cold as in winter.

If by a miracle she succeeded, she would be no more than a fish on the end of a line for Fife to pull up when he looked out and saw her. The notion of letting go and trying to swim out of that roiling current terrified her.

No matter how firmly she reminded herself that she could swim, or told herself that she could do it, the rope was rough and uncomfortable to hold. She had never swum with her clothes on, and she was as certain as she could be that she was not strong enough to reach either shore. She would drown, but she had to try.

Henry having proved skeptical to the notion that Rob had found any handle, the two men labored to clear the three tall rock slabs of accumulated earth and plant life. At last, Rob dug in his shovel into the dirt in front of the central one to see how far they would have to dig to clear away all the dirt in front of the slab. Less than four inches down, its base came into sight, surprisingly straight across.

He looked at Henry and silently raised his eyebrows.

"Sakes," Henry said, stepping closer and bending with his hands on his knees to peer more closely at it. "That looks like masonry underneath it."

Rob nodded. "I think we've found what we were seeking."

"Before we shout our triumph, let's see if we can move that thing."

"I told Adela I'd fetch her if we found an entrance near the waterfall."

"Aye, sure, but we'd best keep working until we know we've found that entrance," Henry said. "Recall that I must meet my ship tomorrow. I'm damned if I'll go without knowing what lies here, so at least, let's find out if we can move that rock before we fetch your lass."

"Aye, sure," Rob agreed. "In any event, with the water running so high and so fast, we'll have to go back to the bridge to cross. A pity, too, since we're nobbut minutes away if we could just swim the horses across."

Henry picked up his shovel and the two cleared the rest of the dirt from the base of the slab. Then, they examined Rob's hand grip on the right side again.

He pulled on it hard with both hands, noting that the exercise had stirred the pain in his left shoulder to life again.

"Mayhap it has a hidden latch like the ones in the cavern," Henry said.

Rob was already searching with his fingertips down that side. At the bottom, where they had cleared the dirt from the base, some still concealed the lowest couple of inches on the side. Feeling his way, using his fingers to dig away the dirt, he said, "I can feel a stone wedge here, I think, like the wooden one at Lestalric."

Taking his dirk from its sheath, he scraped still clinging dirt from the edge of the slab until he had cleared the wedge and was able to remove it.

Rising, he grabbed the edge of the stone again and pulled.

Henry moved next to him to help. "It's moving," he said.

"Wait," Rob said. "Someone's coming!"

Hastily, they pushed the slab back and began kicking dirt in front of it, only to stop when they heard Michael's voice, calling Rob's name.

"Here," Rob shouted over the noise of the river, adding anxiously when Michael came into view, "What's amiss?"

"Fife," Michael said curtly. "My lads tell me he's at Hawthornden by now, with a fighting tail of at least a hundred men."

"I told them to send him to Roslin if he came," Rob said.

"Aye, well, he's had plenty of time to ride there if he was going to, but I'd have heard from others if he had been headed our way. Henry, your people in Edinburgh must have missed his departure. A pair of my own lads saw him a mile east of Polton village, making for Hawthornden, and rode to warn me."

"Sakes, my men should have ridden hard to tell us if he rode anywhere south of Edinburgh," Henry said angrily.

"Don't blame them until we learn that he did not head elsewhere first," Michael said. "He's a sly one, is Fife. He would soon realize it if your lads were trying to follow him everywhere he went."

Henry still frowned, but Rob said urgently, "We must go. Adela is at Hawthornden, and if Fife did not ride on to Roslin, she's in great danger."

"Aye," Michael agreed as the three gathered up the tools and hurried to the horses. "I ordered our lads to assemble at Roslin. They'll be ready when I return."

"How many?" Henry demanded tersely.

"Nearly four score at the castle," Michael said. "I sent men out to collect more and told them to meet us on the way or to follow as soon as they can."

Rob had a sudden, chilling thought. "We showed Adela the sally port."

"No lass would try to escape that way," Henry said bluntly. "Sakes, she would never escape Fife's clutches if he's managed to get inside the castle."

"A Macleod lass might do both," Michael said with the voice of experience.

Rob nodded. "Adela may try, but I doubt she can hold onto that rope. It's thick and rough. Her hands are small and, I think, too delicate to grip it hard enough. Moreover, I don't even know if she can swim. But if she can—"

"Aye," Michael said. "She might think she has no choice."

"Henry, you come with me," Rob said when they

reached the horses. "Michael, collect your men and ride to Hawthornden as fast as you can. Do all you can to suggest a greater force than you have, because you've got to divert Fife's attention in case she's still inside with him when you get there."

"What will you and Henry do?"

"We're going to find my lass if she's fallen in the river," Rob said, his gut clenching as he said the words. "If we see no sign that she made it to the sally port, we'll get to the top of the cliff any way we can. Don't forget to bring those ropes, Henry," he added when he saw him pushing their shovels, torches, and the canvas wrappings under a bush. "We may need them."

The two had not gone far before Henry said, "How the devil are we going to cross this river and get to the top in time to help Michael or anything else?"

"Sakes, Henry, I don't know. But if Adela uses that rope, she won't be able to hang onto it in that swift current. And she can't make landfall on the east side of the river because of those sheer cliffs. Our only hope is if the water sweeps her right onto the west bank. If it does that, she'll be well-nigh drowned and freezing. So, hurry!"

⟋⟍

Adela stepped to the open sally port again, hoping her resolve would stiffen more when she grew more accustomed to how far below her the river was.

As she fought another wave of dizziness at just the thought of looking down, she heard running footsteps on the stairs. Knowing it would be suicidal to leap out or try to hold onto the thick rope and climb down it with any speed, she left the door open and ran along the dark passage to the concealed entrance into the caves below.

The notion of being alone in that dank blackness was terrifying, too, but much less so than facing Fife.

But the door would not open. Despite Rob's insistence that he wanted her to know Hawthornden for her own safety, he had not revealed its secret to her. With a sob more of fury than of fear, she crouched in the darkest corner and waited.

Minutes later, she heard de Gredin's voice.

"*Sacrebleu!*" he exclaimed. "She has escaped!"

Adela shut her eyes tight and prayed.

Fife said coldly, "Don't be an ass. No lass as slight as that one climbed down that rope, certainly not in the clothes she was wearing. In any event, you'd better hope she did not, because if she did, the river has claimed her and you'll have to tell your masters that you've failed. Think what they'll say when you tell them that although you found the woman your cousin abducted and doubtless shared his secrets with, you are unable to produce her or any information extracted from her."

Adela opened her eyes and listened intently, scarcely daring to breathe. Aware of the dirk's sheath against her thigh, she put her hand on it over her skirt, wondering if she dared take the weapon out or could use it if she did.

"It was not I who grew impatient, my lord," de Gredin protested. "Had you not interfered by challenging Lestalric as you did—"

"Be silent," Fife growled. "The one thing we know from this open door is that the lass was here. Before we set my men to searching the whole castle for her, let us first be sure she is not still here. Don't touch that door," he added a moment later. "I want to know where the treasure lies even more than you do. And I'll wager that open door can provide just the incentive the lass will need to tell us all she knows."

Having not the least difficulty deducing what he meant by that, Adela fought another wave of dizziness and pressed hard against the wall, hoping to make herself invisible. The effort was useless, though. She heard them coming, heard them pause near the pit, and then heard Fife's silky voice saying, "Ahhh."

Gathering the dignity she still possessed, she stood and shook out her skirts.

De Gredin, behind Fife, said, "Ah, *merci au bon Dieu.* One feared you had drowned, madame."

"As you see, I still live," Adela said. To the earl, she said, "I do not suppose you will believe I came here looking for my cloak."

"No," he said. "Doubtless you overheard what my indiscreet friend said a moment ago, too. Don't bother to deny it," he added. "It is no more than a dozen feet from this chamber to the one containing the sally port. Indeed, one wonders what purpose this one serves."

Ignoring the chilling thought that he would somehow guess accurately, Adela shrugged and said, "As I've been here only a few nights, I do not know. But I'd surmise that supplies are stored here when the castle is used regularly."

"Yet you knew where the sally port lies."

"I've been tidying the place," she said. "I looked into every chamber first to see how great a task it would be to set the castle to rights."

Realizing she was talking too much, she stopped.

"Come with me now," Fife said, standing back as if to let her go first. "We're going to have a talk."

As she passed close to him, he grabbed her arm in a viselike grip.

She sighed. "Do you fear I shall run from you again, my lord?"

"You should have heeded me when I told you not to make me wait. But before I hang you, you are going to answer my questions. You'll tell me everything, not just about Ardelve but also about the time you spent with your abductor."

"You may ask anything you like, sir, but I can tell you nothing. Waldron of Edgelaw was an evil man. He did not confide in me."

"She's likely telling the truth, my lord," de Gredin said. "As I told you, Waldron was not a man likely to share secrets with anyone, let alone a woman."

"Yet she would have us believe he did not ravish her," Fife said.

Adela said quietly, "He did not believe in ravishing women. He said that God forbade it. Since he believed that in all other instances God would forgive what he did as long as he served His cause, he took care not to defy Him. I'm told you are a religious man, too, my lord," she added, recalling what the abbot had said.

"What else did Waldron tell you? Did he not tell you he sought something stolen long ago from Holy Kirk and from the Pope? Something he meant to return?"

Adela met his steady gaze. "If he did seek such a thing, sir, he did not find it whilst I was with him. And I don't know where it is."

"That is a pity," Fife said. "But we will see if you are telling the truth."

Tightening his grip, he pushed her toward the open door.

"My lord," de Gredin protested. "You cannot really mean to—"

"Shut your mouth," Fife ordered. "I don't know how your masters can have thought you would be at all useful to them, as lily-livered as you are. I will show you how one extracts information from unwilling subjects."

Casting aside dignity, Adela resisted with all her might. But Fife pushed her inexorably toward the open door and the long drop to the river.

Although she would not give him the satisfaction of hearing her scream, she dug in her heels until he lifted her off her feet and strode with her to the opening.

"Now then," he said grimly. "Have a look and tell me if you think the drop is worth continuing to conceal what you know of Waldron and what he learned."

"I've told you," she said through still gritted teeth, "he told me nothing. He did not believe, as you seem to, that I had any reason to know about his business."

"My lord, please," de Gredin said. "We've no cause to disbelieve her. She was his prisoner, after all. How likely is it that he told her anything of value?"

"I told you to be silent," Fife snapped. "You'd believe anything she said. She was with him night and day for a fortnight. How likely is it that she learned nothing? We know what he was seeking. Even a hint of where he looked would be useful. So, lass, just begin at the beginning and talk until you've told us everything, or . . . "

Abruptly, he swung her out through the opening.

Chapter 19

⁓

On the shore opposite the castle, Rob and Henry had seen the dangling rope, the open sally port, and the chevalier de Gredin peering down at the river.

Terrified that Adela had tried to escape by using the rope, Rob was nearly frantic. "I can't lose her, Henry."

"I'm telling you, she did not climb down that rope. Think, lad! I ken fine that you scarcely know the lass—"

"I know her as I know myself," Rob snapped. "I don't know why that is, I just know it. I've known it since my first moment with her."

Henry looked at him without speaking.

The echo of his own words reverberated through Rob's mind then, and he began to relax. "You're right," he said. "I've been comparing her to Isobel and Sorcha, thinking she would act as impulsively as they do. But she doesn't. She thinks first. I've got to get across the river, Henry. Fetch those ropes."

They had to move upriver a short distance, and even as

they tied the ropes together and wrapped one end around a stout tree, Henry remained skeptical. "You'll have to swim hard," he said. "What about your shoulder? Will it serve?"

"It will have to," Rob said, tightening his sword belt across his chest and adjusting the sword snugly in its scabbard on his back so the crossbar on its hilt would keep as much water out as possible. "Sakes, I nearly forgot," he said, pulling off his boot to extract his half of the map. "Keep this for me," he said, handing it to Henry. "And for the love of God don't get caught with it."

Pulling off the other boot, he tossed them both aside then sent his leather jerkin after them. Making a noose, he slipped the rope over his shoulders, and with Henry holding the coil of rope to play out as he swam, he plunged into the river and began to stroke hard for the opposite shore. The water was so icy that it was hard at first to breathe, but at least it numbed the pain in his shoulder.

He came in sight of the sally port just in time to see the Earl of Fife about to throw Adela into the river.

Screaming as Fife swung her out over the river, Adela grabbed him around the neck, hoping to carry him with her if he dropped her. But he did not let go.

By the time she realized that he still held her, de Gredin had grabbed him and was trying to pull him away from the opening.

"My lord, don't be a fool! If you throw her out, we'll learn nothing."

"Let go of me," Fife snapped.

"I beg your pardon," de Gredin said, jerking his hand away. "I have spent much time in France, my lord. In France, they do not threaten women."

"Then go back to France. You are of small use to me, God knows."

Fife turned back toward the doorway, but Adela had had enough. Grabbing his nearly shoulder-length dark hair, she held on tight, wrapping it around her fist and pulling hard. "Put me down, sir, at once!"

"Damnation!" he yelled, dropping her to her feet and angrily reaching to make her release her grip on his hair. His hand clamped hard on hers.

Adela brought her knee up as hard as she could.

Clearly recognizing her intent, he deflected her aim enough to prevent dire consequences to his manhood, but he grunted nonetheless and released his grip.

As she stepped back, however, his free hand swept up and struck her face hard, knocking her toward the open doorway. Terrified that her own momentum would carry her out, she twisted wildly and crashed to the floor.

Fife lunged toward her, but again de Gredin leaped to her defense, catching the earl by an arm.

As Fife turned to strike the younger man, Adela saw that the rope in the doorway had strained tight and was twitching. Without thought for her own safety, she scrambled to her feet and rushed toward the two struggling men.

Another blow from Fife sent her sprawling again, but this time she managed to fall as far from the doorway as possible, landing near the entrance to the pit passage. Leaping to her feet again, she hitched up her skirts and pulled her dirk from its sheath. Straightening, she took a breath to steady herself and held the dirk in a fold of her skirt.

As she did, Fife felled de Gredin near the stairs with a mighty blow, and the chevalier lay on the stone floor where he had landed, unmoving.

"Mercy, have you killed him?"

"Who cares?" Fife said, brushing his hands on his breeks as if to wipe the dust of de Gredin from them. "You have more to answer for now, my lass."

"I am not your lass, sir," she said with dignity, watching his eyes and not looking toward the still twitching, straining rope as she took a step away from him.

"Stay where you are," he said. "You know there is no escape. You have resisted rightful arrest, which in itself is a hanging crime."

"Is it?" She took another step back.

He glanced at de Gredin's still body, then at her. "I should think you'd want to soothe my temper, lass, and evidence suggests that you know ways to do that," he said. "I'll wager Waldron taught you many. If not, surely Lestalric has taught you a few. But if they failed to do so, I'll teach you myself, if not now then when you've told me all I want to know about the treasure and—"

"Treasure! What treasure?"

"That is what you are going to tell me. You will also tell me if Lestalric is hiding the same thing Waldron sought or something more valuable."

"You talk in riddles. What could be worth more than treasure?"

"Mayhap something that will gain me the Scottish crown if I find it."

She still watched his eyes, determined to hold his attention. "How could anything do that?"

"We waste time," he said, and at last, he moved toward her.

Gripping the dirk, she took another step back. She had no idea if the rope still twitched, for she dared not look away from his evil eyes. Logic, and what she had seen of the roiling river below, told her she would have to defend herself. But she had stopped him once. Mayhap, this time, she could stop him permanently.

⁓

Rob heard Fife's words and saw the situation at a glance as he eased himself up the last few inches to peek over the sill of the sally port. If Fife turned or Adela saw him, he would be finished. But if Fife continued to concentrate on Adela, and if de Gredin stayed quietly where he was, he might slip in before Fife saw him.

Because the rope was anchored well up on the wall by the door, climbing over the threshold was no more difficult than climbing up in the first place had been, but he was wet and cold, his muscles resistant to commands from his brain. His fingers, numbed by the icy river water, had made the initial few minutes of his climb more treacherous in their own way than the last ones would be. His clothing was still wet, his body still chilled, but his fingers, hands, and legs would obey him.

His shoulder, surprisingly, scarcely bothered him. He knew the arrow had to have damaged muscle, but he had not noticed any pain as he climbed the rope. He had thought only of getting to Adela, and would have climbed the damned rope with one arm if he'd had to. He gave some credit to the countess's willow bark decoction and her salve, but for the rest, he thanked the Fates.

Adela's right hand twitched where she held it in a fold of her skirt. Knowing instantly what she held, he felt new terror. If she dared to threaten Fife with her wee blade, he would wrest it from her and use it against her if only to teach her a lesson.

And if that happened, Rob would never forgive himself.

As Fife took another step toward her, stalking her now as a beast might stalk its prey, Adela gripped the leather-wrapped hilt of her dirk tighter and backed up step by step. She knew instinctively that he enjoyed the hunt.

"Give me the blade, lassie," he said.

Shivering at his tone, she realized that her movements must have revealed what she held. Still, she said with forced calm, "I prefer to keep it."

"I'm sure you do, but I think I shall enjoy taking it from you, then using it to teach you obedience to my commands."

"If you want to use a blade, Fife, try your own—on me."

Fife whirled, and Adela gave a sigh of relief, recognizing Rob's voice. But as Fife moved, she caught sight of her husband's face, and the fury she saw there sent fresh waves of fear through her body.

It had been one thing to have a vague understanding of what might happen to her if she were to stab one of the

King's sons. But she had known the likelihood was small that she could kill Fife. Not for a moment did she think Rob meant anything other than to cut the earl to pieces—as swiftly as possible.

Fife snatched his sword from its scabbard and leaped forward to engage Rob's blade. Both men used two hands at first to hold their swords, and both swung hard. The sally-port chamber was large enough to allow them to fight, but Adela saw that it left little room for maneuvering.

And the sally port, with its hundred-foot drop to the river, remained open.

Fife lunged, Rob deflected his blade, and the momentum of their thrusts carried each man past the other. As they turned, she realized Rob was barefoot and wore only his shirt. He had taken off his protective heavy leather jack to swim.

Rob faced the open door now. Fife faced Adela.

Looking straight into the earl's eyes, she lifted her skirt and replaced the dirk in its sheath. When Fife's eyes widened, Rob lunged.

Fife seemed to hesitate. But at the last minute, he stepped aside, raised his sword high, and slashed down as Rob's lunge carried him forward.

Adela clapped a hand to her mouth.

Rob leaped sideways, and the heavy blade missed by inches.

Snarling, Fife leaped forward again, and again the men changed places.

With Rob facing her, and still fearing he would kill the Stewart prince, Adela backed deeper into the passageway, seeking anything that might serve to distract Fife or make him stumble. She wanted to render him helpless long enough for Rob to recover his temper. His eyes still burned with fury.

She felt along the wall by the pit. But although she found a sconce there, doubtless to hold a torch, it contained nothing and was bolted to the stone wall.

The clanging continued. Turning back to be sure Rob still held his own, she saw de Gredin begin to stir.

Neither of the other two seemed to notice him.

If he were still inclined to side with her, she did not want to give him away. But if he went for Rob . . .

"So help me," she muttered, "I'll spit the slithersome coof on my dirk."

De Gredin glanced at her. His face showed only relief when their eyes met, so she moved back to that end of the passageway to be near if she could help, and also to keep her eye on the untrustworthy chevalier.

The swordsmen were well matched, which was not reassuring. Fife, being the more treacherous, and dry, would surely hold the edge.

Rob feinted, and when Fife lunged at him, he leaped the other way. Fife's lunge carried him toward the door, but having watched Rob easily avoid that dreadful hazard, Adela felt no surprise when Fife did also, too, pulling himself up well short of the opening.

De Gredin, however, on his feet now, surged forward. With both hands straight out, he slammed into Fife's back.

Off balance, the earl stumbled straight toward the gaping doorway.

Adela cried out, and as she did, Rob leaped to shove

the earl hard, spinning him so he staggered headfirst into the wall beside the doorway instead.

Fife's head cracked against the iron ring that anchored the escape rope. He dropped his sword, collapsed without another sound, and lay still.

"Is he dead?" Adela demanded, rushing forward to see.

"Nay, just clouted himself good," Rob said. Picking up Fife's sword and flinging it through the open sally port, he dropped to a knee beside the earl and pointed to the pulse in Fife's throat, saying, "Sithee, it still beats." He looked up at de Gredin. "You might like to disappear before he wakes."

"Aye, sure, I'd like that," de Gredin said frankly. "But I doubt I'd meet with any success if I tried. He has too many men outside, and they all know me."

"Then lie back down," Adela suggested. "I don't think he saw you get up."

De Gredin shook his head. "I've behaved as a scoundrel toward you, my lady. I'll not make it worse by letting so powerful a prince believe you were the one who tried to shove him into eternity."

Adela felt sad for him. She was grateful that he would tell the truth but fearful, despite all he might have done to harm her, of what could happen to him if he did.

To her surprise, Rob said dryly, "Very noble, Chevalier, but I doubt your confession would do us as much good as you may by remaining unconscious. We may well turn *that* to good account. But first, tell me, did you have aught to do with Ardelve's death or those of my father and brother?"

"Nay, I did not," de Gredin said. "But I cannot prove that, and I do believe Ardelve did not die any more naturally than your kinsmen did. Sithee, Fife had taken strong interest in you, my lady, because I'd told him of Waldron's purpose here. He decided my cousin must have confided in you about what he was seeking. He said if you could tell us nothing else, you could tell us where and how Waldron died."

"You did nowt to harm Ardelve?" Rob's tone remained skeptical.

"I did not, but many guests brought servants, and a horde of gillies were in constant bustle about the high table. I can tell you, too, that my lord Fife was determined to get his hands on Lady Adela before Ardelve took her back to his home. Fife could not seek her there without risking trouble with the Lord of the Isles."

He paused, then said ruefully, "I told him about the solar, my lady, but I never suggested poison. Lord Fife did that and said I could testify to it if the chance arose. He also started those rumors later. I did exaggerate the time you and Ardelve spent in the solar in a regrettable attempt to advance my own cause with Fife. As doubtless you heard him say, the men who trained Waldron and sent him to find the treasure taken from Holy Kirk likewise sent me to discover all I could of what he'd learned. But I lack both Waldron's training and his single-minded sense of purpose. Then, too, I admire you, my lady. Not only are you beautiful and kind but—"

"Enough," Rob growled, his eyes turning flintlike. "Stop whilst you're still alive, Chevalier, and mayhap we will keep you so. What of my father and brother?"

De Gredin grimaced and glanced nervously at Fife. "I know naught of them but what everyone heard," he said. "I do know Fife talked to someone else before me, though. He said I was the second to mention secrets to him in as many weeks."

He glanced again at Fife, who chose that moment to groan.

At hasty gestures from Rob, the chevalier returned swiftly to his erstwhile position on the floor near the stairs and Adela knelt beside the earl.

"Can you tell if you injured him badly, lass?" Rob asked mildly.

Startled, she looked up at him and saw him smile, but the smile was no pleasant one. He had a plan, so she said, "I did not mean to hurt him, sir. I swear it!"

"He will understand that you were only trying to deflect his aim, sweetheart. But mayhap you should run upstairs and fetch some of his men to his side. Just explain to them exactly what happened. We'll face whatever conse—"

"Nay!"

The word came forcefully, although Fife winced as he said it and slowly brought a hand to his brow, already red and bidding fair to show a nasty bruise.

"Let me help you to your feet, my lord earl," Rob said solicitously, placing a hand under Fife's left elbow as the man struggled dizzily to sit up.

Fife shook it off. "I'll help myself. Where's my sword?"

"In the river, I'm afraid," Rob said. "When you stumbled and fell against the wall, you cast it through the sally port. Doubtless we can find you another if you desire to finish our contest. Or we can wait until you feel fit again."

Fife, sitting now, still visibly disoriented, frowned at

the floor and muttered as much to himself as to them, "I did not stumble. Someone pushed me."

Glancing at Rob, who gazed steadily back, Adela said in a small voice, "I'm afraid it was I, sir. I thought you were going to kill poor Rob, and . . . and I threw myself at you to save him. He is my husband, after all, and I care deeply for him." She looked again at Rob, letting him see the truth of those words in her eyes.

Fife, still rubbing his aching head with one hand as he steadied himself with the other, said grimly as he looked up, "Very commendable, I'm sure, madam."

"I agree," Rob said lightly. "You looked ripe for murder, my lord, and considering what effort it took for me to climb that damned rope, I'd expected more respect from you for the effort. Still, my lady wife has explained that you have been laboring under a false belief in some of the worst accusations laid against her. So I can well understand that you might be displeased with us both."

"I suppose you mean to tell me those accusations are all false."

"Aye, sure, for they are. We are certainly married, for which we must both thank you. Had you not terrified the poor lass by making her fear instant arrest, she would never have accepted an offer from such a scapegrace as myself."

"So you are truly married?"

"For nearly a sennight now," Rob said. "The Abbot of Holyrood married us himself, as he will tell you if you ask him. As for murdering Ardelve, I have never even spoken to the man. Nor did I meet her ladyship until after his death."

"You expect me to believe that, when I know you

served Sir Hugo Robison at Roslin before you decided to step forth and claim Lestalric."

"If you know that, you understand why I am most unlikely to have conspired with her ladyship to murder her husband. Not only was Ardelve unknown to me, but surely you know Sir Hugo well enough to be sure he would not introduce a minion like Einar Logan to his sister-by-marriage. Nor would Prince Henry—forgive me, Orkney—or his formidable mother allow such a thing."

Fife grimaced. "Those are excellent arguments which you are fully entitled to make when—"

"My lord Fife, are you still below?"

"Help me up, damn you," Fife growled, reaching for Rob before raising his voice to shout, "Aye, what is it?"

"An army, my lord, approaching under the Douglas banner."

"Rally our men," Fife shouted.

"Sakes, sir, most of them are outside the gates, prey to any Douglas arrow! Aye, and the Roslin banner flies wi' the Douglas, sir. There be dunamany o' them."

"Tell your men to stand down, Fife," Rob said. "You know that the Douglas will follow no order of your giving."

"What the devil is he doing here?"

"He is gathering an army, of course, to keep the damned English in England, something you might aid him with if you want any country left to rule. Or would you prefer to fight his forces and those of Sinclair instead, here and now?"

Giving him a hard, resentful look, Fife shouted at the man above to have his fighting tail prepare to depart as soon as he could join them. Then, with grim intent, he said to Rob, "The Douglas and a few others want bringing to heel."

"Mayhap you can do that," Rob said amiably. "Do you need help up the stairs?"

Curtly declining assistance, Fife turned toward the stairway only to stop when he saw de Gredin still lying there. Without warning, he kicked the man hard.

De Gredin groaned, making what Adela thought was a credible showing of just coming to, but Fife snarled, "Get to your feet, man. We're leaving."

Adela stepped forward, saying urgently, "Surely, you don't want to encumber yourself so, my lord. You can see he's not fit to ride. He is welcome to stay with us until he has recovered from his injury. He suffered a dreadful fall."

Fife had winced after kicking de Gredin, revealing his own painful aftereffects, and he did not argue with her.

As they followed him up the stairs, Rob gave Adela's arm an affectionate squeeze, but she did not respond. She was glad to be safe but still angry with him about the locked door, and she strongly doubted that their troubles were over.

When they reached the courtyard, the scene was frantic. But Fife, despite visible pain and weakness, soon restored order and discipline to his men.

Then, his dignity still apparently intact, he managed to mount his horse with no more assistance than he might normally accept from a gillie, and without looking back, rode out through the gateway to take his place at the head of his fighting tail.

Following him with Rob as far as the gateway, Adela

held her breath until she saw the formidable array of horsemen waiting at the edge of the woods to the south.

Eight abreast, rows of them formed the vanguard of a barely visible, much greater host in the woodland behind them, all waving lances, swords, and banners at the departing royal party.

Douglas and Sinclair banners flanked the leaders.

Only when the last of Fife's men had disappeared over the first hill did several of those leaders spur their mounts forward.

Adela recognized Sir Michael and scanned the rest for familiar faces, trying to remember what the Douglas looked like from her brief glimpse of him at court.

Her jaw dropped when she came to the first face she recognized. "The countess! And I see Isobel and Sidony now, riding up behind them!"

Isobel was grinning. Even the quiet Sidony looked pleased with herself.

Michael explained as he jumped from his horse and hurried to assist the countess, hampered by the shirt of mail and leather breeks that she wore. "I think we've got every horse and every man, woman, and child who can sit one for miles around," he said. "And everyone without one who could carry something to wave came along, too. 'Tis a damned good thing, though, that Fife didn't stay to fight."

"Henry ought to be here soon," Rob said. "He'll be delighted to see this."

"How did you get inside the castle?" Michael asked him.

"We saw the rope hanging from the sally port, so we moved back upriver to a point above the castle, tied me to one of the ropes we'd brought with us, and Henry manned it whilst I swam across and climbed the rope to the sally port."

"I'll wager that sounds easier than it was," Michael said.

"Aye, sure, but Adela had been kind enough to leave the sally port open and throw down the rope, so it seemed a pity to waste it. Scared me witless to see it, I can tell you, thinking she'd tried to use it and had fallen. But then I saw de Gredin."

"So he was there."

"Aye, thank the Fates. I'm thinking he probably saved my lass's life. I saw Fife, too, from the river before I grabbed the rope. He swung her out, threatening to toss her into the river. Had he not been holding her so, he'd have seen me."

"Fife is an evil man, Michael," Adela said. "He wanted to make me talk about"—she glanced at Rob—"about many things. I cannot believe he has simply gone away. He said I was under arrest! I've never been so terrified."

"Never?" Rob said.

She frowned, remembering how clearly she had been able to think. "It was strange," she told him. "At the time, I just thought about how I could foil his plan, whatever it was, and get away. And you, my lord husband," she added sternly, "have much to answer for with respect to the limited choices I had."

"Do I, sweetheart?" he said, putting an arm around her. "As soon as we get rid of all these people, you may have my head for washing."

"You think I won't," she said curtly. "But you had better prepare yourself."

He looked at her, eyes twinkling, and opened his mouth. But apparently he thought better of whatever comment he was about to make, for he shut it again and turned hastily to speak to Michael.

___

The urge to burst into laughzter had surged up without warning, and Rob was having all he could do to control it as he congratulated Michael on the success of his ruse. But he knew Adela would never understand that his need to laugh arose not from amusement but from the joy of having her safe again.

Moreover, he had sensed real anger beneath her words.

He recognized the euphoria of temporary victory, both in her and in himself, and dared to hope she would suffer no more of her nightmares. He had seen such relief before when once-defeated men went on to claim victory. The ills that had settled on them after failure eased as they came to believe in their abilities again and disappeared if they won their next battle. If she was truly angry with him, he would have to address that, but he could not do the task justice until they were alone.

"Judging by the way you're looking at your wife, you'll want to see us gone soon," Michael said. "So I shan't invite everyone to join you for supper."

"I want Henry," Rob said. "We've more to do yet, and I'm thinking we'll want to do it quietly. I don't trust Fife any more now than I did a half hour ago."

"Henry means to return to Edinburgh tonight," Michael said. "But I'll send men now to clear all the approaches to the gorge and guard them. I doubt Fife will return as long as he suspects the Douglas may still be here."

"Where is Douglas, and how did you alert him?"

"Sakes, I don't know where he is. I know only that Henry said he'd left Edinburgh. But the Douglas fighting banner is just a red heart on a white field. My mother was able to conjure up several in less time than it took to gather my army."

Adela was talking with her sisters and the countess, doubtless answering dozens of questions about her marriage and the intervening days. But it occurred to Rob that he knew a sure way to assuage her anger with him, whatever had stirred it. Moving closer to Michael, he said quietly, "I'll be taking Adela with us when Henry and I return to that cut, Michael, so make damn sure we'll be safe."

Michael's jaw hardened before he sighed and said, "You are badly smitten, my friend, to dare to suggest I'd risk Henry's life or yours, let alone Adela's, when I have power to prevent harm to all of you. You know our men are loyal."

"I know that someone told Fife that Einar Logan and I are the same," Rob said. "But it may not have been one of ours, and you're right about my feelings for my lady wife. Seeing her in Fife's arms scared the liver and lights out of me."

"I know," Michael said, looking not at Adela but at his own wife.

"There is one thing more," Rob said. "I don't want

anyone else to be in the gorge with us, or any hint that we're there, for that matter. But I do want a strong tail ready to ride later tonight if I need one."

"You are certainly wearing your baron's mantle more comfortably," Michael said with a wry smile. "You shall have all you request, my lord. Dare I ask why?"

"Because if I find what I expect, I'll want to have a talk with the good Abbot of Holyrood," Rob said. "If I know my lass, she'll insist on riding with me to speak to him, and after what she's accomplished today, she deserves to go."

Chapter 20

Dusk had fallen before Adela, Rob, and Henry made their way into the densely wooded cut, but from that point on, things moved swiftly. The huge central slab pulled away from the other two more easily than they had expected, revealing a three-foot-wide opening in the hillside.

"Sakes, look at this," Henry muttered as he felt the inner edge of the opening. "This slab is hung on hinges, Rob, fixed somehow into that other rock."

"Take this torch, Henry," Rob said, handing it to him. "We'll light mine and keep yours to use if we need it."

While he stepped into the passage to light his, Adela looked back the way they had come. Rob had said Michael and his men were guarding all the approaches to Hawthornden and this part of the gorge, and she knew no one in the castle could see them in the cut, even from the ramparts. Nor could anyone hear them from more than a few feet away over the din of the rushing river. She still felt nervous, although she fairly tingled in anticipation of what they hoped to find.

"Doubtless, one of us should keep watch out here," Henry said. "But I'm damned if I will, and I suspect you won't consent to do so, Rob, or leave Adela."

"We'll trust Michael," Rob said, leading the way and holding the torch high.

Adela followed him into the passageway with Henry right behind her. Compared to the first time she had been in such a place, this was less frightening. The odds that anyone could surprise them now were much smaller.

Rob stopped, and the silence of the passageway closed around them.

"A second passage takes off here," he said, holding his fair copy of the map to the light. "If this is right, we bear left here at this first one."

"Aye, that's right," Henry said, looking at his own map.

Their confidence that it was the right place increased as they proceeded. Men had widened the passage they followed, and the ground was smooth, nearly free of obstacles. Although they had not been walking for long, they had made three turns.

Adela dared not trust her sense of direction, and neither man commented.

Abruptly, the passage opened into a wider chamber.

Rob held the torch higher, and light glittered from crystalline formations. "Wait here," he said. "The path ends here, so there may be pitfalls."

Adela heard water dripping.

"Is there not a symbol on the map at the end of that line?" Adela asked.

"Just a small square," he said.

"Like a treasure chest?" Henry asked.

"Just a square, Henry. God knows what it means." He began walking slowly away from them, holding the torch well out in front of him. He was halfway across the chamber when he stopped still. He did not say a word. He just stood there.

"What is it?" Adela asked quietly.

"Come see," he said.

Rob heard them walk up behind him, but had it been Fife himself coming to arrest him, he could not have taken his gaze from the Stone.

It was dark, either polished marble or basalt, a block as high as his knees. It looked to be about a foot and a half deep, nearly a yard wide, and it was carved and gilded with designs that gleamed eerily in the light of his torch—spirals, a harp, a Pictish boar, and a lion among others. He discerned less visible traces of carved lettering that looked to be Gaelic or Latin. The Stone had feet, balls carved like an eagle's claws, and front corners carved to resemble reptile legs, possibly lizards.

"What are these?" Adela asked, moving closer to touch one of a pair of hooks fixed into the side nearest her. A second pair adorned the opposite side.

Rob and Henry exchanged looks, and Rob said, "I'd guess they are there so men can transport it on two stout poles."

"So this is the true Stone of Scone?"

"Aye," Rob said. "Look here at the seat. It bears a footprint, I think."

"Like the Isles' Footprint Stone," Adela said.

"They were said to be gey similar," Henry said. "What's more, this one looks just like what one sees on official seals made after earlier coronations."

"I've seen the Footprint Stone," Rob said. "Donald stepped onto it barefoot at his installation. This looks as if one is to sit on it, despite the footprint."

"Mayhap one did both," Adela suggested. "That would make sense if the rightful king had to fit the footprint before he could sit."

Henry smiled. "I don't think they had to fit the print," he said. "Some just thought the man they'd selected would make a great ruler if his did. What do you want to do about this, Rob? I'm thinking it may not be safe to leave it here now."

Rob frowned, then said musingly, "It's been safe enough since they brought it here. However, thanks to de Gredin, Fife now believes the Templar treasure is in Scotland. Moreover, he believes the Sinclairs know where it is, and he told Adela he expected his questions of her to reveal whether I also know or if I know the whereabouts of something even more valuable, something that would gain him the Scottish crown if he could find it. I'm guessing the Stone is what he meant by that."

"Aye, sure," Henry said. "To find the Templar treasure would be a grand thing by itself, but the Scottish nobility would not support Fife against Carrick simply because of untold wealth. Indeed, such wealth in his hands would more likely create increased friction. If he found the Stone, though, he could argue that Bruce's notion of passing the succession to the eldest son is wrong, that the son who'd found the true Coronation Stone is proven worthier just by finding it. Most nobles already agree that Fife would make a stronger king than Carrick. They don't like him, but nearly all would support him if he produced the Stone. What I don't understand is why he thinks you might know its whereabouts."

Adela said, "Is it possible he simply thinks the Stone may be hidden with the Templar treasure?" When she saw Rob exchange a look with Henry, she added, "Recall, too, sir, that the chevalier told us that when he first approached Fife, the earl said he was the second one to mention secrets to him in as many weeks."

Rob grimaced. "Will! Doubtless seeking favor of some sort by revealing his own suspicions, though heaven knows why he'd wait so long to do so."

Henry shrugged. "Fife was in no position to grant favors until this past year when he began to take over so many of the King's duties."

"And the King was far less likely to suffer the attentions of such a self-serving sycophant as Will was," Rob said grimly. "But you make a good point, lass, in suggesting that Fife may believe the Stone and the treasure are one and the same."

"Which makes my point that we should move the Stone," Henry said. "If Fife begins his own search in earnest, Roslin Glen is the first place he'll look."

"But how can we move it?" Adela asked.

"Someone moved it here," Rob said.

"Even so, we can't move it tonight. What are you going to do now?"

Rob looked at Henry. "Do you still plan to ride to Edinburgh tonight?"

"Either tonight or early in the morning. Michael did tell me that you'd requested—I think he said 'demanded'—a large fighting tail tonight."

Rob nodded. "Just how sure of himself do you suppose Fife is if neither Douglas nor Sinclair poses an immediate threat to him?"

"As sure as you'd want him to be," Henry said with a twinkle.

"That's what I thought, myself."

⁓

"What else are you thinking?" Adela asked Rob mildly.

His wry smile told her he knew she was still angry with him. But he said only, "I think your gallant chevalier should return to Edinburgh with Henry."

"I hope you have better reason for that than a belief that I shall enjoy his company," Henry said.

"I mean to take him into our confidence," Rob said. "I'll tell him I want him to ride with you as a diversion, in the event that Fife is keeping a watch out for us. I'll say I want to talk with the abbot about information I gained at Lestalric."

"You expect him to tell Fife, and Fife to believe you have the information he wants, whether 'tis treasure, Stone, or both he seeks," Henry said. "But he'll be ripe to murder de Gredin afterward, will he not? Sakes, he's ripe for murder now."

"Then take de Gredin to Orkney with you," Rob suggested. "If you can, I'd like you to leave for town in a couple of hours. Adela and I will follow."

"I can leave whenever you like, but I did intend to slip out and meet my ship at Leith unbeknownst to Fife," Henry reminded him.

"Aye, sure, but I need you."

"You've grown impertinent, sir," Henry said severely.

"Have I?" Rob said. "More than before?"

Henry chuckled.

"You've nowt to worry you, Henry. Even Fife will hesitate to confront *you*. But come now, both of you. We need to close this place up again."

"But what will you do about the Stone?" Adela asked.

"Henry and I must confer about that," Rob said. "But not now."

She nodded, feeling virtuous for not pressing him further. She had said nothing about his having kept the secret of the locked door to the caves from her, not wanting to risk angering him too much lest she miss this expedition. Nor would she risk being left behind when he rode to Edinburgh.

She would hold her peace until she was ready to have it out with him. But have it out with him, she would.

Not much to Rob's surprise, de Gredin agreed at once to ride to town with Henry, assuring him so fervently that he'd not tell a soul about Rob's plans that Rob was tempted to tell him he could inform anyone he liked. He resisted the urge, having no more faith in the chevalier's integrity than he'd had from the outset.

De Gredin was just bait in a trap.

Later, as Rob lifted Adela to her saddle before their ride to Edinburgh, he wondered when she would speak her mind to him. She had chatted amiably enough as they ate supper, but he had sensed her tension then and he still sensed it.

She was biding her time, and although he wondered what he had done to displease her, he was sure she would tell him in her own good time.

Gossamer mist veiled the moon again, but the nights were growing warmer.

As he swung onto his saddle, he realized that although his shoulder ached from the day's exertions, the real pain was nearly gone. Adela had smeared more of the salve on the wound for him, but he'd needed no more of Isabella's willow-bark.

Henry had a large party of men with him, but Rob and Adela had a tail of a dozen well-armed ones, including Archie Tayt, whom Rob decided to send ahead.

"Stay off the main track," he told him. "We want to know if anyone is waiting for us, so be wary. Although we're not carrying torches, they'll be able to see us if they're on the watch, unless this mist thickens till yon moon disappears altogether. Oh, and before you leave, Archie, tell the others to drop back a bit."

"Aye, sir," Archie said.

"Now then, lass," Rob said as soon as he could be sure they were beyond earshot of anyone else. "My head is yours for the washing. What have I done?"

Surprised, Adela looked at him, trying to determine if he was girded for battle or merely curious. Even in the pale light cast by the hazy oval moon, she could see his eyes dancing.

"Would you laugh at me, sir?"

"Nay, lass. 'Tis only that you look so solemn and serene, although I ken fine that you want to shred my character. I don't look forward to it, but if I have done aught to anger you, I should know what it is, should I not?"

"'Tis your secrets again," she said. "You showed me the door to the caves under the castle but not the trick to open it. So when I realized I could not get down that rope before Fife would be upon me—if at all—I had nowhere else to go."

"I don't suppose you considered the pit," he said.

She looked at him.

"Nay, I suppose not." He grimaced. "You are right to be angry, lass. That was a dangerous oversight, and I do apologize for it. You cannot imagine what went through my head when I saw that rope hanging down and the sally port open. All I could think was that if you'd attempted to escape that way and fallen, I'd never forgive myself for having shown you that rope. Little did I realize I'd endangered you more by neglecting to show you the trick of the door. I'll show you how it works as soon as we return to Hawthornden."

Her anger assuaged by his remorse, she said, "I do know that once something becomes a habit, the habit is hard to break."

"Aye," he said. "And I'm still not persuaded that you should know all that I know, but we can discuss that more now or whenever you like. I've a notion I'm going to be tempted to tell you more than I should in any event."

"Do you think so?"

"Aye, for you've magic in you, sweetheart. I'm as wax in your hands."

"You weren't when you refused to let me search with you and Henry."

His eyes narrowed speculatively. "Do you really want to discuss that now?"

Feeling heat flood her cheeks at the mental image of herself, flinging platter and bowl at him, she shook her head.

"I thought not."

Seeking another subject, she said, "Do you think Fife might already be waiting at the abbey for us?"

"Nay, for if he expected us to go anywhere tonight, it would be to Roslin, where he's less likely to lay hands on us. He won't know we're at the abbey until de Gredin tells him, or his spies do. In either event, I don't want a confrontation with him in the open whilst you're with me, so we'll take the woods trail. By doing so, we should also have time to talk to the abbot before Fife finds us."

"If he does," she said.

He changed the subject then, and they continued to chat about nothing in particular. Then, abruptly, he said, "Look there."

They had topped the ridge above the forested plain leading to Edinburgh, and beyond the flat stretch of darkness, lights of the town glimmered like jewels in the mist. The Castle looked silvery atop its dark hillside.

"It is beautiful," she said. "The abbey end looks dark, though."

"The kirkyard will be lighted," he said. "And the abbot will be there."

They skirted Arthur's Seat and entered the abbey woods a short time later, riding silently but for the noise of trappings and the splashy thuds of the horses' hooves on the boggy path. As they entered the rear of the kirkyard, they saw Archie Tayt waiting. Rob raised a hand to halt the men behind him.

"Have you seen Brother Joseph?" he asked Archie.

"Aye, sir. He said to tell ye the abbot would see ye straightaway afore Nocturnes. They've no rung the bell yet, but he did say it wouldna be long now."

"Where is Lord Orkney?"

"He rode right through town, m'lord, but wi' only half his force. I talked wi' one o' his lads as rode through the abbey woods, and he said that his lordship and the chevalier had decided that if ye wanted a stir, they'd give ye one."

Nodding, Rob jumped down and helped Adela dismount. But as the two of them hurried round to the abbey entrance, he muttered, "I warrant Henry's trusting de Gredin more than he should. Sakes, though, I cannot blame him. I nearly told him myself that I wanted Fife to come after us. I hope Henry did not go that far."

"De Gredin did help us," Adela reminded him.

"Aye, lass, but I still don't trust him. If he believes he's in danger, he can go with Henry to Orkney and be safe. As it is, I'm sorry Henry will miss this meeting."

"We did not come here just to test the chevalier or to trap Fife, did we?"

"Nay, but we may have come on a fool's errand."

Entering the abbey kirk, they crossed the candlelit vestibule, and Rob saw the abbot when they stepped into the nave. His bulky person was hard to miss, and he was kneeling where he had been when they'd come before.

Rob put a hand on Adela's arm to stop her, then put his arm around her and drew her close in a warm hug. His body stirred, reminding him of his constant desire for her, making him wonder what would become of them. He did not fear Fife except insofar as the earl threatened Adela. To keep her safe, he would do what he had to do. The Isle of Orkney would provide safety, and not just for de Gredin.

"I gave it up before; I can do it again." When she looked at him, frowning, he realized he'd spoken aloud. "Just talking to myself," he said. "'Twas nowt."

But it was not "nowt," of course, because even as the words left his tongue, he knew he did not want to forfeit Lestalric either. Although he had felt no love for his father or Will, he had cared deeply for his grandfather and all that Sir Walter had represented. In his own mind, Lestalric had been Sir Walter's, was now his own, and would one day be his son's. He had a duty to do all he could to protect it and keep it out of Fife's hands. But he would not risk Adela's safety even for that.

"How may I serve you, my son?"

Rob looked away from his wife's beautiful face to see the abbot striding toward them. Releasing her, he said, "Is there a place we can speak privately, sir?"

"Aye, briefly," the abbot said. "The bell will toll Nocturnes in less than a quarter hour. Is aught amiss, Sir Robert?"

"I don't know, my lord. But I must not say more until we can be sure we will not be heard."

"I see. Then come into this chamber," he added, pushing open a door. "The door lacks a lock, but if her ladyship will condescend to keep watch, we can leave it open. The brothers will not enter the kirk until the bell begins to toll."

When Adela hesitated, Rob understood her as easily as if she had spoken. He said, "I want her ladyship to hear all we say. I know you may be reluctant . . . "

"Nay, my son. According to Holy Kirk, a man and his wife are one. If you wish it, it shall be so. She can stand just inside here to keep watch. That way, she will hear all we say and still be able to warn us if anyone enters the nave. So, now," he said as he led Rob farther into the room. "What is it?"

"We found something of great value today near Hawthornden Castle."

"I see."

The abbot's expression remained neutral, but the fact that he did not ask what they had found bolstered Rob's confidence. The abbot might simply lack curiosity, but Rob's feeling was that he had not asked because he already knew.

"You were here at Holyrood when the English last invaded Scotland, were you not, sir?"

"I was. I served as baillie to the abbot, just as Brother Joseph serves me."

"And you knew my grandfather, did you not?"

"I did, very well, as had my own lord abbot before me."

Rob hesitated. Although he had imagined several such dialogues since the discovery and his subsequent decision to approach the abbot, now that the moment had come, his long-held reluctance to reveal too much put a lock on his tongue.

He glanced at Adela, but she was keeping careful watch over the nave.

The abbot said diffidently into the silence, "This item you found, Sir Robert. If one may ask, what do you intend to do with it?"

Rob looked him in the eye. "I came here to seek your advice, my lord."

"I see. Perhaps you might just tell me what color this item is."

"Black or dark gray. The light was not good enough to be sure."

"Its size?"

"A yard wide, mayhap two feet deep, and as high as my knees."

"Has it legs?"

"Of a sort. They looked reptilian. It also has feet, like eagles' claws."

The abbot nodded. "We need say no more about it, then. Nor will we name this item, for I have sworn not to do so, if only to protect the abbey. It was to protect Holyrood and everyone here that my superior and I first spoke to your grandfather."

"So the item was here?"

"Aye, almost from the first. The Abbot of"—he hesitated—"of another abbey, believing the invaders of his time would proceed directly there, applied to the abbot here. That abbot here, you know, was from Lestalric and thus was as loyal to his country as to his abbey. We are told that he never lied, but of course, failure to tell a complete truth is near enough a lie to require both penance and absolution. Still, he saved this abbey, and he protected the item."

"Then the English came again," Rob said.

"Och, aye. But recall that they occupied this area from 1296 till Bannockburn, when Bruce routed them. Then they threatened to invade again fifteen years later as he lay dying. They crossed into the Borders and severely damaged Melrose Abbey and others, making it clear that they were likely to do the same thing here."

"What did you do?"

"We spoke to the King. No one could doubt Robert the Bruce's feelings for Scotland or his hopes for her destiny. He did all he could to preserve both. It was he who said we could not risk revealing what we knew to anyone else until the Scottish throne was secure and the English no longer a threat. He told us we could entrust what we knew to two men, however, and he named them. Both had proven their loyalty to him. Later, both sacrificed their lives in his service."

"I know who they were," Rob said. "Orkney was with us when we found it."

"Aye, then you likewise know that both Sinclair and Logan passed what they knew to their sons before they left to carry the Bruce's heart to the Holy Land."

"What of the Douglas?" Rob asked. "Did good Sir James not also know?"

"Nay, for as much as Bruce trusted him, he knew the

Douglases harbored hopes of ruling Scotland themselves. And, too, there were fierce factions in that clan then, as there are today. Bruce trusted only Sir James."

"Still, others must have known," Rob said. "No two men could have carried the item two feet, let alone from Holyrood to its present location."

Glibly, the abbot said, "Aye, sure, but there was an organization of outstanding soldiers who had proven their loyalty to Bruce at Bannockburn. He recommended several of them to assist Sinclair and your grandfather, and they did."

"An organization?" Rob said, noting that Adela had turned but keeping his gaze fixed on the abbot. "I believe I know of such an organization, sir."

The abbot gazed steadily back. "I thought you might," he said. "But time is fleeting. You asked for my advice, so I'll tell you what the Bruce told us. At least three men should know the item's whereabouts, but its very presence in Scotland should remain secret until the Scottish throne is secure. Due to the present upheaval within the royal family, and with the English again threatening our border, I'd advise you to continue as we began if the place of concealment remains safe."

"Aye, sure, but I'm nearly certain the Earl of Fife suspects—"

A distant bang interrupted him, and Adela said, "Someone's coming!"

⁓

Fife was the first one through the archway from the vestibule. His grim expression was enough to send shivers through Adela's body, but warm hands on her shoulders reminded her that Rob was there, and the abbot, too.

Fife carried a sword, and when armed men followed him into the nave, Rob gently moved Adela aside and opened the door wide.

Stepping into the nave, he said, "Are you looking for me, my lord earl?"

Adela moved back into the doorway, her heart pounding, determined to see.

Fife's anger was clear as he faced Rob. "You are under arrest, Lestalric, and your lady, too," he said. "I'm told she is here with you."

"Do you always attend Kirk with sword drawn?" Rob asked in a lazy tone.

Fife stiffened, clearly on the verge of losing his temper. "Draw yours, sirrah, and we'll end our contest now," he said.

"I don't draw my weapon in kirk," Rob said, sounding almost sorrowful, Adela thought. "But if you like, I'll meet you in the kirkyard."

"Where is Orkney?"

"What? Do you fear Henry? Doubtless, he's aboard ship on his way home and won't trouble you tonight."

"Nay, I ken fine he was in town but a short while ago, with a large force."

Overhead, the great abbey bell began to toll.

Fife whirled, snapping at one of his followers, "Tell whoever is making that din to stop it until I'm finished here!"

The henchman fled, and Adela felt hands on her shoulders again. She did not jump, knowing them to be the abbot's.

He moved her aside as Rob had done. When he passed her, she stepped back into the doorway as before.

The bell kept tolling, and she saw the hooded monks filing into their stalls.

Sword still out, at the ready, Fife watched Rob and moved toward him, either ignoring the abbot's appearance or not noticing him.

Rob seemed to grow more alert with each step Fife took until finally, when Adela's terror threatened to stop her breathing, Rob reached for his sword.

The abbot put a hand on his, stopping him. Then stepping in front of him, he waited for the tolling to stop before he said sternly, "Put up your weapon, sir."

"Get out of my way, old man," Fife snapped.

"I'm told that, despite your many faults, you are a God-fearing man, my son. Would you, a prince of this realm, befoul His house with violence?"

"That man and his wife are under arrest for acts of violence and murder. If they continue to defy me, I will take them bodily from here and hang them."

"You will not, my son, for this is a sanctuary. To take anyone from here against his will must result in your excommunication. Do you want to burn in Hell for all eternity? Put away your sword."

Fife hesitated, glanced back at his men, who had followed him in, then took another step forward. As he did, noise from the choir stalls drew Adela's attention.

Turning, she saw the monks throwing off their hooded black robes to reveal Rob's twelve men-at-arms. Their weapons remained in their scabbards, but she had as little doubt as Fife must have had that they would draw them if need be.

If Adela was astonished, the abbot was more so, for she saw his eyebrows shoot upward. But he stood his ground, saying calmly to Fife, "Your own family will not support this criminal act, for such it must be. You know that neither Sir Robert nor his lady has committed any crime such as you have described to me."

Without taking his eyes from Fife, Rob said, "He believes a friend of his will testify to the crime of which he accuses my lady and likewise believes that, to protect her, I attacked that friend last Tuesday as the abbey bell tolled Nocturnes."

"Last Tuesday?" The abbot frowned. "Is that what you believe, my son?"

"Aye," Fife snarled. "For that is the truth."

"Nay, it is not," the abbot said. "I married Sir Robert and his lady Tuesday last before all the brothers of this abbey. The bell began to toll Nocturnes just as they were leaving. Where did this attack take place?"

"Near St. Giles," Fife said resentfully.

The abbot looked at Rob. "Might that person testify against her ladyship?"

"You have my word that he will not."

"Then, by God, I'll find ten others who will," Fife growled.

The abbot regarded him sternly. "You give yourself away with such statements, my son. You have no charge, and no crime. I suggest you go home."

One of Fife's men crept up to him and whispered in his ear, whereupon the earl turned without another word and strode from the chamber.

"Mercy," Adela said, staring. "I did not think he would go so quietly."

"Doubtless, he has seen the error of his ways," the abbot said.

"More likely, his man told him Henry and his lads are in the kirkyard," Rob said with a grin. "Also, his own men learned that his charges are untrue. His *friend* the chevalier suffered no attack from anyone but Fife, who is behind all of this, as well as the attack on me near Lestalric. So, I think we have blunted his sword."

"Are we safe then?" Adela asked doubtfully.

"As safe as one ever can be from a vengeful prince," he said. "We have won this skirmish, however. I'm sorry we delayed your service, my lord abbot."

"You must beware, my son," the abbot said. "The Earl of Fife is no great warrior, but he is sly and ever dangerous."

"I'm hoping only that he'll take enough time deciding what to do next to give us enough to do what we must to protect ourselves," Rob said. "I know you must proceed now with your service, but thank you. We won't forget your help."

"Nor will Holyrood forget Lestalric," the abbot said warmly.

Outside, they met Henry in the yard with a large force of his men waiting patiently nearby, far enough away to be out of earshot. They saw no sign of Fife.

"What became of de Gredin?" Rob asked Henry.

He grinned. "He should be aboard my ship by now. He took the precaution of sending a messenger to Fife, saying he thought it best to avoid meeting him."

"I still don't trust that man, Henry."

"My lads will keep an eye on him." Henry nodded toward the abbey kirk. "I trust everything went well inside."

"Well enough," Rob said, briefly describing the episode.

When he had finished, Adela said, "What *will* you two do about the Stone?"

"We'll have to think about that," Rob said.

"I could take it to Orkney," Henry suggested as Rob put Adela on her horse.

"Sakes, Henry, they already suspect that you have the treasure. I'd not be surprised if Fife organized an attack on Orkney to search for it."

"He'd be declaring war on the King of Norway if he did," Henry said.

"He might not think about Norway," Rob said. "However, there is someone else in the Isles powerful enough and honest enough for us to trust with it."

"The Lord of the Isles?" Adela guessed, watching Rob mount his horse.

"Nay, lass," he said. "Donald may be honest. I've no cause to think he is not, but he is the present King's grandson and Fife's nephew. I'd not trust him to keep it secret from them. But Ranald of the Isles is one of the most honest men in Scotland. Furthermore"—he glanced at Henry—"he is a member of what the good abbot called an organization of outstanding soldiers who proved their loyalty at Bannockburn."

Henry nodded. "He is, indeed, and 'tis a good notion. But how can we do it?"

"We've time enough to ponder that," Rob said. "Although Fife suspects I may know something about the Stone, without support from other powerful nobles, he cannot raise an army against me, especially since it won't take me long now to increase and organize my own men-at-arms at Lestalric. It would be different, of course, if his grace had a royal army at his command as English kings do."

"Aye," Henry agreed, "because Fife would soon take command of that army, as he has of so many other things."

"But the King of Scots has to persuade his nobles to provide the men for any army he requires," Adela said.

"He does, indeed," Rob said. "But although that means we can leave the Stone where it is for now, with the Sinclairs guarding it, I'm concerned about the threat of another English invasion. I'd like to see that bit of Scotland's history well away from any path they might take to look for it."

Henry nodded. "We'll give it more thought, then. Are you riding with me?" he added as he turned his horse toward Holyrood's gates.

"Aye," Rob said. "Partway, at least."

Surprised, Adela said, "But is Henry not riding to Leith?"

"Aye, sweetheart," Rob said with a smile. "And we are going home."

Epilogue

Not far from Leith Harbor, six weeks later

Over there," Rob said, pointing toward a series of rock formations that overlooked the Firth of Forth. "Behind that outcropping is a shelf where we'll be out of the wind, with a patch of grass beyond it where our horses can graze."

The shelf was wide enough for comfort. And at the rear, the sloping rock was pleasant to lean against, as Rob remembered from many excursions there as a lad. It had been his secret place, the place he had gone to be alone. He had liked the privacy, and watching for boats. It seemed right to share it with his lass now.

With a sheer drop to the waves below and a sunny blue sky above, dotted with drifting puffy clouds, when they sat and leaned back, it felt as if they were warmly suspended in a world of their own between the sea and the sky.

"Do you like it here, sweetheart?" he asked.

"Aye, it's very pleasant," Adela said. "But I feel guilty

coming out here like this, Rob. They may arrive at any moment, and we should be there to greet them."

"You've thought of nothing but their comfort for a fort-night," he said. "Thanks to Henry's man of affairs, and my own colossal efforts, we now have our own steward, bail-lie, and a decent security force. Moreover, Fife is safely in the Borders, pretending to be helping the Douglas keep the English out of Scotland. And," he added as a clincher, "we know Tam Geddes was not stealing from us. Henry's man said my father just managed his income badly."

"We'll manage better," she said.

"Aye, because I was fortunate enough to marry a lass who knows exactly what she is doing in running a large household even when I do not. And although I've had more training as a warrior than as a farmer or man of af-fairs, I am rapidly learning what I need to know. So I have earned a peaceful afternoon with my wife."

"But what of our guests!"

"Our guests will be astonished at all we have accom-plished."

"The countess is never astonished."

"Aye, well, that's true. And I warrant Lady Clendenen will have all manner of suggestions to make for improv-ing the castle."

"Sorcha will, too. Do you truly think she and Hugo will reach Leith today?"

"He said they would."

"They won't know about the Stone. Will you tell them?"

"I think we must. We've so many related secrets to-gether now that keeping all the bits separate would be im-possible. Moreover, we must seek help from other Templars to move it."

"Fife will be watching Henry's ships, will he not?"

"Aye, but we'll find a way," he said confidently.

"Hugo won't know to look for us here. Should we not go to the harbor?"

"Nay, sweetheart. We'll have had our fill of company by suppertime, I warrant, and they all mean to stay with us for a fortnight. I want an hour with my wife now. And I want her to relax and forget all of her duties, save one."

She smiled. "And that one would be what, sir?"

"To honor her husband, and cherish him."

"I do," she said softly. "You know I do."

He sighed. "I remember that you told Fife you cared deeply for me."

"And you knew I meant that, too," she said.

"Did I?" He pretended to ponder the matter. "As I recall, you were a bit peevish with me at the time."

"You deserved that I should be."

"Perhaps, but now I deserve cherishing."

"Very well," she said, relaxing against him. "I won't mind feeling the sun and the breeze on my face for a short time. I think I'll just close my eyes."

She was silent, and he leaned back, too, feeling comfortably warm and enjoying the lazy flight of gulls overhead. When he turned to look at her, her eyes were still closed, her lips slightly parted. She looked deeply contented.

The sun had brightened the natural color in her cheeks, and her upper lip showed tiny beads of perspiration. She breathed evenly, deeply, her soft breasts rising and falling, enticingly near.

She looked innocently childlike one minute and seductive the next.

He felt overwhelming hunger for her, but something

more, and he knew at last what it was that she satisfied in him. He had thought he just needed someone to care about, a family of his own. But it was more than that. He had needed love, both to give and to savor.

He raised himself on one elbow. The pain from his injury was long gone, and he looked his fill at her, watching the faint pulse in her throat until his gaze drifted back again to her soft breasts. He leaned closer, his lips nearly touching hers.

Her eyes opened, and she gazed back at him.

"You didn't jump," he said quietly.

"Nay, not with you," she murmured. "Never with you. I love you so."

"I know," he said. "I feel it every day."

"And you?"

"I think I fell in love with you when I first saw you at Orkney," he said.

"You did not."

"Well, if it wasn't that first moment, I did when I heard you'd doused Hugo with a basinful of water."

"You jest, sir, but love is serious business."

"Is it, sweetheart? I own, I had thought never to know much about love."

"Aye, well, you know now, and there must be no more secrets between us."

"No more," he said.

"I have a one of my own to tell you," she said.

His heart swelled within him, for he did not have to ask what she meant. "A child, lass? Art certain?"

"Nearly so," she said. "My maid is certain, in any event."

"Then it must be so," he said, kissing her lightly.

The minute his lips touched hers, his body took fire,

and he was lost. He wasted no further time. His hands moved swiftly to unlace and unhook, and her hands were as eager as his.

Her arms slid around him and held him tight before she relaxed back against the slope and he opened her bodice and unlaced her shift to feast on those soft breasts of hers. He imagined a child suckling them.

Her nipples were hard, the skin of her breasts like silk. He savored them, kissing and sucking them, stroking her until he ached for her.

Adela watched him, stroking his hair as he eased downward to kiss and fondle her breasts, enjoying the sensations his lips and fingers ignited through her body as it began to respond to him. Briefly, then, her thoughts shifted to Ardelve.

Whether he had died naturally or not, they did not know, but she was glad she could remember him fondly and with a certainty that if he could see them from where he was, he would cheer her marriage to Rob. He had been a good man, and she had cared for him. But loving Rob as she did, she knew she had been a fool to think she could be happy marrying for no more than kindness and comfort.

Looking out at the water, she saw a distant boat and asked him if he thought people on it might see them. He didn't answer, but he smiled and stroked her belly, his hands moving tantalizingly lower. Then he moved her skirts out of his way and stroked her between her thighs, and all thought of anything else ceased.

She'd murmured something about passing boats, but he paid no heed. And when she responded, arching to meet him, emitting endearing little cries as she did, and clearly having no more concern for boats or anything but him, he touched her where he knew she was most sensitive, stimulating her more and more until she found release. Then he slowed his pace, wanting to savor their time together in that peaceful place for as long as he could.

He pulled her close and began kissing her again, his hands moving over her delicious body at will, gently at first, then more possessively, his mind forming pictures of what the babe she carried might look like.

Would it be a boy that looked like him, or a wee beautiful lassie like herself?

His contrary imagination produced a wee lassie waving a sword in one hand and a dirk in the other, making him chuckle.

"Why do you laugh?" she murmured.

He told her, and she shook her head at him. "The others will surely be there by now," she said with a sigh. "We should go soon."

"Your mind should be on your husband, madam. Kiss me, and do it properly, or I shall have to punish you. As I remember, you once admitted being ticklish."

She laughed and obeyed him with every sign of willingness. When his body leaped to life again, he decided Hugo and the others, even the countess, could wait another hour . . . or two.

Dear Reader,

I hope you enjoyed *Knight's Treasure*. Historic mysteries have fascinated me for many years, and finding an opportunity to connect two of them in one story provided an intriguing challenge.

Sir Robert Logan of Lestalric is a fictional character. Although I based much of his history on that of the first Sir Robert Logan of Restalrig, I found not the slightest suggestion that that gentleman was a Knight Templar. However, with regard to the earlier Logan brothers who accompanied Sir James Douglas and Sir William Sinclair when they attempted to carry the Bruce's heart to the Holy Land, and shared their fate, the likelihood that they shared Sinclair's Templar connection is not beyond the realm of possibility.

Research for this book included topics that ranged from Post Traumatic Stress Disorder (for the lingering effects of Adela's abduction and subsequent loss of her husband) to learning that during the fourteenth century most people considered knighthood to be of greater value than nobility (which basically meant only that the person owned land).

Details about fourteenth-century Edinburgh, Edinburgh Castle, and Holyrood Abbey come from a variety of sources, but one of the most fascinating was Elizabeth Ewan's *Townlife* (sic) *in Fourteenth-Century Scotland* (Edinburgh, 1990).

One interesting bit for the trivia crowd: While the English and many Continental countries surrounded their cities with walls that had gates that shut tight at night, the Scots did not. In the fourteenth century only

Perth and Berwick had walls. They were the exception, and the reason those walls existed at all is that the English occupied both towns for extended periods in the late thirteenth and early fourteenth centuries, and it was English military strategy that maintained them. Most Scottish towns simply relied on the neighboring castle or went without defenses.

With regard to descriptions of Edinburgh, I also relied on a drawing I have of the Castle as it looked from 1377 (when Robert II completed the great tower begun in 1367 by David II) until 1571–73, when cannon destroyed David's Tower during a two-year siege. That tower stood over ninety feet high and comprised three floors of royal accommodations. It survives now only as a ruin consisting of part of the ground floor and a stretch of stone curtain wall. I also have a street plan of the royal burgh and Canongate from a few years later. Those two items helped a great deal.

As for the Stone of Scone, much of the detail I've used with regard to its history and likely fate, and its primary description, came from *Stone of Destiny* by Pat Gerber (Edinburgh, 1997). But I am also indebted to the great Scottish author Nigel Tranter for engaging my interest in this subject through many of his books. Pat Gerber's work supports many details of its history and description in his books.

Mr. Tranter had done a tremendous amount of research on the Stone and was personally involved in the ill-fated 1950 attempt by Scottish Nationalists to take back the stone the English had carted off to Westminster Abbey. He and the others each kept a chip of that stone, and Mr. Tranter kept his "beneath a tiny silver replica of the coronation chair" (Gerber, 184). He thought it absurd that the English had mistaken an eleven-inch-high "lump of Perth sandstone" (*The Islesman*, Nigel Tranter, London, 2003) for the true Scottish Coronation Stone. I agree with him.

Hawthornden Castle is noted for the many caves in the hills around it, and men of the area did indeed use those caves as a base from which to harass the English and raid their supplies during the English invasion of 1335. Nearby Wallace's cave, named for William Wallace, who may have taken refuge there, was also known then.

For more about the Templar treasure, I suggest once again the following sources: *Holy Blood, Holy Grail* by Michael Baigent and Richard Leigh (New York, 1982); *The Temple and the Lodge* by Michael Baigent and Richard Leigh (New York, 1989); *Pirates & the Lost Templar Fleet* by David H. Childress (Illinois, 2003); *The Stone Puzzle of Rosslyn Chapel* by Philip Coppens (Netherlands, 2004); *The Da Vinci Code Decoded* by Martin Lunn (New York, 2004); and *The Lost Treasure of the Knights Templar* by Steven Sora (Vermont, 1999). For more about the Assassins, see *The Assassins* by Bernard Lewis (London, 1967).

Thanks again to Donal Sean MacRae, Laird of Kintail and Fellow of the Society of Antiquaries (Scot) for his continued and much-appreciated generosity in sharing his vast store of knowledge about all things Scottish, particularly this time with regard to titles and historic customs and usage thereof. Also, for his annual haggis and Atholbrose cream, treats beyond compare.

As always, I'd also like to thank my terrific agents,

Lucy Childs and Aaron Priest, as well as the world's most exciting editor and speed reader, Devi Pillai.

If you enjoyed *Knight's Treasure*, please look for *King of Storms*, the story of what fate has in store when quiet, habitually indecisive Lady Sidony Macleod meets a man who will turn her world upside down. It will be at your favorite bookstore in August 2007. In the meantime, *Suas Alba!*

Sincerely,

Amanda Scott

http://home.att.net/~amandascott

About the Author

AMANDA SCOTT, best-selling author and winner of Romance Writers of America's RITA/Golden Medallion and Romantic Times' Awards for Best Regency Author and Best Sensual Regency, began writing on a dare from her husband. She has sold every manuscript she has written. She sold her first novel, *The Fugitive Heiress*—written on a battered Smith-Corona—in 1980. Since then, she has sold many more, but since the second one, she has used a word processor. More than 25 of her books are set in the English Regency period (1810–1820), others are set in fifteenth-century England, and fourteenth-, sixteenth-, and eighteenth-century Scotland. Three are contemporary romances.

Amanda is a fourth-generation Californian who was born and raised in Salinas and graduated with a bachelor's degree in history from Mills College in Oakland. She did graduate work at the University of North Carolina at Chapel Hill, specializing in British History, before obtaining her master's in history from California State University at San Jose. After graduate school, she taught for the Salinas City School District for three years before marrying her husband, who was then a captain in the Air Force. They lived in Honolulu for a year, then in Nebraska for seven years, where their son was born. Amanda now lives with her husband in northern California.